CHILDREN'S TREASURY

CHILDREN'S TREASURY

Fairy Tales,
Nursery Rhymes &
Nonsense Verse

EDITED BY ALICE MILLS

Contents

Aesop's Fables *393–402*

Nonsense Verse *403–35*

Introduction

Fairy tales are openings into a world where life is much simpler than most of us experience it in everyday waking existence, where good and evil are easier to recognise, where the good are rewarded and the bad found out and punished, where animals can talk and ordinary people can become kings and queens, where kingdoms are on offer if only the tasks can be achieved. Life is made up of marvels in fairy tales, and none more marvellous than the promise, in story after story, that life will go on after all the problems, adventures and ordeals ... happily ever after.

The treasure of fairy tales is their call to adventure for everyone who hears or reads them, a call to an adventure of the imagination. The story of the Ugly Duckling, for instance, speaks to everyone who has ever felt lonely or unloved. The story of the Billy-Goats Gruff speaks to everyone who has felt small and weak and inadequate, and not known how to deal with bullies. There are stories of lost children who discover how to make their own way to a new life, a quest that children are set in the course of just growing up, and stories of the smallest and weakest person achieving the most difficult and tricky of tasks—in a fairy story there is always help, an extra inspiration of cleverness, a helpful friend, a dream that hints at the answer, a fairy godmother, a lucky chance. No matter what the problem, there is always a helper. Fairy tales are full of hope.

Once upon a time ... means the right time. The Ugly Duckling has to grow up a year or so until the time is right for him to discover what he really looks like and where he really belongs. Cinderella has to go to the ball three times, Snow White has to wait for the prince to free her throat from the poisoned apple, Sleeping Beauty has to sleep until the right prince comes along, the Beast has to wait for Beauty to learn to love him. In the Arabian Nights, Scheherazade has to find just the right moment to stop telling each story so that everyone who listens will want to hear more the next night. There are characters in fairy tales who never learn the right time to do things—or rather, not to do things, like the Fisherman's Wife who keeps asking for more, or Rumpelstiltskin who chooses the very worst moment to sing and dance and shout out his name ... but it is just the right moment for the Queen's baby to be saved.

All this wealth of hopes and dreams and imaginative freedom is in danger of being forgotten nowadays, as fairy tale and nursery rhyme are being replaced in many children's lives by TV and video and computer games. For too many children, the first rhyme they learn is not a nursery rhyme but an advertising jingle that promises instant happiness if only you buy the product. No need, the jingle tells us, for adventure or challenge or discovery, just buy the fizzy drink or the fashionable pair of jeans. But the jeans or the fizzy drink do not bring lasting happiness. There is always the next advertisement promising more happiness from buying the next thing.

Too many children are brought up on a diet of TV violence in the daily news, the police dramas, the murder mysteries and action films, all of which teach their audience that the world is lethally dangerous and that it is better not to trust. Sooner or later all children will have to face pain and disappointment, loss and death. But TV shows and computer games that sensationalise violence and promote killing as the answer, rarely introduce viewers to their own strengths that might help them through life's problems. Fairy tales offer a balance. There is violence in them, they do mention death, but they also dare to mention love and courage, cleverness and patience, humour, being able to see through appearances, and most of all they mention hope.

Many children today lead lives that are desperately hard and dangerous. For them fairy tales can be a reminder of an inner world where happy endings can be dreamed of, and where everything can be transformed.

Such stories are not an escape in the bad sense of running away from problems, but an escape into the freedom to imagine new answers and new possibilities.

It is from the heart and the imagination, from inner resources, inner knowledge and freedom, that both children and adults can draw strength to deal with their outer world's problems.

There are so many stories that begin with a main character who is just like a child might feel; the weakest, the smallest, the most downtrodden, facing a seemingly hopeless situation. Traditional fairy tales always find a way for them to be accepted, loved and honoured, and these stories offer a hope that can be a first step towards making things better in everyday life. At the end of fairy tales those who have come through the tests are more splendid, more powerful and more loving; shining images of what readers might hardly dare to dream of for themselves. To invite change outside, imagine change inside; and where better to feed the imagination than fairy story and fable?

The joy of nursery rhymes and nonsense verse is their fun. Some of them also have another purpose; as lullabies, to accompany playground games, to help children learn the alphabet or the days of the week or the months of the year or how to count. Some of them have a surprising history. Many people think, for example, that "Ring a Ring of Roses" refers back to a time of plague, to the rose-red marks of infection on the sick person's body, to the posies of flowers that people hoped would drive away the disease with their scent, and to the victims who "all fell down" dead. Some rhymes were written by more recent poets, like Robert Louis Stevenson remembering the days and weeks he spent ill in bed as a child, and how he was free in his imagination but not in his body. The limericks of Edward Lear, master of nonsense, are an invitation for readers to invent more for themselves. But the best gift of all these nonsense verses and nursery rhymes is an enjoyment of sound and rhythm, breaking the boundaries of everyday language, having fun with repetition and jokes and surprise endings.

The rhymes and stories in this book come from traditional sources, brought up to date where necessary while still keeping to the oral tradition of story telling. Children's best chance of learning to love reading comes from being read to, and modelling themselves on someone older who enjoys books. Each fable and fairy tale here is short enough to read aloud at one sitting, and short enough to encourage a beginner reader to read it independently.

There is another way to work the magic of story telling, and that is Scheherazade's way in the Arabian Nights. Try telling a story and breaking off at the most exciting point, so that the listener has to wait for the next instalment, and you may find that children are keen to learn to read just so they can finish the stories for themselves.

The pictures are based on traditional illustration of nursery rhyme and fairy tale, reproducing original artwork by such illustrators as Boyle, Caldecott, Crane, Doyle and Greenaway. Contemporary pictures in similar style have been added, so that the pages are richly and colourfully illustrated throughout. These pictures are especially helpful for the child who cannot yet read, to join in the activity of being read to, and as encouragement for the independent reader.

Whether you are introducing your child to the riches of fairy tale and fable, nursery rhyme and nonsense verse, or whether you are looking for old favourites (and a few surprises) to share, read and enjoy!

Alice Mills

Nursery Rhymes

The Three Little Kittens

Three little kittens they lost their mittens,
And they began to cry,
"Oh, Mammy dear!
"We sadly fear,
"Our mittens we have lost."
"What! lost your mittens, you naughty kittens,
"Then you shall have no pie."
Mew, mew, mew, mew.

Three little kittens they found their mittens,
And they began to cry,
"Oh, Mammy dear,!
"See here, see here!
"Our mittens we have found."
"What! found your mittens, you little kittens,
"Then you shall have some pie."
Purr, purr, purr, purr.

The three little kittens put on their
mittens,
And soon ate up the pie,
"Oh, Mammy dear!
"We greatly fear,
"Our mittens we have soiled."

"What! soiled your mittens, you naughty
kittens."
Then they began to sigh,
"Mew, mew, mew, mew,
Mew, mew, mew, mew."

The three little kittens they washed their mittens,
And hung them up to dry.
"Oh, Mammy dear!
"Look here, look here!
"Our mittens we have washed."

"What! washed your mittens, you darling kittens.
"But I smell a rat close by.
"Hush, hush! mew, mew,
"Mew, mew, mew."

Then all over the room, mammy cat, with a broom,
Chased the rat so nimble and spry;
The kittens ran too, and after him flew,
But none of the lot could come nigh;

So the rat got away, saying pertly, "Good-day,
I am not yet quite ready to die."
"Mew, mew, mew.
"Mew, mew, mew."

A Frog He Would A-Wooing Go

A frog he would a-wooing go,
Heigho! says Rowley,
Whether his mother would let him or no.

With a rowley powley, gammon and
spinach,
Heigho! says Anthony Rowley.

So off he set with his opera hat,
Heigho! says Rowley,
And on the road he met with a rat.
With a rowley powley, gammon and
spinach,
Heigho! says Anthony Rowley.
"Pray, Mr Rat, will you go
with me?"
Heigho! says Rowley,
"Kind Mistress Mousey
for to see!"
With a rowley powley,
gammon and spinach,
Heigho! says
Anthony Rowley.

When they reached the
door of Mousey's hall,
Heigho! says Rowley,
They gave a loud knock,
and they gave a loud call.
With a rowley powley,
gammon and spinach,
Heigho! says
Anthony Rowley.

"Pray, Mistress Mouse,
are you within?"
Heigho! says Rowley,
"Oh, yes, kind sirs,
I'm sitting to spin."
With a rowley powley,
gammon and spinach,
Heigho! says Anthony Rowley.

"Pray, Mistress Mouse, will you give us some beer?"
Heigho! says Rowley,
"For Froggy and I are fond of good cheer."
With a rowley powley, gammon and spinach,
Heigho! says Anthony Rowley.

"Pray, Mr Frog, will you give us a song?"
Heigho! says Rowley,
"But let it be something that's not very long."
With a rowley powley, gammon and spinach,
Heigho! says Anthony Rowley.

"Indeed, Mistress Mouse," replied Mr Frog,
Heigho! says Rowley,
"A cold has made me as hoarse as a hog."
With a rowley powley, gammon and spinach,
Heigho! says Anthony Rowley.

"Since you have caught cold, Mr Frog," Mousey said,
Heigho! says Rowley,
"I'll sing you a song that I have just made."
With a rowley powley, gammon and spinach,
Heigho! says Anthony Rowley.

But while they were all
a merry-making,
Heigho! says Rowley,
A cat with her
kittens came
tumbling in.
With a rowley
powley, gammon
and spinach,
Heigho! says
Anthony Rowley.

The cat she
seized the rat by
the crown,
Heigho! says
Rowley,
The kittens
they pulled the
little mouse
down.
With a rowley
powley, gammon
and spinach,
Heigho! says
Anthony Rowley.

This put Mr Frog in a
terrible fright,
Heigho! says Rowley,
He took up his hat and he wished them
good-night.
With a rowley powley, gammon and
spinach,
Heigho! says Anthony Rowley.

But as Froggy was crossing over a brook,
Heigho! says Rowley,
A lily-white duck came and gobbled
him up.

With a rowley powley, gammon and
spinach,
Heigho! says Anthony Rowley.

So there was an end of one, two, and
three,
Heigho! says Rowley,
The rat, the mouse, and the little frog-gee!
With a rowley powley, gammon and
spinach,
Heigho! says Anthony Rowley.

THE FAT MAN OF BOMBAY

There was a fat man of
  Bombay,
  Who was smoking one
  sunshiny day,
   When a bird, called a snipe
   Flew away with his pipe,
    Which vexed the fat
    man of Bombay.

ONE, TWO, THREE AND FOUR LEGS

Two legs sat upon three legs,
With one leg in his lap;
In comes four legs,
And runs away with one leg.

Up jumps two legs,
Catches up three legs,
Throws it after four legs,
And makes him bring
back one leg.

I HAD A LITTLE DOLL

I had a little doll, the prettiest
ever seen;
She washed up the dishes, and
kept the house clean.
She went to the mill, to fetch
me some flour,
And always got home in less
than an hour.
She baked my bread, she
brewed my ale,
She sat by the fire, and told me
a tale.

I LOVE LITTLE PUSSY

I love little pussy,
Her coat is so warm,
And if I don't hurt her,
She'll do me no harm.

So I'll not pull her tail,
Or drive her away,
But pussy and I
Together will play.

She will sit by my side,
And I'll give her some food,
And she'll like me because
I'm gentle and good.

THREE BLIND MICE

Three blind mice,
See how they run!
They all ran after the farmer's wife,
Who cut off their tails with a carving knife;
Did ever you hear such a thing in your life?
As three blind mice.

A CAT CAME FIDDLING

A cat came fiddling out
of the barn,
With a pair of bagpipes
under her arm;
She could sing nothing
but fiddle-cum-fee
The mouse has married
the humble bee;
Pipe, cat! Dance, mouse!
We'll have a wedding
at our good house.

JACK SPRAT

Jack Sprat could eat no fat,
His wife could eat no lean;
And so between them both,
They licked the platter clean.

BOW, WOW, WOW

Bow, wow, wow
Whose dog art thou?
"Little Tom Tucker's dog,
Bow, wow wow!"

TOM THE PIPER'S SON

Tom he was a piper's son,
He learned to play when he was
young,
But the only tune that he could play,
Was "Over the hills and far away".

Tom with his pipe made such a noise,
That he pleased both the girls and
the boys,
And they all stopped to hear
him play
"Over the hills and far away".

Tom with his pipe did play with such
skill,
That those who heard him could
never stand still,

Whenever they
heard him
they began
to dance,
Even pigs
on their
hind legs
would after
him prance.

He met old Dame Trot with a basket
of eggs—
He used his pipe and she used her
legs;
She danced about till the eggs were
all broke;
She began to fret, but he laughed at
the joke.

He saw a cross fellow
was beating an ass
Heavy laden with
pots, pans, dishes
and glass;
He took out his
pipe and
played them
a tune,
And the
Jackass's load
was lightened
full soon.

THERE WAS AN OLD WOMAN

There was an old woman,
Lived under a hill;
And if she's not gone,
She lives there still.
Baked apples she sold,
And cranberry pies,
And she's the old woman
Who never told lies.

BAA! BAA! BLACK SHEEP

"Baa! baa! black sheep, have you any wool?"

"Yes, sir, yes, sir, three bags full:

One for the master, and one for the dame,

And one for the little boy who lives in our lane."

The Robber Kitten

A kitten once to its mother said,
"I'll never more be good;
But I'll go and be a robber fierce,
And live in a dreary wood,
Wood, wood, wood,
And live in a dreary wood."

So off it went to the dreary wood,
And there it met a cock,
And blew its hat, with a pistol, off,
Which gave it an awful shock!
Shock, shock, shock,
Which gave it an awful shock!

It climbed a tree to rob a nest
Of young and tender owls;
But the branch broke off and the
kitten fell,
With six tremendous howls!
Howls, howls, howls,
With six tremendous howls!

Soon after that it met a cat;
"Now, give to me your purse;
Or I'll shoot you through, and stab
you too,
And kill you, which is worse!
Worse, worse, worse,
And kill you, which is worse."

One day it met a Robber Dog,
And they sat down to drink;
The dog did joke, and laugh, and sing
Which made the kitten wink,
Wink, wink, wink!
Which made the kitten wink!

At last they quarrelled; then they fought,
Beneath the greenwood tree;
Till puss was felled with an awful club,
Most terrible to see!
See, see, see,
Most terrible to see!

When puss got up, its eye was shut,
And swelled, and black, and blue;
Moreover, all its bones were sore,
So it began to mew!
Mew, mew, mew,
So it began to mew!

Then up it rose, and scratched its nose,
And went home very sad;
"Oh! Mother dear, behold me here,
I'll never more be bad,
Bad, bad, bad,
I'll never more be bad."

DOCTOR FOSTER

Doctor Foster went to Glo'ster,
In a shower of rain;
He stepped in a puddle right
up to his middle,
And never went there again.

TEN FINGERS

One, two, three, four, five,
Once I caught a fish alive;
Six, seven, eight, nine, ten,
Then I let him go again.

Why did you let him go?
Because he bit my finger so.
Which finger did he bite?
This little finger on
the right.

THE OLD WOMAN TOSSED UP IN A BASKET

There was an old woman tossed
up in a basket,
Seventeen times as high as the moon;
Where she was going I couldn't
but ask it,
For in her hand she carried a broom.

"Old woman, old woman, old
woman," said I,
"Where are you going up to
so high?"
"To brush the cobwebs off the sky!"
"May I go with thee?"
"Aye, by-and-by."

WHOLE DUTY OF CHILDREN

A child should always say what's true
And speak when he is spoken to,
And behave mannerly at table;
At least as far as he is able.

PETER PIPER

Peter Piper picked a peck of pickled pepper,
A peck of pickled pepper Peter Piper picked;
If Peter Piper picked a peck of pickled pepper,
Where's the peck of pickled pepper Peter Piper picked?

THE RAGGED RASCAL

Round and round the
rugged rocks
The ragged rascal ran.
How many r's are there
in that?
Now tell me if you can.

WEE WILLIE WINKIE

Wee Willie Winkie runs
through the town,
Up stairs and down stairs, in
his night-gown,
Rapping at the window, crying
through the lock:
"Are the children in their beds,
for it's past eight o'clock."

BETTY BOTTER'S BATTER

Betty Botter bought some butter,
But, she said, the butter's bitter:
If I put it in my batter
It will make my batter bitter;
But a bit of better butter
Will surely make my batter better.
So she bought a bit of butter
Better than her bitter butter,
And she put it in her batter
And her batter was not bitter.
So 'twas better Betty Botter
Bought a bit of better butter.

TWO LITTLE DICKY BIRDS

Two little dicky birds
Sat on a wall,
One called Peter,
One called Paul:
Fly away, Peter,
Fly away, Paul!
Come back, Peter,
Come back, Paul.

THE THREE CROWS

Three crows there were
once who sat on a stone,
But two flew away, and
then there was one.
The other crow felt so
timid alone,
That he flew away, and
then there was none.

LADYBIRD, LADYBIRD

Ladybird, ladybird,
Fly away home,
Your house is on fire,
Your children all gone,
All but one, and her name is Ann,
And she crept under the pudding pan.

POLLY, PUT THE KETTLE ON

Polly, put the kettle on,
Polly, put the kettle on,
Polly, put the kettle on,
We'll all have tea.

Sukey, take it off again,
Sukey, take it off again,
Sukey, take it off again,
They've all gone away.

OH, DEAR, WHAT CAN THE MATTER BE?

Oh, dear, what can the matter be?
Dear, dear, what can the matter be?
Oh, dear, what can the matter be?
Johnny's so long at the fair.

He promised to buy me a bunch of blue ribbons,
He promised to buy me a bunch of blue ribbons,
He promised to buy me a bunch of blue ribbons
To tie up my bonny brown hair.

THE OLD WOMAN WHO LIVED IN A SHOE

There was an old woman
who lived in a shoe,
She had so many children
she didn't know what to do;
She gave them some broth
without any bread,
Then spun them all round,
and sent them to bed.

ST VALENTINE'S DAY

Good morning to you, Valentine!
Curl your locks as I do mine,
Two before and three behind,
Good morning to you, Valentine!

JACK BE NIMBLE

Jack be nimble,
Jack be quick,
Jack jump over the candlestick.

THIS LITTLE PIG

This little pig went to market,
This little pig stayed at home;
This little pig had roast beef,
This little pig had none;
And this little pig went
Wee, wee, wee, all the way home.

BLOCK CITY

What are you able to build with your
blocks?
Castles and palaces, temples and
docks.
Rain may keep raining, and others
go roam,
But I can be happy and
building at home.

Let the sofa be mountains, the
carpet be sea,
There I'll establish a city for
me:
A kirk and a mill and a palace
beside,
And a harbour as well where
my vessels may ride.

Great is the palace with pillar and
wall,
A sort of a tower on the top of it all,
And steps coming down in an orderly
way,
To where my toy vessels lie
safe in the bay.

This one is sailing and that one is
moored:
Hark to the song of the sailors on
board!
And see, on the steps of my palace,
the kings,
Coming and going with presents and
things!

Now I have done with it, down let
it go!
All in a moment the town is laid low.
Block upon block lying scattered
and free,
What is there left of my town by
the sea.

Yet as I saw it, I see it again,
The kirk and the palace, the ships
and the men,
And as long as I live and where'er
I may be,
I'll always remember my town by
the sea.

The Spider and the Fly

"Will you walk into my parlour?" said a spider to a fly.
"It is the prettiest parlour that ever you did spy!
You've only got to pop your head just inside the door,

You'll see so many curious things you never saw before.
Will you, will you, will you walk in, pretty fly?
Will you, will you, will you walk in, pretty fly?"

"My fine house is always open," said the spider to the fly.
"I'm glad to have the company of all I see go by."
"They go in but don't come out again— I've heard of you before."
"Oh yes, they do, I always let them out at my back door.
Will you, will you, will you walk in, pretty fly?
Will you, will you, will you walk in, pretty fly?"

"Will you grant me one sweet kiss, dear?" says the spider to the fly.
"To taste your charming lips, I've a curiosity."
Says the fly, "If once our lips did meet, a wager I would lay,

Of ten to one you would not after let them come away."
Will you, will you, will you walk in, pretty fly?
Will you, will you, will you walk in, pretty fly?"

"If not kiss, will you shake hands, then?" says the spider to the fly.
"Before you leave me to myself, with sorrow sad to sigh."
Says the fly, "There's nothing so attractive unto you belongs;
I declare you should not touch me, even with a pair of tongs."
Will you, will you, will you walk in, pretty fly?
Will you, will you, will you walk in, pretty fly?"

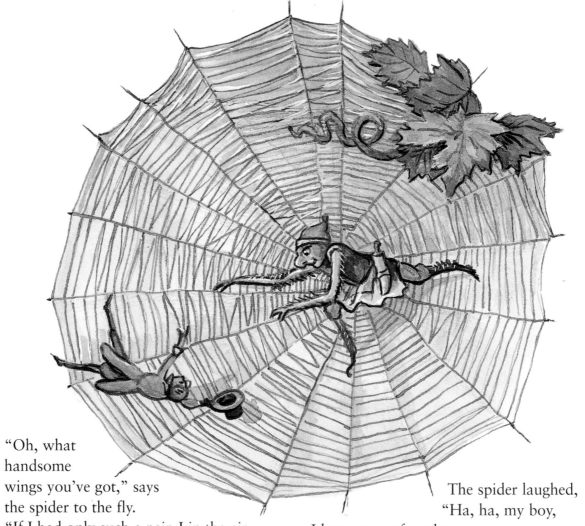

"Oh, what
handsome
wings you've got," says
the spider to the fly.
"If I had only such a pair, I in the air
would fly;
But 'tis useless my repining, and only
idle talk,
You can fly up in the air, while I'm
obliged to walk.
*Will you, will you, will you walk in,
pretty fly?
Will you, will you, will you walk in,
pretty fly?*"

"For the last time now I ask you, will you
walk in, Mister Fly?"
"No, if I do, may I be shot, I'm off so
now goodbye, goodbye, goodbye."
Then up he springs, but both his wings
were in the web caught fast;

The spider laughed,
"Ha, ha, my boy,
I have you safe at last.
*Will you, will you, will you walk out,
pretty fly?
Will you, will you, will you walk out,
pretty fly?*"

"Tell me, pray, how are you now?"
says the spider to the fly.
"You fools will never wisdom get, unless
you dearly buy;
'Tis vanity that ever makes repentance
come too late,
And you who into cobwebs run, right well
deserve your fate.
*Listen, listen, listen, foolish little fly,
Listen, listen to me, foolish,
foolish little fly.*"

My Shadow

I have a little shadow that goes in and out
with me,
And what can be the use of him is
more than I can
see.
He is very,
very like
me from
the heels
up to the
head;
And I
see
him
jump
before me, when I
jump into my bed.

The funniest thing about
him is the way he likes to
grow—
Not at all like proper children,
which is always very slow;
For he sometimes shoots up
taller like an india-rubber ball,
And he sometimes gets so
little that there's none of him
at all.

He hasn't got a notion of how
children ought to play,
And can only make a fool of me in every
sort of way.
He stays so close beside me, he's a coward
you can see;
I'd think shame to stick to nursie as that
shadow sticks to me!

One morning, very early, before the
sun was up,
I rose and found the shining
dew on every buttercup;
But my lazy little shadow, like
an arrant sleepy-head,
Had stayed at home behind me
and was fast asleep in bed.

THE LAZY CAT

Pussy, where have
you been today?
In the meadows
asleep in the hay.
Pussy, you are a
lazy cat,
If you have done
no more than
that.

THREE LITTLE MICE

Three little mice crept out to see
What they could find to have for tea
(For they were dainty, saucy mice,
And liked to nibble something nice).
But pussy's eyes, so big and bright,
Soon sent them scampering off in a fright.

POOR DOG BRIGHT

Poor Dog Bright,
Ran off with all his might,
Because the Cat was after him,
Poor Dog Bright.

Poor Cat Fright,
Ran off with all her might,
Because the Dog was after her,
Poor Cat Fright.

LITTLE JUMPING JOAN

Here am I, little
jumping Joan;
When nobody's
with me,
I'm always alone.

MR AND MRS LAMP

Mr Jacob Lamp and wife,
Both enjoyed the best of life;
They were each quite stout and big,
But they liked to dance and jig.
They could dance a Highland fling,
Also cut a pigeon wing;
So, you see, they made a hit,
With their dancing turns and wit.
Mr Lamp stood on his head,
Till his wife thought he was dead;
But he surely did the trick,
Did it well and did it slick.

THE TIN TAN CELEBRATION

There was a celebration
In Tin Tan Land one night;
They all went out parading,
And, oh! it was a sight!

They sent ten thousand rockets
Clear up into the air;
And all the eyes looked skyward,
Into the fiery glare.

Folks said it was just midnight,
When all the fun was o'er;
But cups and spoons and saucers
Cried, "Oh, we want some more!"

CUPS GO SWIMMING

Cups they would a-swimming go.
Heigh ho!
Cups they would a-swimming go,
For the Icetongs told me so.
Heigh ho!
Rushed and then jumped off the pier.
Heigh ho!
Rushed and then jumped off the pier,
For a bathtub stood quite near.
Heigh ho!
One ran out and made a dive.
Heigh ho!
One ran out and made a dive,
All the rest then made a slide.
Heigh ho!
All dive down, oh, hear them clatter!
Heigh ho!
All dive down, oh, hear them clatter!
What a rough and tumble splatter!
Heigh ho!

THE JOLLY MILK BOTTLES

Children, watch this jolly crowd,
All are healthy, fat and proud,
For they always drink and eat,
Cream and buttermilk and wheat!
All of them have pretty names:
First is Lizzie, then comes James;
Third is Henry, short and fat;
Then comes tall and jolly Jack;
Next is Susie, with her fan;
Last, not least, is Mary Ann.
Yes, they eat whatever they get,
Never scold and never fret,
Always are so good and brave,
Each one knows how to behave—
Do You?

TEA KETTLE JIM

Tea Kettle Jim,
Was the prince of sin,
Had water to burn,
Which he did not earn;
And then they would fill
Him with water, until
He determined to blow
His steam for a show,
And blew off his head,
And painted things red.
He is mighty smart, too,
And a good kettle, who
Will blow off his neck,
And not be a wreck.

PETER THE EGGBEATER

Peter the Eggbeater rubbed his hands
And shook his fearsome pole.
Then he whirled his wheel around,
As he stepped into the bowl.

"They're a crafty set," said he,
As he beat the eggs to foam;
"Oh! these eggs will be a sight,
When I leave the bowl for home."

He whipped and whipped and
beat and stirred,
Until the eggs could hardly stand;
Their cries and moans they say
were heard,
Throughout the town, throughout
the land.

NAUGHTY TEASPOONS

Kettle boils,
Cook's asleep,
Saucers standing
In a heap.
Table set,
Dishes on,
Teaspoons looking
For some fun.
Pull the cloth
On the floor,
Dishes tumble
With a roar.
Cook wakes up,
Mistress comes,
In a fright
Bridget runs.
Cook's discharged,
Teaspoons sneak,
On a lark
For a week.

THE KITCHEN FIRE

Matches tip-toe through the door,
And are quarrelling on the floor.
Pots and kettles, in the dark,
Peeked and yelled: "A spark, a spark!
Matches burning, matches burning!
Wake up, wake up! Fire! Fire!
Pour on water, pour on water!
      Call the pitchers
      And the hose;
      Call the teapot
      And the clothes!
      Stop the fire,
      Put it out
      With a bowl
      And waterspout!"

THE WICKED FLATIRONS

The children stopped to romp and play,
And left the Irons to hold full sway;
They burnt a hole and laughed in glee—
The clothes they were a sight to see.
Boys and girls, don't run away
And let the Tin Tan Irons play;
For, don't you know, they might sit down
Upon your clothes and burn them brown?

The Story of Cruel Frederick

Here is cruel Frederick, see!
A horrid wicked boy was he;
He caught the flies, poor
little things,
And then tore off their
tiny wings.

He killed the birds, and broke
the chairs,
And threw the kitten down
the stairs;
And oh! far worse than
all beside,
He whipped his Mary,
till she cried.

The trough was full, and faithful Tray
Came out to drink one sultry day;
He wagged his tail, and wet his lip,
When cruel Fred snatched up a whip,
And whipped poor Tray till he was sore,
And kicked and whipped him more
and more.
At this, good Tray grew very red,
And growled and bit him till he bled;
Then you should only have been by,
To see how Fred did scream and cry!

So Frederick had to go to bed,
His leg was very sore and red!
The doctor came and shook his head,
And made a very great to-do,
And gave him nasty physic too.

But good dog Tray is happy now,
He has no time to say "bow-wow!"
He seats himself in Frederick's chair,
And laughs to see the nice things there.
The soup he swallows, sup by sup—
And eats the pies and puddings up.

The Story of Flying Robert

When the rain comes tumbling down
In the country or the town,
All good little girls and boys
Stay at home and mind their toys.
Robert thought—"No, when it pours,
It is better out-of-doors."
Rain it *did*, and in a minute,
Bob was in it.
Here you see him, silly fellow,
Underneath his red umbrella.

What a wind! Oh! how it whistles
Through the trees and flowers
and thistles!
It has caught his red umbrella;
Now look at him, silly fellow,
Up he flies
To the skies.
No-one heard his screams and cries;
Through the clouds the rude wind
bore him,
And his hat flew on before him.

Soon they got to such a height,
They were nearly out of sight!
And the hat went up so high,
That it really touched the sky.
No-one ever yet could tell,
Where they stopped, or where
they fell.
Only, this one thing is plain,
Bob was never seen again!

The Story of the Man that Went Out Shooting

This is the man that shoots the hares,
This is the coat he always wears;
With game-bag, powder-horn
and gun,
He's going out to have
some fun.
The hare sits snug in
leaves and grass,
And laughs to see
the green man pass.
He finds it hard,
without a pair
Of spectacles, to
shoot the hare.

Now, as the sun grew
very hot,
And he a heavy gun
had got,
He lay down
underneath a tree,
And went to sleep, as
you may see.
And, while he slept like
any top,
The little hare came,
hop, hop, hop—
Took gun and
spectacles, and then,
On her hind legs went
off again.

The green man wakes and sees her place
The spectacles upon her face,
And now she's trying
all she can,
To shoot the sleepy,
green-coat man.
He cries and screams
and runs away;
The hare runs after
him all day,
And hears him call
out everywhere:
"Help! Fire! Help! The hare! The hare!"

At last he stumbled at the well,
Head over ears, and in he fell.
The hare stopped short, took aim,
and hark!
Bang went the gun—
she missed her mark!

The poor man's wife was drinking up
Her coffee in her coffee cup;
The gun shot cup and saucer through.
"Oh, dear!" cried she, "what shall I do?"
There lived close by the cottage there,
The hare's own child, the little hare,
And while she stood upon her toes,
The coffee fell and burned her nose.
"Oh, dear!" she cried, with spoon in hand,
"Such fun I do not understand."

55

The Story of Johnny Head-in-Air

As he trudged along to school,
It was always Johnny's rule
To be looking at the sky
And the clouds that floated by;
But what just before him lay,
In his way,
Johnny never thought about;

So that everyone cried out—
"Look at little Johnny there,
Little Johnny Head-in-Air!"

Running just in Johnny's way,
Came a little dog one day;
Johnny's eyes were still astray,
Up on high,
In the sky;
And he never heard them cry—
"Johnny, mind, the dog is nigh!"
Bump!
Dump!
Down they fell, with such a thump,
Dog and Johnny in a lump!

Once, with head as high as ever,
Johnny walked beside the river.
Johnny watched the swallows trying
Which was cleverest at flying.
Oh! what fun!
Johnny watched the bright round sun
Going in and coming out;
This was all he thought about.
So he strode on, only think!
To the river's very brink,
Where the bank was high and steep,
And the water very deep;
And the fishes, in a row,
Stared to see him coming so.

One step more! Oh! sad to tell!
Headlong in poor Johnny fell.
And the fishes, in dismay,
Wagged their tails and
ran away.

There lay Johnny on his face,
With his nice red writing-case;
But, as they were passing by,
Two strong men had heard him cry;
And, with sticks, these two strong men,
Hooked poor Johnny out again.

Oh! you should have seen him shiver
When they pulled him from the river.
He was in a sorry plight!
Dripping wet, and such a fright!
Wet all over, everywhere,
Clothes, and arms, and face,
and hair;
Johnny never will forget,
What it is to be so wet.

And the fishes, one, two, three,
Are come back again, you see;
Up they came the moment after,
To enjoy the fun and laughter.
Each popped out his little head,
And, to tease poor Johnny, said:
"Silly little Johnny, look,
You have lost your writing-book!"

Shock-Headed Peter

Just look at him! There he stands,
  With his nasty hair and hands.
See! his nails are never cut;
They are grimed as black
      as soot;

And the sloven, I declare
Never once has combed his hair;
    Anything to me is sweeter
      Than to see Shock-Headed
      Peter.

LITTLE JACK HORNER

Little Jack Horner sat in a corner,
Eating a Christmas pie;
He put in his thumb, and pulled out a plum,
And said, "What a good boy am I!"

DIDDLTY, DIDDLTY, DUMPTY

Diddlty, diddlty, dumpty,
The cat ran up the plum tree;
Give her a plum, and down she'll come,
Diddlty, diddlty, dumpty.

ELSIE MARLEY

Elsie Marley has grown so fine,
She won't get up to serve the swine;
But lies in bed till eight or nine,
And surely she does take her time.

LITTLE BO-PEEP

Little Bo-Peep, she lost her sheep,
And didn't know where to find them;
Leave them alone, they'll all come home,
And bring their tails behind them.

Little Bo-Peep fell fast asleep,
And dreamt she heard them bleating;
But when she awoke, she found it a joke,
For they were still a-fleeting.

Then up she took her little crook,
Determined for to find them;

She found them indeed, but it made her heart bleed,
For they'd left their tails behind them.

It happened one day as Bo-Peep did stray,
Into a meadow nearby;
There she espied their tails side by side,
All hung on a tree to dry.

She heaved a sigh and wiped her eye,
Then went over hill and dale;
And tried what she could, as a shepherdess should,
To tack to each sheep its tail.

LITTLE BOY BLUE

Little Boy Blue, come blow your horn,
The sheep's in the meadow, the cow's in the corn.
Where's the boy who looks after the sheep?
He's under the haystack fast asleep.
Will you wake him? No, not I!
For if I do, he'll be sure to cry.

TEA FOR TWO

You see, merry Phillis, that dear little maid,
Has invited Belinda to tea;
Her nice little garden is shaded by trees—
What pleasanter place could there be?

There's a cake full of plums, there are strawberries too,
And the table is set on the green;
I'm fond of a carpet all daisies and grass—
Could a prettier picture be seen?

SOMEWHERE TOWN

Which is the way to Somewhere Town?
Oh, up in the morning early;
Over the tiles and the chimney pots,
That is the way, quite clearly.

And which is the door to Somewhere Town?
Oh, up in the morning early;
The round red sun is the door to
go through,
That is the way, quite clearly.

THE PROUD GIRL

Yes, that's the girl who struts about,
She's very proud—so very proud!
Her *bow-wow's* quite as proud
as she:
They both are very wrong to be
So proud—so very proud.

See, Jane and Willy laugh at her,
They say she's very proud!
Says Jane, "My stars!—they're very silly;"
"Indeed they are," cries little Willy,
"To walk so stiff and proud."

PRINCE FINIKIN

Prince Finikin and his mamma
Sat sipping their bohea;
"Good gracious!" said his
Highness, "why,
What girl is this I see?

"Most certainly it cannot be
A native of our town;"

And he turned him round to his
mamma,
Who set her teacup down.

But Dolly simply looked at them,
She did not speak a word;
"She has no voice!" said Finikin;
"It's really quite absurd."

Then Finikin's mamma
observed,
"Dear Prince, it seems to me,
She looks as if she'd like to
drink
A cup of my bohea."

So Finikin poured out her tea,
And gave her currant pie;
Then Finikin said, "Dear
Mamma,
What a kind prince am I!"

THE DAISIES

You very fine Miss Molly,
What will the daisies say,
If you carry home so many
Of their little friends today?

Perhaps you take a sister,
Perhaps you take a brother,
Or two little daisies who
Were fond of one another.

THE DANCING FAMILY

Pray let me introduce you to
This little dancing family;
For morning, afternoon and night,
They danced away so happily.

They twirled round about,
They turned their toes out;
The people wondered what the noise,
            Could all be about.

        They danced from
          early morning,
        Till very late at night;
        Both in-doors and
        out-of-doors,
      With very great delight.

And every sort of dance they knew,
From every country far away;
And so it was no wonder that,
They should keep dancing all the day.

So dancing—dancing—dancing,
In sunshine or in rain;
And when they all left off,
Why then—they all began again.

WHEN WE WENT OUT WITH GRANDMAMMA

When we went out with
Grandmamma—
Mamma said for a treat—
Oh, dear, how stiff we had to walk
As we went down the street.

One on each side we had to go,
And never laugh or loll;
I carried Prim, her Spaniard dog,
And Tom—her parasol.

THE CATS HAVE COME TO TEA

What did she see—oh, what did she see,
As she stood leaning against the tree?
Why, all the cats had come to tea.

What a fine turnout—from round about,
All the houses had let them out,
And here they were with scamper and shout.

"Mew—mew—mew!" was all they could say,
    And, "We hope we find you well today."

    Oh, what should she do—oh, what should
    she do?
What a lot of milk they would get through,
    For here they were with "Mew—mew—
        mew!"

    She didn't know—oh, she didn't know,
    If bread and butter they'd like or no,
    They might want little mice, oh! oh! oh!

    Dear me—oh, dear me,
    All the cats had come to tea.

THE FOUR PRINCESSES

Four princesses lived in a green
tower—
A bright green tower in the middle
of the sea;
And no-one could think—
oh, no-one could think—
Who the four princesses could be.

One looked to the north, and one to
the south,
And one to the east, and one to the
west;
They were all so pretty, so very pretty,
You could not tell which was the
prettiest.

Their curls were golden—their eyes
were blue,
And their voices were sweet as a
silvery bell;
And four white birds around
them flew,
But where they came from—
who could tell?

Oh, who could tell? for no-one knew,
And not a word could you hear
them say.
But the sound of their singing, like
church bells ringing,
Would sweetly float as they passed
away.

For under the sun, and under
the stars,
They often sailed on
the distant sea;
Then in their green
tower and roses
bower
They lived
again—
a mystery.

JACK AND JILL

Jack and Jill went up the hill,
To fetch a pail of water;
Jack fell down and broke his crown,
And Jill came tumbling after.

Then up Jack got and home did trot,
As fast as he could caper;
Dame Jill had the job to plaster
his nob
With vinegar and brown paper.

Jill came in, and she did grin
To see his paper plaster;
Her mother, vexed, did scold her next
For laughing at Jack's disaster.

This made Jill pout, and she ran out,
And Jack did quickly follow;
They rode dog Ball, till Jill did fall,
Which made Jack laugh and holler.

THE LITTLE JUMPING GIRLS

Jump–jump–jump–
Jump away
From this town into
The next, today.

Jump–jump–jump–
Jump over the moon;
Jump all the morning;
And all the noon.

DICKERY, DICKERY, DARE!

Dickery, dickery, dare!
The pig flew up in the air;
The man in brown
Soon brought him down,
Dickery, dickery, dare!

THE CROOKED SONG

There was a crooked man, and
he walked a crooked mile,
He found a crooked sixpence
beside a crooked stile,
He bought a crooked cat,
which caught a crooked mouse,
And they all lived together in a
little crooked house.

GOOSEY, GOOSEY, GANDER

Goosey, goosey, gander,
Where shall I wander?
Up stairs, down stairs,
And in my lady's chamber:
There I met an old man,
Would not say his prayers;
Take him by the left leg,
Throw him down the stairs.

TOAD AND FROG

"Croak," said the toad,
"I'm hungry I think,
Today I've had nothing to
eat or to drink;
I'll crawl to a garden and
jump through the pales,
And there I'll dine nicely on
slugs and on snails."

"Ho, ho! said the frog,
"is that what you mean?
Then I'll hop away to the
next meadow stream,
There I will drink, and eat
worms and slugs too,
And then I shall have a
good dinner like you."

LITTLE ROBIN REDBREAST

Little robin redbreast sat
upon a tree,
Up went pussy cat and down
went he.
Down came pussy cat, and
away robin ran,
Says little robin redbreast:
"Catch me if you can."

SHAVE A PIG

Barber, barber, shave a pig,
How many hairs will make a wig?
"Four and twenty, that's enough,"
Give the barber a pinch of snuff.

LITTLE MISS MUFFET

Little Miss Muffet,
She sat on a tuffet,
Eating her curds and whey;
Down came a spider,
Which sat down beside her,
And frightened Miss Muffet away.

TWINKLE, TWINKLE, LITTLE STAR

Twinkle, twinkle, little star,
How I wonder what you are,
Up above the world so high,
Like a diamond in the sky.
Twinkle, twinkle, little star,
How I wonder what you are.

When the blazing sun is gone,
When he nothing shines upon,
Then you show your little light,
Twinkle, twinkle, all the night.
Twinkle, twinkle, little star,
How I wonder what you are.

Then the traveller in the dark,
Thanks you for your tiny spark.
Could he see which way to go
If you did not twinkle so?
Twinkle, twinkle, little star,
How I wonder what you are.

In the dark blue sky you keep,
While you through my curtains peep,
And you never shut your eye
Till the sun is in the sky.
Twinkle, twinkle, little star,
How I wonder what you are.

THERE WAS A LITTLE GIRL

There was a little girl
And she had a little curl
Right in the middle of her
forehead,
And when she was good
She was very, very good,
And when she was bad she was
horrid.

ONE MISTY, MOISTY MORNING

One misty, moisty morning, when cloudy was the weather,
There I met an old man clothed all in leather;
He began to compliment and I began to grin,
How do you do? how do you do? how do you do again?

DIDDLE DIDDLE DUMPLING

Diddle diddle dumpling, my son John,
Went to bed with his trousers on;
One shoe off, and one shoe on,
Diddle diddle dumpling, my son John.

OLD WOMAN, OLD WOMAN

"Old woman, old woman, shall we go a-shearing?"
"Speak a little louder, sir, I'm very hard of hearing."
"Old woman, old woman, shall I kiss you dearly?"
"Thank you, kind sir, I hear you very clearly."

BED IN SUMMER

In winter I get up at night,
And dress by yellow
candle-light.
In summer, quite the
other way,
I have to go to bed by day.

I have to go to bed and see,
The birds still hopping on
the tree,
Or hear the grown-up
people's feet,
Still going past me in the
street.

And does it not seem hard
to you,
When all the sky is clear
and blue,
And I should like so much
to play,
To have to go to bed day?

STAR LIGHT, STAR BRIGHT

Star light, star bright,
First star I see tonight,
I wish I may,
I wish I might,
Have the wish
I wish tonight.

THE FARMER AND HIS DAUGHTER

A farmer went trotting upon
his grey mare,
Bumpety, bumpety, bump!
With his daughter behind him
so rosy and fair,
Lumpety, lumpety, lump!

A raven cried "croak" and they
all tumbled down,
Bumpety, bumpety, bump!
The mare broke her knees,
and the farmer his crown,
Lumpety, lumpety, lump!

The mischievous raven flew
laughing away,
Bumpety, bumpety, bump!
And vowed he would serve
them the same the next day,
Lumpety, lumpety, lump!

GOOD-FRIDAY SONG

Hot-cross buns!
Hot-cross buns!
One a penny, two a penny,
Hot-cross buns!

Hot-cross buns!
Hot-cross buns!
If you have no daughters,
Give them to your sons.

THE COW

The friendly cow all red and white,
I love with all my heart;
She gives me cream with all her might,
To eat with apple tart.

She wanders lowing here and there,
And yet she cannot stray,
All in the pleasant open air,
The pleasant light of day.

And blown by all the winds that
pass,
And wet with all the showers,
She walks among the meadow
grass,
And eats the meadow flowers.

NEST EGGS

Birds all the sunny day
Flutter and quarrel,
Here in the arbour-like
Tent of the laurel.

Here in the fork
The brown nest
is seated,
Four little blue
eggs
The mother keeps
heated.

While we stand
watching her
Staring like gabies,
Safe in each egg
are the
Bird's little babies.

Soon the frail eggs they shall
Chip, and upspringing,

Make all the April woods
Merry with singing.

Younger than we are
O children, and frailer,
Soon in blue air they'll be,
Singer and sailor.

We, so much older,
Taller and stronger,
We shall look down on the
Birdies no longer.

They shall go flying
With musical speeches,
High overhead in the
Tops of the beeches.

In spite of our
wisdom
And sensible talking,
We on our feet must go
Plodding and walking.

GEORGIE PORGIE

Georgie Porgie,
pudding and pie,
Kissed the girls and
made them cry;
When the girls
came out to play,
Georgie Porgie
ran away.

MARY'S CANARY

Mary had a pretty bird,
Feathers bright and yellow;
Slender legs—upon my word,
He was a pretty fellow.
The sweetest note he always sung,
Which much delighted Mary;
She often, where the cage was hung,
Sat hearing her canary.

ONE, TWO, BUCKLE MY SHOE

One, two,
Buckle my shoe;

Three, four,
Knock at the door;

Five, six,
Pick up sticks;

Seven, eight,
Lay them straight;

Nine, ten,
A good fat hen;

Eleven, twelve,
Dig and delve;

Thirteen, fourteen,
Maids a-courting;

Fifteen, sixteen,
Maids in the kitchen;

Seventeen, eighteen,
Maids a-waiting;

Nineteen, twenty,
My plate's empty.

PICTURE STORY-BOOKS IN WINTER

Summer fading, winter comes —
Frosty mornings, tingling thumbs,
Window robins, winter rooks,
And the picture story-books.

Water now is turned to stone,
Nurse and I can walk upon,
Still we find the flowing brooks,
In the picture story-books.

All the pretty things put by,
Wait upon the children's eye,
Sheep and shepherds, trees and crooks,
In the picture story-books.

We may see how all things are,
Seas and cities, near and far,
And the flying fairies' looks,
In the picture story-books.

How am I to sing your praise,
Happy chimney-corner days,
Sitting safe in nursery nooks,
Reading picture story-books?

LITTLE MAID, PRETTY MAID

"Little maid,
pretty maid,
Where are you
going today?"
"Down to the
meadow to milk
my cow,
And I will be
gone all day."
"Shall I go with
you little maid,
pretty maid?"
"No, no, you
must wait right
here in the
shade."

SEE-SAW, MARGERY DAW

See-saw,
Margery Daw,
Jack shall have
a new master,
He shall have
but a penny
a day,
Because he
won't work
any faster.

Mother Tabbyskins

Sitting at a window,
In her cloak and hat,
I saw Mother Tabbyskins,
The real old cat!

Very old, very old,
Crumplety and lame;
Teaching kittens how to scold—
Is it not a shame?

Kittens in the garden,
Looking in her face,

Learning how to spit and swear,
Oh, what a disgrace!

Very wrong, very wrong,
Very wrong, and bad;
Such a subject for our song,
Makes us all too sad.

Old Mother Tabbyskins,
Sticking out her hand,
Gave a howl, and then a yowl,
Hobbled off to bed.

Very sick, very sick,
Very savage, too;
Pray send for a doctor quick,
Any one will do!

Doctor mouse came creeping,
Creeping to her bed;
Lanced her gums and felt her pulse,
Whispered she was dead.

Very sly, very sly,
The real old cat,
Open kept her weather eye—
Mouse! beware of that!

Old Mother Tabbyskins,
Saying "Serves him right,"
Gobbled up the doctor,
With infinite delight.

"Very fast, very fast,
Very pleasant, too—
What a pity it can't last!
Bring another, do."

Doctor Dog comes running,
Just to see her begs;
Round his neck a comforter,
Trousers on his legs.

Very grand, very grand—
Golden-headed cane
Swinging gaily from his hand,
Mischief in his brain!

"Dear Mother Tabbyskins,
And how are you now?
Let me feel your pulse—so, so;
Show your tongue—bow wow."

"Very ill, very ill."
"Please attempt to purr;
Will you take a draught or pill?
Which do you prefer?"

Ah, Mother Tabbyskins,
Who is now afraid?
Of poor little Doctor Mouse
You a mouthful made.

Very nice, very nice,
Little doctor he,
But for Doctor Dog's advice
You must pay the fee.

Doctor Dog comes nearer,
Says she must be bled;
I heard Mother Tabbyskins
Screaming in her bed.

Very close, very close,
Scuffling out and in;
Doctor Dog looks full and gross—
Where is Tabbyskin?

I will tell the moral
Without any fuss;
Those who lead the young astray,
Always suffer thus.

Very nice, very nice,
Let our conduct be;
For all doctors are not mice,
Some are dogs, you see!

Good King Wenceslas

Good King Wenceslas looked out,
On the feast of Stephen;
When the snow lay round about,
Deep and crisp and even.

Brightly shone the moon that night,
Though the frost was cruel,
When a poor man came in sight,
Gathering winter fuel.

"Hither page, and stand by me,
If thou know'st it, telling;
Yonder peasant, who is he?
Where and what his dwelling?"
"Sire, he lives a good league hence,
Underneath the mountain,
Right against the forest fence,
By Saint Agnes' fountain."

"Bring me meat, and bring me wine,
Bring me pine-logs hither;
Thou and I shall see him dine,
When we bear them thither."
Page and monarch, forth they went,
Forth they went together,
Through the rude wind's wild lament,
And the bitter weather.

"Sire, the night is darker now,
And the wind blows stronger;
Fails my heart, I know not how:
I can go no longer."
"Mark my footsteps, good my page,
Tread thou in them boldly;
Thou shalt find the winter's rage
Freeze thy blood less coldly."

In his master's steps he trod,
Where the snow lay dinted;
Heat was in the very sod
Which the saint had printed.
Therefore, Christian men, be sure,
Wealth or rank possessing,
Ye who now will bless the poor,
Shall yourselves find blessing.

The House that Jack Built

This is the house that Jack built.

This is the malt
That lay in the house that
Jack built.

This is the rat,
That ate the malt
That lay in the house that
Jack built.

This is the cat,
That killed the rat,
That ate the malt
That lay in the house that
Jack built.

This is the dog,
That worried the cat,
That killed the rat,
That ate the malt
That lay in the house that
Jack built.

This is the cow with the
crumpled horn,
That tossed the dog,
That worried the cat,
That killed the rat,
That ate the malt
That lay in the house that
Jack built.

This is the maiden all forlorn,
That milked the cow with the crumpled horn,
That tossed the dog,
That worried the cat,
That killed the rat,
That ate the malt
That lay in the house that Jack built.

This is the man all tattered and torn,
That kissed the maiden all forlorn,
That milked the cow with the crumpled horn,
That tossed the dog,
That worried the cat,
That killed the rat,
That ate the malt
That lay in the house that Jack built.

This is the priest all shaven and shorn,
That married the man all tattered and torn,
That kissed the maiden all forlorn,
That milked the cow with the crumpled horn,
That tossed the dog,
That worried the cat,
That killed the rat,
That ate the malt
That lay in the house that Jack built.

This is the cock that crowed in the morn,
That waked the priest all shaven and shorn,
That married the man all tattered and torn,
That kissed the maiden all forlorn,
That milked the cow with the crumpled horn,
That tossed the dog,
That worried the cat,
That killed the rat,
That ate the malt
That lay in the house that Jack built.

This is the farmer sowing his corn,
That kept the cock that crowed in the morn,
That waked the priest all shaven and shorn,
That married the man all tattered and torn,
That kissed the maiden all forlorn,
That milked the cow with the crumpled horn,
That tossed the dog,
That worried the cat,
That killed the rat,
That ate the malt
That lay in the house that Jack built.

The Milkmaid

A lady said to her son—a poor young squire:
"You must seek a wife with a fortune!"

"Where are you going, my pretty maid?"
"I'm going a-milking, sir," she said.

"Shall I go with you, my pretty maid?"
"Oh, yes, if you please, kind sir," she said.

"What is your father, my pretty maid?"
"My father's a farmer, sir," she said.

"Shall I marry you, my pretty maid?"
"Oh, thank you, kindly, sir," she said.

"But what is your fortune, my pretty maid?"
"My face is my fortune, sir," she said.

"Then I can't marry you, my pretty maid!"
"Nobody asked you, sir!" she said.

"Nobody asked you, sir!" she said.
"Sir!" she said.
"Nobody asked you, sir!" she said.

The Queen of Hearts

The Queen of Hearts,
She made some tarts,

All on a summer's day;

The Knave of Hearts,
He stole those tarts,

And took them right away.

The King of Hearts,
Called for those tarts,

And beat the Knave
full sore;

The Knave of Hearts,
Brought back those tarts,

And vowed he'd steal
no more.

Sing a Song of Sixpence

Sing a song of sixpence,
a pocket full of rye,

Four and twenty
blackbirds baked in
a pie,

When the pie was
opened the birds began
to sing,

Wasn't that a dainty dish
to set before a king?

The King was in his
counting-house,
counting out his money,

The Queen was in the
parlour, eating bread
and honey,

The maid was in the garden, hanging
out the clothes,
Along came a blackbird and pecked
off her nose.

Hey! Diddle, Diddle

Hey! diddle, diddle,
The cat and the fiddle,

The cow jumped over
the moon;
The little dog laughed
To see such fun,

And the dish ran away
with the spoon.

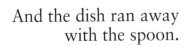

The Little Land

When at home alone I sit
And am very tired of it,
I have just to shut my eyes,
To go sailing through the skies—
To go sailing far away
To the pleasant Land of Play;
To the fairy land afar,
Where the little people are;
Where the clover-tops are trees,
And the rain-pools are the seas,
And the leaves, like little ships,
Sail about on tiny trips;
And above the daisy tree
Through the grasses,
High o'erhead the bumble bee
Hums and passes.

In that forest to and fro
I can wander, I can go;
See the spider and the fly,
And the ants go marching by,
Carrying parcels with their feet
Down the green and grassy street.
I can in the sorrel sit
Where the ladybird alit.
I can climb the jointed grass
And on high
See the greater swallows pass
In the sky,
And the round sun rolling by
Heeding no such things as I.

Through that forest I can pass
Till, as in a looking-glass,
Humming fly and daisy tree
And my tiny self I see,
Painted very clear and neat
On the rain-pool at my feet.
Should a leaflet come to land
Drifting near to where I stand,
Straight I'll board that tiny boat
Round the rain-pool sea to float.

Little thoughtful creatures sit
On the grassy coasts of it;
Little things with lovely eyes,
See me sailing with surprise.
Some are clad in armour green—
(These have sure to battle been!)—
Some are pied with ev'ry hue,
Black and crimson, gold and blue;
Some have wings and swift are gone—
But they all look kindly on.

When my eyes I once again
Open, and see all things plain:
High bare walls, great bare floor;
Great big knobs on drawer and door;
Great big people perched on chairs,
Stitching tucks and mending tears,
Each a hill that I could climb,
And talking nonsense all
the time—
Oh, dear me,
That I could be
A sailor on the
rain-pool sea,
A climber in the
clover tree,
And just
come back,
a sleepy-head,
Late at night
to go to bed.

GOING TO ST IVES

As I was going to St Ives,
I met a man with seven wives;
Every wife had seven sacks,
Every sack had seven cats,
Every cat had seven kits,
Kits, cats, sacks and wives,
How many were there going
to St Ives?

THE LIGHT-HEARTED FAIRY

Oh, who is so merry, so merry,
heigh ho!
As the light-hearted fairy, heigh
ho, heigh ho?
He dances and sings
To the sound of his wings,
With a hey, and a heigh,
and a ho!

Oh, who is so merry, so merry,
heigh ho!
As the light-hearted fairy, heigh
ho, heigh ho?

His nectar he sips
From a primrose's lips,
With a hey, and a
heigh, and a ho!

Oh, who is so
merry, so merry,
heigh ho!
As the
light-footed
fairy, heigh ho,
heigh ho?
His night is
the noon,
And his sun is
the moon,
With a hey, and a
heigh, and a ho!

THREE MEN IN A TUB

Rub-a-dub-dub,
Three men in a tub,
And who do you think they be?

The butcher, the baker,
The candlestick-maker,
Turn 'em out, knaves all three!

THE LION AND THE UNICORN

The lion and the unicorn were
fighting for the crown;
The lion beat the unicorn
all round about the
town.

Some gave them
white bread, and
some gave them
brown;

Some gave them
plum cake, and
sent them out of
town.

THE CHILD AND THE STAR

Little star that shines so bright,
Come and peep at me tonight,
For I often watch for you
In the pretty sky so blue.

Little star! Oh, tell me, pray,
Where you hide yourself all day?
Have you got a home like me,
And good friends so kind to see?

Little child! at you I peep
While you lie so fast asleep;
But when morn begins to break,
I my homeward journey take.

For I've many friends on high,
Living with me in the sky;
They love me as I love you,
And they love and watch you too.

I HAD A LITTLE PONY

I had a little pony,
His name was Dapple-Grey,
I lent him to a lady,
To ride a mile away.
She whipped him, she lashed him,
She rode him through the mire,
I would not lend my pony now,
For all the lady's hire.

EARLY TO BED, EARLY TO RISE

Cocks crow in the morn
To tell us to rise,
And he who lies late
Will never be wise;

For early to bed
And early to rise,
Is the way to be healthy
And wealthy and wise.

LULLABY

When little birdie bye-bye goes,
Quiet as mice in churches,
He puts his head where no-one knows,
On one leg he perches.

When little baby
bye-bye goes,
On mamma's arm
reposing,
Soon he lies beneath
the clothes,
Safe in the cradle
dozing.

When pretty pussy
goes to sleep,
Tail and nose together,
Then little mice
around her creep,
Lightly as a feather.

When little baby goes to sleep,
And he is very near us,
Then on tip-toe softly creep,
That baby may not hear us.

THE UNSEEN PLAYMATE

When children are playing alone
on the green,
In comes the playmate that never
was seen.
When children are happy and
lonely and good,
The Friend of the Children
comes out of the wood.

Nobody heard him and nobody
saw,
His is a picture you never could
draw,
But he's sure to be present,
abroad or at home,
When children are happy and
playing alone.

He lies in the laurels, he runs on
the grass,
He sings when you tinkle the
musical glass;
Whene'er you are happy
and cannot tell why,

The Friend of
the Children is
sure to be by!

He loves to be
little, he hates to
be big,
'Tis he that
inhabits the caves
that you dig;
'Tis he
when you
play with
your soldiers of tin,
That sides with the Frenchmen
and never can win.

'Tis he, when at night you go off
to your bed,
Bids you go to your sleep and
not trouble your head;
For wherever they're lying, in
cupboard or shelf,
'Tis he will take care of your
playthings himself!

RING-A-RING-A-ROSES

Ring-a-ring-a-roses,
A pocket full of posies,
A-tishoo, A-tishoo
We all fall down.

SINGING

Of speckled eggs the birdie sings,
And nests among the trees;
The sailor sings of ropes and things,
In ships upon the seas.

The children sing in far Japan,
The children sing in Spain;
The organ with the organ man,
Is singing in the rain.

COMICAL FOLK

In a cottage in Fife
Lived a man and his wife,
Who, believe me, were comical folk;
For, to people's surprise,
They both saw with their eyes,
And their tongues moved whenever
they spoke.

When they were asleep,
I'm told—that to keep
Their eyes open
they could not
contrive;
They both walked
on their feet,
And 'twas thought
what they eat,
Helped, with drinking,
to keep them alive.

SOLOMON GRUNDY

Solomon Grundy,
Born on a Monday,
Christened on Tuesday,
Married on Wednesday,
Took ill on Thursday,
Worse on Friday,
Died on Saturday,
Buried on Sunday,
And that is the end of
Poor Solomon Grundy.

A, B, C, TUMBLE DOWN D

A, B, C, tumble down D,
The cat's in the cupboard and can't see me.

GIRLS AND BOYS COME OUT TO PLAY

Girls and boys come out
to play,
The moon does shine as
bright as day,
Leave your supper
and leave your sleep,
And join your
playfellows in the street.

Come with a whoop and
come with a call,
And come with a
good-will or not at all,
Up the ladder and down
the wall,
A penny loaf will serve us all.

THOMAS A'TATTAMUS

Thomas A'Tattamus took two T's,
To tie two tups to two tall trees.
To frighten the terrible Thomas
A'Tattamus,
Tell me how many T's there are in
all that.

MISTER SUNFLOWER

In your dress of brown
and yellow

What a stiff-necked,
long-legged fellow!

Must you stare,
although the bees

Settle on your face
and tease?

Can't you turn your
big flat head

Till the sun has gone
to bed?

OLD MAID
HOLLYHOCK

Old maid hollyhock,
tall, and slim,

Upright, dignified,
stiff-necked prim!

All the flowers you
keep in order,

Stern-faced governess
of the border.

MONSIEUR RENARD'S GLOVES

Monsieur Renard gaily dressed,
Dons his fox-gloves of the best,
"Rabbits in the fern!" cries he,
"I'll invite myself to tea!"

ALDERMAN POPPY

"I see you, Alderman!" cries the wee maid—
"Alderman Poppy, asleep in the shade!"

FROGGY'S BANQUET

The sun is burning in
the sky,
Go fill the King-cup!
Fill it high!
I'm very thirsty in July,
I'll drink until the
pond is dry.

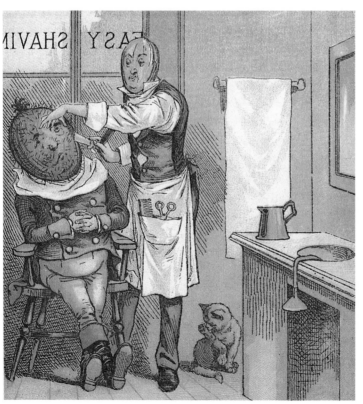

MISTER GOOSEBERRY'S BARBER

Says the gooseberry red
to the gooseberry green,
"Shave me quickly, kind sir,
I'm not fit to be seen;
I'm too hairy, too rough
and too purple in hue,
And I want to be pallid and
smooth faced like you!"

112

THE DOORMOUSE JUGGLER

Wee doormouse juggler,
I think you play
With nuts and acorns
for balls all day;
And the birds come
flocking to see the fun,
While the woodpecker
taps on the tree
"Well done!"

SUNFLOWER CYMBALS

Sunflowers, oh! so round
and flat!
See me curry-comb
the cat!
Sunflowers, oh! so flat
and round!
Cymbals, if they made
a sound!

GENERAL COCK-A-DOODLE

Cock-a-doodle-doo!
The top of the morning to you!
Generalissimo,
Crowing fortissimo
Cock-a-doodle-doo!

THE BATTLE OF THE BEE AND THE SNAPDRAGON

"Come, snapdragon!" says the bee,
"Give your honey up to me!
Though you threaten to devour,
I will never yield to flower!

Snap then, dragon, snap at me!
Like a new Saint George I'll be—
Buzz! Buzz! Buzz! and victory!"

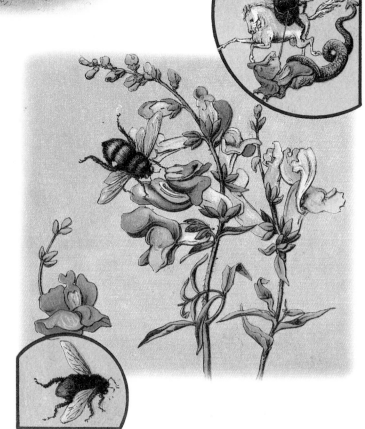

THE COBWEB HARP

Hark! The droning beetle
sings,
To his harp of cobweb
strings,
Perched upon his
cup-moss seat,
While the glow-worm
at his feet,
Lights the insects as
they pass,
Through the tangle of the
grass.

THE BUTTERFLIES
LAWN TENNIS

When a game at lawn tennis the
butterflies sought,
"I," said the snail, "I will mark out
the court."
"I," said the bee, "for a racquet will
bring
Some lazy old drone's cast off
gossamer wing."
"For your balls," said the fuchsia,
"I've dewdrops in store."
"As for me," said the fly, "let
me buzz out the score."
"I," said the spider, "will spin
you a net."
So the bright butterflies made
up a set.

Old Mother Hubbard

Old Mother Hubbard
Went to her cupboard,
To give her poor dog a bone;
When she came there
The cupboard was bare,
And so the poor dog had none.

She went to the baker's
To buy him some bread;
When she came back
The dog was dead!

She went to the
undertaker's
To buy him a coffin;
When she came back
The dog was laughing.

She took a clean dish
To get him some tripe;
When she came back
He was smoking his pipe.

She went to the ale-house
To get him some beer;
When she came back
The dog sat in a chair.

She went to the tavern
For white wine and red;
When she came back
The dog stood on his head.

She went to the hosier's
To buy him some hose;
When she came back
He was dressed in his
clothes.

The dame made a
curtsy,
The dog made a bow;
The dame said,
"Your servant,"
The dog said,
"Bow-wow!"

She went to the hatter's
To buy him a hat;
When she came back
He was feeding the cat.

She went to the cobbler's
To buy him some shoes;
When she came back
He was reading the news.

She went to the sempster's
To buy him some linen;
When she came back
The dog was spinning.

Simple Simon

Simple Simon met a pie-man,
Going to the fair;
Says Simple Simon to the pie-man,
"Let me taste your ware."

Says the pie-man unto Simon,
"First give me a penny."
Says Simple Simon to the pie-man,
"I have not got any."

He went to catch a dicky-bird,
And thought he could not fail,
Because he had got a little salt,
To put upon his tail.

He went to ride a spotted cow,
That had got a little calf;
She threw him down upon the ground,
Which made the people laugh.

Then Simple Simon went a-hunting,
For to catch a hare;
He rode a goat about the street,
But could not find one there.

He went for to eat honey,
Out of the mustard-pot;
He bit his tongue until he cried,
That was all the good he got.

Simple Simon went a-fishing,
For to catch a whale;
And all the water he had got,
Was in his mother's pail.

He went to take a bird's nest,
Was built upon a bough;
A branch gave way, and Simon fell,
Into a dirty slough.

He went to shoot a wild duck,
But the wild duck flew away;
Says Simon, "I can't hit him,
Because he will not stay."

Once Simon made a great snowball,
And brought it in to roast;
He laid it down before the fire,
And soon the ball was lost.

He went to slide upon the ice,
Before the ice would bear;
Then he plunged in above his knees,
Which made poor Simon stare.

He went to try if cherries ripe,
Grew upon a thistle;
He pricked his finger very much,
Which made poor Simon whistle.

He washed himself with
blacking-ball,
Because he had no soap;
Then, then, said to his mother,
      "I'm a beauty now, I hope."

He went for water
  in a sieve,
    But soon it all ran
    through;
    And now poor
    Simple Simon
    Bids you all adieu.

THE WIND

I saw you toss the kites on high,
And blow the birds about the sky,
And all around I heard you pass,
Like ladies' skirts across the grass—
O wind, a-blowing all day long,
O wind, that sings so loud a song.

I saw the different things you did,
But always you yourself you hid.
I felt you push, I heard you call,
I could not see yourself at all—
O wind, a-blowing all day long,
O wind, that sings so loud a song.

O you that are so strong and cold,
O blower, are you young or old?
Are you a beast of field and tree,
Or just a stronger child than me?
O wind, a-blowing all day long,
O wind, that sings so loud a song.

THE SWING

How do you like to go up in a swing,
Up in the air so blue?
Oh, I do think it the pleasantest thing
Ever a child can do!

Up in the air and over the wall,
Till I can see so wide,
Rivers and trees and cattle and all
Over the countryside—

Till I look down on the garden green,
Down on the roof so brown—
Up in the air I go flying again,
Up in the air and down!

THE MOON

The moon has a face like the clock
in the hall;
She shines on thieves on the
garden wall,
On streets and fields and harbour
quays,
And birdies asleep in the forks
of the trees.

The squalling cat and the
squeaking mouse,
The howling dog by the door
of the house,
The bat that lies in bed at noon,
All love to be out by the light
of the moon.

But all of the things that belong
to the day,
Cuddle to sleep to be out of her way;
And flowers and children close
their eyes,
Till up in the morning the sun
shall rise.

A GOOD PLAY

We built a ship upon the stairs
All made of the back-bedroom chairs,
And filled it full of sofa pillows
To go a-sailing on the billows.

We took a saw and several nails
And water in the nursery pails;
And Tom said, "Let us also take
An apple and a slice of cake" —
Which was enough for Tom and me
To go a-sailing on, till tea.

We sailed along for days and
days,
And had the very best of
plays;
But Tom fell out and hurt
his knee,
So there was no-one left but me.

MARY HAD A LITTLE LAMB

Mary had a little lamb,
Its fleece was white as snow,
And everywhere that Mary went,
The lamb was sure to go;
He followed her to school one day,
That was against the rule,
It made the children laugh and play,
To see a lamb at school.

So the teacher turned him out,
But still he lingered near,
And waited patiently about,
Till Mary did appear;
And then he ran to her and laid
His head upon her arm,
As if he said: "I'm not afraid,
You'll keep me from all harm."

"What makes the lamb love Mary so?"
The eager children cry.

"O, Mary loves the lamb you know,"
The teacher did reply.
"And you each gentle animal,
In confidence may bind,
And make them follow at your call,
If you are always kind."

ROUND AND ROUND
THE GARDEN

Round and round the garden
Like a teddy bear;
One step, two step,
Tickle you under there.

"When I get rich," say the bells
of Shoreditch.

"When will that be?" say
the bells of Stepney.
"I do not know," says the
great bell of Bow.
"Pancakes and fritters,"
say the bells of Saint Peter's.
"Two sticks and an apple,"
say the bells of
Whitechapel.

ORANGES AND LEMONS

"Oranges and lemons," say
the bells of Saint Clement's.
"You owe me five farthings,"
say the bells of Saint Martin's.
"When will you pay me?" say
the bells of Old Bailey.

"Old father Bald-pate," say the
slow bells of Aldgate.
"Pokers and tongs," say the bells
of Saint John's.
"Kettles and pans," say the bells
of Saint Anne's.
"Brickbats and tiles," say the bells
of Saint Giles.

EYE WINKER

Eye winker,
Tom tinker,
Nose smeller,
Mouth eater,
Chin chopper,
Guzzlewopper.

THE FLOWERS

All the names I know from
nurse:
Gardener's garters, shepherd's
purse,
Bachelor's buttons, lady's smock,
And the lady hollyhock.

Fairy places, fairy things,
Fairy woods where the wild
bee wings,
Tiny trees for tiny dames —
These must all be fairy names!

Tiny woods below whose
boughs,
Shady fairies weave a house;
Tiny tree-tops, rose or thyme,
Where the braver fairies climb!

Fair are grown-up people's trees,
But the fairest woods are these;
Where, if I were not so tall,
I should live for good and all.

LAVENDER'S BLUE

Lavender's blue, diddle, diddle!
Lavender's green;
When I am king, diddle, diddle!
You shall be queen.

Call up your men, diddle, diddle!
Set them to work;
Some to the plough, diddle, diddle!
Some to the cart.

Some to make hay, diddle, diddle!
Some to cut corn;
While you and I, diddle, diddle!
Keep ourselves warm.

CHRISTMAS

Christmas is coming, the geese are getting fat,
Please to put a penny in an old man's hat;
If you haven't got a penny, a ha'penny will do,
If you haven't got a ha'penny, God bless you.

A LITTLE COCK SPARROW

A little cock
sparrow sat on a
green tree,
And he chirruped and chirruped,
so merry was he,
But a naughty boy came with a
small bow and arrow,
Determined to shoot this little
cock sparrow.

"This little cock sparrow shall
make me a stew,"
Said this naughty boy.
"Yes, and a little pie, too."
"Oh! no," said the sparrow,
"I won't make a stew,"
So he fluttered his wings and
away he flew.

THE DAYS OF THE MONTH

Thirty days has September,
April, June and November;
February has twenty-eight alone,
All the rest have thirty-one,
Except in leap-year, when's the time,
That February has twenty-nine.

THE MULBERRY BUSH

Here we go round the mulberry bush,
The mulberry bush,
The mulberry bush;
Here we go round the mulberry bush,
On a cold and frosty morning.

This is the way we wash our hands,
We wash our hands,
We wash our hands;
This is the way we wash our hands,
On a cold and frosty morning.

This is the way we dry our hands,
We dry our hands,
We dry our hands;
This is the way we dry our hands,
On a cold and frosty morning.

This is the way we clap our hands,
We clap our hands,
We clap our hands;
This is the way we clap our hands,
On a cold and frosty morning.

This is the way we warm our
hands,
We warm our hands,
We warm our hands;
This is the way we
warm
our hands,
On a cold and frosty
morning.

FOREIGN LANDS

Up into the cherry
tree
Who should climb
but little me?
I held the trunk with
both my hands
And looked abroad
on foreign lands.

I saw the next door
garden lie,
Adorned with flowers,
before my eye,
And many pleasant
places more
That I had never seen
before.

I saw the dimpling
river pass,
And be the sky's blue
looking-glass;
The dusty roads go
up and down
With people tramping in
to town.

If I could find a higher tree
Farther and farther I should see,
To where the grown-up river slips,
Into the sea among the ships.

To where the roads
on either hand,
Lead onward into
fairy land,
Where all the children
dine at five,
And all the playthings
come alive.

LITTLE POLLY FLINDERS

Little Polly Flinders
Sat among the
cinders
Warming her
pretty little toes;
Her mother came
and caught her
And scolded her
daughter
For spoiling her
nice new clothes.

THE LOVING BROTHERS

I love you well, my little
brother,
And you are fond of me;
Let us be kind to one
another,
As brothers ought to be.
You shall learn to play
with me,
And learn to use my toys;
And then I think that we
shall be,
Two happy little boys.

LOOKING-GLASS RIVER

Smooth it glides
upon its travel,
Here a wimple, there
a gleam—
O the clean gravel!
O the smooth
stream!

Sailing blossoms,
silver fishes,
Paven pools as clear
as air—
How a child wishes
To live down there!

We can see our
coloured faces,
Floating on the
shaken pool,
Down in cool places,
Dim and very cool.

Till a wind or water
wrinkle,
Dipping marten, plumping trout,

Spreads in a twinkle,
And blots all out.

See the rings pursue each other;
All below grows black as night—
Just as if mother,
Had blown out the light!

Patience, children, just a
minute—
See the spreading circles die;
The stream and all in it,
Will clear by-and-by.

The Thievish Mouse

A story sad I've got to tell about a little mouse
With bright brown eyes who used to scamper up and down the house:
No cheese was safe, no birthday cake on either shelf or ground,
For mouse would surely find it out, and nibble it all round.

I cannot tell you how each night this naughty mouse would roam,
Her little nose thrust into things she should have left alone:

It mattered not where they were put, in cupboard or on shelf,
This cunning mouse would sniff them out, and coolly help herself.

Aunt Mary said, "It is no use to hide the cakes and pies,
For someone finds them all, and slyly feasts upon the prize.
A thief there surely is secreted somewhere in the house."
But Grandpapa (the wise old man) declared it was a mouse.

Said he, "We'll get a trap, and then you soon will find I'm right,
Just toast a bit of cheese and make all ready for tonight,
And when our little friend arrives, prepared to help herself,
She'll find, instead of pie and cake, there's mischief on the shelf."

Poor mousey! little did she think while scampering along,
How dearly she would have to pay, that night for doing wrong.
She tasted pie and cake, then seized the cheese with eager greed.
Alas! the trap closed with a spring, and she was caught indeed.

Now little folks believe me, when you do a wicked thing,
Sometime or other it is sure, its punishment to bring,
And nothing can be worse you know, in people small or grown,
Than that of taking anything which is not quite their own.

You see, if mouse had stayed at home, nor cared to pry and peep,
And had not trotted out to steal, while others were asleep,
She'd now have been alive and well, and happy with her friends,
Instead of being caught and killed, to prove how stealing ends.

The Death and Burial of Cock Robin

Who killed Cock Robin?
"I," said the sparrow,
"With my bow and arrow,
I killed Cock Robin."

Who'll make his shroud?
"I," said the beetle,
"With my thread and needle,
I'll make his shroud."

Who saw him die?
"I," said the fly,
"With my little eye,
I saw him die."

Who'll bear the torch?
"I," said the linnet,
"Will come in a minute,
I'll bear the torch."

Who caught his blood?
"I," said the fish,
"With my little dish,
I caught his blood."

Who'll be the clerk?
"I," said the lark,
"I'll say Amen in the dark,
I'll be the clerk."

Who'll dig his grave?
"I," said the owl,
"With my spade and trowel,
I'll dig his grave."

Who'll carry his coffin?
"I," said the kite,
"If it be in the night,
I'll carry his coffin."

Who'll be the parson?
"I," said the rook,
"With my little book,
I'll be the parson."

Who'll be chief mourner?
"I," said the dove,
"I mourn for my love,
I'll be chief mourner."

Who'll sing his dirge?
"I," said the thrush,
"As I sing in a bush,
I'll sing his dirge."

Who'll toll the bell?
"I," said the bull,
"Because I can pull,
I'll toll the bell."

All the birds of the air,
Fell sighing and sobbing,
When they heard the bell toll
For poor Cock Robin.

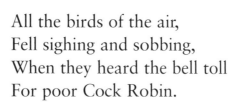

North-West Passage

1. Good-Night

Then the bright lamp is carried in,
The sunless hours again begin;
O'er all without, in field and lane,
The haunted night returns again.

Now we behold the embers flee,
About the firelit hearth; and see
Our faces painted as we pass,
Like pictures, on the window-glass.

Must we to bed indeed? Well then,
Let us arise and go like men,
And face with an undaunted tread
The long black passage up to bed.

Farewell, O brother, sister, sire!
O pleasant party round the fire!
The songs you sing, the tales you tell,
Till far tomorrow, fare ye well!

3. In Port

Last, to the chamber where I lie,
My fearful footsteps patter nigh,
And come from out the cold and gloom
Into my warm and cheerful room.

There, safe arrived, we turn about,
To keep the coming shadows out,
And close the happy door at last
On all the perils that we past.

Then, when mamma goes by to bed,
She shall come in with tip-toe tread,
And see me lying warm and fast
And in the Land of Nod at last.

2. Shadow March

All round the house is the jet-black
night,
It stares through the
window-pane;
It crawls in the corners,
hiding from the light,
And it moves with the
moving flame.

Now my little heart goes
a-beating like a drum,
With the breath of the
Bogie in my hair;
And all round the candle
the crooked shadows come,
And go marching along
up the stair.

The shadow of the
balusters, the shadow of
the lamp,
The shadow of the child
that goes to bed—
All the wicked shadows
coming, tramp, tramp,
tramp,
With the black night
overhead.

I HAD A LITTLE NUT TREE

I had a little nut tree, nothing
would it bear,
But a silver nutmeg and a
golden pear;
The King of Spain's daughter
came to visit me,
And all for the sake of my
little nut tree.

THERE WAS A LADY LOVED A SWINE

There was a lady loved a swine,
"Honey!" said she,
"Pig-hog, will you be mine?"
"Hunc!" said he.

"I'll build you a silver sty,
"Honey!" said she,
"And in it you shall lie!"
"Hunc!" said he.

"Pinned with a silver pin,
"Honey!" said she,
"That you may go out and in,"
"Hunc!" said he.

"Will you have me now,
"Honey?" said she,
"Speak, or my heart will break,"
"Hunc!" said he.

GOOD KING ARTHUR

When good King Arthur ruled this land,
He was a goodly king,
He stole three pecks of barley meal,
To make a bag pudding.

A bag pudding the Queen did make,
And stuffed it well with plums,
And in it put great lumps of fat
As big as my two thumbs.

The King and Queen did eat thereof,
And noblemen beside,
And what they could not eat that night
The Queen next morning fried.

OLD KING COLE

Old King Cole was a merry old soul,
And a merry old soul was he;
He called for his pipe, and he called
for his bowl,
And he called for his fiddlers three.
Every fiddler had a fiddle,
And a very fine fiddle had he.
Tweedle dee, tweedle dee, tweedle dee,
tweedle dee,
Tweedle dee, tweedle dee, went the
fiddlers three;
Oh, there's none so rare as can compare
With King Cole and his fiddlers three.

HUSH-A-BYE BABY

Hush-a-bye baby on the tree-top,
When the wind blows the cradle will rock;
When the bough breaks the cradle will fall,
And down will come baby, cradle and all!

MR DUCK AND MR TURKEY

Mister Duck went to call on
Mister Turkey,
And he walked with a wobble,
wobble, wobble;
When he said, "How d'ye do,"
to Mister Turkey,
Mister Turkey said:
"Gobble, gobble, gobble."

Mister Duck then answered,
"Quack, quack, quack,"
And turned around to go right back;
Mister Turkey said: "I'll go with you,"
And they looked so very odd,
those two;
Mister Duck was walking wobble,
wobble, wobble;
Mister Turkey talking,
"Gobble, gobble, gobble."

MR FROG

Mister Frog came out of
the pond one day,
And found himself in the rain;
Said he: "I'll get wet, and
I may catch cold,"
So he jumped in the pond again.

THE CATERPILLAR

Fuzzy old fellow,
Brown and yellow,
Will you be a butterfly some
summer day?
Your dusty brown
Turned to golden brown,
And with wings to fly away,
with wings to fly away.

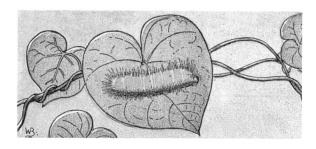

THE WHALE

In the South Sea lives a whale,
With a very broad back,
And a great big tail, a great big tail;
He said: "I shall spend my life at sea,
For it's just the place for me."

So if ever you get to the great
South Sea,
Be sure to go for a sail;
And if you sing this song
He may come along,
And you'll see that great big whale.

HUMPTY DUMPTY

Humpty Dumpty sat on a wall,
Humpty Dumpty had a great fall;
All the King's horses and
all the King's men,
Couldn't put Humpty
together again.

PAT-A-CAKE

Pat-a-cake, pat-a-cake,
baker's man!
Bake me a cake as fast
as you can,
Prick it and nick it and
mark it with B,
And there will be plenty
for baby and me.

MARY, MARY, QUITE CONTRARY

"Mary, Mary, quite contrary,
How does your garden grow?"
"With silver bells and
cockle shells,
And pretty maids all
in a row."

LUCY LOCKET

Lucy Locket lost her pocket,
Kitty Fisher found it;
Not a penny was there in it
But a ribbon round it.

PUSSY CAT, PUSSY CAT, WHERE HAVE YOU BEEN?

"Pussy cat, pussy cat,
where have you been?"
"I've been to London to
see the new Queen."
"Pussy cat, Pussy cat, what
did you there?"
"I caught a little mouse
under her chair."

THE HAYLOFT

Through all the pleasant
meadow-side,
The grass grew shoulder-high,
Till the shining scythes went far
and wide,
And cut it down to dry.

Those green and sweetly
smelling crops,
They led in waggons home,
And they piled them here in
mountain tops,
For mountaineers to roam.

Here is Mount Clear, Mount
Rusty-Nail,
Mount Eagle and Mount High—
The mice that in these
mountains dwell,
No happier are than I!

Oh, what a joy to clamber there,
Oh, what a place for play,
With the sweet, the dim, the
dusty air,
The happy hills of hay!

OH, WHERE, OH, WHERE IS
MY LITTLE DOG GONE?

Oh, where, oh, where is my little dog gone?
Oh, where, oh, where can he be?
With his ears cut short, and his tail cut long,
Oh, where, oh where is he?

MONDAY'S CHILD

Monday's child is fair of face,
Tuesday's child is full of grace,
Wednesday's child is full of woe,
Thursday's child has far to go,
Friday's child is loving and giving,
Saturday's child works hard for its living,
But the child that is born on the Sabbath day,
Is bonny and blithe and good and gay.

DING DONG BELL

Ding dong bell!
Pussy's in the well!
Who put her in?
Little Tommy Lin.
Who pulled her out?
Little Tommy Stout.
What a naughty boy was that
To drown poor pussy cat,
Who never did any harm,
But killed all the mice in father's barn.

RIDE A COCK-HORSE

Ride a cock-horse to
Banbury Cross,
To see a fine lady ride on a
white horse;
With rings on her fingers,
And bells on her toes,
So she shall have music
wherever she goes.

HICKORY, DICKORY DOCK!

Hickory, dickory, dock!
The mouse ran up the clock;
The clock struck one,
The mouse ran down,
Hickory, dickory, dock!

Fairy Tales

Thumbelina

There was once a woman who wanted to have a tiny little child, but she did not know where to get one from. So one day she went to an old witch and said to her: "I should so much like to have a tiny little child; can you tell me where I can get one?"

"Oh, we have just got one ready!" said the Witch. "Here is a barley-corn for you, but it's not the kind the farmer sows in his field, or feeds the hens with, I can tell you. Put it in a flower pot, and then you will see something happen."

"Oh, thank you!" said the woman, and gave the Witch a shilling, for that was what it cost. Then she went home and planted the barley-corn; immediately there grew out of it a large and beautiful flower, which looked like a tulip, but the petals were tightly closed.

"What a beautiful flower!" exclaimed the woman, and she kissed the red and yellow petals; as she kissed them the flower burst open. It was a real tulip, but in the middle of the blossom, sat a pretty little girl. She was scarcely half a thumb in height; so they called her Thumbelina. A polished walnut shell served Thumbelina as a cradle, the petals of a violet were her mattress, and a rose leaf her cover. There she lay at night, but in the daytime she used to play about on the table; here the woman had put a bowl, in the middle of which floated a tulip petal, and on this Thumbelina sat, and sailed from one side of the bowl to the other, rowing herself with two white horse hairs for oars. She could sing, too, with a voice more soft and sweet than had ever been heard before.

One night, when Thumbelina was lying in her pretty little bed, an old toad crept in through a broken pane in the window. "This would make a beautiful wife for my son," said the ugly old toad, taking up the walnut shell, with Thumbelina inside, and hopping with it through the window into the garden.

There flowed a great wide stream; here the toad lived with her son. Ugh! how ugly and clammy he was, just like his mother! "Croak, croak, croak!" was all he could say when he saw the pretty little girl in the walnut shell.

"Don't talk so loud, or you'll wake her," said the old toad. "She might escape us even now; she is as light as a feather. We will put her at once on a broad waterlily leaf in the stream. That will be quite an island for her; she is so small and light. She can't run away from us there."

Outside in the brook grew a great number of waterlilies with broad green leaves, which looked as if they were swimming about on the water. The leaf farthest away was the largest, and to this the old toad swam with Thumbelina in her walnut shell.

The tiny Thumbelina woke up early in the morning, and when she saw where she was she began to cry bitterly; for on every side of the great green leaf was water, and she could not get to the land.

The old toad swam out with her ugly son to the leaf where Thumbelina lay. The old toad bowed low in the water before her, and said: "Here is my son; you shall marry him, and live in great magnificence down under the marsh."

"Croak, croak, croak!" was all the son could say. Then the old toad and her son swam away; but Thumbelina sat alone on

The tiny Thumbelina woke up very early in the morning, and when she saw where she was she began to cry bitterly; for on every side of the great green leaf was water, and she could not get to the land.

the green leaf and wept, for she did not want to live with the clammy old toad, or marry her ugly son.

The little fishes swimming about under the water had seen the toad quite plainly, and heard what she had said; so they put up their heads to see the little girl. They thought her so pretty that they were very sorry she should go down to live with the ugly toad. They assembled in the water round the green stalk which supported the leaf on which she was sitting, and nibbled the stem in two. Away floated the leaf down the stream, bearing Thumbelina far beyond the reach of the toad.

A great big cicada came flying past; he caught sight of little Thumbelina, and in a moment had put his arms round her slender waist, and had flown off with her to a tree. Oh dear! how terrified poor little Thumbelina was; he sat down with her on a large green leaf, and told her that she was very pretty, although she wasn't in the least like a cicada. Later on, all the other cicadas who lived in the same tree came to pay calls; they examined Thumbelina closely, and then remarked, "Why, she has only two legs! How very miserable!"

"She has no feelers!" cried another.

"How ugly she is!" said all the female cicadas, even though poor Thumbelina was really very pretty.

The cicada who had stolen her knew this very well; but when he heard all the ladies saying she was ugly, he began to think so too, and would not keep her. So he flew down from the tree with her and put her on a daisy. There she sat and wept, because she was so ugly that the cicada would have nothing to do with her; and yet she was the most beautiful creature imaginable, so soft and delicate, like the loveliest rose leaf.

All through the summer poor little Thumbelina lived all alone in the great wood. She plaited a soft bed for herself of blades of grass, and hung it up under a clover leaf, so that she was protected from the rain; she gathered honey from the flowers for food, and drank the dew on the leaves every morning. Thus summer and autumn passed, but then came winter—the long, cold winter. The trees shed their leaves, all the flowers died; the clover leaf under which she had lived curled up, and nothing remained of it but the withered stalk. She was terribly cold, for her clothes were ragged, and she was so small and thin. Poor little Thumbelina! She would surely be frozen to death. It began to snow, and every snowflake that fell on her was to her as a whole shovelful thrown on one of us, for we are so big and she was so tiny. She wrapped herself round in a dead leaf, but it was torn in the middle and gave her no warmth; she was trembling with cold.

Once she came across the door of a fieldmouse, who had a little hole under the snow. There the fieldmouse lived warm and snug, with a storeroom full of corn. Poor little Thumbelina went up to the door and begged for a little piece of barley, for she had not had anything to eat for the last two days.

"Poor little creature!" exclaimed the fieldmouse, for she was a kind-hearted old thing. "Come into my nice warm room and have some dinner with me."

As Thumbelina pleased her, she said: "You may spend the winter with me; but you must keep my room clean and tidy, and tell me stories, for I like that very much." And Thumbelina did all that the kind old fieldmouse asked, and did it remarkably well too.

The swallow flew down with Thumbelina, and set her upon one of the broad leaves. There, to her astonishment, she found a tiny little man sitting in the middle of a flower, he had the prettiest golden crown on his head, and the most beautiful wings on his shoulders.

"Now I am expecting a visitor," said the fieldmouse; "my neighbour comes to call on me once a week. If you could only marry him, you would be well provided for. But he is blind. You must tell him all the prettiest stories you know."

But Thumbelina did not trouble her head about him, for he was only a mole. He came and paid them a visit in his black velvet coat.

"He is so rich," the fieldmouse told her. "His house is at least twenty times larger than mine; he possesses great knowledge, but he cannot bear the sun and the beautiful flowers, and speaks slightingly of them, for he has never seen them."

Thumbelina sang so prettily that the mole fell in love with her and made up his mind to marry her. A short time before he had dug a long passage through the ground from his own house to that of his neighbour; in this he gave the fieldmouse and Thumbelina permission to walk as often as they liked. But he begged them not to be afraid of the dead bird that lay in the passage; it was a real bird with feathers and a beak, and must have died a little time ago, and now lay buried just where he had made his tunnel. The mole took a piece of rotten wood in his mouth, for that glows like fire in the dark, and went in front, lighting the way through the long dark passage.

When they came to the place where the dead bird lay, the mole put his broad nose up against the ceiling and pushed a hole through, so that the daylight could shine down. In the middle of the path lay a dead swallow, his pretty wings pressed close to his sides, his claws and head drawn under his feathers; the poor bird had evidently died of cold. Thumbelina was very sorry, for she was very fond of all little birds. But the mole kicked him with his bandy legs and said: "Now he can't sing any more! It must be very miserable to be a little bird! Birds always starve in winter."

"Yes, you speak like a sensible man," said the fieldmouse.

Thumbelina did not say anything; but when the other two had passed on she bent down to the bird, brushed the feathers from his head, and kissed his closed eyes gently. "Perhaps it was he that sweetly sang to me in the summer," she thought.

The mole closed up the hole which let in the light, and then escorted the two ladies home. But Thumbelina could not sleep that night; so she got out of bed, and plaited a great big blanket of straw, and spread it over the dead bird, so that the poor little thing should lie warmly buried.

"Farewell, pretty little bird!" she said. "Farewell, and thank you for your beautiful songs in the summer, when the trees were green, and the sun shone down so warmly on us!" Then Thumbelina lay her head against the bird's heart. But the bird was not dead: he had been frozen, but now that she had warmed him, he was coming to life again.

In autumn the swallows fly far away to foreign lands; but there are some who are late in starting, and then they get so cold that they drop down as if dead, and the snow comes and covers them over. Poor Thumbelina trembled, she was so frightened; for the bird was very large in comparison with herself. But she took courage, fetched her own cover and laid it over the poor bird's head.

The next night she crept out again to him. There he was alive, but very weak; he could only open his eyes for a moment and look at Thumbelina, who was standing in front of him with a piece of rotten wood in her hand, for she had no other lantern.

"Thank you, pretty little child!" said the swallow to her. "I am so beautifully warm! Soon I shall regain my strength, and then I shall be able to fly out again into the warm sunshine."

"Oh!" she said, "it is very cold outside; it is snowing and freezing! Stay here in your warm bed; I will take care of you!"

The whole winter he remained down there, and Thumbelina looked after him and nursed him tenderly. Neither the mole nor the fieldmouse learnt anything of this, for they could not bear the poor swallow.

When the spring came, and the sun warmed the earth again, the swallow said farewell to Thumbelina, who opened the hole in the roof for him which the mole had made. The sun shone brightly down upon her, and the swallow asked her if she would go with him; she could sit upon his back.

"We will fly far away from the ugly mole and his dark house, over the great mountains, to the warm countries, where it is always summer, and there are always beautiful flowers. Do come with me, dear little Thumbelina, who saved my life when I lay frozen in the dark tunnel!"

"Yes, I will go with you, my friend," said Thumbelina, and got on the swallow's back, placing her feet on one of his out-stretched wings. Up he flew into the air, over woods and seas, over the great mountains where the snow is always lying. And if she was cold she crept under his warm feathers, only keeping her little head out to admire all the beautiful things in the world beneath. At last they came to warm lands. Under the most splendid green trees beside a blue lake stood a glittering white marble castle. There were many swallows' nests, and in one of these lived the swallow who was carrying Thumbelina.

"Here is my house!" he said. "But it won't do for you to live with me; I am not tidy enough to please you. Find a home for yourself in one of the lovely flowers that grow down there."

"That will be splendid!" she replied clapping her little hands.

Then the swallow flew down with little Thumbelina, and set her upon one of the broad leaves. There, to her astonishment, she found a tiny little man sitting in the middle of a flower, he had the prettiest golden crown on his head, and the most beautiful wings on his shoulders; he himself was no bigger than Thumbelina. He was the spirit of the flower. In each blossom there dwelt a tiny man or woman; but this one was the King.

"Oh, how handsome he is!" whispered Thumbelina to the swallow.

The little Prince was very frightened at the swallow, for in comparison with one so tiny as himself he seemed a giant. But when he saw Thumbelina, he was happy, for she was the most beautiful girl he had ever seen. So he took his golden crown from his head and put it on hers, asking her if she would be his wife. Yes! he was a different kind of husband to the son of the old toad and the mole with the black velvet coat. So she agreed to marry him. And out of each flower came a lady and gentleman, each so tiny and pretty that it was a pleasure to see them. Each brought Thumbelina a present, but the best of all was a beautiful pair of wings which were fastened on to her back, and now she too could fly from flower to flower. They all wished Thumbelina and the little Prince joy, and the swallow sat above in his nest and sang the wedding march.

Andersen, *The Yellow Fairy Book*

The Snow Queen

There was once a wicked troll, a very wicked troll, the wickedest of trolls, who made a magic mirror. Everything good and beautiful reflected in the mirror shrank to nothing, and everything ugly and useless looked much worse and much bigger. Kind people's faces looked foolish and warped, and good thoughts always made them look even worse. The other trolls carried the mirror from country to country to mock at everything there, and at last they carried it up to the sky. But the higher they went the more the magic mirror grinned, until they dropped it. The mirror broke into millions and billions of pieces, some as small as a grain of sand, and these flew about in the air and got into people's eyes so that they saw only the evil in the world. If a piece of mirror got into someone's heart, the heart turned to ice. If a piece of mirror was made into spectacles, the person was never able to see properly and judge things well. The evil Troll laughed at all this, but there were still plenty of pieces of the broken mirror flying about in the air.

In the middle of the great city, where there are so many houses and people that there is no room for each person to have his own little garden, and where most must therefore be contented with flower pots, there were two poor children nevertheless who *did* have a garden somewhat bigger than a flower pot. Gerda and Kay were neighbours who loved each other like brother and sister. They lived up in the garrets of two adjoining roofs, with the gutter running between them, and there were two little windows projecting from the roofs, and facing each other, so that one only had to step over the gutter to get from one window to the other.

The two families each had a big wooden box outside, where they grew pot herbs as well as a little rose bush. The two rose bushes sent out long shoots that climbed up the windows and bent towards each other. The children were often allowed to step out and sit on their small stools under the roses, and there they enjoyed themselves thoroughly.

In the winter, though, the windows were shut and frozen over, and the children had to climb the stairs down and up again to visit one another. When the snow fell, Kay's grandmother told him that the white bees were swarming, and in their midst the Snow Queen who never rests on the ground but always flies up in a black cloud.

"Could the Snow Queen come in here?" asked Gerda.

"If she comes in," said Kay, "I will put her on the stove and she will melt."

That night, Kay looked out through a little hole that he had melted in the ice covering the window, and outside he saw a snowflake falling. It grew and grew outside the window until it turned into a beautiful woman totally made of ice, gleaming and glittering, and her eyes shining like stars. There was no peace or rest in those eyes, and she beckoned to Kay to open the window. He jumped down from his chair in fear, and a shadow passed over the window like a big bird flying past.

Spring finally came, and then summer; the two rose bushes bloomed better than ever that summer. One sunny day Gerda and Kay were looking at a picture-book

At last the boat passed close by a cottage with a cherry orchard. Out came an old woman leaning on a crutch. She hooked her crutch in the boat and drew it closer, and then she lifted Gerda out.

together when all of a sudden Kay cried out, "Something is hurting in my heart! And something is in my eye!"

Gerda looked into his eye but she could see nothing there. "I think it is gone," he said, but it was still there. It was a piece of the broken mirror, that magic mirror that makes everything good seem worthless and mean, and everything worthless and mean seem even worse. Kay had a splinter of the mirror in his heart too, that would turn it to ice. Even though the pain went away, the mirror worked its magic inside him.

"Why are you crying, Gerda?" he said. "You look so ugly when you cry! There is nothing wrong with me."

He said that the picture-book was only for babies and when his grandmother was telling them stories he stood behind her and made faces. He started to imitate everyone in the street and to mock at them cruelly. The neighbours thought he was clever, but it was all the glass splinter's doing. It was the splinter of glass that made him spiteful to poor Gerda all the time, even though she loved him dearly.

When the snowflakes fell Kay looked at them with a magnifying glass and told Gerda that they were much more beautiful than flowers. "For flowers are not perfect, and snowflakes are so well made!" Then he took his sled and went off to play with the other boys and left poor Gerda behind.

The boldest boys would tie their sleds to the farmer's carts to get pulled along. In the middle of their game, someone covered in white furs came along driving a large sled. Kay tied his sled to it and was pulled along the streets a couple of times, but then the sledge drove off, faster and faster. Every time Kay began to untie his little sled, the driver turned and nodded to him in a friendly way as if telling him to stay.

They drove out of town, and the snow began to fall so thickly that Kay could see nothing, not even his own hand. He tried to untie his sled, but the big sled pulled it along as if by magic. When he called out for help, no-one heard him. The snowflakes were getting bigger and bigger until they looked like big white hens.

At last the big sled stopped and the driver stood up. The white furs were all made of snow, and the driver was none other than the Snow Queen. She was tall and slender and very white. "No-one likes to freeze," she said. "Come here and creep under my bearskin."

She put him in her sled, and covered him with the bearskin. It felt just like lying under the snow.

"Are you still cold?" asked the Snow Queen, and then she kissed him on the forehead. It was a cold kiss, colder than ice, and it went to his heart, which was already half frozen. He felt as though he was dying, just for a moment, and then the pain went away and he felt quite warm.

Then she kissed him again, and Kay forgot Gerda and his grandmother and his home. They drove on into the night, high in the cold sky, through storm and cloud, over sea and land. All night Kay looked down in the moonlight, and all day he slept at the Snow Queen's feet.

Gerda asked everyone where Kay had gone but no-one knew. The boys thought he was drowned and dead, but she did not believe them. When spring came she decided to go in search of him. She put on her new shoes and went to ask the river if it had taken Kay away from her. "I will give you my red shoes," she said, "if you will give him back to me." She took off her shoes and threw them into the water, but the river carried them back to her. Gerda thought she had not thrown them far enough, and she got into a boat to reach further out over the water. Then she threw her shoes into the river again, and as she did so the boat began to drift downstream. Soon it was too far from land for Gerda to escape, and she was carried along for hours with her red shoes floating behind.

At last the boat passed close by a little cottage with a cherry orchard. Out came an old woman leaning on a crutch. Then she hooked her crutch in the boat and drew it closer, and then she lifted Gerda out. "Tell me who you are, and what you are doing so far away along the river," she said, and Gerda told her everything.

"Have you seen Kay?" she asked.

The old woman said she had not seen him, but some day he would come there. Then she invited Gerda to come inside and eat cherries and have her hair combed. The more the old woman combed her hair, the more Gerda forgot Kay. The old woman was a witch, you see, and wanted Gerda to stay with her. She made all the roses in her garden disappear under the ground so that Gerda would not see them and remember her friend Kay.

Gerda walked out into the beautiful garden to play, and then came indoors to a pretty bedroom to sleep, and the next day

The more the old woman combed her hair, the more Gerda forgot Kay. The old woman was a witch, you see, and wanted Gerda to stay with her.

she played in the garden again, and the next day, until all summer was gone. Gerda thought that one flower was missing from the garden, but she could never remember which one.

One day she was looking at the old woman's hat, all painted with flowers, and she saw a rose painted there, that the Witch had forgotten to cover up. Suddenly Gerda could remember the roses at home and then she remembered Kay and wept. When her tears fell on the ground, the roses began to grow and bloom again.

"I have been here too long," said little Gerda. "Roses, do you know where Kay is? Is he dead?"

"No, he is not dead," replied the roses, "for we have been under the ground and Kay was not buried there." And none of the other flowers knew where he was.

"I must find Kay," exclaimed Gerda, and away she ran barefoot out of the garden and into the wide world. In the Witch's garden it was always summer, but outside it was almost winter.

"I have wasted so much time," Gerda thought to herself. Her bare feet hurt, and she was cold and wet, and she could find nothing good to eat, but on she went looking for Kay.

First she met a crow who told her that Kay was married to a princess and living in a palace, but when Gerda went to find him it was not Kay at all. Still, the Prince and Princess gave little Gerda a carriage and a horse and good boots and fur gloves to keep her hands warm, and on she drove to find her playmate Kay.

Then she went through a dark wood where robbers lived. The robbers stopped the carriage and were going to kill Gerda and eat her, but a little robber girl wanted Gerda for a pet.

"She will play with me," said the little robber girl, "and I shall have her boots and gloves and her dress to wear. No-one will kill her if I want her to live. And she will stay alive as long as I do not get angry with her. Are you a princess?" she asked Gerda.

"No," said little Gerda, and then she told all her story, how she was looking for Kay and had been tricked by the Witch in the cherry orchard. The little robber girl showed Gerda all the animals and birds that she had trapped and kept in her cave as pets. There was even a reindeer, who was afraid of the robber girl's knife that she stroked along his neck every night.

When Gerda talked about Kay the animals listened too. Then the wood-pigeons told Gerda that they had seen the Snow Queen in her sled with Kay, travelling to Lapland in the far north. The reindeer said that the Snow Queen's summer palace was in Lapland and her winter castle was at the North Pole, as far north as you can go.

The little robber girl decided to help Gerda escape, and she lifted her onto the reindeer's back and tied her on. She returned Gerda's boots but kept the warm gloves. In their place, to keep Gerda's hands warm, she gave her her mother's big gloves that reached up to Gerda's elbows. Then she tied onto the reindeer's back two loaves of bread and a ham, and said, "Away you go to Lapland, and take care of the little girl."

Away the reindeer ran, through the forest, over the moor, north to Lapland. Gerda ate the bread and all the ham, and then they were in Lapland.

The reindeer took her to a wise woman who lived in a little hut, and asked her to help with some magic against the Snow Queen. But the wise woman informed the reindeer that Gerda was stronger than any magic she could offer, for she was good and innocent, so that human beings and animals would all help her. All that the reindeer could do now, she said, was to take Gerda to the Snow Queen's garden, as close to her palace as he could go. Then she lifted Gerda onto the reindeer's back again, and away he ran.

"Stop! I have forgotten my boots and gloves," cried little Gerda, but it was too late. The reindeer ran on until he reached the Snow Queen's garden and there he put Gerda on the ground, kissed her and ran back. She was all alone in the snow and ice, with no shoes and no gloves to keep her feet and hands warm. She ran on in the snow storm and saw that the snowflakes were getting bigger. They were the Snow Queen's guards.

Gerda began to pray, and as she did so the mist from her breath in the cold air turned into angels, all standing around her with spears in their hands to protect her. They touched her hands and feet and then she did not feel the cold as she walked towards the Snow Queen's palace of snow and ice.

The palace was cold and empty, except for the Snow Queen sitting in the middle of a frozen lake that was all broken into pieces of ice, and Kay trying to fit the pieces together to make words. The lake was the mirror of reason, the Queen told him, and if he could make the word 'Eternity' out of the pieces of ice, he would be free and she would give him the whole world and a pair of skates. But that was the one word Kay could never make.

"I am going south to spread frost and snow," said the Snow Queen, and off she went, leaving Kay alone beside the lake of ice, just as still and stiff as if he were frozen too.

Gerda ran into the room and over to Kay. "Kay, dear Kay! I have found you at last!" she said, but Kay sat still and said nothing to her.

Then Gerda cried because he was so unkind. Her tears fell just where his heart was, and they thawed the ice and melted the splinter of the magic mirror. Suddenly Kay started to cry too, for now he remembered Gerda.

"Where am I?" he asked, as he looked around the cold room. "How cold and empty it all is!"

Then Gerda laughed for joy, and so did all the pieces of ice until they made up the word 'Eternity'; the word that the Snow Queen had promised Kay his freedom for. When Gerda kissed Kay's face and hands, he suddenly became warm again instead of cold as ice.

Outside the reindeer was waiting with another reindeer to take them home, past the wise woman's hut, past the robbers' hall where the little robber girl said goodbye to them, past the Princess's palace and the cherry orchard. At last they came to their own town, only now Kay and Gerda were grown up, and it seemed to them that the Snow Queen's palace was only a weary dream. Kay's grandmother was waiting for them, and they sat happily together, and it was summer again.

Andersen, retold by Alice Mills

The Travelling Companion

John's mother was dead, and he had no brother or sister, and so he was left all alone when his good father died too. "You have always been a good son," his father said just before he died, "and God will surely help you and be by your side." John sat and wept beside the bed where his dead father lay, and at last he fell asleep and dreamed a wonderful dream. The sun and moon greeted him, and there was his father alive and well and laughing for joy. John saw a beautiful girl wearing a crown, holding out her hand to him. "What a fine princess you are marrying," said John's father, and then poor John woke up all alone and sad again.

After his father was buried, John set out to find his fortune in the world, and all that he took was a little bundle of clothes, fifty dollars and a few silver pennies. It was all that he had. First he went to the churchyard to say goodbye to his dear father, and then he walked through the flowering fields, to villages and people that were new to him.

The first night he slept in a haystack, and it seemed to him the best bed in the world, with the moon for a lantern and the sky for a ceiling and the stream for his bath. The next morning he came to another churchyard where the graves had not been cared for, and they were all overgrown. John pulled up the grass and straightened the gravestones, for he thought that someone might do the same for his own dear father's grave some day also.

Outside the churchyard was an old beggar on crutches, and John gave him the silver pennies.

The morning was sunny but by nightfall it was stormy and wet, and there were no buildings to shelter in except a lonely church. Outside the cold rain fell and the thunder roared, but John said his prayers and went quietly to sleep.

In the middle of the night he woke up. The storm was over and the moon was shining. He could see an open coffin in the middle of the church and in it the body of a man who had not yet been buried. John was not afraid, for he had done no wicked deeds, and he knew that the dead hurt nobody. It is bad people who hurt others, and two bad men were in the church wanting to hurt the poor dead body by throwing it out of its coffin, out of the church, onto the ground outside.

"What are you doing?" asked John.

"He was a bad man," they said to him, "he owed us money and could not pay us, and now he is dead and we will never get our money back. That is why we are now throwing him out of the church."

John answered, "You can have my fifty dollars, all the money I have, if you will leave the dead man in peace."

The two bad men took the money and laughed as they went away, thinking what a fool John was. But John carefully put the body back in the coffin, said goodbye to it and walked happily on his way in the moonlight.

The next day someone shouted to him from behind, "Where are you going?"

John told him that he was seeking his fortune, and that he was all alone in the world now that his father was dead. "I am going into the world too," said the man,

When John arrived at the castle door, the King himself greeted him. He was very unhappy about his daughter's behaviour and begged John to forget the Princess and go home.

"would you like me to go with you?" John agreed. The stranger was good company; he knew so many things, John thought he must have visited every country in the world.

As they ate their breakfast together, an old woman came by on crutches, carrying a bundle of firewood and three little bundles of ferns and twigs. As she passed by, she fell and broke her leg. John jumped up to help carry her home, but his friend said that he had an ointment that would mend any leg. He would mend the old woman's leg, but only if she gave him the three bundles of ferns and twigs. "You want high payment, sir doctor," said the old woman, but she would give them to him if only he would mend her broken leg with his ointment. And so he did.

John and his friend walked on and came to an inn. Inside there was a man with puppets ready to perform a play. There was a king puppet and a queen and all their court, and the play was just beginning when a dog sprang up and took the queen puppet in his mouth so roughly that he bit her almost in two. The puppet master was so sad that he was nearly in tears, but John's Companion said that he could mend her better than new with his ointment. And so he did, and now she could dance and walk all by herself.

In the night there was a strange sound. It was the other puppets weeping and sighing because they could only move when someone else pulled their strings. The puppet master offered John's Companion all his money if he would put his magic ointment on the rest of the puppets, but he said that all he wanted was a large sword that the puppet master wore by his side. Then he rubbed the puppets with the ointment, and they could dance and walk just like the queen.

Next morning John and his friend were walking together when they saw a white swan lying dead on the ground. "See the beautiful wings," said the Companion, and he cut them off with his new sword and took them with him. "So you see, John," he said, "the sword came in useful after all."

They walked on until they came to a castle where a king lived with his beautiful daughter. She was a wicked Princess, and she said that she would only marry the man who could tell her three times what she was thinking. Any man who tried and could not tell her the answer must die. Many Princes had died, and yet she was so beautiful that still more men came to try to win her. And one of them was John, for he saw her as she rode by, and she was just like the beautiful Princess of his dream. So he told his Companion that he planned to go to the palace to win the Princess, even though the Companion begged him not to go.

"I love you dearly," he said to John, "and I do not want to lose you. But let us be merry tonight, for I shall have time enough to be sad when you are gone."

He ordered the innkeeper to bring them a bowl of punch so that they could drink the Princess's health, but in it he put a powder and when John drank he fell asleep at once.

Then the Companion put the swan wings onto his shoulders and took one of the bundles of ferns and flew through the night to the palace. He hid himself close by the Princess's bedroom, and at midnight he saw her flying out through her window into the night on long black wings. He made himself invisible and followed her, waving his ferns in the air and summoning all the winds to blow so that the Princess was buffeted and cold. She flew on until

The princess in her pleasure-ground. All the flowers were tied up to human bones instead of sticks, and grinning skulls served as flower pots.

she reached a cave in the mountain; it was full of spiders and poisonous snakes, glow worms and bats. In the middle of the cave was a throne made out of bones. There sat a monstrous troll, who told the Princess to sit beside him.

"I have a new suitor," said the Princess. "What shall I think of tomorrow when he comes to win me?"

"Think of something simple and he will never guess it," said the Troll. "Think of your shoe. Then you can cut off his head like all the rest, and bring it to me for supper."

The Princess promised to do so, and off she flew back to the palace. Close behind her flew John's Companion, and this time he waved his ferns so that the wind blew colder and stronger and the Princess could hardly reach her window.

In the morning John woke up and the Companion told him he had dreamed a strange dream. In this dream the Princess was thinking of her shoe. He asked John to give this answer when the Princess questioned him.

When John arrived at the castle door, the King himself greeted him. He was very unhappy about his daughter's behaviour and begged John to forget the Princess and go home. When John persisted, the King took him to the pleasure-ground of the Princess, and a horrid sight there was there! In every tree there hung three or four princes who had come to woo the Princess, but had not been able to guess her thoughts. The skeletons clattered so in every gust of wind that all the small birds were scared away and never dared enter that garden. All the flowers were tied up to human bones instead of sticks, and grinning skulls served as flower pots. What a garden for a princess!

"Now you can see it for yourself!' said the old King. "This is the end you will come to, just like those whom you see here. Then please leave it alone, you make me quite miserable, I take it so much to heart!"

John kissed the hand of the good old King and said he felt sure it must all go well, he was so very much in love with the beautiful Princess.

The King took John inside and soon the Princess and all her ladies entered the room. She looked lovely, and John fell more deeply in love with her. No, she could never be the cruel wicked witch that people called her! The Princess asked John to name what she was thinking of, and when he said "Your shoe" she looked pale and ill, but she could not deny that this was the right answer.

The next night, as soon as John was asleep, his Companion flew on the swan wings to the palace, and then to the Troll's cave after the wicked Princess. This time he waved the sticks and called up the rain, so that the Princess was wet through when she came to the Troll. They agreed that when John came to her the next morning she should think of her glove.

In the morning the Companion told John of his dream, and John went to the Princess and guessed that she was thinking of her glove, and so it was.

The next night, as soon as John was asleep, his Companion took up his sword and fastened on the swan wings and flew to the palace, and then to the Troll's cave after the Princess. This time he waved the ferns and the sticks and called up a hailstorm to beat the Princess all the way to the Troll's cave so that she could hardly fly. Then the Princess told the Troll that John had guessed right twice now, and if he guessed right a third time she would have to marry him and lose all her magic. "What must I think of this time?" she asked the Troll. And she wept bitterly.

"This time I will take you back to your palace window," said the Troll, and when they had flown there, with the Companion close behind, the Troll whispered to the Princess that she must think of his head. Off the Princess flew through the window, but the Troll never flew back to his cave, for the Companion cut off his head with the sword. He threw the body into the sea, but the head he wrapped in a black silk handkerchief and took back to the inn.

In the morning he gave the bundle to John and told him not to look inside until the Princess had asked him the third question. And so he did, and saw the Troll's big ugly head, and the Princess saw it too. She wept and cried, but she could not deny that it was the right answer, and now she must marry John that evening and lose all her magic powers.

John could tell that she did not love him, and that she was only going to marry him because she must. He went to the Companion and begged him to find a way for the Princess to fall in love with him and smile when he was near. The Companion gave him a little bottle and three feathers from the swan wings. He told John to wet the feathers in the water from the bottle and then sprinkle the Princess with the water from each feather, and then she would be free from the spell. And so he did.

When he sprinkled her with the first feather, she turned into a black swan with fiery eyes. Then John sprinkled the black swan with the second feather and she turned into a white swan, but it had a black ring around its throat. Then he wetted the third feather and sprinkled the water over the swan, and she turned into his own Princess free from enchantment and smiling at him with love. She told him that the Troll had caught her and cast a wicked spell on her, and that even the Troll's death had not been enough to free her.

While the Princess and John were preparing for the marriage, the Companion came to the palace to say good-bye. John begged him to stay and live with them and share their happiness. The Companion replied, "No, now I have paid my debt and must go. Do you remember the dead man in the coffin that you protected from the wicked men who wanted to throw his body outside the church, because he could not pay them? You gave all you had so that he could rest in peace. I am that dead man." And the next minute he disappeared, leaving John both sad and happy.

Andersen, retold by Alice Mills

The Wild Swans

There once lived a king and queen who had eleven sons and one daughter, called Elise. But the mother died and the King married a second wife, a wicked queen who hated her stepchildren. She sent Elise away into the country and cast a spell on the eleven Princes, turning them into white swans. "Now fly away, into the wide world, far away from me," she said, and away they flew out of the palace window.

Early in the morning they flew past the peasant cottage where their sister was living, called out and flapped their wings, but nobody noticed. They were forced to fly far away to the forest.

When Elise was fifteen, her father sent for her to come to the palace. She was so beautiful that the wicked Queen had grown jealous of her and wanted to turn her into a swan also, but she was afraid of her husband the King. So instead she cast a spell on the Princess.

She hid three toads in the bath, saying to one, "Sit on Elise's forehead so that she turns stupid and muddled." She said to the next, "Sit on Elise's face so that she turns ugly and her father does not recognise her." And to the third toad she said, "Sit over Elise's heart so that she turns to evil ways." And when the Princess sat in her bath and the toads came to her forehead and face and heart, the spell had no power because the Princess was so good, and she was not turned ugly or stupid or evil.

So the wicked Queen stained Elise's skin with walnut juice and tangled her hair and rubbed dirt over her face, so that her father did not recognise her. Poor Elise wept and wondered where her eleven brothers were.

She was so unhappy that she decided to go in search of her brothers, and she wandered far until she came to the forest.

All night long in the dark forest she dreamed of her brothers, and in the morning she found a path to the water's edge. Elise looked at her reflection in the water and did not recognise herself, but when she washed in the water all the stain left her, and the dirt washed away. There was no king's daughter more beautiful than she.

She wandered in the forest all day and dreamed again of her brothers at night. The next morning she met an old woman with a basket of berries who gave her some to eat. Elise asked the old woman if she had ever seen eleven princes in the wood. "No," said the old woman, "but I have seen eleven white swans with gold crowns on their heads, swimming in a stream near here."

She took the Princess to the stream, and Elise wandered along the bank until she came to the sea. There she saw eleven swan feathers lying on the sand and picked them up. She waited there all day. At sunset the eleven swans came flying towards the land, and she hid while they came lower and landed. They were each wearing a golden crown on their heads. As the sun set, the eleven swans all turned into princes, Elise's lost brothers.

She called out their names and the Princes recognised their lost sister. They told one another all that had happened, and the swan Princes said that they were swans as long as the sun was in the sky, but as soon as the sun set they were men again. They did not live at sea, nor in the dark forest, but far across the sea in another

Elise did not want to leave her brothers, but the King lifted her onto his horse and rode away towards the palace.

country. It was so far to fly that it took them two days, and there was a little island to rest on at night in the middle of the sea, a little rock just big enough for them all to stand side by side. Only once a year were they allowed to visit their homeland, and they could spend eleven days only flying to and fro over the castle, calling out to the King and looking for their dear sister. There were two days left before they must go back over the sea.

"How can we take you with us, dear little sister?" asked the brothers.

They talked together all night, but the next day as the sun rose the Princes all turned back to swans and all of them except the youngest flew away. He stayed with his sister all day until his brothers came back at sunset.

"How can we take you with us?" they said again. "Tomorrow we must fly away and not come back for another year. Are we strong enough to carry you with our wings, dear little sister?"

Elise and her brothers spent the whole night weaving a mat of grass and reeds. In the morning, when the Princes had become swans again, they picked up the mat with their beaks and flew into the sky with their sister while she was asleep. Her youngest brother flew high overhead and shaded her from the sun with his wings.

They flew all day and she could see no island to rest upon. The swans were flying more slowly than usual, because they were carrying their sister. It was almost sunset and the sky grew dark and stormy, and Elise was afraid that they would all be drowned for her sake. But just as it was time for the brothers to change from swans to men, they saw the little rock in the sea and flew down to it. There was just room for them all to stand close together all night, and the rain fell and the wind blew, but they held each other tightly so that they would all be safe.

In the morning they flew on, and by sunset they reached a land of mountains where the swan Princes lived in a cave. That night Elise dreamed that the old woman who had given her the berries said to her, "I am the fairy Morgana, and I know how you can release your brothers from the spell if you are brave and patient. Do you see the stinging nettles that I am carrying in my hands? There are many nettles like this growing round the cave, and it is these nettles that you must weave into shirts for your brothers, these and no others except the nettles that grow around the churchyard graves. You must pick them with your delicate hands and trample them with your feet to make them into yarn. Then you must weave eleven shirts with long sleeves and throw them over the swans' backs, and the spell will be broken. But you must not speak a word until the shirts are finished or your brothers will die."

When Elise woke up, she began to gather nettles although they stung her hands to blisters. She trampled them with her feet until she made yarn. Her brothers came back at sunset and could not understand why she said nothing to them. They saw the blisters on her hands and feet, and then they knew that she was trying to save them.

The next day she worked at the yarn until she had made one of the shirts. Then she heard the noise of a horn. It was the King's hunting party close by, and Elise was afraid of the dogs. She ran into the cave with the shirt and her bundle of nettles.

The King's dog ran into the cave and the King ran after it. He had never before seen a maiden more beautiful, and he said to her, "Where did you come from, beautiful child?" But Elise said nothing.

"Come with me," said the King, "and if you are as good as you are beautiful, I will marry you and you will be my queen and live in my palace."

Elise did not want to leave her brothers, but the King lifted her onto his horse and rode away towards the palace. When the sun was setting, the splendid royal city with its towers and domes lay before them. The King led her into the palace, where fountains splashed in the high marble halls, and where walls and ceilings glowed with paintings. But Elise had no eyes for it all. She silently wept and scarcely knew that the women were decking her in royal array, braiding her hair with pearls, and gently drawing soft gloves upon her poor blistered fingers.

As she stood there in all her splendour, her beauty was so dazzling that the Court bowed low before her, and the King proclaimed her his bride, even though the Archbishop thought that she was a witch who had enchanted him. All the while she held the shirt that she had woven and the bunch of nettles, and the King let her keep them to comfort her in her weeping.

By this time Elise realised that the King was kind and perhaps she would be able to

Bocca fermala

As she stood there in all her splendour, her beauty was so dazzling that the Court bowed low before her, and the King proclaimed her his bride.

finish her brothers' shirts, so she agreed to marry him. She said nothing, though, even at her wedding.

Every day she loved the King more and more, but every night she went into a corner and wove her nettles into shirts, until she had made seven shirts and there were no more nettles in her bundle.

She remembered what the old woman had said to her, that the only nettles she could use grew near the cave or by the churchyard graves. She went out secretly one night to the churchyard to gather more nettles, and the Archbishop saw her there. Now he was certain that she was a witch, and he ran to the King and told him.

The King did not believe him, but he watched Elise every night and saw her treading the nettles and weaving them into shirts. He was angry with his wife and asked her what she was doing, but she still said nothing to him. She wove the nettles until she had made ten shirts, but the nettles were all used up and there was still another shirt to be made.

Elise went out in the dark night to the churchyard graves and the King and the Archbishop followed her. "See, it is as I told you, she is a witch and she must be burned as a witch tomorrow," said the Archbishop. This time the King believed him. He sent his wife into a dark prison where the bitter wind whistled through the grated window. Instead of silks and velvets, he threw the nettles after her for her to use as a pillow, and the shirts for her to use as blankets.

The Princess trod the nettles and began to weave them into a shirt. Then she heard the sound of swans' wings above her prison. Her brothers were close by and waiting for the moment when the spell would be broken.

Elise worked all night on the shirt of nettles and in the morning, just before sunrise, her eleven brothers came to the palace and tried to speak to the King, to tell him what their sister was doing. But he would see no-one until sunrise, and the brothers waited until they had to fly away as swans.

In the morning the King sent for his wife to be burned as a witch. A wretched horse drew the cart; and there she sat, clothed in a coarse dress of sackcloth; her beautiful long hair hung loose around her shapely head; her cheeks were deadly white. All the way through the city she wove the nettles into the last shirt, and the people shouted, "Look at the witch! She is weaving spells with nettles!"

The people wanted to tear the nettles from her, and they thronged in upon her. Suddenly the eleven white swans flew close; they alighted round about her on the cart, and flapped with their great wings, and the crowd drew back in fear. The people were ashamed and thought it was a sign from heaven that she was innocent. But they were afraid to say anything aloud.

Just as the headsman took hold of the Princess to burn her, she quickly threw the shirts over the swans and eleven princes stood in their place. But the youngest had one wing still, for she had not had time to weave all of the last nettle shirt.

"Now I can tell you," she said, "I am not a witch." And the people who saw what had taken place bowed before her. But her troubles and cares had become too much to bear, and she sank lifeless in her brothers' arms.

"Yes! She is innocent!" Elise's eldest brother called out, and he explained to the King and to the people why she had been silent and why she had woven shirts out of nettles. While he spoke, every piece of

The King gathered the white rose and laid it on Elise's breast, and she awoke and lived.

wood that had been heaped up to burn her turned into a rose tree laden with red roses. High above the rest grew a lovely white rose, shining like a star, dazzling and full of perfume. The King gathered the white rose and laid it on Elise's breast, and she awoke and lived.

All the church bells rang by themselves, and the birds came flocking to celebrate with the people. Back to the palace went the procession, more magnificent than any king had ever enjoyed before, and everyone except the Archbishop danced for joy.

Andersen, retold by Alice Mills

The Little Mermaid

Far away and deep in the sea there lived a sea king with his six daughters in a palace of coral and amber and pearl. They were all looked after by their grandmother, a mermaid who wore twelve oysters on her tail because she was the King's mother. The youngest mermaid was the prettiest; her eyes were as blue as the sea and her skin as delicate and fair as a rose petal. Just like all the other mermaids, she had a human body that ended in a fish's tail instead of human legs and feet.

The daughters of the sea king played in their father's palace, where the walls grew flowers and the amber windows opened into the deep sea. Fish would swim in through these windows just as birds can fly in through the windows of human houses. But these fish swam up to the mermaid Princesses, and ate from their hands and allowed themselves to be stroked.

All the Princesses had gardens under the sea, where they made their flower beds in the shape of whales and mermaids, but the littlest mermaid made hers in the shape of the sun, and she chose to have only those flowers that shone like the sun.

The littlest mermaid was different from her five sisters, quieter and more thoughtful. They ornamented their gardens with the strangest items that they had discovered in wrecked ships, but she put nothing in her sun-garden except a single marble statue. The statue was made of fine white marble, and shaped like a beautiful boy, and it had sunk to the bottom of the sea with a sinking ship. Next to the boy she planted a rose-red weeping willow that grew well and spread its branches over his head.

The Princesses were not allowed to go up to the top of the sea until their fifteenth birthday, and then, one by one, year after year, they went up and came home again to tell of the wonders that they had seen. One of them saw the moonlight on the calm sea, and one of them saw the sunset and swans flying overhead, and the bravest Princess swam up a river and saw children at play, and was scared by a dog in the water.

At last it was the turn of the littlest mermaid, on her fifteenth birthday. Her grandmother made her wear eight oysters on her tail, because she was a princess.

"You must suffer, to be fashionable," she said, when the Little Mermaid complained that the oysters hurt her tail.

Up she went to see the world above the water. It was just after sunset, and she could see a sailing ship close by where a prince was celebrating his birthday too, only he was a year older than the Little Mermaid. She could see his big black eyes and his handsome face whenever the waves lifted her up, but when the fireworks began she was afraid and hid under the water.

Then a storm began to blow. This time it was not the Little Mermaid but the sailors who were frightened, and with good reason, for the wind blew and the waves tossed until the ship was wrecked and the men all jumped into the water to save themselves. She could see the Prince sinking into the sea, and at first she was glad that he was coming to live in her palace, but then she remembered that men could not live under the water, and that he must be lifted up or he would die. She dived down among the wreckage that might well have

The bravest Princess swam up a river and saw children at play.

crushed her, and took hold of the young Prince and lifted up his head so that he could breathe.

All night long she held his head above the water, and at sunrise she could see the land, but the Prince's eyes were shut and he did not feel the Little Mermaid kissing his face. She took him towards the land, and there she could see tall blue mountains with white snow on their crests. To the Little Mermaid the snow looked like white swans lying there. Closer to the shore was a green wood, and a building with a garden of orange and lemon trees, and tall palm trees in front of its gates. The sea had shaped a small bay here, with a narrow beach of pure white sand under a cliff, and the water in the bay was calm and smooth and very deep. The Little Mermaid swam up and then hid in the water and waited. A young girl came down to the shore and found the Prince, just as he was waking, and he smiled at her. But the Little Mermaid was sad, for the Prince had not smiled at her, and he did not know that she was the one who had rescued him from drowning.

Then she swam home sadly, and every morning and every evening she went back to the place where she had taken the Prince, but he was never there. Her sisters kept asking what was troubling her, and at last she told them.

"Come, dear little sister," they said, "we know where the Prince lives, far away from here, and we will take you to look at his palace."

It was a palace of marble and gold with marble steps down to the sea. Now that the Princess knew where the Prince lived, she went there again and again, to see him and to listen to the people talking about him and saying how good he was to them. The Little Mermaid longed to live on the land like people, and she asked her grandmother what it would be like to be a human being and not a mermaid.

"Do human beings live for ever if they do not drown?" she said.

"No," said her grandmother, they die like us, but we live for three hundred years and their lives are shorter. But when we die we turn to foam of the sea, for we have no souls. Human beings have immortal souls that live on for ever in heaven."

"Why do we have no souls?" asked the Little Mermaid sadly. "I would give my three hundred years for a day of human life and a soul."

"Better to live as your sisters do, and be happy here. The only way to have a soul is to share a human being's soul, if someone were to love you and marry you, but that is impossible. They do not think our tails are beautiful and they can only love people who have those clumsy legs instead."

The Little Mermaid looked at her tail and wished for human legs. That night a ball was held, more splendid than any ball ever held by humans on the land. The walls of the great ballroom were of crystal. There were hundreds of mussel shells that served as lamps, glowing red and green, sending out jets of bright blue flame until the hall

was full of light and so was the sea outside, for the crystal walls let the light through. There were too many fishes to count, fish of all sizes and shapes, golden, silvery, their scales gleaming in the light, all swimming close by the walls. A stream flowed through the centre of the ballroom, wide and rippling, and just as the stream made its water music as it danced along, the mermaids and mermen all made their own music as they danced. Their voices were more beautiful than any voices heard on the land or in the sky. The Little Mermaid sang more sweetly than anyone else, and when they clapped their hands for her singing, her heart sang with joy too, for she knew that she had the most beautiful voice of all, in the sea, in the air or on the land. But then she began to think sadly of the world above her. She could not forget the handsome Prince, and she remembered her longing to have an immortal soul like his. She stole out of her father's palace and went to visit the Sea Witch to ask for her help.

The Witch lived at the bottom of a whirlpool in the sea, in the middle of a sea forest of snaky creatures, half plant and half hungry animal, that took hold and would not let go of everything that went past. But the Little Mermaid tied back her hair and swam past the snaky things and the bones of all that they had caught and killed.

The Sea Witch was waiting for her. "You are a fool, Little Mermaid," she said, "to want legs instead of a tail, hoping to make the Prince fall in love with you and give you half of his soul. Still, I will help you. I will make a drink for you, and you must swim to the land and drink it there before the sun rises, and your pretty tail will turn to legs as you drink. People will think that you are beautiful, and you will walk and dance more beautifully than anyone, but each time your feet touch the ground it will be like treading on a knife."

"I am willing to suffer the pain of sharp knives to win a soul," said the Princess.

"But the spell comes at a price," said the Sea Witch. "You can never come home again, and if the Prince does not love you and marry you, you will not win an immortal soul. The day after he marries someone else, you will die from a broken heart and turn to foam on the sea."

"I am willing to take the risk," said the Princess.

"But the spell has another price," said the Sea Witch. "You have the most beautiful voice of all the sea people, and I want it for myself. You must let me cut out your tongue, and only then will I make up the potion for you to drink."

"But if I give you my voice," answered the Princess, "how will the Prince come to love me?"

"You will have your beauty to win him by. Put your tongue out, it is only a little price to pay, and I will give you the potion."

So the Little Mermaid bravely put out her tongue for the Sea Witch to cut off, and then the Witch gave her the drink that shone in its bottle like a star. The Little Mermaid swam back through the forest of snaky creatures easily, for they were afraid of the star-drink, and she swam through the whirlpool and back to her father's palace. How sad she was, for she could not speak to them to say goodbye, and she knew she was leaving them for ever.

She swam to the shore where the Prince's marble steps came down to the sea, and there she drank the potion. It hurt her throat like a sword cutting her, and she fainted and lay on the steps until daylight. Then the Prince found her lying there, wrapped only in her hair, and asked who

she was and where she had come from, but she could not speak to tell him.

He took her into the palace and dressed her in fine clothes, and she danced for him on her new feet more beautifully than any human being could dance. Every step she took, the pain was like treading on a knife, but she walked so beautifully that no-one could tell. The Prince told her that she must stay with him always, to be his companion, for he loved her.

He loved her like a child, but he had no thought of marrying her, and one day he told her that he was in love with a beautiful girl from a faraway land who had saved him from the dark sea when he had almost drowned, on the night of his sixteenth birthday. The Little Mermaid longed to tell him that it was she who had saved him, and not the girl who had found him on the seashore. She could say nothing, however, for she had given her voice to the Sea Witch.

The King and Queen wanted their son to marry, and were sending him to a faraway country to meet a princess. The Prince told the Little Mermaid that he

The Sea Witch was waiting for her.

would never marry this Princess that he did not know or love, for his heart was given to the girl who had rescued him from the sea.

"If I marry, it will be to you," he said to the Little Mermaid, and he kissed her.

Next day they set sail for the faraway country, and the Prince asked the Little Mermaid if she was afraid. She laughed to think of the storms she had swum in, and then she was sad when she looked deep into the water and saw her father's palace and her grandmother and sisters looking sadly up at her.

At last the ship arrived at the palace where the Princess was waiting. As soon as the Prince saw her, he said, "You are the beautiful girl who saved me when I nearly drowned. I have always loved you and it is my dearest wish to marry you." Then he turned to the Little Mermaid, and said, "You will stay with us and be happy too."

But the Little Mermaid felt her heart breaking, so that she would surely die in the morning and turn to foam on the sea.

In the evening the Prince and his bride sailed on the sea, and the Little Mermaid went with them. There was a feast and a dance to celebrate the marriage, and the Little Mermaid danced more beautifully than ever. At every step she felt the pain of sharp knives cutting her feet, but the pain in her heart was worse.

Late into the night they feasted and danced, but at last the Prince and his bride and all the sailors were ready to rest. Only the Little Mermaid stayed awake and watched the sea all night, until it was almost dawn when she would turn to foam on the sea as she died. Then she saw her five sisters come up from the depths of the sea, and their flowing hair was all gone. They had sold it to the Sea Witch so that she would make a spell to rescue the Little Mermaid.

"The Witch gave us a knife, so that you might kill the Prince before sunrise. When his blood runs over your feet, they will become a tail again and you will live with us three hundred years in the sea. You must be quick, sister!"

The Little Mermaid went to the bed where the Prince and his bride were sleeping. She looked at the Prince, and then she threw the knife into the sea just as the sun was rising, and threw herself after it into the water. She could feel herself turning to foam of the sea.

In the sunlight, above the sea, she could see hundreds of spirits floating in the air and singing. She felt herself rising up out of the foam to join them.

"Who are you?" she said, and now she had a voice again, as beautiful as theirs.

"We are the daughters of air," they told her. "Like the sea people, we have no souls, but we can create a soul for ourselves by doing good. After three hundred years, if we have tried our best to do good, we win an immortal soul and go to heaven. Little Mermaid, you have tried to do good, you have endured pain for the sake of love, and so you have won a place with us."

The Prince and his bride looked sadly down into the sea foam for the Little Mermaid's body. She kissed the bride and smiled at the Prince, but they could not see her or feel her kiss. Then she flew up with the daughters of air into the sky, to do good deeds and win an immortal soul.

"Perhaps it will be less than three hundred years," the daughters of the air said to her. "Whenever we find a child who is good and loving, a year is taken from the three hundred. But whenever we find a wicked child, we weep, and for every tear we must wait out another day."

Andersen, retold by Alice Mills

The Ugly Duckling

A duck had built herself a warm nest, and now she was sitting all day on six eggs. Five of them were white but the sixth, which was larger than the others, was an ugly grey colour. Other birds might have thought that when the duck went down in the morning and even to the water to stretch her legs in a good swim, some lazy mother might have popped her egg into the nest. But ducks are not clever at all, and are not quick at counting, so this duck did not worry herself about the matter, but just took care that the big egg should be as warm as the rest.

This was the first set of eggs that the duck had ever laid and, to begin with, she was very pleased and proud, and laughed at the other mothers, who were always neglecting their duties to gossip with each other or to take little extra swims besides the two in the morning and evening that were necessary for health. But at length she grew tired of sitting there all day; and she pined for a little amusement also. Still, she knew that if she left her eggs and the ducklings in them to die, none of her friends would ever speak to her again; so there she stayed, only getting off the eggs several times a day to see if the shells were cracking—which may have been the very reason why they did not crack sooner.

She had looked at the eggs at least a hundred and fifty times when, to her joy, she saw a tiny crack on two of them, and scrambling back to the nest she never moved for the whole of that day. Next morning she was rewarded by noticing cracks in the whole five eggs, and by midday two little yellow heads were poking out from the shells. She sat steadily for a whole night upon the nest, and before the sun rose the five white eggs were empty, and ten pairs of eyes were gazing out upon the green world.

Day after day went on, and the big egg showed no signs of cracking, and the duck grew more and more impatient. "I will give it one more chance," sighed the duck, "and if it does not come out of its shell in another twenty-four hours, I will just have to leave it alone and teach the rest of them to swim properly and to find their own food. I really can't be expected to do two things at once." And with a fluff of her feathers she pushed the egg into the middle of the nest.

All through the next day she sat on the egg. In the evening, she thought she saw a tiny crack in the upper part of the shell. When she woke with the first streaks of light she felt something stirring under her. Yes, there it was at last; and as she moved, a big awkward bird tumbled head first on the ground.

There was no denying it was ugly, even the mother was forced to admit that to herself, though she only said it was "large" and "strong", with a glance of surprise at the dull brown which covered his back, and at his long naked neck.

A few days later, the ducklings were taken into the duckyard so they could pay their respects to the very old duck sitting in the middle of the yard. The rest of the ducks looked on discontentedly and said to each other: "Did you ever see anything as ugly as that great tall creature? He is a disgrace to any brood. I shall go and chase him out!" and an angry duck put up her feathers, and running to the big Duckling bit his neck.

The Duckling gave a loud quack; it was the first time he had felt any pain, and at the sound his mother turned quickly.

"Leave him alone," she said fiercely to the duck, "or I will send for his father. He was not troubling *you*."

"No; but he is so ugly and awkward no-one can put up with him."

"It certainly is a great pity he is so different from these beautiful darlings. If he could only be hatched over again!"

The poor little fellow drooped his head, and did not know where to look, but was comforted when his mother answered: "He may not be as handsome as the others, but he swims better, and is very strong; I am sure he will make his way in the world as well as anybody."

The Duckling was snapped at by everyone when they thought his mother was not looking. Even the turkey-cock, who was so big, never passed him without mocking words, and his brothers and sisters, who would not have noticed any difference unless it had been put into their heads, soon became as rude and unkind as the rest.

At last the Duckling could bear it no longer, and one day he fancied he saw signs of his mother turning against him too; so that night he stole away through an open door, and scrambled on till he reached a wide grassy moor, full of soft marshy places where the reeds grew. Here he lay down, but he was too tired and too frightened to sleep, and with the earliest peep of the sun the reeds began to rustle, and he saw that he had blundered into a colony of wild ducks. But as he could not run away again he stood up and bowed politely before them.

"You *are* ugly," said the wild ducks, when they had looked him over. "However, it is no business of ours, unless you wish to marry one of our daughters, and that we should not allow." The Duckling answered that he wanted nothing but to be left alone after his long journey.

So for two whole days he lay quietly among the reeds, till he felt himself quite strong again. He wished he might stay where he was forever, he was so comfortable and happy, with nobody to bite him and tell him how ugly he was.

Two young ganders caught sight of him as they were having their evening splash among the reeds, looking for their supper. "We are getting tired of this moor," they said, "and tomorrow we think of trying another, where the lakes are larger and the feeding better. Will you come with us?"

"Is it nicer than this?" asked the Duckling doubtfully. The words were hardly out of his mouth, when "Pif! paf!" and the two newcomers were stretched dead beside him.

At the sound of the gun the wild ducks in the rushes flew into the air, and for a few minutes the firing continued. Luckily for himself the Duckling could not fly, and he floundered along through the water till he could hide himself among some tall ferns. But before he got there he met a huge dog, who stood and gazed at him with a long red tongue hanging out of his mouth. The Duckling grew cold with terror, and tried to hide his head beneath his little wings; but the dog sniffed at him and passed on, and he was able to reach his place of shelter.

"I am too ugly even for a dog to eat," he said to himself. "Well, that is a great mercy." And he curled himself up in the soft grass till the shots died away in the distance.

When all had been quiet for a long time, and there were only the stars to see him, he

The duckling remained for three weeks in the cottage with the old woman, her cat and a hen.

crept out and looked about him. He would never go near a pool again, *never ever,* he thought; and seeing that the moor stretched far away in the opposite direction, he went bravely on till he got to a small cottage, which seemed too tumbledown for the stones to hold together many hours longer. Even the door only hung upon one hinge, and the Duckling edged himself cautiously in and lay down under a chair close to the broken door, from which he could get out if necessary. But no-one seemed to see him or smell him; so he spent the rest of the night in peace.

Now in the cottage dwelt an old woman, her cat and a hen. The next morning, when it grew light, they noticed their visitor, who stood trembling before them, with his eye on the door ready to escape at any moment. They did not, however, appear very fierce, and the Duckling became less afraid as they approached him.

"Can you lay eggs?" asked the hen. And the Duckling answered meekly: "No; I don't know how." The hen turned her back, and the cat came forward.

"Can you ruffle your fur when you are angry, or purr when you are pleased?" she asked. And again the Duckling had to admit that he could do nothing but swim.

So the cat and the hen went straight off to the old woman, who was still in bed. "A useless creature has taken refuge here," they said. "It calls itself a duckling; but it can neither lay eggs nor purr! What should we do with it?"

"Keep it, to be sure!" replied the old woman briskly. "It is all nonsense about it not laying eggs. Anyway, we will let it stay here for a bit and see what happens."

So the Duckling remained in the old cottage for three weeks, and shared the food of the cat and the hen; but nothing in the way of eggs happened at all. Then the sun came out, and the air grew soft, and the Duckling wanted with all his might to have a swim.

"What is the matter?" asked the hen; and the Duckling told her.

"I am so longing for the water again. You can't think how delicious it is to put your head under the water and dive straight to the bottom."

"I don't think *I* should enjoy it," replied the hen doubtfully. And the cat agreed there was nothing she would hate so much.

"I can't stay here any longer, I *must* get to the water," repeated the Duckling. And the cat and the hen, who felt hurt and offended, answered: "Very well then, go."

They both turned their backs on him, so he went out of the rickety door feeling rather sad. But he could not help a thrill of joy when he was out in the air and water once more, and cared little for the rude glances of the creatures he met. For a while he was quite happy and content; but soon the winter came on, and snow began to fall. And the Duckling soon found that it is one thing to enjoy being in the water, and quite another to like being damp on land.

The river, to the Duckling's bewilderment, was getting hard and slippery, when he heard a sound of whirring wings, and high up in the air a flock of swans were flying. They were as white as the snow which had fallen during the night, and their long necks with yellow bills were stretched southwards, for they were going to a land where the sun shone all day. Oh, if he could only have gone with them! But that was not possible, of course; and besides, what sort of companion could an ugly thing like him be to those beautiful beings? So he walked sadly down to a sheltered pool and dived to the very bottom, and tried to think it was the greatest happiness he could dream of. But, all the same, he knew it wasn't!

And every morning it grew colder and colder, and the Duckling had to work hard to keep himself warm. Indeed, it would be truer to say that he never was warm at all. He never could tell afterwards exactly how he had spent the winter. He only knew that he was very miserable and that he never had enough to eat. But by and by things grew better. The earth became softer, the sun hotter, the birds sang, and the flowers once more appeared in the grass. When he stood up, he felt different somehow. His body seemed larger and his wings stronger. Something pink looked at him from the side of a hill. He thought he would fly towards it and see what it was.

Oh, how glorious it felt to be rushing through the air, wheeling first one way and then the other! The Duckling was almost sorry when he drew near the pink cloud and found it was made up of apple blossoms growing beside a cottage whose garden ran down to the banks of a canal. He fluttered slowly to the ground, and while he was gazing about him a flock of the same beautiful birds he had seen so many months ago swam down the canal, and floated quietly upon the waters as if they were part of them.

"I will follow them," said the Duckling to himself; "ugly though I am, I would rather be killed by them than suffer all I have suffered from cold and hunger, and from the ducks who should have treated me kindly." And flying down to the water, he swam after them as fast as he could.

Directly they saw him coming some of the younger ones swam out to meet him with cries of welcome, which the Duckling hardly understood. He approached them

He beheld beneath him a beautiful white swan!

glad, yet trembling, and turning to one of the older birds, he said: "If I am going to die, I would rather you should kill me. I don't know why I was ever hatched, for I am too ugly to live." And as he spoke, he bowed his head and looked down into the water. Reflected there he saw many white shapes, with long necks and golden bills, and he looked for the dull grey body and the awkward skinny neck. But no such thing was there. Instead, he beheld beneath him a beautiful white swan!

"The new one is the best of all," said the children when they came down to feed the swans in the evening. "His feathers are whiter and his beak more golden than the rest." When he heard that, the Duckling thought it was worthwhile having undergone all the persecution and loneliness that he had passed through, as otherwise he would never have known what it was to be really happy.

Andersen, *The Orange Fairy Book*

The Story without an End

I

There was once a young child who lived in a little hut, and in the hut there was nothing but a little bed and a looking-glass which hung in a dark corner. Now the child cared nothing about the looking-glass, but as soon as the first sunbeam glided softly through the casement and kissed his sweet eyelids, and the finch and the linnet woke him merrily with their morning songs, he arose and went out into the green meadow. And he begged flour of the primrose, and sugar of the violet, and butter of the buttercup; he shook dew-drops from the cowslip into the cup of a harebell; spread out a large lime-leaf, set his little breakfast upon it, and

And the child cared nothing about the looking-glass.

feasted daintily. Sometimes he invited a humming-bee, more often a bright butterfly, to partake of his feast; but his favourite guest was the blue dragon-fly. The bee murmured a good deal, in a solemn tone, about his riches; but the child thought that if *he* were a bee, heaps of treasure would not make him happy; and that it must be much more delightful and glorious to float about in the free and fresh breezes of spring, and to hum joyously in the web of the sunbeams, than, with heavy feet and heavy heart, to stow the silver wax and the golden honey into cells.

To this the butterfly assented; and he told how, once upon a time, he too had been

The sunbeams stole in to kiss him.

180

greedy and sordid; how he had thought of nothing but eating, and had never once turned his eyes upwards to the blue sky. At length, however, a complete change had come over him; and instead of crawling spiritless about the dirty earth, half dreaming, he all at once awakened as out of a deep sleep. And now he could rise into the air—and it was his greatest joy sometimes to play with the light, and to reflect the sky in the bright eyes of his wings; sometimes to listen to the soft language of the flowers, and catch their secrets. Such talk delighted the child, and his breakfast was the sweeter to him, and the sunshine on leaf and flower seemed to him more bright and cheering.

But when the bee had flown off to beg from flower to flower, and the butterfly had fluttered away to join his play-fellows, the dragon-fly still remained, poised on a blade of grass. Her slender and burnished body, more brightly and deeply blue than the deep blue sky, glistened in the sunbeam; and her fragile net-like wings laughed at the flowers because *they* could not fly, but must stand still and abide the wind and the rain. The dragon-fly sipped a little of the child's clear dew-drops and blue violet honey, and then whispered her winged words. And the child finished his breakfast, closed his dark blue eyes, bent down his beautiful head, and listened to the sweet prattle.

Then the dragon-fly told much of the merry life in the green wood; how sometimes she played hide-and-seek with her playfellows under the broad leaves of the oak and the beech trees, or hunt-the-hare along the surface of the still waters; sometimes quietly watched the sunbeams as they flew busily from moss to flower and from flower to bush, and shed life and warmth over all. But at night, she said, the moonbeams glided softly around the wood, and dropped dew into the mouths of all the thirsty plants; and when the dawn pelted the slumberers with the soft roses of the sky, some of the half-drunken flowers looked up and smiled; but most of them could not so much as raise their heads for a long, long time.

Such stories did the dragon-fly tell; and as the child sat motionless, with his eyes shut, and his head rested on his little hand, she thought he had fallen asleep—so she poised her double wings and flew into the rustling wood.

II

But the child was only sunk into a dream of delight, and was wishing *he* were a sunbeam or a moonbeam; and he would have been glad to hear more and more, for

But he was only sunk in a dream of delight.

181

ever. But at last, as all was still, he opened his eyes and looked around for his guest; but she had flown far away; so he could not bear to sit there any longer alone, and he got up and went to the gurgling brook. It gushed and rolled so merrily; and tumbled so wildly along as it hurried to throw itself head-over-heels into the river, just as if the great massy rock out of which it sprang were close behind it, and could only be escaped by a break-neck leap.

Then the child began to talk to the little waves, and asked them where they came from. They would not stay to give him an answer, but danced away, one over another; till at last, that the sweet child might not be grieved, a drop of water stopped behind a piece of rock. From this drop of water the child heard strange histories, but he could not understand them all, for she told him about her former life, and about the depths of the mountain.

"A long, long while ago," she said, "I lived with my countless sisters in the great ocean, in peace and unity. We had all sorts of pastimes; sometimes we mounted up high into the air, and peeped at the stars; then we sank plump down deep below, and looked how the coral builders work till they are tired, that they may reach the light of day at last. But I was conceited, and thought myself much better than my sisters. And so one day, when the sun rose out of the sea, I clung fast to one of his hot beams, and thought that now I should reach the stars, and become one of them. But I had not ascended far, when the sunbeam shook me off, and, in spite of all I could say or do, let me fall into a dark cloud. And soon a flash of fire darted through the cloud, and now I thought I must surely die; but the whole cloud laid itself down softly upon the top of a mountain, and so I escaped with

The stars are far, far away!

my fright and a black eye. Now I thought I should remain hidden, when, all of a sudden, I slipped over a round pebble, fell from one stone to another, down into the depths of the mountain, till at last it was pitch dark, and I could neither see nor hear anything. Then I found, indeed, that 'pride goes before a fall'. I resigned myself to my fate, and, as I had already laid aside all my pride in the cloud my portion was now the salt of humility; and after undergoing purifications from the hidden virtues of metals and minerals, I was at length permitted to come up once more into the free, cheerful air; and now will I run back to my sisters, and there wait patiently till I am called to something better."

However, she had hardly finished when the root of a forget-me-not caught the drop of water by her hair and sucked her in, that she might become a floweret, and twinkle brightly as a blue star on the green firmament of earth.

III

The child did not very well know what to think of all this; he went thoughtfully home and laid himself on his little bed; and all night long he was wandering about on the ocean, and among the stars, and over the dark mountain. But the moon loved to look on the slumbering child as he lay with his little head softly pillowed on his right arm. She lingered a long time in front of his window, and went slowly away to lighten the dark chamber of some sick person.

As the moon's soft light lay gently on the child's eyelids, he fancied he sat in a golden boat, on a great, great water; countless stars swam glittering on the dark mirror. He stretched out his hand to catch the nearest star, but it had vanished, and the water sprayed up against him. Then he saw clearly

The child fancied he sat on a golden boat on a great, great water.

that these were not the real stars: he looked up to the sky, and wished he could fly there.

But in the meantime the moon had wandered on her way; and now the child was led in his dream into the clouds and he thought he was sitting on a white sheep, and he saw many lambs grazing around him. He tried to catch a little lamb to play with, but it was all mist and vapour; and the child was sorrowful, and wished himself down again in his own meadow, where his own lamb was sporting gaily about.

Meanwhile the moon was gone to sleep behind the mountains, and all around was dark. Then the child dreamt that he fell down into the dark, gloomy caverns of the mountain, and at that he was so frightened, that he suddenly awoke, just as morning opened her clear eye over the nearest hill.

IV

The child started up and, to help himself recover from his fright, went into the flower garden behind his cottage, where the beds were surrounded by ancient palm trees, and where he knew that the flowers would nod kindly at him. However, behold, the tulip turned up her nose, and the ranunculus held her head as stiffly as possible, that she might now bow good morning to him. The rose, with her fair round cheek, smiled and greeted the child lovingly; so the child went up to her and gently kissed her fragrant mouth. And then the rose tenderly complained that he so seldom came into the garden, and that she gave out her bloom and her lovely fragrance the live-long day in vain; for the other flowers could not see her, because they were too low, or did not care to look at her because they themselves were so rich in bloom and fragrance. But she was

183

most delighted when she glowed in the blooming head of a child, and she could pour out all her heart's secrets to him in sweet odours. Among other things, the rose whispered in his ear that she was the fullness of beauty.

And in truth the child, while looking at her beauty, seemed to have quite forgotten to go on; till the blue larkspur called to him, and asked whether he cared nothing more about his faithful friend: she said that she was unchanged, and that even when she was dying she would look upon him with eyes of unfading blue.

The child thanked the larkspur for her true-heartedness, and passed on to the blue hyacinth, who stood near the puffy, gaudy tulips. Even from a distance the hyacinth

The garden of ancient palms.

sent forth kisses to him, for she knew not how to express her love. Although she was not remarkable for her beauty, yet the child felt himself wondrously attracted by her, for he thought no flower loved him so well. But the hyacinth poured out her full heart and wept bitterly, because she stood so lonely; the tulips indeed were her countrymen, but they were so cold and unfeeling that she was ashamed of them. The child gave her encouragement, and told her he did not think things were so bad as she fancied. The tulips spoke their love in bright looks, while she uttered hers in fragrant words; that these, indeed, were lovelier and certainly more intelligible, but that the others were not to be despised.

Then the hyacinth was comforted, and said she would be content; and the child went on to the powdered auricula who, in her bashfulness, looked kindly up to him, and would gladly have given him more than kind looks, had she had more to give. But the child was quite satisfied with her modest greeting; he felt that he was poor too, and he saw the deep, thoughtful colours that lay beneath her golden dust. But the humble flower, of her own accord, sent him to her neighbour, the lily, whom she willingly acknowledged as her queen. And when the child came to the lily, the slender flower waved to and fro, and bowed her pale head with gentle pride and stately modesty, and sent forth a fragrant greeting to him. The child knew not what had come to him: it reached his inmost heart, so that his eyes filled with soft tears.

The child was so moved that he slipped, and would have fallen, had not the branch of a currant bush caught and held him; he took some of the bright berries for his morning's meal, and went back to his hut and stripped the little branches.

V

In the hut he stayed not long, all was so gloomy, close, and silent within; and abroad everything seemed to smile, and to rejoice in the clear and unbounded space. Therefore the child went out into the green wood, of which the dragon-fly had told him such pleasant stories. But he found everything far more beautiful and lovely even than she had described it; for all about, wherever he went, the tender moss pressed his little feet, and the delicate grass embraced his knees, and the flowers kissed his hands, and even the branches stroked his cheeks with a kind and refreshing touch, and the high trees threw their fragrant and cooling shade around him.

There was no end to the child's delight. The little birds warbled and sang, and fluttered and hopped about, and the delicate wood-flowers gave out their beauty and their odours; and every sweet sound took a sweet odour by the hand, and thus walked through the open door of the child's heart, and held a joyous nuptial dance therein. But the nightingale and lily of the valley led the dance; for the nightingale sang of nothing but love, and the lily breathed of nothing but innocence, and he was the bridegroom and she was the bride. And the nightingale was never weary of repeating the same thing a hundred times over, for the spring of love which gushed from his heart was ever new; and the lily bowed her head bashfully, that no-one might see her glowing heart. And yet the one lived so solely and entirely in the other, that no-one could see whether the notes of the nightingale were floating lilies, or the lilies visible notes, falling like dew-drops from the nightingale's throat.

The child's heart was so full of joy that he felt it might burst. He sat himself down,

When the child came to the lily, the slender flower waved to and fro.

and he almost thought he should like to take root there, and live for ever among the sweet plants and flowers, and so become a true sharer in all their gentle pleasures. For he felt a deep delight in the still, secluded, twilight existence of the mosses and small herbs, which felt not the storm, nor the frost, nor the scorching sunbeam; but dwelt quietly among their many friends and neighbours, feasting in peace and good fellowship on the dew and cool shadows which the mighty trees shed upon them. To them it was a high festival when a sunbeam chanced to visit their lowly home; whilst the tops of the lofty trees could find joy and beauty only in the purple rays of morning or evening.

Sarah Austin

The History of
Jack the Giant-Killer

In the reign of the famous King Arthur there lived in Cornwall a lad named Jack, who was a bold fellow and took delight in hearing or reading of conjurers, giants and fairies; and used to listen eagerly to stories of the deeds of the knights of King Arthur's Round Table.

In those days there lived on St Michael's Mount, off Cornwall, a huge giant called Cormoran; his fierce and savage looks were the terror of all who beheld him. He dwelt in a gloomy cavern on the top of the mountain, and used to wade over to the mainland in search of prey; he would throw half-a-dozen oxen upon his back, and tie three times as many sheep and hogs round his waist, and march back to his own abode. Cormoran had done this for many years when Jack resolved to destroy him.

Jack took a horn, a shovel, a pickaxe, his armour, and a dark lantern, and one winter's evening he went to the mount. There he dug an enormous pit. He covered the top over so as to make it look like solid ground. He then blew such a tantivy on his horn that the Giant awoke and came out of his den, crying out: "You saucy villain! you shall pay for this. I shall broil you for my breakfast!"

He had just finished, when, taking one step further, he tumbled headlong into the pit, and Jack struck him a blow on the head with his pickaxe which killed him. Jack then returned home to cheer his friends with the news.

Another giant, called Blunderbore, vowed to be revenged on Jack if ever he should have him in his power. Blunderbore kept an enchanted castle in the midst of a lonely wood; and some time after the death of Cormoran, Jack was passing through a wood, and being weary sat down and went to sleep. The Giant, passing by and seeing Jack, carried him to his castle, where he locked him up in a large room, the floor of which was covered with the bodies, skulls and bones of men and women. A short while later the Giant went to fetch his brother, who was likewise a giant, to take a meal off his flesh; and Jack saw with terror through the bars of his prison the two Giants approaching.

Jack, perceiving in one corner of the room a strong cord, took courage, and making a slip-knot at each end, he threw them over their heads, and tied it to the window bars; he then pulled till he had choked them. When they were black in the face he slid down the rope and stabbed them to the heart.

Jack next took a great bunch of keys from the pocket of Blunderbore, and went into the castle again. He made a search through all the rooms, and in one of them found four ladies tied up by the hair of their heads, and almost starved to death. They told him that their husbands had been killed by the evil Giants, who had then condemned them to be starved to death, because they would not eat the flesh of their own dead husbands.

"Ladies," said Jack, "I have put an end to the monster and his wicked brother; and I give you this castle and all the riches it contains, to make some amends for the dreadful pains you have felt." He then very politely gave them the keys of the castle, and went further on his journey to Wales.

As Jack had very little money, he went on as fast as possible. At length he came to a handsome house. Jack knocked at the door, and there came forth a giant with two heads. Jack said he was a traveller who had lost his way, and the Giant made him welcome, and let him into a room where there was a good bed to sleep in.

Jack took off his clothes quickly, but though he was weary he could

back to his own room, thinking he had broken all Jack's bones.

Early in the morning Jack put a bold face upon the matter, and walked into the Giant's room to thank him for his lodging. The Giant started when he saw him, and began to stammer out: "Oh! dear me; is it you? Pray how did you sleep last night? Did you hear or see anything in the dead of the night?"

"Nothing worth speaking of," answered Jack carelessly: "a rat, I believe, gave me three or four slaps with its tail, and disturbed me a little; but I soon went to sleep again."

The Giant wondered more and more at this: yet he did not answer a word, but

not go to sleep. Soon after this he heard the Giant walking to and fro in the next room, and saying to himself:

> "*Though here you lodge with me this night,*
> *You shall not see the morning light;*
> *My club shall dash your brains out quite.*"

"Say you so?" thought Jack. "Are these your tricks upon travellers? But I hope to prove as cunning as you are." Then, getting out of bed, he groped about the room, and at last found a large thick billet of wood. He laid it in his own place in the bed, and then hid himself in a dark corner of the room.

The Giant, about midnight, entered the apartment, and with his bludgeon struck many blows on the bed, in the very place where Jack had laid the log; and then he went

knife, plunged it into his own stomach, and in a moment dropped down dead. Jack, having been successful in all his undertakings, resolved not to be idle in future; he therefore furnished himself with a horse, a cap of knowledge, a sword of sharpness, shoes of swiftness, and an invisible coat, the better to perform the wonderful enterprises that lay before him. He travelled over high hills, and on the third day he came to a large and spacious forest through which his road lay. Scarcely had he entered the forest when he beheld a monstrous giant dragging along by the hair of their heads a handsome knight and his lady. Jack alighted from his horse and, tying him to an oak tree, put on his invisible coat, under which he carried his sword of sharpness.

When he came up to the Giant he made several strokes at him, but could not reach his body. However, he wounded his thighs in several places; and at length, putting

went to bring two great bowls of hasty pudding for their breakfast. Jack wanted to make the Giant believe that he could eat as much as himself, so he contrived to button a leather bag inside his coat, and slip the hasty pudding into this bag, while he seemed to put it into his mouth.

When breakfast was over he said to the Giant: "Now I will show you a fine trick. I can cure all wounds with a touch: I could cut off my head in one minute, and the next put it sound again on my shoulders. You shall see an example." He then took hold of the knife, ripped up the leather bag, and all the hasty pudding tumbled out upon the floor.

"Ods splutter hur nails!" cried the Welsh Giant, who was ashamed to be outdone by such a little fellow as Jack, "hur can do that hurself;" so he snatched up the

Jack alighted from his horse and, putting on his invisible coat, approached and aimed a blow at the Giant's head, but missing his aim he only cut off his nose. On this the Giant seized his club and laid about him most unmercifully. "Nay," said Jack, "if this be the case I'd better dispatch you!" so jumping on the block, he stabbed him in the back, and the Giant dropped down dead.

both hands to his sword and aiming with all his might, he cut off both his legs. Then Jack, setting his foot upon his neck, plunged his sword into the Giant's body, and the monster gave a groan and expired.

The Knight and his Lady thanked Jack for their deliverance, and invited him to their house to receive a proper reward for his services.

"No," said Jack, "I cannot be easy till I have found out where this monster lives." So taking the Knight's directions, he mounted his horse, and soon after came in sight of another giant, who was sitting on a block of timber waiting for his brother's return.

Jack continued on his travels, performing heroic deeds along the way. Eventually he arrived at the castle of the Knight whom he had delivered from the power of the Giant and, recollecting his invitation, he went in and was received with every demonstration of joy imaginable, by both the Knight and his Lady. They gave a splendid entertainment in honour of Jack's victory, which lasted many days and to which all the nobility and gentry of that part of the country were invited. When the company were assembled, the Knight related the noble exploit of Jack and presented him, as a token of gratitude, with a beautiful ring, on which was engraved a picture of the Giant dragging along the unfortunate Knight and his Lady by the hair.

However, suddenly a herald, breathless with haste and terror,

rushed into the midst of the company and cried out that Thundol a ferocious giant, having heard of the death of his kinsmen, had come from the north to be revenged on Jack, and that he was only a short distance from the house. The country people all flew before him in the greatest terror like chaff before the wind. At these tidings, the very boldest of the guests humbled with confusion and dismay; while the undaunted Jack brandished his sword and cried, "Let him come; for I have a rod to chastise him." The good Knight's house was surrounded by a deep moat, over which was a drawbridge. Jack employed two men to cut the bridge almost to the middle and then, putting on his invisible coat, he went

immense body and the tremendous steps that he took, it broke and he tumbled into the water, and rolled about like a large whale. Jack, standing by the moat, laughed and jeered at him for some time. At last he ordered a cart rope to be brought to him, and he cast it over the Giant's head. With the help of a great number of horses, he dragged him to the edge, and then in the presence of the Knight and his guests, he snapped off the monster's head and, before he ate or drank, sent them to the court of King Arthur. He then returned to the company, and the remainder of the day was spent in mirth, good cheer, and the congratulations of all the company.

After staying with the Knight for some time, Jack began to grow weary of such an idle life, and so he set out again in search of

out to meet the Giant with his sword of sharpness. As Jack came close to him (though the Giant could not see him on account of his invisible coat) he was aware of some impending danger, and roared out in a voice that was quite terrible:

> "Fe, fi, fo, fum,
> I smell the blood of an Englishman.
> Be he living, or be he dead,
> I'll grind his bones to be my bread."

"You must catch me first," said Jack; and throwing off his invisible coat, and putting on his shoes of swiftness, he began to run. The furious Giant stalked after him like a moving castle, making the earth shake at every step he took. Jack ran over the drawbridge, the Giant still pursuing him with his club. As the Giant reached the middle, where the bridge had been cut by Jack's order, with the very great weight of his

new adventures. He travelled over hills and dales till he arrived at the foot of a high mountain. He knocked at the door of a lonely house, and an old man let him in.

When Jack was seated the hermit said to him: "My son, on the top of this mountain is an enchanted castle, kept by the Giant Galligantus and a vile magician. I lament the fate of a duke's daughter, whom they seized as she was walking in her father's garden, and carried her away in a chariot drawn by two fiery dragons, and transformed her into a deer."

Jack promised that in the morning, at the risk of his life, he would break the enchantment; and after a sound sleep he rose early, put on his invisible coat, and got ready for the attempt.

When he had climbed to the top of the mountain he saw two fiery dragons; but he passed between them without the least fear of danger, for they could not see him because he had on his invisible coat. On the castle gate he found a golden trumpet, under which were written these lines:

Whoever can this trumpet blow
Shall cause the Giant's overthrow.

As soon as Jack had read this he seized the trumpet and blew a shrill blast, which made the gates fly open and the very castle itself tremble.

The Giant and the Magician now knew that their wicked course was at an end, and they stood biting their thumbs and shaking with fear. Jack, with his sword of sharpness, soon killed the Giant, and the Magician

was then carried away by a whirlwind; and every knight and beautiful lady who had been changed into birds and beasts returned to their proper shapes. They flocked around their gallant deliverer and thanked him most gratefully for their happy escape. The castle vanished away like smoke, and the head of the Giant Galligantus was then sent to King Arthur.

The knights and ladies rested that night at the old man's hermitage, and next day they set out for the Court. Jack then went up to the King, and gave his Majesty an account of all his fierce battles.

Jack's fame had now spread through the whole country, and at the King's desire the Duke gave him his daughter in marriage, to the joy of all his kingdom. After this the King gave him a large estate, on which he and his wife lived the rest of their days in joy and contentment.

Anon., *The Blue Fairy Book*
and *Jack the Giant Killer*

The Pied Piper of Hamelin

I

Hamelin Town's in Brunswick,
  By famous Hanover city;
The river Weser, deep and wide,
Washes its wall on the southern side;
A pleasanter spot you never spied;
But, when begins my ditty,
Almost five hundred years ago,
To see the townsfolk suffer so
From vermin, was a pity.

II

Rats!
They fought the dogs and killed the cats,
And bit the babies in the cradles,
And ate the cheeses out of the vats.
And licked the soup from the cook's
own ladles,

Split open the kegs of salted sprats,
Made nests inside men's Sunday hats,
And even spoiled the women's chats,

By drowning their speaking
With shrieking and squeaking
In fifty different sharps and flats.

III

At last the people in a body
To the Town Hall came flocking:
"'Tis clear," cried they, "our Mayor's a noddy;
"And as for our Corporation—shocking.
"To think we buy gowns lined with ermine
"For dolts that can't or won't determine
"What's best to rid us of our vermin!
"You hope, because you're old and obese,
"To find in the furry civic robe ease?
"Rouse up, sirs! Give your brains a racking
"To find the remedy we're lacking,
"Or, sure as fate, we'll send you packing!"
At this the Mayor and Corporation
Quaked with a mighty consternation.

IV

An hour they sate in council,
At length the Mayor broke silence:
"For a guilder I'd my ermine gown sell;
"I wish I were a mile hence!
"It's easy to bid one rack one's brain—
"I'm sure my poor head aches again,
"I've scratched it so, and all in vain.
"Oh for a trap, a trap, a trap!"
Just as he said this, what should hap
At the chamber door but a gentle tap?
"Bless us," cried the Mayor, "what's that?"
(With the Corporation as he sat,
Looking little though wondrous fat;
Nor brighter was his eye, nor moister
Than a too-long-opened oyster,
Save when at noon his paunch grew mutinous
For a plate of turtle green and glutinous)
"Only a scraping of shoes on the mat?
"Anything like the sound of a rat
"Makes my heart go pit-a-pat!"

V

"Come in!"—the Mayor cried, looking bigger:
And in did come the strangest figure!
His queer long coat from heel to head
Was half of yellow and half of red,
And he himself was tall and thin,
With sharp blue eyes, each like a pin,
And light loose hair, yet swarthy skin
No tuft on cheek or beard on chin,
But lips where smiles went out and in;
There was no guessing his kith and kin:
And nobody could enough admire
The tall man and his quaint attire.
Quoth one: "It's as my great-grandsire,
"Starting up at the Trump of Doom's tone,
"Had walked this way from his painted tombstone!"

VI

He advanced to the council-table:
And, "Please your honours," said he, "I'm able,
"By means of a secret charm, to draw
"All creatures living beneath the sun,
"That creep or swim or fly or run,
"After me so as you never saw!
"And I chiefly use my charm
"On creatures that do people harm,
"The mole and toad and newt and viper;
"And people call me the Pied Piper."
(And here they noticed round his neck
A scarf of red and yellow stripe,
To match with his coat of the self-same cheque;
And at the scarf's end hung a pipe;
And his fingers they noticed were ever straying
As if impatient to be playing
Upon this pipe, as low it dangled
Over his vesture so old-fangled.)

196

Like a candle-flame where salt is
sprinkled;
　And ere three shrill notes the pipe
　　uttered,
　You heard as if an army muttered;
　And the muttering grew to a
　　grumbling;
　And the grumbling grew to a
　　mighty rumbling;
　And out of the houses the rats
　　came tumbling.
　　　　Great rats, small rats,
　　　　lean rats, brawny rats,
　　　　Brown rats, black rats,
　　　　grey rats, tawny rats,
　　　　Grave old plodders, gay
　　　　young friskers,
　　　　Fathers, mothers, uncles,
　　　　cousins,
Cocking tails and pricking whiskers,
Families by tens and dozens,
Brothers, sisters, husbands, wives—
Followed the Piper for their lives.
From street to street he piped advancing,
And step for step they followed dancing,

"Yet," said he, "poor Piper as I am,
"In Tartary I freed the Cham,
"Last June, from his huge swarms of gnats,
"I eased in Asia the Nizam
"Of a monstrous brood of vampyre-bats:
"And as for what your brain bewilders,
"If I can rid your town of rats
"Will you give me a thousand guilders?"
"One? fifty thousand!"—was the
exclamation
Of the astonished Mayor and
Corporation.

VII

Into the street the Piper stept,
Smiling first a little smile,
As if he knew what magic slept
In his quiet pipe the while;
Then, like a musical adept,
To blow the pipe his lips he wrinkled,
And green and blue his sharp eyes
twinkled,

Until they came to the river Weser
Wherein all plunged and perished!
—Save one who, stout as Julius Caesar,
Swam across and lived to carry
(As he, the manuscript he cherished)
To Rat-land home his commentary:
Which was, "At the first shrill notes of the pipe,

"I heard a sound as of scraping tripe,
"And putting apples, wondrous ripe,
"Into a cider-press's gripe:
"And a moving away of pickle-tub-boards,
"And a leaving ajar of conserve-cupboards,
"And a drawing the corks of train-oil-flasks,
"And a breaking the hoops of butter-casks:
"And it seemed as if a voice

"(Sweeter far than by harp or by psaltery
"Is breathed) called out, 'Oh rats, rejoice!
" 'The world is grown to one vast drysaltery!
" 'So munch on, crunch on, take your nuncheon,
" 'Breakfast, supper, dinner, luncheon!'
"And just as a bulky sugar-puncheon,
"All ready staved, like a great sun shone
"Glorious scarce an inch before me,
"Just as methought it said, 'Come, bore me!'
"—I found the Weser rolling o'er me."

VIII

You should have heard the Hamelin people
Ringing the bells till they rocked the steeple.
"Go," cried the Mayor, "and get long poles,
"Poke out the nests and block up the holes!
"Consult with carpenters and builders,
"And leave in our town not even a trace
"Of the rats!"—when suddenly up the face
Of the Piper perked in the market-place,
With a, "First, if you please, my thousand guilders!"

IX

A thousand guilders! The Mayor looked blue;
So did the Corporation too.
For council dinners made rare havoc
With Claret, Moselle, Vin-de-Grave, Hock;
And half the money would replenish
Their cellar's biggest butt with Rhenish.
To pay this sum to a wandering fellow
With a gipsy coat of red and yellow!
"Beside," quoth the Mayor with a knowing wink,

"Our business was done at the river's
brink;
"We saw with our eyes the vermin sink,
"And what's dead can't come to life, I
think.
"So, friend, we're not the folks to shrink
"From the duty of giving you something to
drink,
"And a matter of money to put in your
poke;
"But as for the guilders, what we spoke
"Of them, as you very well know, was
in joke.
"Beside, our losses have made us thrifty.
"A thousand guilders! Come, take fifty!"

X

The Piper's face fell, and he cried,
"No trifling! I can't wait, beside!
"I've promised to visit by dinner-time
"Bagdad, and accept the prime
"Of the Head-Cook's pottage, and he's
rich in,
"For having left, in the Caliph's kitchen,
"Of a nest of scorpions no survivor:
"With him I proved no bargain-driver,
"With you, don't think I'll bate a stiver!
"And folks who put me in a passion
"May find me pipe after another fashion."

XI

"How?" cried the Mayor, "d'ye think I
brook
"Being worse treated than a Cook?
"Insulted by a lazy ribald
"With idle pipe and vesture piebald?
"You threaten us, fellow? Do your
worst,
"Blow your pipe there till you
burst!"

XII

Once more he stept into the street,
And to his lips again
Laid his long pipe of smooth straight cane;
And ere he blew three notes
(such sweet
Soft notes as yet musician's cunning
Never gave the enraptured air)
There was a rustling, that seemed like a
bustling
Of merry crowds justling at pitching and
hustling,
Small feet were pattering, wooden shoes
clattering,
Little hands clapping and little tongues
chattering,
And, like fowls in a farm-yard when
barley is scattering,
Out came the children running.
All the little boys and girls,
With rosy cheeks and flaxen curls,
And sparkling eyes and teeth like pearls,

Tripping and skipping, ran merrily after
The wonderful music with shouting and
laughter.

XIII

The Mayor was dumb, and the Council
stood
As if they were changed into blocks of
wood,
Unable to move a step, or cry
To the children merrily skipping by.
—Could only follow with the eye
That joyous crowd at the Piper's back.
But how the Mayor was on the rack,
And the wretched Council's bosoms beat,
As the Piper turned from the High Street

To where the Weser rolled its waters
Right in the way of their sons and
daughters!
However he turned from South to West,
And to Koppelberg Hill his steps addressed,
And after him the children pressed;
Great was the joy in every breast.
"He never can cross that mighty top!
"He's forced to let the piping drop,
"And we shall see our children stop!"
When, lo, as they reached the
mountain-side,
A wondrous portal opened wide,
As if a cavern was suddenly hollowed;
And the Piper advanced and the children
followed,

And when all were in to the very last,
The door in the mountain-side shut fast.
Did I say, all? No! One was lame,
And could not dance the whole of
the way;
And in after years, if you would blame
His sadness, he was used to say,—
"It's dull in our town since my
playmates left!
"I can't forget that I'm bereft
"Of all the pleasant sights they see,
"Which the Piper also promised me.
"For he led us, he said, to a joyous land,
"Joining the town and just at hand,
"Where waters gushed and fruit-trees
grew,

"And flowers put forth a fairer hue,
"And everything was strange and new;
"The sparrows were brighter than
peacocks here,
"And their dogs outran our fallow deer,
"And honey-bees had lost their stings,
"And horses were born with eagles'
wings:
"And just as I became assured
"My lame foot would be speedily
cured,
"The music stopped and I stood still,
"And found myself outside the hill,
"Left alone against my will,
"To go now limping as before,
"And never hear of that country more!"

XIV

Alas, alas for Hamelin!
There came into many a burgher's pate
A text which says that Heaven's gate
Opens to the rich at as easy rate
As the needle's eye takes a camel in!
The Mayor sent East, West, North,
and South,
To offer the Piper, by word of mouth,
Wherever it was men's lot to find him,
Silver and gold to his heart's content,
If he'd only return the way he went,
And bring the children behind him.
But when they saw 'twas a lost endeavour,
And Piper and dancers were gone for ever,
They made a decree that lawyers never
Should think their records dated duly
If, after the day of the month and year,
These words did not as well appear,
"And so long after what happened here
"On the Twenty-second of July,
"Thirteen hundred and seventy-six:"
And the better in memory to fix
The place of the children's last retreat,
They called it, the Pied Piper's Street—
Where any one playing on pipe or tabor,
Was sure for the future to lose his labour.
Nor suffered they hostelry or tavern
To shock with mirth a street so solemn;
But opposite the place of the cavern
They wrote the story on a column,
And on the great church-window painted
The same, to make the world acquainted
How their children were stolen away,
And there it stands to this very day.
And I must not omit to say
That in Transylvania there's a tribe
Of alien people that ascribe
The outlandish ways and dress
On which their neighbours lay
such stress,
To their fathers and mothers having risen
Out of some subterraneous prison
Into which they were trepanned
Long time ago in a mighty band
Out of Hamelin town in Brunswick land,
But how or why, they don't understand.

XV

So, Willy, let me and you be wipers
Of scores out with all men—especially
pipers!
And, whether they pipe us free from rats
or from mice,
If we've promised them aught, let us keep
our promise!

Browning, *The Pied Piper of Hamelin*

202

Cinderella

There was once an honest gentleman who took for his second wife a lady, the proudest and most disagreeable in the whole country. She had two daughters exactly like herself in all things. The gentleman also had one little girl, who resembled her dead mother, the best woman in all the world.

Scarcely had the second marriage taken place than the stepmother became jealous of the good little girl, who was so great a contrast to her own two daughters. She gave her all the dirty work of the house; compelled her to wash the floors and staircases, to dust the bedrooms and clean the grates; and while her sisters slept in carpeted chambers hung with mirrors, where they could see themselves from head to foot, this poor little girl was sent to sleep in an attic, on an old straw mattress, with only one chair and not a looking-glass in the room.

She suffered all in silence, not daring to complain to her father, who was entirely ruled by his new wife. When her daily work was done, she used to sit down in the chimney-corner among the ashes; and so the two sisters gave her the nickname of Cinderella. But Cinderella, however shabbily clad, was handsomer than they were with all their fine clothes.

Now it happened that the King's son gave a number of balls, to which were invited all the nobles and the fashionable people of the city, and among the rest the two elder sisters. They were very proud and happy, and occupied their whole time in deciding what they should wear.

This was a source of new trouble to Cinderella, whose duty it was to get ready their fine linen and laces, and who never could please them however much she tried.

The two sisters talked of nothing but their clothes.

"I," said the elder, "shall wear my velvet gown and my trimmings of English lace."

"And I," added the younger, "will have only my ordinary silk petticoat to wear, but I shall adorn it with an upper skirt of flowered brocade, and shall put on my diamond tiara, which is a great deal finer than anything of yours."

Here the elder sister grew very angry, and the dispute ran so high that Cinderella, who was known to have excellent taste, was called upon to decide between them. She gave them the best advice she could, and offered to dress them herself, and to arrange their hair, which she could certainly do very well.

The important evening came, and she exercised all her skill to adorn the two young ladies. While she was combing out the elder's hair, this ill-natured girl said sharply, "Cinderella, do you not wish you were going to the ball?"

"Ah, madam," (they obliged her always to say madam when addressing them), "you are only mocking me; it is not my fortune to have any such pleasure."

"You are right; people would only laugh to see a little cinder-girl at a ball."

Any other than Cinderella would have arranged the hair all awry, but she was good and arranged it perfectly even and smooth, and as prettily as she could.

The sisters had scarcely eaten for two days in trying to make themselves slender; but tonight they lost their tempers over and over again before they had finished dressing. When at last the happy moment arrived, Cinderella followed them to the coach; after it had whirled them away, she sat herself down by the kitchen fire and began to cry.

Immediately her godmother, who was a fairy, appeared beside her. "What are you crying for, my little maid?"

"Oh, I wish—I wish—". Cinderella's sobs stopped her.

"You wish to go to the ball; isn't it so?" Cinderella nodded.

"Well, then, be a good girl, and you shall go. First run into the garden and fetch me the largest pumpkin you can find."

Cinderella did not see what this had to do with her going to the ball, but being obedient and obliging she went. Her godmother took the pumpkin, and having scooped out all its inside, struck it with her wand; at once it became a splendid gilt coach, lined with rose-coloured satin.

"Now fetch me the mouse-trap out of the pantry, my dear."

Cinderella brought it; it contained six of the fattest, sleekest mice you ever saw. The Fairy lifted up the wire door, and as each mouse ran out, she struck it and changed it into a beautiful black horse.

"But what shall I do for your coachman, Cinderella?"

Cinderella said that she had seen a large black rat in the rat-trap, and he might do for want of anything better.

"You are right; go and look again for the rat."

He was found, and the Fairy made him into a most respectable coachman, with a pair of very fine whiskers. She took six lizards from behind the pumpkin frame and changed them into six footmen, all in splendid livery, who immediately jumped up behind the carriage, as if they had been footmen all their days. "Well, Cinderella," she said, "now you can go to the ball."

"What, in these old clothes?" replied Cinderella piteously, looking down on her ragged frock.

Her godmother laughed, and touched her also with the wand; at which her wretched threadbare jacket became stiff with gold, and sparkling with jewels; her woollen petticoat changed into a gown of sweeping satin, from underneath which peeped out her little feet, no longer bare, but covered with silk stockings and the prettiest glass slippers in the world.

"Now, Cinderella, depart; but remember, if you stay one instant after midnight, your carriage will become a pumpkin, your coachman a rat, your horses mice, and your footmen lizards; while you yourself will be the little cinder-girl you were an hour ago."

Cinderella promised without fear, because her heart was so full of joy.

When she arrived at the palace, the King's son was standing at the door, ready to receive her. Someone, probably the Fairy, had told him to await the coming of an uninvited princess whom nobody had met before.

He offered her his hand, and led her with the utmost courtesy through the rows of guests, who stood aside to let her pass, whispering to one another, "Oh, how beautiful she is!" It might have turned the head of anyone but poor Cinderella, who was so used to being despised, that she took it all as if it were something happening in a dream.

Her triumph was now complete; even the old King said to the Queen, that never since her Majesty's young days had he seen so charming and elegant a person. All the court ladies scanned her eagerly, clothes and all, meaning to have theirs made next day of exactly the same pattern.

The King's son himself led her out to dance, and she danced so gracefully that he admired her more and more. Indeed at supper, which was fortunately early, his admiration quite took away his appetite. As for Cinderella herself, she sought out her sisters; placed herself beside them and

offered them all sorts of attentions, which, coming as they supposed from a complete stranger, and so fine a woman, filled them with delight.

While she was talking with them she heard the clock strike a quarter to twelve, and taking leave of the royal family, she re-entered her carriage, escorted tenderly by the King's son, and arrived in safety at her own door. There she found her godmother, who smiled at her, and she begged permission to go to a second ball, the following night, to which the Queen had invited her. Then the two sisters were heard knocking at the gate, and the Fairy Godmother vanished, leaving Cinderella sitting in the chimney-corner.

"Ah," exclaimed the eldest sister, "it has been the most delightful ball; and there was present the most beautiful princess I have ever seen, who was very polite to us both."

"Was she?" replied Cinderella quietly; "and who might she be?"

"Nobody knows, though everybody would give their eyes to know, especially the King's son."

"Indeed!" replied Cinderella, a little more interested; "I should like to see her. Miss Javotte"—that was the elder sister's name—"will you not let me go tomorrow, and lend me your yellow gown that you wear on Sundays?"

"What, lend my yellow gown to a cinder-girl! I am not so foolish as that;" At this refusal Cinderella did not complain, for if her sister really had lent her the gown she would have been rather put out.

The next night came, and the two young ladies, richly dressed, went to the ball. Cinderella, more splendidly attired and beautiful than ever, followed them shortly after. "Now remember twelve o'clock," was her godmother's parting speech; and the girl thought she certainly should.

But on this evening the Prince's attentions to her were greater even than on the first one, and in the delight of listening to his pleasant talk time slipped by. While she was sitting happily beside him in a lovely alcove, and looking at the moon from under a bower of fragrant orange blossoms, she heard a clock strike the first stroke of twelve. She started up, and fled away as lightly as a deer.

The Prince followed, but could not catch her. Indeed he missed his lovely Princess altogether, and only saw running out of the palace doors a little dirty girl whom he had never beheld before, and of whom he certainly would never have taken the least notice.

Cinderella arrived home breathless and weary, ragged and cold, without carriage, or footmen, or coachman; the only thing left to remind her of the ball being one of her little glass slippers—the other slipper she had dropped in the ballroom as she ran away.

When the two sisters returned they were full of this strange adventure—how the beautiful lady had appeared at the ball more beautiful than ever, and enchanted every one who looked at her; how as the clock was striking twelve she had suddenly risen up and fled through the ballroom, disappearing no-one knew how or where, and dropping one of her glass slippers behind her in her flight; and how the King's son had been very sad until he chanced to pick up the little glass slipper, which he carried away in his pocket, and was seen to take it out continually and look at it, with the air of a man very much in love.

Cinderella listened in silence, turning her face to the kitchen fire, and perhaps it was that which made her look so rosy; but nobody ever noticed or admired her at home, so it did not matter, and next morning she went to her weary work again just as she did each day.

A few days later the whole city was attracted by the sight of a herald going round with a little glass slipper in his hand, publishing, with a flourish of trumpets, that the King's son had ordered this slipper to be fitted on the foot of every lady in the kingdom, and that he wished to marry the lady whom it fitted best, or who owned a glass slipper like it.

Princesses, duchesses, countesses and simple gentlewomen all tried it on, but being a fairy slipper, it fitted nobody; and besides this, nobody could show the matching slipper, which lay all the time safely in the pocket of Cinderella's old gown.

At last the herald came to the house of the two sisters, and though they knew only too well neither of themselves was the beautiful lady, they made every attempt to get their clumsy feet into the glass slipper, but all in vain.

"Let me try it on," said Cinderella from the chimney-corner.

"What, you?" cried the others, bursting into shouts of laughter; but Cinderella only smiled, and held out her hand.

Her two sisters could not prevent her, since the command was that every young maiden in the city should try on the slipper, in order that no chance might be left untried, for the Prince was nearly breaking his heart; and his father and mother were afraid that, though he was a prince, he would actually die for love of the beautiful unknown lady.

So the herald told Cinderella to sit down on a three-legged stool in the kitchen, and himself put the slipper on her pretty little foot, which it fitted exactly; she then drew from her pocket the matching slipper, which she also put on, and stood up—for with the touch of the magic shoes all her dress was changed likewise—no longer the poor despised cinder-girl, but the beautiful lady whom the King's son loved.

Her sisters knew her at once. Filled with astonishment, mingled with no little alarm, they threw themselves at her feet, begging her pardon for all their former unkindness. She raised and embraced them; told them she forgave them with all her heart, and only hoped they would love her always. Then she departed with the herald to the King's palace, and told her whole story to his Majesty and the royal family, who were not in the least surprised, for, of course, everybody believed in fairies, and everybody longed to have a fairy godmother.

As for the young Prince, he found the girl more lovely and lovable than ever, and insisted upon marrying her immediately. Cinderella never went home again, but she sent for her two sisters to the palace, and with the consent of all parties married them shortly afterwards to two rich gentlemen of the Court, though, to tell the truth, they scarcely deserved this good fortune.

Perrault, *The Milk-White Thorn*

The Twelve Dancing Princesses

Once upon a time there lived a young shepherd, without either father or mother. His real name was Michael, but he was always called the Star Gazer, because he went along with his head in the air, gaping at nothing.

The village girls used to cry after him, "Well, Star Gazer, what are you doing?" and Michael would answer, "Oh, nothing," and go on his way without even turning to look at them. He thought them very ugly, with their sunburnt necks, their great red hands, their coarse petticoats and their wooden shoes. He had heard that somewhere in the world there were girls whose necks were white and whose hands were small, who were always dressed in the finest silks and laces, and were called princesses, and while his companions round the fire saw nothing in the flames but common everyday fancies, he dreamt that he had the great happiness to marry a princess.

One morning, just at midday when the sun was hottest, Michael ate his dinner of a piece of dry bread, and went to sleep under an oak.

He dreamt that there appeared before him a beautiful woman, who said to him: "Go to the castle of Beloeil, and there you shall marry a princess."

That evening the young shepherd told his dream to the farm people. But they only laughed at him.

The next day the beautiful woman appeared to him a second time, and said: "Go to the castle of Beloeil, and you shall marry a princess."

Michael told his friends of his second dream but they only laughed at him more than before. "Never mind," he thought to himself; "if the woman appears to me a third time, I will do as she tells me." And so it happened.

There lived in the castle of Beloeil twelve princesses of wonderful beauty, and as proud as they were beautiful. They led exactly the lives that princesses ought to lead, sleeping far into the morning, and never getting up till midday. They had twelve beds all in the same room, but though they were locked in by triple bolts, every morning their satin shoes were found worn into holes. When they were asked what they had been doing all night, they always answered that they had been asleep; and indeed, no noise was ever heard in the room, yet the shoes could not wear themselves out alone!

At last the Duke of Beloeil ordered a proclamation to be made that whoever could discover how his daughters wore out their shoes should choose one of them for his wife. A number of princes arrived at the castle to try their luck. They watched all night long behind the open door of the Princesses, but when the morning came they had all disappeared, and no-one could tell what had become of them.

When he reached the castle, Michael went straight to the gardener and offered his services. He was told that when the Princesses got up he was to present each one with a bouquet, and Michael thought that if he had nothing more unpleasant to do than that he should get on very well.

He gave one to each of the sisters, and they took them without even deigning to look at the lad, except Lina the youngest, who fixed her large black eyes as soft as velvet on him, and exclaimed, "Oh, how pretty he is—our new flower boy!" The rest all burst out laughing, and the eldest pointed out that a princess ought never to lower herself by looking at a garden boy.

Even so, the beautiful eyes of Princess Lina inspired him with a longing to try his fate. Unhappily he did not dare to come forward, being afraid that he should only be jeered at, or even turned away from the castle on account of his impudence.

Nevertheless, in a little while the Star Gazer had another dream. The woman appeared to him once more, holding in one hand two young laurel trees, a cherry laurel and a rose laurel, and in the other hand a little golden rake, a little golden bucket and a silken towel. She said: "Plant these two laurels in two large pots, rake them over with the rake, water them with the bucket, and wipe them with the towel. When they have grown as tall as a girl of fifteen, say to each of them, 'My beautiful laurel, with the golden rake I have raked you, with the golden bucket I have watered you, with the silken towel I have wiped you.' Then ask anything you choose, and the laurels will give it to you."

When he woke up he found the two laurel trees had been placed beside him. So he carefully obeyed the orders he had been given by the woman.

The trees grew very fast, and when they were as tall as a girl of fifteen he said to the cherry laurel, "My lovely cherry laurel, with the golden rake I have raked you, with the golden bucket I have watered you, with the silken towel I have wiped you. Kindly teach me how to become invisible." There instantly appeared on the laurel a pretty white flower, which Michael stuck into his button-hole.

That evening, when the Princesses went upstairs to bed, he followed them barefoot, so that he might make no noise, and hid himself under one of the twelve beds. The Princesses began at once to open their wardrobes and boxes. They took out of them the most magnificent dresses which they put on before their mirrors, and when they had finished, turned themselves round and round to admire their appearances.

Michael could see nothing from his hiding place, however he listened to the Princesses laughing. At last the eldest said, "Be quick, my sisters, our partners will be impatient." He peeped out and saw the twelve sisters in their splendid garments, with their satin shoes on their feet.

Then the eldest Princess clapped her hands three times and a trapdoor opened. All twelve Princesses disappeared down a secret staircase, and Michael followed them. As he was following on the steps of Princess Lina, he carelessly trod on the back of her dress.

"There is somebody behind me," cried the Princess; "they are holding my dress."

"You foolish thing," said her eldest sister, "it is only a nail which caught you."

They went down, down, down, till at last they came to a passage with a door at one end. The eldest Princess opened it, and they found themselves immediately in a lovely little wood, where all the leaves were spangled with drops of silver which shone in the brilliant light of the moon. They next crossed another

211

wood where the leaves were sprinkled with gold, and after that another still, where the leaves glittered with diamonds. At last the Star Gazer perceived a large lake, and twelve little boats, in which were seated twelve princes, grasping their oars.

Each princess entered one of the boats, and Michael slipped into that which held the youngest. The boats glided along rapidly, but Lina's, from being heavier, was always behind the rest. "We never went so slowly before," said the youngest Princess; "what can be the reason?"

"I don't know," answered the Prince. "I am rowing as hard as I can."

On the other side of the lake was a beautiful castle splendidly lit. From the castle came the lively music of fiddles, kettles, drums and trumpets. In a moment they touched land, and the company jumped out of the boats; and the princes gave their arms to the Princesses and conducted them to the castle.

Michael entered the ballroom in their train. He placed himself out of the way, admiring the grace and beauty of the Princesses. Some were fair and some were dark; some had chestnut hair, or curls darker still, and some had golden locks. But the one who the shepherd thought the most beautiful was the little Princess with the velvet eyes.

The poor boy envied those handsome young men with whom Lina danced so gracefully, but he did not know how little reason he had to be jealous of them. The young men were really the princes who had tried to steal the Princesses' secret. The Princesses had made them drink a philtre, which froze the heart and left nothing but the love of dancing.

They danced on and on till the shoes of the Princesses were worn into holes.

The dancers all went back to their boats. They crossed again the wood with the diamond-spangled leaves, the wood with gold-sprinkled leaves, and the wood whose leaves glittered with drops of silver, and Michael broke a small branch from a tree in the last wood. Lina turned as she heard the noise made by the breaking of the branch.

"What was that noise?" she said.

"Oh, it was nothing," replied the eldest Princess; "it was only the screech of the barn-owl."

While she was speaking Michael was able to slip in front, and he reached the Princesses' room first. He flung open the window, and sliding down the vine which climbed up the wall, found himself in the garden just as the sun was beginning to rise, and it was time for him to set to his work.

That day, Michael hid the branch with the silver drops in the bouquet for the youngest Princess. When Lina discovered it she was much surprised. However she said nothing to her sisters.

The same evening the twelve sisters went again to the ball, and the Star Gazer again followed them and crossed the lake in Lina's boat. This time it was the Prince who complained that the boat seemed very heavy. During the ball Lina looked everywhere for the gardener's boy, but she never saw him.

As they came back, Michael gathered a branch from the wood with the gold-sprinkled leaves, and now it was the eldest Princess who heard the noise.

"It is nothing," said Lina; "only the cry of the owl."

As soon as she got up she found the branch in her bouquet. When the sisters went down she stayed behind and said to the young shepherd: "Where does this branch come from?"

"Your Royal Highness knows only too well," answered Michael.

"So you have followed us?"

"Yes, Princess."

"How did you manage it?"

"I hid myself," replied the Star Gazer quietly.

"You know our secret!—keep it." And she flung the boy a purse of gold.

"I do not sell my silence," answered

Michael, and he left without picking up the purse.

For three nights Lina neither saw nor heard anything extraordinary; on the fourth she heard a rustling among the diamond-spangled leaves. That day there was a branch of the trees in her bouquet.

Lina's sisters had seen her talking to the little garden boy, and jeered at her for it.

"What prevents your marrying him?" asked the eldest, "You could live in a cottage at the end of the park, and when we get up you could bring us our bouquets."

Princess Lina was very angry, and when the Star Gazer presented her bouquet, she received it in a disdainful manner. She made up her mind then and there to tell everything to her eldest sister.

"What!" said she, "this rogue knows our secret, and you never told me! I must lose no time in getting rid of him."

Then the youngest sister declared that if they laid a finger on the little garden boy, she would herself go and tell their father the secret of the holes in their shoes.

At last it was decided that they would take Michael to the ball, and give him the philtre which was to enchant him just as it had the princes.

They sent for the Star Gazer, and the eldest sister gave him the order they had agreed upon. He only answered: "I will obey."

He had really been present, invisible, at the council of princesses, and had heard all; but he had made up his mind to drink of the philtre, and sacrifice himself to the happiness of the girl he loved.

Not wishing, however, to cut a poor figure at the ball by the side of the other dancers, he went to the laurels, and said: "My lovely rose laurel, with the golden rake I have raked you, with the golden bucket I have watered you, with a silken towel I have dried you. Dress me like a prince." A beautiful pink flower appeared. Michael gathered it, and found himself clothed in velvet, which was as black as the eyes of the little Princess, with a cap to match, and a blossom of the rose laurel in his button-hole.

The twelve Princesses went upstairs to bed. Michael followed them and waited behind the open door till they gave the signal for departure.

This time he did not cross in Lina's boat. He gave his arm to the eldest sister, danced with each in turn, and was so graceful that everyone was delighted with him. At last the time came for him to dance with the little Princess. She said to him in a mocking voice: "Here you are at the summit of your wishes; you are being treated like a prince."

"Don't be afraid, Lina," replied the Star Gazer gently. "You shall never be a gardener's wife."

The little Princess stared at him with a frightened face, and he left her without waiting for an answer.

When the satin slippers were worn through the fiddles stopped.

The eldest sister made a sign, and one of the pages brought in a large golden cup.

"The enchanted castle has no more secrets for you," she said to the Star Gazer. "Let us drink to your triumph."

He cast a lingering glance at the little Princess, and then without hesitation lifted the cup.

"Don't drink!" she suddenly cried out; "I would rather marry a gardener." And she burst into tears.

Michael fell at Lina's feet. The rest of the princes fell likewise at the knees of the Princesses, each of whom chose a husband

and raised him to her side. The charm was broken.

They went straight to the Duke of Beloeil, who had just woken up. Michael held in his hand the golden cup, and he revealed the secret of the holes in the shoes.

"Choose, then," said the Duke, "whichever you prefer."

"My choice is already made," replied the garden boy, and he offered his hand to the youngest Princess, who blushed and lowered her eyes.

Princess Lina did not become a gardener's wife; it was the Star Gazer who became a Prince: but before the marriage ceremony the Princess insisted that her lover should tell her how he came to discover the secret. So he showed her the two laurels which had helped him, and she, thinking they gave him too much advantage over his wife, cut them off at the root and threw them in the fire.

Grimm, *The Red Fairy Book*

The Princess and the Pea

There was once upon a time a prince who wanted to marry a princess, but she must be a true princess. So he travelled through the whole world to find one, but there was always something against each. There were plenty of princesses, but he could not find out if they were in fact true princesses. In each and every case there was a little fault, which showed that the genuine article was not yet found. So he came home again in very low spirits, for he had wanted very much to have a true princess. One night there was a dreadful storm; there was thunder and lightning and the rain streamed down in torrents. It was fearful! There was a knocking heard at the palace gate, and the old King went to open it.

There stood a princess outside the gate; but oh, in what a sad plight she was in from the rain and the storm! Water was running down from her hair and her dress into the tips of her shoes and out at the heels again. And yet she said she was a true princess!

"Well, we shall soon find out!" thought the old Queen. But she said nothing, and went into the bedroom, took off all the bedclothes, and laid a pea on the bottom of the bed. Then she put twenty mattresses on top of the pea, and twenty eiderdown quilts on the top of the mattresses. And this was the bed in which the Princess was to sleep.

The next morning she was asked how she had slept.

"Oh, very badly!" said the Princess. "I scarcely closed my eyes all night! I am sure I don't know what was in the bed. I laid on something so hard that my whole body is black and blue. It is dreadful!"

Now they perceived that she was indeed a true princess, because she had felt the pea through the twenty mattresses and the twenty eiderdown quilts. No-one but a true princess could be so sensitive.

So the Prince married her, for now he knew that at last he had a true princess. And the pea was put into the Royal Museum, where it is still to be seen if no-one has stolen it.

Andersen, *The Yellow Fairy Book*

The Tale of a Youth who Set Out to Learn what Fear Was

A father had two sons, the eldest was clever and bright; but the youngest was stupid. Now when there was anything to be done, the eldest had always to do it; but if something was required late or in the night-time, and the way led through the churchyard or some such ghostly place, he always replied: "Oh! no, Father: nothing will induce me to go there, it makes me shudder!" for he was afraid. Or, when they sat of an evening round the fire telling stories which made one's flesh creep, the listeners sometimes said: "Oh! it makes one shudder," the youngest sat in a corner, and could not understand what it meant. "They are always saying it makes one shudder! Nothing makes me shudder. It's probably an art quite beyond me."

His father said to him one day: "You there in the corner; you

are growing big and strong, and you must learn to earn your own bread. Look at your brother, what pains he takes; but all the money I've spent on your education is thrown away."

"My dear Father," he replied, "I will gladly learn—in fact, if it were possible I should very much like to learn to shudder; I don't understand that a bit yet." The eldest laughed when he heard this, and thought to himself: "Good heavens! what a ninny my brother is! he'll never come to any good."

The father sighed, and answered him: "You will soon learn to shudder; but that won't help you to make a living."

When the sexton came to pay them a visit, the father told him what a bad hand his youngest son was at everything he did: he knew nothing and learnt nothing. "Only think! when I asked him how he purposed gaining a livelihood, he actually asked to be taught to shudder."

"If that's all he wants," said the sexton, "I can teach him that; just you send him to me and I'll soon polish him up." The father was pleased with the proposal, because he thought: "It will be a good discipline for the youth." So the sexton took him into his house, and told him that his duty was to toll the bell.

After a few days he woke him at midnight, and told him to rise up and climb into the tower and toll. "Now, my friend, I'll teach you to shudder," he thought. He stole forth secretly in front, and when the youth was at the top of the tower, and had turned round to grasp the bell-rope, he saw, standing opposite him, a white figure. "Who is there?" he called out, but the figure gave no answer, and neither stirred nor moved. "Answer," cried the youth, "or begone; you have no business here at this hour of the night." However, the sexton remained motionless, so that the youth might think it he saw a ghost. The youth called out the second time: "What do you want here? Speak if you are an honest fellow, or I'll knock you down the stairs."

The sexton thought: "He can't mean that in earnest," and stood as though he were made of stone. Then the youth shouted out to him the third time, and as that too had no effect he made a dash at the spectre and knocked it down the stairs, so that it fell about ten steps and remained lying in a corner. The youth tolled the bell, then went home to bed without saying a word, and fell asleep.

The sexton's wife waited a long time for her husband. At last she became anxious, and woke the youth and asked: "Don't you know where my husband is? He went up to the tower in front of you."

"No," answered the youth; "but someone stood at the top of the stairs up there, and because he wouldn't answer me, or go away, I took him for a rogue and knocked him down."

The wife ran and found her husband, who was lying groaning in a corner, with his leg broken. She carried him down, and then hurried to the house of the youth's father. "Your son," she cried; "threw my husband downstairs so that he broke his leg. Take the good-for-nothing wretch out of our house."

The father was horrified, hurried to the youth, and gave him a scolding.

"Father," he replied, "Only listen to me; I am quite guiltless. He stood there in the night, like one who meant harm. I didn't know who it was, and warned him three times to speak or to begone."

"Oh!" groaned the father, "you'll bring me nothing but misfortune; get out of my sight, I won't have anything more to do with you."

"Yes, dear Father, willingly; I'll set out and learn how to shudder, and in that way I shall be master of an art which will gain me a living."

"Learn what you will," said the father, "it is all the same to me. Here are fifty dollars for you, set forth into the wide world with them."

When day broke the youth set out on the hard high road, and kept muttering to himself: "If I could only shudder! if I could only shudder!"

In the evening he reached an inn. Then, just as he was entering the room, he said again, quite loudly: "Oh! if I could only shudder! if I could only shudder!" The land-lord laughed and told him that in the neigh-bourhood stood a haunted castle, where one could easily learn to shudder if one only kept watch in it for three nights. The King had promised the man who dared to do this thing his daughter as wife, and she was the most beautiful maiden under the sun. There was also much treasure hidden in the castle, guarded by evil spirits, which would then be free. Many had already gone in, but so far none had ever come out again.

So the youth went to the King and spoke: "If I were allowed, I should much like to watch for three nights in the castle." The King looked at him, and because he pleased him he said: "You can ask for three things, none of them living, and those you may take with you into the castle."

Then the youth answered: "Well, I shall beg for a fire, a turning lathe, and a carving bench with the knife attached."

On the following day the King had everything put into the castle; and when night drew on the youth lit a bright fire in one of the rooms, placed the carving bench with the knife close to it, and sat himself down on the turning lathe. "Oh! if I could only shudder!" he said; "but I shan't learn it here either." Towards midnight he heard a shriek from a corner: "Ou, miou! miou! how cold we are!"

"You fools!" the youth cried; "Why do you scream? If you are cold, come here and sit beside the fire and warm yourselves." As he spoke two enormous black cats sprang fiercely forwards and sat down, one on each side of him, and gazed wildly at him with their fiery eyes. After some time, when they had warmed themselves, they said:

"My friend, shall we play a little game of cards?"

"Why not?" he replied; "but first let me take a look at your paws." Then they stretched out their claws. "Ha!" said he; "what long nails you've got! Wait a minute: I must first cut them off." He seized them by the scruff of their necks, lifted them on to the carving bench, and screwed down their paws firmly. "After watching you very closely," said the youth, "I no longer feel any desire to play cards with you;" and with these words he struck them dead and threw them out into the water.

Out of every nook and corner came forth black cats and black dogs in such swarms that he couldn't possibly get away from them. They yelled in the most ghastly manner, jumped upon his fire, scattered it all, and tried to put it out. He looked on quietly for a time, but when it got beyond a joke he seized his carving knife and called out: "Be off, you rabble rout!" and let fly at them. Some of them fled away, and the others he struck dead and threw them out into the pond below.

He blew up the sparks of the fire once more, and warmed himself. And as he sat in this way his eyes refused to keep open any longer. Then he looked around him and beheld in the corner a large bed. "The very thing I need," he said, and laid himself down in it. But the bed began to move all by itself, and ran all round the castle. "Capital," he said, "only a little quicker." Then the bed sped on as if drawn by six horses, up this way and down that. All of a sudden—crish, crash! with a bound it turned over, upside down, and lay like a mountain on top of him. But he tossed the blankets and pillows in the air, emerged from underneath, lay down at his fire, and slept till daylight.

In the morning the King arrived, and when he beheld him lying on the ground he imagined the ghosts had been too much for him. Then he said: "What a pity! and such a fine fellow as he was."

The youth heard this, got up, and said: "It's not come to that yet." Then the King was astonished, but very glad, and asked how it had fared with him. "First-rate," he answered; "and now I've survived the one night, I shall certainly get through the other two also."

The second night the youth went up again to the old castle, sat down at the fire, and began his old refrain: "If I could only shudder!" As midnight approached, a noise and din broke out, then all was quiet for a few minutes, and at length, with a loud scream, half of a man dropped down the chimney and fell in front of him. "Hi, up there!" shouted he; "there's another half wanted down here, that's not enough;" then there was a shrieking and a yelling, and then the other half fell down. "Wait a bit," he said; "I'll stir up the fire for you." When he had done this and again looked round, the two pieces had united, and a horrible-looking man was sitting on his seat. "Come now," said the youth, "the seat is mine." The man tried to shove him away, but the youth wouldn't allow it for a moment, and, pushing him off by force, sat down in his place again.

Then more men dropped down, one after the other, who fetched nine skeleton legs and two skulls, put them up and proceeded to play ninepins with them. The youth thought he would like to play too, and said: "Look here; do you mind if I join the game?"

"No, not if you have money."

"I've money enough," he replied, "but your balls aren't very round." Then he took the skulls, placed them on his lathe, and turned them till they were round. "Now they will roll along better," said he, "and houp-la! now the fun begins." He played with them and lost some of his money, but when the hour of twelve struck everything vanished before his eyes. He lay down and slept peacefully.

The next morning the King arrived, anxious for news. "How have you got on this time?" he asked, to which the youth replied, "I played ninepins, and lost a few pence."

"Didn't you shudder then?"

"No such luck," he said; "I made myself merry. If I only knew how to shudder!"

On the third night he sat down again on his bench, and said, in the most desponding way: "If I could only shudder!" When it got late, six big men came in carrying a coffin. Then he cried: "Ha! ha! that's most likely my little cousin who only died a few days ago;" and beckoning with his finger he called out: "Come, my small cousin, come." They placed the coffin on the ground, and he approached it and took off the cover. In it lay a dead man. He felt his face, and it was as cold as ice. "Wait," he said, "I'll heat you up a bit," went to the fire, warmed his hand, and laid it on the man's face, but the dead man remained cold. Then he lifted him out, sat down at the fire, laid him on his knee, and rubbed his arms that the blood should circulate again. When that too had no effect it occurred to the youth that if two people lay together in bed they warmed each other; so he put his cousin into the bed, covered him up, and lay down beside him; after a time the corpse became warm and began to move. Then the youth said: "Now, my little cousin, what would have happened if I hadn't warmed you?"

However, the dead man rose up and cried out: "Now I will strangle you."

"What!" said he, "is that all the thanks I get? You shall be put straight back into your coffin," lifted him up, threw him in, and closed the lid. Then the six men came and carried him out again. "I simply can't shudder," he said, "and it is clear I shan't learn it in a lifetime here."

The next morning the King came and said: "You have freed the castle from its

curse, and you shall marry my daughter."

"That's all charming," he said; "but I still don't know what it is to shudder."

Then the wedding was celebrated, but the young King, though he loved his wife dearly, and though he was very happy, still kept on saying: "If I could only shudder! if I could only shudder!"

At last he reduced her to despair. Then her maid said: "I'll help you; we'll soon make him shudder." So she went out to the stream that flowed through the garden, and had a pail full of little fish brought to her. At night, when the young King was asleep, his wife had to pull the clothes off him, and pour the pail over him, so that the little fish swam all about him. Then he awoke and cried out: "Oh! how I shudder, how I shudder, my dear Wife! Yes, now I know what shuddering is."

The Tinder Box

A soldier came marching along the high road—left, right! left, right! He had his knapsack on his back and a sword by his side, for he had been to the wars and was now returning home.

An old witch met him on the road. She was very ugly to look at. "Good evening, Soldier!" she said. "What a fine sword and knapsack you have! You are a very fine soldier! You ought to have as much money as you would like to carry!"

"Thank you, old Witch," answered the Soldier.

"Do you see that great tree there?" said the Witch, pointing to a tree beside them. "It is hollow inside. You must climb up to the top, then you will see a hole through which you can let yourself down into the tree. I will tie a thick rope round your waist, so that I may be able to pull you up again when you call."

"What shall I do down there?" asked the Soldier.

"Get money!" answered the Witch. "Listen! When you reach the bottom of the tree you will find yourself in a large hall; it is light there, for there are more than three hundred lamps burning. Then you will see three doors, which you can open—the keys are in the locks. If you go into the first room, you will see a great chest in the middle of the floor with a dog sitting upon it; he has eyes as large as saucers, but you need not trouble about him. I will give you my blue-check apron, which you must spread out on the floor, and then go back quickly and fetch the dog and set him upon it; open the chest and take as much money as you like. It is copper there. If you would rather have silver, you must go into the next room, where there is a dog with eyes as large as mill-wheels. But don't take any notice of him; just

224

set him upon my apron, and help yourself to the money. If you prefer gold, you can get that too, if you go into the third room, and as much as you like to carry. But the dog that guards the chest there has eyes as large as the Round Tower at Copenhagen! He is a savage dog, I can tell you; but you need not be afraid of him either. Only, put him on my apron and he won't touch you, and you can take out of the chest as much gold as you like!"

"This is not bad!" said the Soldier. "But what am I to give you in return, old Witch; for surely you are not going to do this for nothing?"

"Yes, I am!" replied the Witch. "Not a single farthing will I take! For me you shall bring nothing but an old tinder box which my grandmother forgot last time she was down there."

"Well, tie the rope round my waist!" said the Soldier.

"Here it is," said the Witch, "and here is my blue-check apron."

Then the Soldier climbed up the tree, let himself down through the hole, and found himself standing, as the Witch had said, underground in the large hall, where the more than three hundred lamps were burning.

Well, he opened the first door. Ugh! there sat the dog with eyes as big as saucers glaring at him. "You are a fine fellow!" said the Soldier, and put him on the Witch's apron, took as much copper as his pockets could hold; then he shut the chest, put the dog on it again, and went into the second room.

Sure enough there sat the dog with eyes as large as mill-wheels.

"You had better not stare at me so hard!" said the Soldier, "or your eyes will come out of their sockets!" And then he set the dog on the apron. When he saw all the silver in the chest, he threw away the copper he had taken, and filled his pockets and knapsack with nothing but silver.

Then the Soldier went into the third room. Horrors! the dog there had two eyes, each as large as the Round Tower at Copenhagen, spinning round in his head like wheels.

"Good evening!" said the Soldier and saluted, for he had never seen a dog like this before. But when he had examined him more closely, he thought to himself: "Now then, I've had enough of this!" and put him down on the floor, and opened the chest.

Heavens! what a heap of gold there was! With all that he could buy up the whole town, and all the sweet things, all the tin soldiers, whips and rocking-horses in the whole world. Now he threw away all the silver with which he had filled his pockets and knapsack, and filled them with gold instead—yes, all his pockets, his knapsack, cap and boots even, so that he could hardly walk. Now he was rich indeed. He put the dog back upon the chest, shut the door, and then called up through the tree: "Now pull me up again, old Witch!"

"Have you got the tinder box also?" asked the Witch.

"Botheration!" said the Soldier, "I had clean forgotten it!" And then he went back and fetched it.

The Witch pulled him up, and there he stood again on the high road, with his pockets, knapsack, cap and boots filled with gold.

"What do you want to do with the tinder box?" asked the Soldier.

"That doesn't matter to you," replied the Witch. "You have got your money, give me my tinder box."

"We'll see!" said the Soldier. "Tell me at once what you want to do with it, or I will draw my sword and cut off your head!"

"No!" screamed the Witch.

The Soldier immediately cut off her head. That was the end of the old Witch! But he tied up all his gold in her apron, slung it like a bundle over his shoulder, put the tinder box in his pocket, and set out towards the town.

It was a splendid town! He walked into the finest inn, ordered the best room and his favourite dinner; for now that he had so much money he was really rich.

It certainly occurred to the servant who had to clean his boots that they were astonishingly old boots for such a rich lord. But that was because he had not yet bought new ones; next day he appeared in respectable boots and fine clothes. Now, instead of a common soldier he had become a noble lord, and the people told him about all the grand doings of the town and the King, and what a beautiful princess his daughter was.

"How can one get to see her?" asked the Soldier.

"She is never to be seen at all!" they told him; "she lives in a great big copper castle, surrounded by many walls and towers! No-one except the King may go in or out, for it is prophesied that she will marry a common soldier, and the King simply cannot submit to that."

"I should very much like to see her," thought the Soldier; but he could not get permission.

Now he lived very pleasantly, went to the theatre, drove in the King's garden, and gave the poor a great deal of money, which was very nice of him; he had experienced in former times how hard it is not to have a farthing in the world. Now he was rich, wore fine clothes, and made many friends, who all said that he was an excellent man, a real nobleman. And the Soldier liked that. But as he was always spending money and never made any more, at last the day came when he had nothing left but two shillings, and he had to leave the beautiful rooms in which he had been living, and go into a little attic under the roof, and clean his own boots, and mend them with a darning needle. None of his friends came to visit him there, for there were too many stairs to climb.

It was a dark evening, and he could not even buy a light. But all at once it flashed across him that there was a little end of tinder in the tinder box, which he had

taken from the hollow tree into which the Witch had helped him down. He found the box with the tinder in it; but just as he was kindling a light, and had struck a spark out of the tinder box, the door burst open, and the dog with eyes as large as saucers, which he had seen down in the tree, stood before him and said: "What does my lord command?"

"Whatever is the meaning of this?" exclaimed the Soldier. "This is a wonderful kind of tinder box, if I can get whatever I want like this. Get me money!" he cried to the dog, and hey, presto! he was off and back again, holding a great purse full of money in his mouth.

Now the Soldier knew what an excellent tinder box this was. If he rubbed once, the dog that sat on the chest of copper appeared; if he rubbed twice, there came the dog that watched over the silver chest; and if he rubbed three times, the one that guarded the gold appeared. Now, the Soldier went down again to his beautiful rooms,

and appeared once more in splendid clothes. His friends immediately recognised him again, as though he were the person they liked best in the world.

One day he thought to himself: "It is very strange that no-one can get to see the Princess. They all say she is very pretty, but what's the use of that if she has to sit for ever in the great copper castle with all the towers? Can I not manage to see her somehow? Where is my tinder box?" and so he struck a spark, and, presto! there came the dog with eyes as large as saucers.

"It is the middle of the night, I know," said the Soldier; "but I should very much like to see the Princess for a moment."

The dog was already outside the door, and before the Soldier could look around, in he came with the Princess. She was lying asleep on the dog's back and was so beautiful that anyone could see she was a real princess. The Soldier could not refrain from kissing her, for he was such a thorough soldier. Then the dog ran back with the

Princess. But when it was morning, and the King and Queen were drinking tea, the Princess said that the night before she had had such a strange dream about a dog and a soldier: she had ridden on the dog's back, and the soldier had kissed her.

"That is certainly a fine story," replied the Queen. But the next night one of the ladies-in-waiting was told to watch at the Princess' bed, to see if it was only a dream, or if it had actually happened.

The Soldier once again had an overpowering longing to see the Princess again, and so the dog came in the middle of the night and fetched her, running as fast as he could. But the lady-in-waiting put on her slippers and followed them. When she saw them disappear into a large house, she thought to herself: "Now I know where it is;" and made a large cross on the door with a piece of chalk. Then she went home and lay down, and the dog came back also, with the Princess. But when he saw that a cross had been made on the door of the house where the Soldier lived, he took a piece of chalk also, and made crosses on all the doors in the town; and that was very clever, for now the lady-in-waiting could not find the right house, as there were crosses on all the doors.

Early next morning the King, Queen, ladies-in-waiting, and officers came out to see where the Princess had been. "There it is!" exclaimed the King, when he saw the first door with a cross on it.

"No, there it is, my dear!" exclaimed the Queen, when she also saw a door with a cross on it.

"But here is one, and there is another!" they all exclaimed; wherever they looked there was a cross on the door. Then they realised that the sign would not help them at all.

However, the Queen was an extremely clever woman, who could do a great deal more than just drive in a coach. She took her great golden scissors, cut up a piece of silk, and made a pretty little bag of it. This she filled with the finest buckwheat grains, and tied it round the Princess' neck; she cut a little hole in the bag, so that the grains would strew the whole road wherever the Princess went.

In the night the dog came again, took the Princess on his back and ran away with her to the Soldier, who was very much in love with her, and would have liked to have been a prince so that he might have had her for his wife.

The dog did not notice how the grains were strewn right from the castle to the Soldier's window, where he ran up the wall with the Princess.

In the morning the King and the Queen saw plainly where their daughter had been, and they took the Soldier and put him into prison. There he sat. How dark and dull it was there! And they told him: "Tomorrow you are to be hanged." Hearing that did not exactly cheer him, and he had left his tinder box in the inn.

Next morning he could see through the iron grating in front of his little window how all the people were hurrying out of the town to watch him hanged. He heard the drums and saw the soldiers marching; all the people were running to and fro. Just below his window was a shoemaker's apprentice, complete with leather apron and shoes; he was skipping along so merrily that one of his shoes flew off and fell against the wall, just where the Soldier was sitting peeping through the iron grating.

"Oh, shoemaker's boy, you needn't be in such a hurry!" said the Soldier to him. "There's nothing going on till I arrive. But if you will run back to the house where I lived and fetch me my tinder box, I will give you four shillings. But you must put your best foot foremost."

The shoemaker's boy was very willing to earn four shillings, and fetched the tinder box, gave it to the Soldier, and—yes—now you shall hear.

Outside the town a great scaffold had been erected, and all round were standing the soldiers, and hundreds of thousands of people. The King and Queen were sitting on a magnificent throne opposite the judges and the whole council.

The Soldier was already standing on the top of the ladder; but when they wanted to put the rope round his neck, he said that the fulfilment of one innocent request was always granted to a poor criminal before he underwent his punishment. He told them he would so much like to smoke a small pipe of tobacco; it would be his last pipe in this world.

The King could not refuse him this, and so he took out his tinder box, and rubbed it once, twice, three times. And lo, and behold! there stood all three dogs—the one with eyes as large as saucers, the second with eyes as large as mill-wheels, and the third with eyes each as large as the Round Tower at Copenhagen.

"Help me now, so that I may not be hanged!" cried the Soldier. And thereupon all three dogs fell upon the judges and the whole council, seized some by the legs, others by the nose, and threw them so high into the air that they fell to the ground and were smashed into pieces.

"I won't stand this!" said the King; but the largest dog seized him too, and the Queen as well, and threw them up after the others. This frightened the soldiers, and all the people cried: "Good Soldier, you shall be our King, and marry the Princess!"

Then they put the Soldier into the King's coach, and the three dogs danced in front, crying "Hurrah!" and all the boys whistled and the soldiers presented arms.

The Princess came out of the copper castle, and became Queen; and that pleased her very much.

The wedding festivities lasted for eight days, and the dogs sat at table and made eyes at everyone.

Andersen, *The Yellow Fairy Book*

229

The Story of the Fisherman and his Wife

There was once a fisherman and his wife who lived together in a little hut close to the sea, and the Fisherman used to go down every day to fish. Now, once the line was pulled deep under the water, and when he hauled it up he hauled a large flounder with it. The Flounder said to him, "Listen, Fisherman. I implore you to let me go; I am not a real flounder, I am an enchanted prince. What good will it do you if you kill me—I shall not taste nice. Put me back into the water and let me swim away."

"Well," replied the man, "you need not make so much noise about it; I am sure I had much better let a flounder that can talk swim away." He put him back again into the shining water, and the Flounder sank to the bottom.

Then the Fisherman got up, and went home to his wife in the hut.

"Husband," said his wife, "have you caught nothing today?"

"No," answered the man. "I caught a flounder who said he was an enchanted prince, so I let him swim away again."

"Did you wish nothing from him?" said his wife.

"No," said the man; "what should I have wished from him?"

"Ah!" said the woman, "it's dreadful to have to live all one's life in this hut that is so small and dirty; you ought to have wished for a cottage. Go now and call him; tell him that we choose to have a cottage, and he will certainly give it to you."

"Alas!" said the man, "why should I go down there again?"

"Why," said his wife, "you caught him, and then let him go again, so he is sure to give you what you ask. Go down quickly."

The man did not like going at all, but he went down to the sea. When he came there the sea was quite green and yellow, and was no longer shining. So he stood on the shore and said:

"Once a prince, but changed
you be
Into a flounder in the sea.
Come! for my wife, Ilsebel,
Wishes what I dare not tell."

Then the Flounder came swimming up and said, "Well, what does she want?"

"Alas!" said the man, "my wife tells me I ought to have kept you and wished something from you. She does not want to live any longer in the hut; she would like a cottage."

"Go home, then," said the Flounder; "she has it."

So the man went home, and there was his wife no longer in the hut, but in its place was a beautiful cottage, and his wife was sitting in front of the door on a bench. Inside the cottage was a tiny hall, and a beautiful sitting room, and a bedroom, a kitchen and a dining room all furnished with the best of everything. And outside was a little yard in which were chickens and ducks, and also a little garden with vegetables and fruit trees.

"See," said his wife, "isn't this nice?"

"Yes," answered her husband; "here we shall remain and live very happily."

"We will think about that," said his wife.

All went well for a week or a fortnight, then his wife said: "Listen, Husband; the cottage is much too small, and so is the yard and the garden; the Flounder might just as well have sent us a larger house. Go down to the Flounder, and tell him to send us a castle."

"Ah, Wife!" said the Fisherman, "the cottage is good enough; why do we choose to live in a castle?"

"Why?" said his wife, "You go down; the Flounder can quite well do that."

The Fisherman's heart was heavy, and he did not like going. He said to himself, "It is not right." Still, he went down.

When he came to the sea, the water was all violet and dark blue, and dull and thick, and no longer green and yellow, but it was still smooth. So he stood there and said:

"Once a prince, but changed
you be
Into a flounder in the sea.
Come! for my wife, Ilsebel,
Wishes what I dare not tell."

"What does she want now?" asked the Flounder.

"Ah!" answered the Fisherman, half ashamed, "she wants to live in a great stone castle."

"Go home; she is standing before the door," said the Flounder.

The Fisherman went home and there stood a great stone palace, and his wife was standing on the steps waiting for him. And outside the house was a large courtyard with horse and cow stables—and a splendid garden with the most beautiful flowers and fruit, and everything one could ever wish for.

"Now, Husband," said his wife, "isn't this beautiful?"

"Yes, indeed," replied the Fisherman. "Now we will stay here and live in this beautiful castle, and be very happy."

"We will consider the matter," said his wife, and they went to bed.

The next morning his wife woke up first at daybreak, and looked out of the bed at the beautiful country stretched before her. Her husband was still sleeping, so she dug her elbows into his side and said: "Get up, Husband, and look out of the window. Could we not become the king of all this land? Go down to the Flounder and tell him we choose to be king."

"Ah, Wife!" replied her husband, "why should we be king? *I* certainly don't want to be king."

"Well," said his wife, "if you don't want to be king, *I* will be king. Go down to the Flounder; I will be king."

So the Fisherman went. "It is not right! It is not right," he thought. He did not wish to go, yet he went.

When he came to the sea, the water was a dark grey colour, and it was heaving against the shore. So he stood and said:

"Once a prince, but changed
you be
Into a flounder in the sea.
Come! for my wife, Ilsebel,
Wishes what I dare not tell."

"What does she want now?" asked the Flounder.

"Alas!" said the Fisherman, "she wants to be king."

"Go home; she is that already," said the Flounder.

The Fisherman went home, and when he came near the palace he saw that it had become much larger. And when he went into the palace, he found everything was of pure marble and gold, and the curtains were made of damask with tassels of gold. Then the doors of the hall flew open, and there stood the whole Court round his wife, who was sitting on a high throne of gold and diamonds.

So he said: "Let that be enough, Wife, now that you are king! Now we have nothing more to wish for."

"Nay, Husband," said his wife restlessly, "my wishing powers are boundless. Go down to the Flounder; king I am, now I must be emperor."

"Ah, Wife," he said, "he cannot make you emperor; I don't like to ask him that. There is only one emperor in the kingdom."

"If he can make king," said his wife, "he can make emperor, and emperor I must and will be. Go!"

So he had to go. But as he went, he felt quite frightened, and he thought to himself, "This can't be right; to be emperor is too ambitious; the Flounder will be tired out at last."

The sea was quite black and thick, and it was breaking high on the beach. The Fisherman was chilled with fear. He stood and said:

"Once a prince, but changed
you be
Into a flounder in the sea.
Come! for my wife, Ilsebel,
Wishes what I dare not tell."

"What does she want now?" asked the Flounder.

"Alas! Flounder," he said, "my wife wants to be emperor."

"Go home," said the Flounder; "she is that already."

So the Fisherman went home, and when he came there he saw the whole castle was made of polished marble. Before the gate soldiers were marching, blowing trumpets and beating drums. And when he entered, he saw his wife upon a throne which was made out of a single block of gold. She had on a very tall golden crown which was set with brilliants and sparkling gems. The Fisherman went up to her quietly and said: "Wife, are you emperor now?"

"Yes," she said, "I am emperor."

He stood looking at her magnificence, and when he had watched her for some time, said: "Ah, Wife, let that be enough, now that you are emperor."

"Ah, Husband," she said, "why are you standing there? I am emperor now, and I want to be pope too, so go down to the Flounder."

"Alas! Wife," said the Fisherman, "You cannot be pope; there is only one pope in Christendom, and the Flounder cannot make you that."

"Husband," she said, "I *will* be pope. Go down quickly; I must be pope today."

So he was frightened and went out; but he felt quite faint, and trembled and shook, and his knees and legs began to give way under him. The wind was blowing fiercely across the land, and the clouds flying across the sky looked as gloomy as if it were night;

the water was foaming and seething and dashing upon the shore. Still the sky was very blue in the middle, although at the sides it was an angry red as in a great storm. So he stood shuddering in anxiety, and said:

"Once a prince, but changed
    you be

Into a flounder in the sea.
Come! for my wife, Ilsebel,
Wishes what I dare not tell."

"Well, what does she want now?" asked the Flounder.

"Alas!" said the Fisherman, "she wants to be pope."

"Go home, then; she is that already," said the Flounder.

Then he went home, and when he came there he saw a large church surrounded by palaces. He pushed his way through the people. The interior was lit up with thousands and thousands of candles, and his wife was sitting on a much higher throne, and she wore three great golden crowns. All the emperors and kings were on their knees before her, and were kissing her foot. "Wife," said the Fisherman, looking at her, "are you pope now?"

"Yes," she said; "I am pope." So he stood staring at her, and it was as if he were looking at the bright sun. He said: "Ah, Wife, let it be enough now that you are pope."

But she sat as straight as a tree, and did not move or bend the least bit.

The woman was not content; that night her greed would not allow her to sleep, and she kept on thinking and thinking what she could still become. The Fisherman slept well and soundly, for he had done a great deal that day, but his wife could not sleep at all, and turned from one side to another the whole night long, and thought and thought, till she could think no longer, what more she could become. Then the sun began to rise, and she thought, "Ha! could I not make the sun and moon rise?"

"Husband," she said, poking him in the ribs with her elbows, "wake up. Go down to the Flounder; I will be a god."

The Fisherman was still half asleep, yet he was so frightened that he fell out of bed. He thought he had not heard right, and opened his eyes wide and said: "What did you say, Wife?"

"Go down at once; I will be a god."

"Alas! Wife," pleaded the Fisherman, falling down on his knees before her, "the Flounder cannot do that. Emperor and pope he can make you. I implore you, be content and remain pope."

Then she flew into a rage, her hair hung wildly about her face, she pushed him with her foot and screamed: "I am not contented, and I shall not be contented! Will you go?"

So he hurried on his clothes as fast as possible, and ran away as if he were mad. But the storm was raging so fiercely that he could scarcely stand. The sky was as black as ink, it was thundering and lightening, and the sea was tossing in great waves as high as church towers and mountains, and each had a white crest of foam. So he shouted, not able to hear his own voice:

"Once a prince, but changed
you be
Into a flounder in the sea.
Come! for my wife, Ilsebel,
Wishes what I dare not tell."

"Well, what does she want now?" asked the Flounder.

"Alas!" he said, "she wants to be a god."

"Go home, then; she is sitting again in the hut." And there they are sitting to this day.

Grimm, *The Green Fairy Book*

Beauty and the Beast

Once upon a time, there lived a rich merchant with six daughters. One day a most unexpected misfortune befell them. Their house caught fire and was burnt to the ground, and this was only the beginning of their troubles. Their father suddenly lost every ship he had upon the sea, his clerks in distant countries, whom he trusted entirely, proved unfaithful; and at last from great wealth he fell into the direst poverty.

All that he had left was a little house in a desolate place in the midst of a dark forest. The girls regretted unceasingly the luxuries and amusements of their former life; only the youngest tried to be brave and cheerful. Because she was not as doleful as her sisters, they declared that this miserable life was all she was fit for. But she was really far prettier and cleverer than they were; indeed, she was so lovely that she was always called Beauty.

After two years, their father received the news that one of his ships had come safely into port with a rich cargo. All the daughters at once thought that their poverty was at an end, and wanted to set out immediately for the town; but their father determined to go himself to make inquiries. Only the youngest daughter had any doubt but that they would soon again be as rich as before. So they all loaded their father with commissions for jewels and dresses which it would have taken a fortune to purchase; only Beauty did not ask for anything. Her father said: "And what shall I bring for you, Beauty?"

"The only thing I wish for is to see you return home safely," she answered. Her father was pleased, but he insisted that she choose something.

"Well, dear Father," she said, "as you insist upon it, bring me a rose."

So the merchant set out only to find that his former companions, believing him to be dead, had divided between them the goods which the ship had brought; and after six months of trouble and expense he found himself just as poor as when he started. To

make matters worse, he was obliged to leave the town in the most terrible weather. Night overtook him, and the deep snow and bitter frost made it impossible for his horse to carry him any further. Snow had covered up every path, and he did not know which way to turn.

At length he made out some sort of track, and though at the beginning it was rough and slippery it presently became easier and led him into an avenue of trees which ended in a splendid castle. It seemed to the merchant very strange that no snow had fallen in the avenue. When he reached the castle he saw before him a flight of agate steps and went up them, and passed through several magnificently furnished rooms. The pleasant warmth of the air revived him, and he felt very hungry; but there seemed to be nobody in all this vast and splendid palace whom he could ask to give him something to eat. At last, tired of roaming through empty rooms, he stopped in a room where a fire was burning and a couch was drawn up cosily close to it. Thinking that this must be prepared for someone who was expected, he sat down to wait till he should come, and very soon fell into a sweet sleep.

When his extreme hunger woke him after several hours he was still alone; but a little table, upon which was a good dinner, had been drawn up close to him and, as he had eaten nothing for twenty-four hours, he lost no time at all in beginning his meal, hoping that he might soon have the opportunity of thanking his considerate entertainer. But no-one appeared, and he resolved to search once more through all the rooms; but it was of no use, there was no sign of life in the palace! Then he went down into the garden, and though it was winter everywhere else, here the sun shone, and the birds sang, and all the spring and summer flowers bloomed.

In spite of being so cold and weary when he reached the castle, he had taken his horse to the stable and fed it. Now he thought he would saddle it for his homeward journey, and he turned down the path which led to the stable. This path had a hedge of roses on each side of it. They reminded him of his promise to Beauty, and he stopped and had just gathered one to take to her when he was startled by a strange noise behind him. Turning round he saw a frightful Beast, which seemed to be very angry and said, in a terrible voice: "Who told you that you might gather my roses? Was it not enough that I allowed you to be in my palace and was kind to you? This is the way you show your gratitude, by stealing my flowers! But your insolence shall not go unpunished."

"Alas!" thought the merchant, "if my daughter Beauty could only know what danger her rose has brought me into!" And in despair he began to tell the Beast all his misfortunes, and the reason for his journey, not forgetting to mention Beauty's request.

"A king's ransom would hardly have procured all that my other daughters asked for," he said; "but I thought that I might at least take Beauty her rose. I beg you to forgive me, for I meant no harm."

The Beast considered for a moment, and then he said, in a less furious tone: "I will forgive you on one condition—that you will give me one of your daughters."

"Ah!" exclaimed the merchant, "if I were cruel enough to buy my own life at the expense of one of my children's, what excuse could I invent to bring her here?"

"No excuse would be necessary," the Beast answered. "If she comes at all she must come willingly. On no other condition will I have her. I give you a month to see if one of your daughters will come back with you and stay here, to let you go free. If none of them is willing, you must come alone, for then you will belong to me. And do not imagine that you can hide from me, for if you fail to keep your word I will come and fetch you!"

The merchant accepted this proposal, though he did not really think any of his daughters would be persuaded to come.

He mounted his horse, which carried him off so swiftly that in an instant he had lost sight of the palace, and he was still wrapped in gloomy thoughts when it stopped before the door of the cottage.

His daughters rushed to meet him, eager to know the result of his journey. But he hid the truth from them at first, only saying sadly to Beauty as he handed her the rose: "Here is what you asked me to bring you; you little know what it has cost."

However, this excited their curiosity so greatly that presently he told them his adventures from beginning to end, and then they were all very unhappy. The girls were very angry with Beauty and said it was all her fault, and that if she had asked for something sensible this would never have happened.

Poor Beauty said to her sisters: "I have indeed caused this misfortune, but I assure you I did it innocently. Who could have guessed that to ask for a rose would cause so much misery? But as I did the mischief, I will go back with my father to keep his promise."

When the fatal day came she encouraged and cheered her father as they rode back. Her father tried to persuade her to go back, but in vain. Night fell, and then splendid fireworks blazed out before them; all the forest was illuminated by them, and

the air even felt pleasantly warm, though it had been bitterly cold before. When Beauty and her father got nearer to the palace they saw that it was illuminated from the roof to the ground, and music sounded softly from the courtyard.

"The Beast must be very hungry," said Beauty, trying to laugh, "if he makes all this rejoicing over the arrival of his prey." But, in spite of her anxiety, she could not help admiring all the wonderful things she saw.

When the Beast really appeared, though she trembled at the sight of him, she made a great effort to hide her horror, and saluted him respectfully.

"Have you come willingly?" asked the Beast. "Will you be content to stay here when your father goes away?"

Beauty answered bravely that she was quite prepared to stay.

"I am pleased with you," said the Beast.

The merchant was forced to bid Beauty a hasty farewell; and as soon as he had mounted his horse he went off at such a pace that she lost sight of him in an instant. Then Beauty began to cry, and wandered sadly into the castle. But she soon found that she was very sleepy, and she lay down and instantly fell asleep. And then she dreamed that she was walking by a stream bordered with trees, and lamenting her sad fate, when a young prince, handsomer than anyone she had ever seen, and with a voice that went straight to her heart, came and said to her, "Ah, Beauty! you are not so unfortunate as you suppose. Here you will be rewarded for all you have suffered elsewhere. Your every wish shall be gratified. Only try to find me out, no matter how I may be disguised, as I love you dearly, and in making me happy you will find your own happiness."

"What can I do, Prince, to make you happy?" asked Beauty.

"Only be grateful," he answered, "and do not trust too much to your eyes. And, above all, do not desert me until you have saved me from my cruel misery."

Beauty found her dreams so interesting that she was in no hurry to wake up, but presently the clock roused her by calling her name softly twelve times, and then she got up and found her dressing-table set out with everything she could possibly want; and dinner was waiting in the room next to hers. She began to think about the charming Prince she had seen in her dream.

"He said I could make him happy," said Beauty to herself. "It seems then that this horrible Beast keeps him a prisoner. How can I set him free? But it was only a dream, so why should I trouble myself about it? I had better go and find something to do to amuse myself."

So she got up and began to explore the palace. The first room she entered was lined with mirrors, and Beauty saw herself reflected on every side, and thought she had never seen such a charming room. She went further on into a gallery of pictures, where she soon found a portrait of the handsome Prince. It was so cleverly painted that he seemed to smile kindly at her. Tearing herself away from the portrait at last, she passed through into a room which contained every musical instrument under the sun, and here she amused herself for a long while in trying some of them. The next room was a library, and she saw everything she had ever wanted to read, and it seemed to her that a whole lifetime would not be enough even to read the names of all the books, there were so many. It was growing dusk, and wax candles in diamond and ruby candlesticks were beginning to light themselves in every room.

Beauty found her supper served just at the time she preferred to have it, but she did not see anyone or hear a sound and, though her father had warned her that she would be alone, she began to find it rather dull. Presently she heard the Beast coming, and wondered tremblingly if he meant to eat

her up now. However, as he did not seem at all ferocious, and only said gruffly: "Good evening, Beauty," she answered cheerfully and managed to conceal her terror. Then he asked if she thought she could be happy in his palace; and Beauty answered that everything was so beautiful that she would be very hard to please if she could not be happy here.

Then he got up to leave her, and said in his gruff voice: "Do you love me, Beauty? Will you marry me?"

"Oh! what shall I say?" cried Beauty, for she was afraid to make the Beast angry by refusing.

"Say 'yes' or 'no' without fear," he replied.

"No, Beast," said Beauty hastily.

"Since you will not marry me, good night, Beauty," he said.

She answered: "Good night, Beast," very glad to find that her refusal had not provoked him.

After he was gone she was very soon in her bed and asleep, and dreaming of her unknown Prince. She thought he came and said to her: "Ah, Beauty! why are you so unkind to me? I fear I am fated to be unhappy for many a long day still."

And then her dreams changed, but the charming Prince figured in them all. When morning came her first thought was to look at the portrait in the gallery of pictures and see if it was really like him, and she found that it certainly was.

Every evening after supper the Beast came to see her, and always asked her in his terrible gruff voice: "Beauty, will you marry me?" And it seemed to Beauty that when she said, "No, Beast," he went away quite sad. But her happy dreams of the handsome young Prince soon made her forget the poor Beast, and the only thing that at all disturbed her was to be constantly told to allow her heart guide her, and not her eyes.

So everything went on for a long time until at last Beauty began to long for the sight of her father and sisters; and one night, seeing her look very sad, the Beast asked her what was the matter. Now she knew that he was really gentle in spite of his ferocious looks and his dreadful voice. So she answered that she was longing to see her home once more. The Beast cried miserably.

"Beauty, have you the heart to desert an unhappy Beast like this? What more do you want to make you happy? Is it because you hate me that you want to escape?"

"No, my dear Beast," answered Beauty softly, "I do not hate you, and I should be very sorry never to see you any more, but I long to see my father again. Only let me go for two months, and I promise to come back to you and stay here for the rest of my life."

The Beast replied: "I cannot refuse you anything, even though it should cost me my life. But remember your promise and come back when the two months are over. If you do not return you will find your faithful Beast dead. You will not need any chariot to bring you back. When you have gone to bed turn this ring round upon your finger and say: "I wish to go back to my palace and see my Beast again." Good night, Beauty. Fear nothing, sleep peacefully, and before long you shall see your father once more."

Beauty went to bed, but could hardly sleep for joy. When at last she did begin to dream of her beloved Prince she was grieved to see him sad and weary, and not like himself.

"What is the matter?" she cried.

But he looked at her reproachfully and asked: "How can you ask me, cruel one? Are you not leaving me to my death by chance?"

"Don't be so sorrowful," cried Beauty; "I am only going to assure my father that I am safe and happy. I have promised the

Beast faithfully that I will come back, and he would die of grief if I did not keep my word!"

"What would that matter to you?" said the Prince. "Surely you would not care?"

"Indeed I should be most ungrateful if I did not care for such a kind Beast," cried Beauty indignantly. "I would die to save him from pain. It is not his fault that he is so ugly."

Just then a strange sound woke her—someone was speaking not very far away; and opening her eyes she found herself in a room which was certainly not nearly so splendid as those she was used to in the Beast's palace. Where could she be? Then she heard her father's voice, and rushed out and greeted him joyfully. Her sisters were all astonished at her appearance, as they had never expected to see her again. But when they heard that she had only come to be with them for a short time, and then must go back to the Beast's palace forever, they lamented loudly.

Over the following two months Beauty found that nothing amused her very much; and she often thought of the palace where she was so happy, especially as at home she never once dreamed of her dear Prince, and she felt quite sad without him. But she loved her father dearly, and he seemed so grieved at the thought of her departure that she had not the courage to say goodbye until she had a dismal dream which helped her to make up her mind. She thought she was wandering in a lonely path in the palace gardens, when she heard groans and found the Beast stretched out upon his side, apparently dying.

Beauty was so terrified by this dream that the next morning she announced her intention of going back at once, and that very night she said goodbye to her father and sisters, and as soon as she was in bed she turned her ring round upon her finger, and said: "I wish to go back to my palace and see my Beast again," as she had been told to do.

Then she fell asleep, and only woke up to hear the clock saying, "Beauty, Beauty" twelve times in its musical voice, which told her at once that she was really in the palace once more. Everything was just as before, but Beauty thought she had never known such a long day, for she was so anxious to see the Beast again that she felt as if supper time would never come.

But when it did come and no Beast appeared she was really frightened; so she ran down into the garden to search for him. Up and down the paths and avenues ran poor Beauty, calling him in vain, for no-one answered, and not a trace of him could she find; until at last she saw that she was standing opposite the shady path she had seen in her dream. She rushed down it, and there lay the Beast—asleep, or so Beauty thought. She ran up and stroked his head, but to her horror he did not move or open his eyes.

"He is dead; and it is all my fault," said Beauty, crying bitterly. But then she fancied he still breathed and, hastily fetching some water from the nearest fountain, she sprinkled it over his face, and to her great delight he began to revive.

"Beast, how you scared me!" she cried. "I never knew how much I loved you until just now, when I feared I was too late to save your life."

"Can you really love such an ugly creature?" asked the Beast faintly.

"Beauty, you only came just in time. I was dying because I thought you had forgotten your promise. But go back now, I shall see you again by and by."

Beauty, who had half expected that he would be angry with her, was reassured by his gentle voice, and went back to the palace, where supper was awaiting her; and afterwards the Beast came in as usual, and talked about the time she had spent with her father.

And when at last the time came for him to go, and he asked, as he had often asked before: "Beauty, will you marry me?" she answered softly, "Yes, my dear Beast."

As Beauty spoke a blaze of light sprang up before the windows of the palace; fireworks crackled and guns banged, and across the avenue of orange trees, in letters all made of fireflies, was written: 'Long live the Prince and his Bride'. Turning to ask the Beast what it could all mean, Beauty found that he had disappeared, and in his place stood her long-loved Prince! The marriage was celebrated the next day with the utmost splendour, and Beauty and the Prince lived happily ever after.

De Villeneuve, *The Blue Fairy Book*

241

The Three Little Pigs

There was once a Mother Pig with three Little Pigs, and she told them that they must each build a house to protect them from the Wolf. But she did not tell them how to do it.

The first Little Pig built his house out of straw, for there was plenty of straw in the fields in the autumn, and he would be snug all through the winter. He did not think about the Wolf at all.

The second Little Pig built his house out of twigs and branches, for there was plenty of wood lying about in the forest in the autumn, and he would be snug all winter. He hoped that the big branches would keep him safe from the Wolf.

The third Little Pig built his house out of bricks. It was hard and slow making the bricks and building them up, but he thought of the Wolf's teeth and the Wolf's claws and he knew he would be safe.

One day in winter the Wolf was hungry and went looking for a nice plump pig for dinner. He saw the first Little Pig's house all made of straw, and he knocked on the door, calling out: "Little Pig, Little Pig, let me in, let me in!"

The first Little Pig saw the Wolf's big claws through a gap in the straw, and he replied, "Not by the hairs on my chinny-chin-chin!"

"Then I'll huff and I'll puff and I'll blow your house down," growled the Wolf, and he huffed and he puffed and he blew down the house of straw. Then he ate up the first Little Pig, and off he went.

Next day the Wolf was feeling hungry again, and this time he saw the second Little Pig's house all made of twigs and branches. The Wolf knocked on the door, calling out: "Little Pig, Little Pig, let me in, let me in!"

The second Little Pig saw the Wolf's big teeth through a gap in the branches. and he replied, "Not by the hairs on my chinny-chin-chin!"

"Then I'll huff and I'll puff and I'll blow your house down," growled the Wolf, and he huffed and he puffed and he blew down the house of twigs and branches. Then he ate up the second Little Pig, and off he went.

Next day the Wolf was feeling hungry again, and this time he saw the third Little Pig's house all made of bricks. The Wolf knocked on the door, calling out: "Little Pig, Little Pig, let me in, let me in!"

The third Little Pig saw the Wolf's big eyes through the keyhole, and he replied, "Not by the hairs on my chinny-chin-chin!"

"Then I'll huff and I'll puff and I'll blow your house down," growled the Wolf, and he huffed and he puffed, and he huffled and he puffled, and he gasped and he rasped, and still he could not blow down the house of bricks. So then he thought that he would trick the pig into coming out. "Little Pig," he called out, "do you know where the turnips are just ready for eating?"

"No," said the third Little Pig, "tell me where that might be."

"It is Farmer Smith's field," said the Wolf, trying to make his voice sound friendly, "if you like I will take you there tomorrow. Be ready at six in the morning."

"Thank you," said the Little Pig, "I will be ready at six." But he was ready at five, and went to the turnip field and dug up the turnips, and was home again eating them for breakfast by the time the Wolf came by.

"How late you are," he called out to the Wolf, "you have lost your chance for a turnip feast by staying too long in bed!"

The Wolf was furious, but he wanted to trick the Little Pig out of his house, so he said, "I don't much care for turnips, myself, but do you know where the apples are just ripe for eating?"

"No," said the Little Pig, "tell me where that might be."

"It is Farmer Smith's orchard," said the Wolf, and although he tried hard to sound friendly his voice was growly, "if you like I will take you there tomorrow. Be ready at five in the morning."

"Thank you," said the Little Pig, "I will be ready at five." But he was ready at four, and off he went to the orchard and picked a big basket of apples, and was up the tree eating apples when the Wolf came by.

"How late you are," he called out to the Wolf, "you have lost your chance for a feast of apples by staying so long in bed!"

"Are they juicy apples?" the Wolf growled up to him, trying to sound friendly.

"Try one!" said the Little Pig, and threw an apple

so far away that the Wolf had to run to find it. And while the Wolf was searching in the grass for the apple, the Little Pig had time to jump down and get safely home to his house of bricks.

The Wolf was furiously angry and he wanted to eat the Little Pig more than ever. Next morning he went to the house of bricks and knocked at the door, and called out in his friendliest voice, "Little Pig, come to the fair with me this afternoon and I will give you a present."

The Little Pig agreed, but he did not wait for the afternoon. As soon as the Wolf was gone, away went the Little Pig to the fair to enjoy himself. He bought a big butter churn and by afternoon he was ready to go home again with it. But on the way he saw the Wolf coming up the hill towards him, with his big claws and his big teeth and his angry eyes and his growly voice. There was nowhere to hide except in the churn.

Down the hill rolled the churn, rolling over and over and dashing and crashing and bumping and thumping, and away the Wolf ran, for he was afraid of getting squashed.

The next day the Wolf knocked on the Little Pig's door again to trick him into coming out, but this time the Little Pig would not come out at all. The Wolf tried this trick and that, telling him of puddings and pies and good things in the kitchen, but the Little Pig said no to all of it.

At last the Wolf was so angry that he said, "I will climb up on your roof and come down your chimney and then I will eat you up!"

"Not by the hairs on my chinny-chin-chin!" said the Little Pig, and then he ran to the fireplace and lit a fire and on it he put a big pot full of water. The fire grew hot and the water started to boil, and just then the Wolf came tumbling down the chimney, into the pot, and the Little Pig boiled him up and ate him for supper.

Halliwell, retold by Alice Mills

244

The Gingerbread Man

There was once an old husband and his wife who lived in a little cottage, and most of the time they were happy and sometimes they were not. One day the wife thought that she would please her husband by cooking him some gingerbread, and she made two gingerbread men and cooked them in the oven.

When they were ready the husband picked up one of the gingerbread men to have a taste of it, and the other Gingerbread Man saw him take a big bite out of it. This is no place for me, thought the second Gingerbread Man, and he jumped off the table onto the floor and ran out of the door.

The old man and the old woman tried to catch the Gingerbread Man; but he was too quick for them and away he went before they could hobble after him. The Gingerbread Man called after them:

"You can run and run as fast as
you can,
But you won't catch me, I'm the
Gingerbread Man."

Away he went into the world, until he came to a tailor's shop, and in he went to see what he could see. There were three tailors sitting sewing in the shop, and as soon as they caught sight of the Gingerbread Man they dropped their needles and thread and tried to catch him to eat him.

But he was too quick for them, and away he went before they could get the stiffness out of their hands in order to catch him. The Gingerbread Man called after them:

"You can run and run as fast as
you can,
But you won't catch me, I'm the
Gingerbread Man."

Away he went into the world, until he came to a weaver's shop, and in he went to see what he could see. There was the weaver working at his loom, and his wife winding the wool, and as soon as they caught sight of the Gingerbread Man they dropped their wool and tried to catch him to eat him. But he was too quick for them, and he ran in between the loom and the wool until it was all tangled, and the weaver and his wife tripped over the tangle and away went the Gingerbread Man. He called after them:

*"You can run and run as
fast as you can,
But you won't catch me,
I'm the Gingerbread Man."*
Away he went into the world,
until he came to a farmhouse where
the farmer's children were churning butter
in a big churn. As soon as they caught sight
of the Gingerbread Man they wanted to
eat him with the butter they had made,
and they ran to and fro trying to catch him.
But he was too quick for them, and he ran
between their feet and knocked over the
churn, and away he went as they were picking it up. He called after them:
*"You can run and run as fast as
you can,
But you won't catch me, I'm the
Gingerbread Man."*
Away he went into the world, until he
came to a mill where the miller was grinding flour. As soon as he caught sight of the
Gingerbread Man, the miller wanted to
eat him. "Sit down with me, Gingerbread
Man," he said, "I like the thought of gingerbread and cheese." But the Gingerbread
Man was too quick for him, and he ran out
of the door while the miller was cutting up
his cheese. The Gingerbread Man called
after him:
*"You can run and run as fast as
you can,
But you won't catch me, I'm the
Gingerbread Man."*

Away he went once more, until he came
to a house where the mother was stirring a
pot of steaming hot soup. "Sit down with
us, Gingerbread Man," the mother said,
"Gingerbread will be welcome after we
have finished eating our soup." But the
Gingerbread Man was too quick for her,
and he knocked over the pot and out he ran
while she threw the big soup spoon after
him. The Gingerbread Man called after her:
*"You can run and run as fast as
you can,
But you won't catch me, I'm the
Gingerbread Man."*
Away he went into the world again,
until he came to a house where the man
and his wife were about to go to bed. The
man was just taking his trousers off when
they caught sight of the Gingerbread Man
and wanted to eat him. "Throw your
trousers over him," shouted the wife to her
husband, and so he did, but the Gingerbread
Man was too quick for them and ran away.
The wife tripped over the trousers, and the
husband ran after the Gingerbread Man with
his legs all naked in the cold night air, and
they ran and they ran until it was too dark to
see where they were going. The Gingerbread
Man called after them:
*"You can run and run as fast as
you can,
But you won't catch me, I'm the
Gingerbread Man."*
Then the husband went back home all
cold and hungry, but the Gingerbread Man
went on into the world until he was tired
out. In the end he came across a hole in
the ground, and into it he went. But it was
a fox's hole, and the Fox said to him,
"Whoever you are, you are welcome here!"
and ate him all up. So that was the end of
the Gingerbread Man.

Anon., retold by Alice Mills

246

The Goose-Girl

Once upon a time there was a little princess whose father was dead. Her mother, the Queen, was alive, and she loved her little daughter very dearly.

When the Princess grew up she was to be married to a young prince who lived in a far-off country. At last the day came when she was to leave her mother and her home and set off to the distant country in which her Prince lived.

Her mother gave her all kinds of rich and beautiful things—gold and silver cups and dishes, diamonds and pearls, and fine dresses of silk. Then she gave her daughter a maid to travel with her, and two horses to carry them. One of the horses was a fairy gift. His name was Falada, and he could speak almost as well as you can.

Just before the Princess set out on her journey, her mother gave her a thin leaf of gold with some strange writing on it. "Dear child," she said, "take care of this, and it will take care of you. Keep it carefully, and it will keep you from harm."

The Princess put the charm close to her heart. Then the Queen kissed her daughter again and again. At last, with many tears, they said farewell to each other. The Princess and her maid mounted their horses and set off.

The sun was hot and the road was dusty. As they trotted along the Princess felt very thirsty. She said to her maid, "Please get down and bring me some water from that brook in my golden cup."

Now the maid was a very saucy, sly girl. She knew that she was a long way from the Queen, and she began to be rude to the Princess. She said, "Get down yourself, if you are thirsty, and drink at the brook. I am not going to wait on you."

The Princess was so thirsty that she got off her horse. She knelt by the side of the brook, and bent her head to drink. She was very much hurt by her maid's rudeness, and wept. "I wonder what will become of me," she cried.

Then the charm close to her heart said:
"Alas! alas! did thy mother know,
Heavy indeed would her fond
heart grow."

The Princess was comforted. She rode on her way without saying a word to her saucy maid.

Again the Princess grew very hot and thirsty. Once more she said to her maid, "Please get down and bring me some water from that brook in my golden cup."

Again the maid was very rude. She said, "Get down yourself; I am not going to wait on you."

Once more the Princess got off her horse, and bent her head over the running stream. Her tears fell into the water, and she said, "What will become of me?" But the charm close to her heart said:

"Alas! alas! did thy mother know,
Heavy indeed would her fond
heart grow."

Then she bent her head to drink. As she did so the charm fell out and floated away on the water. The Princess did not see it, but the maid did. *She* laughed aloud with wicked glee, for she knew that the Princess was now in her power.

When the Princess had finished drinking, she tried to mount her horse again; but the maid pushed her aside, and said, "No, this horse is mine. Falada belongs to me. You will ride on the other horse or stay where you are."

The meek, gentle Princess was forced to agree. Then the maid made her mistress strip off her beautiful riding dress. This the maid put on, and then made the Princess dress herself in the clothes of a servant.

They rode on, and the maid pretended that she was the Princess. "If you tell anybody that I am *not* the Princess," she said, "I will kill you." The poor little Princess was afraid, and she had to promise that she would not tell. She wept, for she thought that she now had no friends.

She really had one friend, and that was the horse Falada. He saw and heard all that took place.

At last they reached the King's palace, and the false princess entered the courtyard amidst the loud sound of trumpets. The King himself ran forward to welcome his son's bride. He lifted the maid who pretended to be the Princess from her horse, and kissed her hand. Then he led her into the palace.

Nobody took any notice of the real Princess. She wandered forlornly about the courtyard and wondered what was to become of her.

The false princess was taken to an upper room. Here she changed her riding dress for a lovely robe made of cloth of gold. Meanwhile the old King looked out of the window and saw the real Princess down in the courtyard. She looked sweet and pretty, but very sad. Anybody could tell that she was the daughter of a queen, even though she wore shabby clothes. "I wonder who she is?" said the old King. "She looks like a princess pretending to be a maid."

When the false bride appeared in her fine dress, the King asked her who the strange girl was. "Oh," she replied, "she is only a servant. She is very idle, and I hope you will give her some rough, hard work to do."

"I don't know what work to give her," said the old King. "Wait! she shall help the lad who looks after the geese."

"That will do," said the false princess. "Any kind of work is good enough for her." So the real Princess was sent to help the goose-herd, whose name was Conrad.

Then the false bride sat by the Prince who was soon to be her husband. They talked of many things. At last she said, "Dear Prince, will you do something just for me?"

"Anything," he replied. "Ask what you will, it shall be done."

"Then," said she, "get one of your men to cut off the head of the horse on which I rode here. It is a wild, fierce animal, and not fit to live."

The truth was that she was afraid the horse would speak. She thought he would tell the servants that she was nothing but a maid, and that the real Princess was helping the goose-herd.

The Prince told his men to kill Falada, and that night the deed was done. When the real Princess heard the sad news, she wept bitterly, for she loved her horse very much. Then she went to the man who had killed her horse. She promised him a gold piece which she found in her pocket if he would nail up the horse's head over the city gate. She wished to see the head of her friend as she went to and fro to her work.

Next morning, as the real Princess and Conrad drove the geese to the field, she saw Falada's head nailed up over the gate, and she said:

> "Falada, Falada, thou art dead,
> And all the joy of my life is fled."

To this the head answered:

> "Alas! alas! did thy mother know,
> Heavy indeed would her fond
> heart grow."

Then they took the geese out to the meadow, and sat down to watch them. Soon the Princess let down her hair, and the long tresses gleamed like gold in the sunshine. Conrad was so pleased that he tried to pull out one of the locks. At this the Princess sang:

> "Blow, ye breezes, blow, I say,
> Blow the goose-herd's hat away;
> Blow it high and blow it low,
> After it let Conrad go.
> Blow it here and blow it there,

> While I comb my flowing hair;
> Do not let him catch it, pray,
> Till my hair is combed today."

At once a breeze sprang up, and blew Conrad's hat over hill and dale. The lad ran after it; and while he was chasing it from place to place, the Princess combed her beautiful hair and tied it up until not a lock was out of place.

When Conrad came back he was very glum and sulky, and would not speak to her all day. When the sun sank they called their geese, and drove them towards the town.

Next morning, as they passed under the gate, the poor girl once more looked at the horse's head. Then she said:

> "Falada, Falada, thou art dead,
> And all the joy of my life is fled."

To this the head replied:

> "Alas! alas! did thy mother know,
> Heavy indeed would her fond
> heart grow."

Then they continued on their way to the meadow. Sitting down on a bank, the Princess began to comb out her beautiful hair. Once more Conrad wanted to pull out a lock, and once more she called on the breezes to blow. They did so, and blew Conrad's hat over hill and dale. He did not catch it until her hair was combed. Conrad was just as sulky as before, and together they watched the geese until it grew dark.

When they got home, Conrad went to the old King, and said to him, "My lord, I will no longer keep your geese with that girl as helper."

"Why not?" asked the King.

"Because she teases me all day," said the lad. "She makes my life not worth living."

Then the King asked Conrad to tell him all about the strange girl.

He told the King that she spoke to the horse's head every morning, and that it answered her. Then he said that every day she let down her hair, which shone like pure gold. When he wished to pull out a lock or two, she called on the wind to blow his hat off. This it did, and he had to chase his hat over hill and dale. While he was away she did up her hair again, so that not a lock was out of place.

Next day the King went to the meadow without being seen by anybody. He hid himself in a bush by the side of the bank on which the Princess sat. Here he could see and hear all that went on without being seen. He saw Conrad and the goose-girl drive the geese to the meadow, and then he saw the girl begin to let down her lovely hair. Conrad was quite right, it *did* shine like pure gold.

Then he saw Conrad try to steal a lock, and heard the girl sing:

> "Blow, ye breezes, blow, I say,
> Blow the goose-herd's hat away;
> Blow it high and blow it low,
> After it let Conrad go.
> Blow it here and blow it there,
> While I comb my flowing hair;
> Do not let him catch it, pray,
> Till my hair is combed today."

Then the King felt the breeze blow, and saw that it blew Conrad's hat ever so far away. The lad had to run a long way to catch it. He saw, too, that while the lad was chasing his hat the girl was combing her hair. It was all in order by the time he came back. Though the King saw all this, he did not let the goose-girl see him.

That night he called her to him and asked her who she was and what these strange doings meant. The goose-girl wept and said: "I dare not tell you, for if I do I shall be killed."

"Nonsense," said the King. "Tell me all about it, and I will see that you come to no harm." He looked so kind that the girl told him the whole story.

"I am really a queen's daughter," she said, "and a false servant has taken my place. She has ridden my horse and killed him. She wears my clothes, and now sits with my Prince, while I tend the geese in the field. O, my lord! send me back to my mother. If she knew of my sad plight, her heart would break."

When she had finished her sad tale, the King kissed her, and dried her eyes. Then he ordered his servants to dress her like the princess she really was.

As she walked down the stairs in her beautiful dress, anybody with half an eye could tell she was a princess; she looked so sweet, and carried herself so nobly.

Then the King called his son and told him that his bride was no princess, but a cheat. He said that she was not a queen's daughter, but a maid who had stolen the real Princess' horse and clothes. "Here," he said, "stands the real Princess, your bride."

At once the Prince saw that he had been cheated. He knelt to kiss the hand of the lovely but ill-treated Princess, who smiled upon him.

Then a great feast was made, and all sat down to it. The King sat at the head of the table, the false princess on the one side and the real Princess on the other. During the feast the King told the story of the wronged Princess. He asked the false bride what should be done to the one who had acted in such a wicked way.

"She should be locked up for life in a dark prison," said the maid. "Nothing would be too bad for her."

"You are right," replied the old King. "You are the person who has done so wickedly. You have judged your own case, and said what shall be your own punishment. So be it."

So they shut up the false princess in a dark prison, because she had so wickedly wronged the real Princess, and had cheated them all.

Then the Prince and Princess were married amidst the joy of all the people. They lived happily ever afterwards. I am glad to tell you that a good fairy brought Falada back to life again, and that the good horse carried his mistress for many a year.

Grimm, *The Milk-White Thorn*

Snow-White and Rose-Red

A poor widow once lived in a little cottage with a garden in front of it, in which grew two rose trees, one bearing white roses and the other red. She had two daughters, who were just like the two rose trees; one was called Snow-White and the other Rose-Red, and they were the sweetest and best children in the world, always diligent and always cheerful; but Snow-White was quieter and more gentle than Rose-Red. Rose-Red loved to run about the fields and meadows, and to pick flowers and catch butterflies; but Snow-White sat at home with her mother and helped her in the household, or read aloud to her when there was no work to do. The two children loved each other so dearly that they always walked about hand-in-hand whenever they went out together, and when Snow-White said to her sister: "We will never desert each other," Rose-Red answered: "No, not as long as we live;" and the mother added: "Whatever one gets she shall share with the other."

They often roamed about in the woods gathering berries and no beast offered to hurt them; the little hare would eat a cabbage leaf from their hands, the deer grazed beside them, the stag would bound past them merrily, and the birds remained on the branches

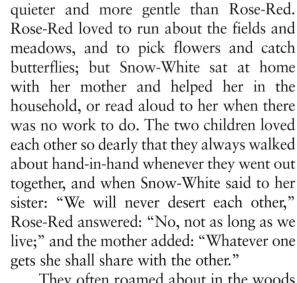

and sang to them with all their might. No evil ever befell them; if they lingered in the wood and night overtook them, they lay down together on the moss and slept till morning, and their mother knew they were quite safe, and never felt anxious about them. Once, when they had slept the night in the wood and had been wakened by the morning sun, they saw a beautiful child in a shining white robe sitting close to their resting place. The figure got up, looked at them kindly, but said nothing, and vanished into the wood. When the sisters looked round about them they became aware that they had slept quite close to a precipice, over which they would certainly have fallen had they gone on a few steps further in the darkness. When they went home and told their mother of their adventure, she said what they had seen must have been the angel that guards good children.

Snow-White and Rose-Red kept their mother's cottage so beautifully clean and neat that it was a pleasure to go into it. In summer Rose-Red looked after the house, and every morning before her mother awoke she placed a bunch of flowers before the bed, from each tree a rose. In winter Snow-White lit the fire and put on the kettle, which was made of brass but so beautifully polished that it shone like gold. In the evening when the snowflakes fell their mother said: "Snow-White, close the shutters;" and they drew round the fire, while the mother put on her spectacles and read aloud from a big book and the two girls sat and listened. Beside them on the ground lay a little lamb, and behind them perched a little white dove with its head tucked under its wings.

One evening as they sat cosily together someone knocked at the door as though he wanted to come in. The mother said:

"Rose-Red, go and open the door quickly; it must be some traveller seeking shelter." Rose-Red hastened to unbar the door, and thought she saw a poor man standing in the darkness outside; but it was no such thing, only a bear, who poked his thick brown head through the door. Rose-Red screamed aloud and sprang back in terror, the lamb began to bleat, the dove flapped its wings, and Snow-White ran and hid behind her mother's bed. But the Bear began to speak, and said: "Don't be afraid; I won't hurt you. I am half frozen, and I only wish to warm myself a little."

"My poor Bear," said the mother, "lie down by the fire, only take care you don't burn your fur."

Then she called out: "Snow-White and Rose-Red, come out; the Bear will do you no harm: he is a good, honest creature." So they both came out of their hiding places, and gradually the lamb and dove drew near too, and they all forgot their fear. The Bear asked the children to beat the snow out of his fur, and they fetched a brush and scrubbed him till he was dry. Then the beast stretched himself in front of the fire, and growled quite happily and comfortably. The children soon grew quite at their ease with him, and led their helpless guest a fearful life. They tugged his fur with their hands, put their small feet on his back, and rolled him about here and there, or took a hazel wand and beat him with it; and if he growled they only laughed. The Bear submitted to everything with the best possible good-nature, only when they went too far he cried: "Oh! children, spare my life!

Snow-White and Rose-Red,
Don't beat your darling dead."

When it was time to retire for the night, and the others went to bed, the mother said to the Bear: "Lie there on the hearth; it will be shelter for you from the cold and wet." As soon as day dawned the children let him out, and he trotted over the snow into the wood. From this time on the Bear came every evening at the same hour, and lay down by the hearth and let the children play what pranks they liked with him; and they got so accustomed to him that the door was never shut till their brown friend had made his appearance. When spring came, and all outside was green, the Bear said one morning to Snow-White: "Now I must go away, and not return again the whole summer."

"Where are you going to, dear Bear?" asked Snow-White.

"I must go to the wood and protect my treasure from the wicked dwarfs. In winter, when the earth is frozen solid, they are obliged to remain underground, for they can't work their way through; but now, when the sun has thawed and warmed the ground, they break through and come up above to spy the land and steal what they can: what once falls into their hands and into their caves is not easily brought back to light."

Snow-White was quite sad over their friend's departure. When she unbarred the door for him, the Bear, stepping out, caught a piece of his fur in the door-knocker, and Snow-White thought she caught sight of glittering gold beneath it, but she couldn't be certain; and the Bear ran hastily away, and soon disappeared behind the trees.

A short time after this the mother sent the children into the wood to collect firewood. They came in their wanderings upon a big tree which lay felled on the ground, and on the trunk among the long grass they noticed something jumping up and down, but what it was they couldn't tell. When they approached nearer they saw a dwarf with a wizened face and a very long beard. The end of the beard was jammed into a cleft of the tree, and the little man sprang about like a dog on a chain, and didn't seem to know what he was to do. He glared at the girls with his fiery red eyes, and screamed out: "What are you standing there for? can't you come and help me?"

"What were you doing, little man?" asked Rose-Red.

"You stupid, inquisitive goose!" replied the Dwarf; "I wanted to split the tree, in order to get little chips of wood for our kitchen fire; those thick logs that serve to make fires for coarse,

greedy people like yourselves burn up all the little food we need. I had successfully driven in the wedge, and all was going well, but the cursed wood was so slippery that it suddenly sprang out, and the tree closed up so rapidly that I had no time to take my beautiful white beard out, so here I am stuck fast, and I can't get away; and you silly, smooth-faced, milk-and-water girls just stand and laugh! Ugh! what wretches you are!"

The children did all in their power, but they just couldn't get the beard out; it was wedged in far too firmly. "I'll run and fetch somebody," said Rose-Red.

"You crazy blockheads!" snapped the Dwarf; "what's the good of calling anyone else? You're already two too many for me. Does nothing better occur to either of you than that?"

"Don't be so impatient," said Snow-White, "I'll see you get help;" and taking her scissors out of her pocket she cut the end off his beard.

As soon as the Dwarf felt himself free he seized a bag full of gold which was hidden among the roots of the tree, lifted it up and muttered out loud: "Curse these rude wretches for cutting off a piece of my splendid beard!" With these words he swung the bag over his back, and disappeared without as much as a glance at the children again.

Shortly after this Snow-White and Rose-Red went out to get a dish of fish. As they approached the stream they saw something which looked like an enormous grasshopper, springing towards the water as if it were going to jump in. They ran forward and recognised their old friend the Dwarf. "Where are you going to?" asked Rose-Red; "you're surely not going to jump into the water?"

"I am not such a fool," screamed the Dwarf. "Don't you see that cursed fish is trying to drag me in?" The little man had been sitting on the bank fishing, when unfortunately the wind had entangled his beard in the line; and when immediately afterwards a big fish bit, the feeble little creature had no strength to pull it out; the fish had the upper fin, and dragged the Dwarf towards him. The poor Dwarf clung on with all his might to every reed and

When the Dwarf saw what they were doing he yelled to them: "Do you call that manners, you two toadstools! to disfigure a fellow's face? It wasn't enough that you shortened my beard before, but you must now cut off the best bit of it with your stupid old scissors. I can't appear like this before my own people. I wish you'd been at Jericho first." Then he fetched a sack of pearls that lay among the rushes, and without saying another word he dragged it away and disappeared behind a stone.

It happened that soon after this the mother sent the two girls to the town to buy needles, thread, laces and ribbons. Their road led over a heath where huge boulders of rock lay scattered here and there. While trudging along they saw a big bird hovering in the air, circling slowly above them, but always descending lower, till at last it settled on a rock not far from them. It was an eagle in search of prey, and it had landed on top of something or someone small, but the girls could not see clearly what it had caught. They heard a sharp, piercing cry. They ran forward, and saw with horror that the eagle had pounced on their old friend the Dwarf, and was about to carry him off. The tender-hearted children seized hold of the little man, and struggled so long with the bird that at last he let go his prey and flew off in disgust, with his talons empty. When the Dwarf had recovered from the first shock he screamed in his screeching voice: "Couldn't you have treated me more carefully? You have torn my thin little coat all to shreds, useless, awkward girls that you are!" Then he took a bag of precious stones and vanished under the rocks into his cave. The two girls were accustomed to his ingratitude, and went on their way to town.

blade of grass, but it didn't help him much; he had to follow every movement of the fish, and was in great danger of being drawn into the water. The girls came up just at the right moment, held him firm, and did all they could to disentangle his beard from the line; but in vain, beard and line were in a hopeless muddle. Nothing remained but to produce the scissors and cut the beard, by which a small part of it was sacrificed.

On their way home, as they were again passing the heath, they surprised the Dwarf pouring out his precious stones on an open space, for he had thought no-one would pass by at so late an hour. The evening sun shone on the glittering stones, and they glanced and gleamed so beautifully that the children stood still and gazed on them.

"What are you standing there gaping for?" screamed the Dwarf, and his ashen-grey face became quite scarlet with rage. "I suppose you are planning to steal all this treasure from me, you nasty thieves." He was about to go off with these angry words when a sudden growl was heard, and a brown bear trotted out of the wood. The Dwarf jumped up in a great fright, but he hadn't time to reach his place of retreat, for the Bear was already close to him. Then he cried in terror: "Dear Mr Bear, spare me! I'll give you all my treasure. Look at those beautiful precious stones lying there. Spare my life! What pleasure would you get from a poor feeble little fellow like me? You won't feel me between your teeth. There, lay hold of these two wicked girls, they will be a tender morsel for you, as fat as young quails; eat *them* up." But the Bear, paying no attention to his words, gave the evil little creature one blow with his paw, and he never moved again.

The girls had run away, but the Bear called after them: "Snow-White and Rose-Red, don't be afraid; wait, and I'll come with you." Then they recognised his voice and stood still, and when the Bear was quite close to them his skin suddenly fell off, and a beautiful man stood beside them, all dressed in gold. "I am a king's son," he said, "and have been doomed by that unholy little Dwarf, who had stolen my treasure, to roam about the woods as a wild bear till his death should set me free.

Now at last he has got the punishment he truly deserves."

Snow-White married the Prince, and Rose-Red his brother, and they divided the great treasure the Dwarf had collected in his cave between them. The old mother lived for many years peacefully with her children. She kept the two rose trees with her, and they stood in front of her window, and every year they bore the finest red and white roses.

Grimm, *The Blue Fairy Book*

The Brave Little Tailor

One summer's day a little tailor sat on his table by the window in the best of spirits, and sewed for dear life. As he was sitting a peasant woman came down the street, calling out: "Good jam to sell, good jam to sell." This sounded sweetly in the Tailor's ears; he put his frail little head out of the window and shouted: "Up here, my good woman, and you'll find a willing customer."

The woman climbed up the three flights of stairs with her basket to the Tailor's room, and he made her spread out all the pots in a row before him. He examined them all, and smelt them, and said at last: "This jam seems good, weigh me four ounces of it, my good woman; and even if it's a quarter of a pound I won't stick at it."

The peasant woman, who had hoped to find a good market for her jam, gave him what he wanted, but went away grumbling wrathfully.

"Now heaven shall bless this jam for my use," declared the Little Tailor, "and it shall sustain and strengthen me." He went to fetch some bread out of a cupboard, cut a slice off the loaf and spread the jam on it. "That won't taste amiss," he said; "but I'll finish that waistcoat first before I take a bite." He placed the bread beside him, went on sewing, and out of the lightness of his heart kept on making his stitches bigger and bigger.

In the meantime the smell of the sweet jam rose to the ceiling, where heaps of flies were sitting lazily, and attracted them to such an extent that they swarmed on to it in masses. "Ha! who invited you?" said the Tailor, and chased the unwelcome guests away. But the flies, who didn't understand English, refused to let themselves be warned off, and returned again in even greater numbers. At last the Little Tailor, losing all patience, reached out of his chimney corner for a duster, and exclaiming: "Wait, I'll give it to you," he beat them mercilessly with it. When he left off he counted the slain, and no fewer than seven lay dead before him with outstretched legs.

"Oh, what a desperate fellow I am!" he said, and was filled with admiration at his own courage. "The whole town must know about this;" and in haste the Little Tailor cut out a belt, hemmed it, and embroidered on it in big letters, 'Seven at a blow'.

"What did I say, the town? No, the whole world shall hear of it," he said; and his heart beat for joy.

The Tailor strapped the belt round his waist and set out into the wide world, for he considered his workroom too small a field for his prowess. Before he set forth he looked round about him, to see if there was anything in the house he could take with him on his journey; but he found nothing except a mouldy old cheese, which he took possession of. In front of the house he observed a bird that had been caught in some bushes, and this he put into his bag beside the cheese. Then he went on his way merrily, and being light and agile he never felt tired.

His way led up a hill, on the top of which sat a powerful giant, who was calmly surveying the landscape. The Little Tailor went up to him, and greeting him cheerfully said: "Good-day to you, friend; there you sit at your ease viewing the whole wide world. I am just on my way there. What do you say to accompanying me?"

The Giant looked contemptuously at the Tailor and said: "What a poor wretched little creature you are!"

"Well, that's a good joke," answered the Little Tailor, and unbuttoning his coat he showed the Giant the belt. "There now, you can read what sort of a fellow I am."

The Giant read: 'Seven at a blow'; and thinking they were human beings the Tailor had slain, he conceived a certain respect for the little man. But first he thought he'd test him, so taking up a stone in his hand, he squeezed it till some drops of water ran out. "Now you do the same," said the Giant, "if you really wish to be thought strong."

"Is that all?" said the Little Tailor; "that is child's play to me," so he dived into his bag, brought out the cheese and pressed it till the whey ran out. "My squeeze was better than yours," he said.

The Giant didn't know what to say, for he couldn't have believed it of the little fellow. To prove him again, the Giant lifted a big stone and threw it so high that the eye could hardly follow it. "Now, my little pygmy, let me see you do that."

"Well thrown," said the Tailor; "but, after all, your stone fell to the ground; I'll throw one that won't come down at all." He dived into his bag again, and grasping the bird in his hand, he threw it up into the air. The bird, delighted to be free, soared up

into the sky, and flew away never to return. "Well, what do you think of that little piece of action, friend?" asked the Tailor.

"You can certainly throw," replied the Giant; "but now let's see if you can carry a proper weight." With these words he led the Tailor to a huge oak tree which had been felled to the ground and said: "If you are strong enough, help me to carry the tree out of the wood."

"Most certainly," said the Little Tailor: "just you take the trunk on your shoulder; I'll bear the top and branches, which is certainly the heaviest part."

The Giant laid the trunk on his shoulder, but the Tailor sat at his ease among the branches; and the Giant, who couldn't see what was going on behind him, had to carry the whole tree, and the Little Tailor into the bargain. There he sat behind in the best of spirits, whistling a tune, as if carrying the tree were mere sport.

After dragging the heavy weight for a long time, the Giant could carry on no further and shouted out: "Hi! I must let the tree fall."

The Tailor sprang nimbly down, seized the tree with both hands as if he had carried it the whole way, and said to the Giant: "Fancy a big lout like you not being able to carry a tree!"

They continued on their way together, and as they passed by a cherry tree the Giant grasped the top of it, where the ripest fruit hung, handed the branches to the Tailor, and told him to eat. But the Tailor was far too weak to hold the tree down, and when the Giant let go the tree swung back into the air, bearing the Little Tailor with it. When he had fallen to the ground again without hurting himself, the Giant exclaimed: "What! do you mean to tell me you haven't the strength to hold down a feeble twig?"

"It wasn't strength that was wanting," answered the Tailor; "do you think that would have been anything for a man who has killed seven at a blow? I jumped over the tree because the huntsmen are shooting among the branches near us. You do the same if you dare."

The Giant made an attempt, but couldn't get over the tree, and stuck fast in the branches, so that here too the Little Tailor had the better of him.

"Well, you're a fine fellow, after all,' said the Giant; "come and spend the night with us in our cave."

The Little Tailor willingly consented to do this, and following his friend they went on till they reached a cave where several other Giants were sitting round a fire, each holding a roast sheep in his hand, of which he was eating. The Little Tailor looked about him, and thought: "Yes, there's more room to turn round in here than in my workshop." The Giant showed him a bed, and told him to lie down and have a good sleep. But the bed was too big for the Little Tailor, so he didn't get into it, but crept away into the corner. At midnight, when the Giant thought the Little Tailor was fast asleep, he rose up, and taking his big iron walking stick, he broke the bed in two with a blow, and thought he had made an end of the little grasshopper.

At early dawn the Giants went off to the wood and forgot about the Little Tailor, till all of a sudden they met him trudging along in the most cheerful manner. The Giants were terrified at the apparition, and, fearful lest he should slay them, they all took to their heels as fast as they could.

The Little Tailor continued to follow his nose, and after he had wandered about for a long time he came to the courtyard of a royal palace, and feeling tired he lay down on the grass and fell asleep. While he lay there the people came, and looking him all over read on his belt: 'Seven at a blow'. "Oh!" they said, "what can this hero of a hundred fights want in our peaceful land? He must indeed be a man of valour." They went and told the King about him, and said what an important and useful man he'd be in time of war, and that it would be well to secure him at any price.

This counsel pleased the King, and he sent one of his Courtiers to the Little Tailor, to offer him, when he awoke, a commission in their army. The messenger stood by the sleeper, and waited till he stretched his limbs and opened his eyes, when he tendered his proposal.

"That's the very thing I came here for," he answered; "I am quite ready to enter the King's service." So he was received with all honour, and given a special house of his own to live in.

However, the other officers resented the success of the Little Tailor, and wished him a very long way away. "What's to come of

it all?" they asked each other; "if we quarrel with him, he'll strike out at us, and at every blow seven will fall. There'll soon be an end of us." So they resolved to go in a body to the King, and all to send in their commissions. "We are not made," they protested, "to hold out against a man who kills seven at a blow."

The King was grieved at the thought of losing all his faithful servants for the sake of one man, and he wished heartily that he had never set eyes on the Tailor, or that he could get rid of him. But he didn't dare to send the Tailor away, for he feared he might kill him along with his people, and place himself on the throne. The King pondered long and deeply over the matter, and finally came to a conclusion. He sent to the Tailor and told him that, seeing what a great and warlike hero he was, he was about to make him an offer. In a certain wood of his kingdom there dwelt two Giants who did much harm; by the way they robbed, murdered, burnt and plundered everything about them; no-one could approach them without endangering his life. But if he could overcome and kill these Giants he should have his only daughter for a wife, and half his kingdom into the bargain; he might have a hundred horsemen, too, to back him up.

"That's the very thing for a man like me," thought the Little Tailor; "one doesn't get the offer of a beautiful princess and half a kingdom every day."

"Done with you," he answered; "I'll soon put an end to the Giants. But I haven't the smallest need of your hundred horsemen; a fellow who can slay seven men at a blow need not be afraid of two."

The Little Tailor set out, and the hundred horsemen followed him. When he came to the outskirts of the wood he said to his followers: "You wait here, I'll manage the Giants by myself;" and he went on into the wood, casting his sharp little eyes right and left about him. After a while he spied the two Giants lying asleep under a tree, and snoring till the very boughs bent with the breeze. The Little Tailor lost no time in filling his bag with stones, and then climbed up the tree under which they lay. When he got to about the middle of it he slipped along a branch till he sat just above the sleepers, when he threw down one stone after the other on the nearest Giant.

The Giant felt nothing for a time, but at last he woke and, pinching his companion, said: "What did you strike me for?"

"I didn't strike you," replied the other, "you must be dreaming."

They both lay down to sleep again, and the Tailor threw down a stone on the second Giant, who sprang up and cried: "Why did you throw something at me?"

"I didn't throw anything," growled the first one.

They wrangled on for a time, till, as both were tired, they made up the matter and fell asleep again. The Little Tailor began his game once more, and flung the largest stone he could find in his bag with all his force, and hit the first Giant on the chest. "This is too much!" the Giant yelled and, springing up like a madman, he knocked his companion against the tree till he trembled. He gave, however, as good as he got, and they became so enraged that they tore up trees and beat each other with them, till they both fell dead at once on the ground.

Then the Little Tailor jumped down. He drew his sword and gave each of the Giants a fine thrust or two on the breast, and then went to the horsemen and said: I've put an end to the two of them; but I assure you it has been no easy matter, for they even tore up trees in their struggle to defend themselves; but all that's of no use against one who slays seven men at a blow."

"Weren't you wounded at all?" asked the horsemen. "No fear," said the Tailor; "they haven't touched a hair of my head." But the horsemen wouldn't believe him till they rode into the wood and found the Giants weltering in their blood.

The Little Tailor now demanded the promised reward from the King, but he repented his promise, and pondered once more how he could rid himself of the hero.

"Before you obtain the hand of my daughter and half my kingdom," he said to him, "you must do another deed of valour. A unicorn is running about in the wood, and doing much mischief; you must catch it."

"I'm even less afraid of one unicorn than of two giants; seven at a blow, that's my motto."

He took a piece of cord and an axe with him, went out to the wood, and again told the men who had been sent with him to remain outside. He hadn't to search long, for the unicorn soon passed by and, on perceiving the Tailor, dashed straight at him as though it were going to spike him on the spot. "Gently, gently," he said, "not so fast, my friend;" and standing still he waited till the beast was quite near, when he sprang lightly behind a tree; the unicorn ran with all its force against the tree, and rammed its horn so firmly into the trunk that it had no strength left to pull it out again, and was thus successfully captured.

"Now I have caught my bird," said the Tailor, and he came out from behind the tree, placed the cord round its neck first, then struck the horn out of the tree with his axe, and when everything was in order led the beast before the King.

Still the King didn't want to give him the promised reward, and made a third demand. The Tailor was to catch a wild boar for him that did a great deal of harm in the wood; and he might have the huntsmen to help him.

"Willingly," said the Tailor."

However, he didn't take the huntsmen into the wood. As soon as the boar saw the Tailor, it ran at him with foaming mouth and gleaming teeth and tried to knock him down; but our alert little friend ran into a chapel that stood nearby, and got out of the window again with a jump. The boar

pursued him into the church, but the Tailor skipped round to the door, and closed it securely. So the raging beast was caught, for it was far too heavy and unwieldy to spring out of the window. The Little Tailor summoned the huntsmen together, that they might see the prisoner with their own eyes. Then the hero went to the King, who was obliged now, whether he liked it or not, to keep his promise, and hand him over his daughter and half his kingdom. Had he known that no hero-warrior but only a little tailor stood before him, it would have troubled his heart even more. So the wedding was celebrated with much splendour and little joy, and the Tailor became a king.

After a time the Queen heard her husband saying one night in his sleep: "My lad, make that waistcoat and patch these trousers, or I'll box your ears." Thus she learnt in what rank the young gentleman had been born, and next day she poured forth her woes to her father, and begged him to help her to get rid of a husband who was nothing more nor less than a tailor. The King comforted her, and said: "Leave your bedroom door open tonight, my servants shall stand outside, and when your husband is fast asleep they shall enter, bind him fast, and carry him on to a ship, which shall sail away out into the wide ocean."

The Queen was well satisfied with the idea, but the armour-bearer, who had overheard everything, being much attached to his young master, went straight to him and revealed the whole plot. "I'll soon put a stop to the business," said the Tailor.

That night he and his wife went to bed at the usual time; and when she thought he had fallen asleep she got up, opened the door, and then lay down again. The Little Tailor, who had only pretended to be asleep, began to call out in a clear voice: "My lad, make that waistcoat and patch those trousers, or I'll box your ears. I have killed seven at a blow, slain two giants, led a unicorn captive, and caught a wild boar, then why should I be afraid of those men standing outside my door?" When they heard the Tailor saying these words, the men were so terrified that they fled as if pursued by a wild army, and didn't dare go near him again. So the Little Tailor was and remained a king all the days of his life.

Grimm, *The Blue Fairy Book*

Rapunzel

Once upon a time there lived a man and his wife who were very unhappy because they had no children. These good people had a little window at the back of their house, which looked into the most lovely garden, full of all manner of beautiful flowers and vegetables; but the garden was surrounded by a high wall, and no-one dared to enter it, for it belonged to a witch of great power, who was feared by the whole world. One day the woman stood at the window overlooking the garden, and saw there a bed full of the finest endive; the leaves looked so fresh and green that she longed to eat them. The desire grew day by day, and just because she knew she couldn't possibly get any, she pined away and became quite pale and wretched. Then her husband grew alarmed and said: "What ails you, dear wife?" "Oh," she answered, "if I don't get some endive to eat out of the garden behind the house, I know I shall die." The man, who loved her dearly, thought to himself, "Come! rather than let your wife die you shall fetch her some endive, no matter the cost." So at dusk he climbed over the wall into the Witch's garden and, hastily gathering a handful of endive leaves, he returned with them to his wife. She made them into a salad, which tasted so good that her longing for the forbidden food was greater than ever. If she were to know any peace of mind, there was nothing for it but that her husband should climb over the garden wall again, and fetch her some more. So at dusk over he climbed, but when he reached the other side he drew back in terror, for there, standing before him, was the old Witch.

"How dare you," the Witch said, with a wrathful glance, "climb into my garden and steal my endive like a common thief? You shall suffer for your foolhardiness."

"Oh!" he implored, "please forgive me; necessity alone drove me to the deed. My wife saw your endive from her window, and conceived such a desire for it that she would certainly have died if her wish had not been gratified." The Witch's anger was a little appeased, and she said:

"If it's as you say, you may take as much endive with you as you like, but on one condition only—that you give me the child your wife will shortly bring into the world. All shall go well with it, and I will look after it like a mother."

The man in his terror agreed to everything she asked, and as soon as the child was

born the Witch appeared, and having given it the name of Rapunzel, which is the same as endive, she carried it off with her.

Rapunzel was the most beautiful child under the sun. When she was twelve years old the Witch shut her up in a tower in the middle of a great wood, and the tower had neither stairs nor doors, only high up at the very top a small window. When the old Witch wanted to get in she stood underneath and called out:

"Rapunzel, Rapunzel,
Let down your golden hair,"

for Rapunzel had wonderful long hair, and it was as fine as spun gold. Whenever she heard the Witch's voice she unloosed her plaits, and let her hair fall down out of the window, and the old Witch climbed up by it.

After they had lived like this for a few years, it happened one day that a prince was riding through the wood and passed by the tower. As he drew near it the Prince heard someone singing so sweetly that he stood still, spellbound, and listened. It was Rapunzel in her loneliness trying to while away the time by letting her sweet voice ring out into the wood. The Prince longed to see the owner of the voice, but he sought in vain for a door in the tower. He rode home, but he was so haunted by the song he had heard that he returned every day to the wood and listened. One day, when he was standing behind a tree, he saw the Witch approach and heard her call out:

"Rapunzel, Rapunzel,
Let down your golden hair."

Then Rapunzel let down her plaits, and the Witch climbed up by them.

"So that's the staircase, is it?" said the Prince. "Then I too will climb it and try my luck."

So the following day, at dusk, he went to the foot of the tower and cried:

"Rapunzel, Rapunzel,
Let down your golden hair,"

and as soon as she had let it down the Prince climbed up.

At first Rapunzel was terribly frightened when a man came in, for she had never seen one before; but the Prince spoke to her so kindly, and told her at once that his heart had been so touched by her singing, that he felt he should know no peace of mind till he had seen her. Very soon Rapunzel forgot her fear, and when the Prince asked her to marry him she consented at once. "For," she thought, "he is young and handsome, and I'll certainly be happier with him than with the old Witch." So she put her hand in his and said: "Yes, I will gladly go with you, only how am I to get down out of the tower? Every time you come to see me you must bring a skein of silk with you and I will make a

ladder of them, and when it is finished I will climb down by it, and you will take me away on your horse." They arranged that, till the ladder was ready, he was to come to her every evening, because the old woman was with her during the day. The old Witch, of course, knew nothing of what was going on, till one day Rapunzel, not thinking, turned to the Witch and said:

"How is it, good Mother, that you are so much harder to pull up than the young Prince? He is always with me in a moment."

"Oh! you wicked child," cried the Witch. "What is this I hear? I thought I had hidden you safely from the whole world, and in spite of it you have managed to deceive me."

In her anger the Witch seized Rapunzel's beautiful hair, wound it round and round her left hand, and then grasping a pair of scissors in her right, snip snap, off it came, and the beautiful plaits lay on the ground. And, worse than this, she was so hard-hearted that she took Rapunzel to a lonely desert place, and there left her to live in loneliness and misery.

But on the evening of the day in which she had driven poor Rapunzel away, the Witch fastened the plaits on to a hook in the window, and when the Prince came and called out:

"Rapunzel, Rapunzel,
Let down your golden hair,"
she let them down, and the Prince climbed up as usual, but instead of his beloved Rapunzel he found the old Witch, who fixed her evil, glittering eyes on him, and cried mockingly:

"Ah, ah! you thought you would find your lady love, but the pretty bird has flown and its song is dumb; the cat caught it, and will scratch out both your eyes too. Rapunzel is lost to you forever—you will never see her again."

The Prince was beside himself with grief, and in his despair he jumped right down from the tower, and, though he escaped with his life, the thorns among which he fell pierced his eyes. Then he wandered, blind and miserable, through the wood, eating nothing but roots and berries, and weeping and lamenting the loss of his lovely bride. So he wandered about for some years, as wretched and unhappy as he could be, and at last he came to the lonely desert place where Rapunzel was living. All of a sudden he heard a voice which seemed strangely familiar to him. He walked eagerly in the direction of the sound, and when he was quite close, Rapunzel recognised him and fell on his neck and wept. But two of her tears touched his eyes, and in a moment they became quite clear again, and he saw as well as he had ever done. Then he led her to his kingdom, where they were welcomed with great joy, and lived happily ever after.

Grimm,
The Red Fairy Book

266

Puss in Boots; or, the Master Cat

There was a miller who died and left to his three sons his mill, his ass and his cat. The eldest had the mill, the second the ass, and the youngest nothing but the cat.

The unfortunate young fellow was quite comfortless at having so poor a lot. "My brothers," said he, "may get their living handsomely enough by joining together their stocks; but, for my part, when I have eaten up my cat, and made gloves out of his skin, I must die of hunger."

The Cat, who heard all this, but pretended he did not, said to him with a grave and serious air: "Do not trouble yourself, my good master, for you have nothing else to do but to give me a bag, and get a pair of boots made for me, in which I may scamper through the dirt and the brambles, and you shall see that you have not so bad a bargain of me as you imagine."

The Cat's master did not rely very much upon what he said; he had, however, often seen him play a great many cunning tricks to catch rats and mice; when he used to hang by the heels, or hide himself in the flour, and pretend that he were dead; so that

he did not altogether despair that the Cat might help him in his miserable condition. When the Cat had what he asked for, he booted himself very gallantly, and, putting his bag about his neck, he held the strings of it in his two fore paws, and went into a

warren where there were plenty of rabbits. He put bran and thistle into his bag, and, stretching out at length, as if he were dead, he waited for some young rabbits, not yet acquainted with the deceits of the world, to come and rummage in his bag for what he had put into it.

Scarcely had he lain down but he had what he wanted: a rash and foolish young rabbit jumped into his bag, and Monsieur Puss in Boots, immediately drawing close the strings, took and killed him without pity. Proud of his prey, he went with it to the palace, and asked to speak with his Majesty. He was shown upstairs into the King's apartment, and, making a low bow, said to him: "I have brought you, sir, a rabbit of the warren, which my noble Lord, the Master of Carabas [for that was the title which Monsieur Puss in Boots was pleased to give his master] has commanded me to present to your Majesty with his compliments."

"Tell your master," said the King, "that I thank him, and that he gives me a great deal of pleasure."

Another time he went and hid himself among some wheat, holding still his bag open; and, when a brace of partridges ran into it, he drew the strings, and so caught them both. He went and made a present of these to the King, as he had done before. The King received the partridges with great pleasure also.

The Cat continued for two or three months to carry his Majesty, from time to time, game of his master's taking. One day in particular, when he knew for certain that he was to take the air along the riverside, with his daughter who was the most beautiful princess in the world, he said to his master: "If you will follow my advice your fortune is made. You have nothing else to do but wash yourself in the river, where I shall show you, and leave the rest to me."

The Marquis of Carabas did what the Cat advised him to, without knowing why or wherefore. While he was washing, the King passed by, and the Cat began to cry out: "Help! help! My Lord Marquis of Carabas is going to be drowned."

At this noise the King put his head out of the coach window, and, finding it was the Cat who had so often brought him such good game, he commanded his guards to run immediately to the assistance of his Lordship the Marquis of Carabas. While they were drawing the poor Marquis out of the river, the Cat came up to the coach and told the King that, while his master was washing, there came by some rogues, who went off with his clothes, though he had cried out: "Thieves! thieves!" several times, as loud as he could.

This cunning Cat had hidden them under a great stone. The King immediately commanded the officers of his wardrobe to run and fetch one of his best suits for the Lord Marquis of Carabas.

The King was amazingly friendly to him, and as the fine clothes set off his good looks, the King's daughter took a secret inclination towards him, and the Marquis of Carabas had no sooner cast two or three respectful and somewhat tender glances but she fell in love with him. The King insisted on having him come into the coach and take part in the trip. The Cat, quite overjoyed to see his project begin to succeed, marched on ahead, and, meeting with some countrymen who were mowing a meadow, he said to them: "Good people, you who are mowing, if you do not tell the King that the meadow you mow belongs to my Lord Marquis of Carabas, you shall be chopped as small as herbs for the pot."

The King did not fail to ask the mowers who the meadow they were mowing belonged to. "Why, to my Lord Marquis of Carabas," they answered all together, for the Cat's threats had made them terribly afraid.

"You see, sir," said the Marquis, "this is a meadow which never fails to yield a plentiful harvest every year."

The Master Cat, who went on ahead, met with some reapers, and said to them: "Good people, you who are reaping, if you do not tell the King that all this wheat belongs to the Marquis of Carabas, you shall be chopped up as small as herbs for the pot."

The King, who passed by a moment later, insisted on knowing who all that wheat which he then saw, belonged to. "To my Lord Marquis of Carabas," replied the reapers, and the King was very well pleased with it, as well as the Marquis. The Master Cat, who went always ahead said the same words to all he met, and the King was astonished at the vast estates of my Lord Marquis of Carabas.

Monsieur Puss came at last to a stately castle, the master of which was an ogre, the richest had ever been known; for all the lands which the King had then gone over belonged to this castle. The Cat, who had taken care to inform himself who this ogre was and what he could do, asked to speak with him, saying he could not pass so near his castle without having the honour of paying his respects to him.

The ogre received him as politely as an ogre could do, and made him sit down.

example, to change yourself into a rat or a mouse; but I must admit to you I take this to be impossible."

"Impossible!" cried the ogre; "you shall see that at once." And at the same time he changed himself into a mouse, and began to run about the floor. Puss no sooner saw this than he fell upon him and ate him up.

Meanwhile the King, who saw, as he passed, this fine castle of the ogre's, had a mind to go into it. Puss, who heard the noise of his Majesty's coach running over the drawbridge, ran out, and with a low bow said to the King: "Your Majesty is most welcome to this castle of my Lord Marquis of Carabas."

"What! my Lord Marquis," cried the King, "and does this castle also belong to you? There can be nothing finer than this court and all the stately buildings which surround it; let us go into it, if you please."

The Marquis offered his hand to the Princess, and followed the King, who went first. They passed into a splendid spacious hall, where they found a magnificent feast, which the ogre had prepared for his friends, who were that very day to visit him, but dared not to enter, knowing the King was there. His Majesty was perfectly charmed with the good qualities of my Lord Marquis of Carabas, as was his daughter, who had fallen desperately in love with him, and, seeing the vast estate he possessed, said to him: "It will be owing to yourself only, my Lord Marquis, if you are not my son-in-law."

The Marquis, making several low bows, accepted the honour which his Majesty conferred upon him, and forthwith, that very same day, married the Princess. Puss became a great lord, and never ran after mice any more except for his amusement.

Perrault, *The Blue Fairy Book*

"I have been assured," declared the Cat, "that you have the gift of being able to change yourself into all sorts of creatures you have a mind to; you can, for example, transform yourself into a lion, or elephant, and the like."

"That is true," answered the ogre very briskly; "and to convince you, you shall see me now become a lion."

Puss was so terrified at the sight of a lion so near him that he immediately got into the gutter, not without a great deal of trouble and danger, because of his boots, which were of no use at all to him in walking upon the tiles. A little while later, when Puss saw that the ogre had resumed his natural form, he came down, and admitted he had been very much frightened.

"I have been also informed," said the Cat, "but I do not know how to believe it, that you have also the power to take on you the shape of the smallest animals; for

The Story of the Emperor's New Clothes

Many years ago there lived an emperor who was so fond of new clothes that he spent all his money on them in order to be beautifully dressed. He did not care about his soldiers, he did not care about the theatre; he only liked to go out walking to show off his new clothes. He had a coat for every hour of the day; and just as they say of a king, "He is in the council chamber," they always said here, "The Emperor is in the wardrobe."

In the great city in which he lived there was always something going on; every day many strangers came there. One day two impostors arrived at the city gates who said they were weavers, and that they knew how to manufacture the most beautiful cloth imaginable. Not only were the texture and pattern uncommonly beautiful, but the clothes which were made of the stuff possessed this wonderful property that they were invisible to those who were not fit for their position, or who were unpardonably stupid.

"Those must undoubtedly be splendid clothes," thought the Emperor. "If I had them on I could find out which people in my kingdom are unfit for the positions they hold; I could distinguish the wise from the stupid! Yes, this cloth must be woven for me at once." And he gave both the impostors much money, so that they might begin their work.

They obtained two weaving looms and began to behave as if they were working, but they had not the least thing on the looms. They also demanded the finest silk and the best gold, which they put in their pockets, and worked at the empty looms till late into the night.

"I should like very much to know how far they have got with the cloth," thought the Emperor. But he remembered when he thought about it that whoever was stupid or not fit for his position would not be able to see it. Now he certainly believed that he had nothing to fear for himself, but he wanted first to send somebody else in order

271

to see how fit he was for his position in life. Everybody in the whole town knew what a wonderful power the cloth had, and they were all curious to see how bad or how stupid their neighbour was.

"I will send my old and most honoured minister to visit the weavers," thought the Emperor. "He can judge best the cloth's qualities, for he has intellect, and no-one understands his work better than he."

Now the good old minister went into the hall where the impostors sat working at the empty weaving looms. "Dear me!" thought the old minister, opening his eyes wide, "I can see nothing!" But he did not say so.

Both the impostors begged him to be so kind as to step closer, and asked him if it were not a beautiful texture and lovely colours. They pointed to the empty loom, and the poor old minister went forward rubbing his eyes; but he could see nothing, for there was nothing there.

"Oh dear!" thought the minister, "can I be stupid? I have never thought that, and nobody must know it! Can I be not fit for my position? No, I must certainly not say that I cannot see the cloth!"

"Have you nothing to say about it?" asked one of the men who was weaving.

"Oh, it is most lovely!" answered the old minister, looking through his spectacles. "What a texture! What colours! Yes, I will tell the Emperor that it pleases me very much."

"Now we are delighted at that," said both the weavers, and they named the colours and explained the texture. The old minister paid great attention, so that he could tell the same to the Emperor when he came back to him, which he did.

The two impostors now wanted more money, more silk, and more gold to use in their weaving. They put it all in their own pockets, and no threads appeared on the loom, but they went on as they had done before, working at the empty loom. The Emperor soon sent another worthy statesman to see how the weaving was proceeding, and whether the cloth would soon be finished. It was the same with him as the first one; he looked and looked, but because there was nothing on the empty loom he could see nothing.

"Is it not a beautiful piece of cloth?" asked the two impostors, and they pointed to and described the splendid material which was not there.

"Stupid I am not!" thought the man, "so it must be my good position for which I am not fitted. It is strange, certainly, but no-one must be allowed to notice it." And so he praised the cloth which he did not see, and expressed to them his delight at the beautiful colours and the splendid texture. "Yes, it is quite beautiful," he said to the Emperor.

Everybody in the town was talking of the magnificent cloth.

Now the Emperor wanted to see it himself while it was still on the loom. With a great crowd of select followers, among whom were both the worthy statesmen who had already been there before, he went to the cunning impostors, who were now weaving with all their might, but without fibre or thread.

"Is it not splendid!" exclaimed both the old statesmen who had already been there. "See, your Majesty, what a texture! What colours!" Then they pointed to the empty loom, for they believed that all the others could see the cloth quite well.

"What!" thought the Emperor, "I can see nothing! This is indeed horrible! Am I stupid? Am I not fit to be Emperor? That would be the most dreadful thing that could happen to me. "Oh, it is very beautiful," he said. "It has my gracious approval." And then he nodded pleasantly, and examined the empty loom, for he would not say that he could see nothing.

His whole Court round him looked and looked, and saw no more than the others; but they said like the Emperor, "Oh! it is beautiful!" And they advised him to wear these new and magnificent clothes for the first time at the great procession which was soon to take place. "Splendid! Lovely! Most beautiful!" travelled from mouth to mouth; everyone seemed delighted over them, and the Emperor gave to the impostors the title of Court Weavers to the Emperor.

Throughout the entire night before the morning on which the procession was to take place, the impostors were up and were working by the light of more than sixteen candles. The people could see that they were very busy getting the Emperor's new clothes ready. They pretended they were taking the cloth from the loom, cut with huge scissors in the air, sewed with needles without thread, and then said at last, "Now the clothes are finished!"

The Emperor came himself with his most distinguished knights. Each impostor held up his arm as if he were holding something, and said, "See! here are the trousers! Here is the coat! And here is the cloak!" and so on.

"Spun clothes are so comfortable that one would imagine one had nothing on at all; but that is the beauty of it!"

"Yes," agreed all the knights, but they could see nothing at all, for of course there was nothing there.

"Will it please your Majesty graciously to take off your clothes," said the impostors, "then we will put on the new clothes, here before the mirror."

The Emperor took off all his clothes, and the impostors placed themselves before him as if they were putting on each part of his new clothes, and the Emperor turned and bent himself in front of the mirror.

"How beautifully they fit! How well they sit!" said everybody. "What material! What colours! It is a gorgeous suit!"

"They are waiting outside with the canopy which your Majesty has borne over you in the great procession," announced the Master of the Ceremonies.

"Look, I am ready," said the Emperor. "Doesn't it sit well!" And he turned himself again to the mirror to see if his finery was on all right.

The chamberlains who were used to carry the train put their hands near the floor as if they were lifting up the train; then they behaved as if they were holding something in the air. They would not have it noticed that they could see nothing.

So the Emperor went along in the procession under the splendid canopy, and the people in the streets and at the windows said, "How matchless are the Emperor's new clothes! That train fastened to his back, how beautifully it hangs!"

No-one wished it to be noticed that he could see nothing, for then he would have been unfit for his work, or else very stupid. None of the Emperor's clothes had met with such approval as these had.

"But he has nothing on!" declared a little child at last.

"Just listen to the innocent child!" said the father, and each one whispered to his neighbour what the child had said.

"But he has nothing on!" the whole of the people called out at last. This struck the Emperor, for it seemed to him as if they were right; but he thought to himself, "I must go on with the procession now." And the chamberlains walked along still more uprightly, holding up the train which was not there at all.

Andersen,
The Yellow Fairy Book

Hansel and Gretel

A poor woodman once dwelt near a forest in which he cut wood every day. He had two children—Hansel, the boy, and Gretel the girl. Their mother was dead, and their father had married again. Unhappily, their stepmother did not love them.

Times were hard; there was a famine in the land, and the woodman could not earn enough money to buy bread for his wife and children, who were very hungry and miserable. They went to bed, and the poor man, who was too wretched to sleep, said, "What will become of us? You and I and the children will certainly starve."

Then his wife said, "We cannot feed four mouths, but we may feed two; so let us take the children early tomorrow into the thickest part of the wood and leave them there. We will make a fire and give them each a piece of bread, and then they must take care of themselves."

"No, no," said the husband; "I cannot leave my children to be torn to pieces by wild beasts. I would rather die first."

"Then die you will," said his wife, "and so shall I; but little you will care for that."

She stormed and wept and gave him no peace, until at last he agreed to her cruel plan. The two children, however, were too hungry to sleep, and were lying awake in the next room. They overheard all that was said, and then Gretel began to weep; but Hansel said, "Don't be afraid, Gretel. I will take care of you." Then he got up, slipped on his jacket, and quietly opened the door. The full moon was shining on the white pebbles in the road and making them look like pieces of silver. Hansel filled his pockets with them, and then crept back to bed. "Go to sleep now," he said to his sister. "It will be all right."

Early next morning, even before the sun was up, the stepmother woke the children roughly, and gave them each a piece of bread. "That is for your dinner," she said. "If you eat it now you will have nothing for the rest of the day. Come along; we are going into the forest to chop wood."

Gretel carried her bread in her apron, and she put Hansel's with it because his pocket was full of pebbles. As they walked along, Hansel lagged behind and kept

stopping to drop one after another of the pebbles out of his pocket on the path. At last they came to the thickest part of the forest, and the woodman told the children to collect wood for a fire. This they did, and soon a little fire was burning brightly. "Sit down by the fire," said the stepmother to the children. Your father and I are going to chop wood over there. We will come and call you when it is time to go home."

The children sat by the fire until noon, when they ate their bread. They were not afraid, because they thought they heard the blows of their father's axe. But what they really heard was a branch blown to and fro by the wind against the trunk of a tree. The father had bound the branch to the tree in this way so that the children should not know when he and his wife went home and left them alone in the forest.

They waited all the long afternoon until evening, but no-one came for them, and then Gretel began to cry. Hansel comforted her as best he could, and said, "Just wait until the moon rises, and I will take you home."

When the moon shone forth, Hansel and Gretel set off hand in hand. They found their way home quite easily, for the moon shone brightly on the pebbles which Hansel had dropped by the way, and showed them the road very plainly. Early in the morning they reached their cottage, and their father was very glad to see them again, for he had been full of sorrow at leaving them alone. The stepmother seemed glad too, but she was only pretending.

Well, a little while later there was again no bread for the family to eat, and Hansel and Gretel once more heard their step-mother say, "We shall starve if we do not get rid of the children. This time they must be taken so far into the wood that they *cannot* find the way out."

"No, no," answered the father; "we will share our last crust with the children, and then we will all die together."

But the wife stormed and scolded until the poor man gave way, and said he would do as she wished. Once more the children overheard what was said, and once more Hansel got up quietly and crept to the door, meaning to fill his pocket with pebbles. His stepmother, however, had locked the door, and he could not get out.

"Never mind," he said to his sister. "Go to sleep. I will find out a way."

Next morning the stepmother pulled the children roughly out of bed, handed them each a piece of bread, and led them away into the forest. As they walked on, Hansel crumbled his bread in his pocket, and every now and then stopped to drop a crumb on the path.

On they walked, but Hansel kept on dropping the crumbs. At last they got into the thickest part of the forest, and the step-mother felt sure that the children could not find their way back this time. Once more a fire was lighted, and once more the parents went off to chop wood, and told the children they would fetch them in the evening.

Gretel shared her bread with her brother, who had crumbled his up and strewn it on the path as they walked along. Then the children went to sleep until evening. When they woke, no-one came to fetch them. They decided to wait till the moon came out so they could see the crumbs of bread that would lead them home.

Alas! when the moon shone, they could not find any crumbs, for the birds had been busy all day picking them up. The children realised that they were really lost.

All night and all next day they trudged along, trying to find a way out of the wood; but all in vain. Oh, how hungry and tired they were! They were so weary that they lay down under a tree and fell asleep.

In the afternoon of the third day they felt so weak that they thought they were going to die. Just then they saw a beautiful snow-white bird on a bough. It sang to them sweetly and then flew off. Tired as they were, the children followed it, and soon came to a cottage—the most wonderful cottage they had ever seen, for it was made of gingerbread, with a roof of cake, and windows of barley sugar.

"Hurrah!" said Hansel. "Now we can have a feast." He reached up and broke a small piece off the roof, and Gretel had just broken a pane of barley sugar when a sweet voice from within called out:

"Tip, tap! who goes there?"

The children answered:

"The wind, the wind,
That flows through the air."

Hansel filled his mouth with the cake, and Gretel sucked away at the barley sugar, when suddenly the door opened and an ugly old woman came out. She was bent double with age, and was leaning on a big stick. Hansel and Gretel were frightened but the woman spoke kindly to them, and said: "My dear children, what are you doing here? Come inside and live with me. I will take care of you and make you very happy." The children went inside the cottage, and there

on the table was plenty to eat: milk and pancakes, sugar, apples, nuts, and lots of other things that children love. When they had eaten their fill, the old woman led them into the back room and showed them two nice little beds on which they were to sleep. Hansel and Gretel lay down and soon were fast asleep.

Now this ugly old fairy was really a witch, and a spiteful witch, and her house of gingerbread, cake and barley sugar was only a trap to entice children. When she got them inside her house she fed them until they were fat, and then killed them, cooked them, and gobbled them up!

Early in the morning she hobbled into the room where the children were sleeping, and looked at them. But their sweet faces did not make her feel a bit sorry for them, and she said, "The boy will make a good meal." So she roused Hansel, and put him in a big chicken-coop by himself. Then she roused Gretel, and sent her to the well for some water, and told her to cook breakfast. "Your brother," she said, "is shut up over there. I shall feed him well, and when he is nice and fat I shall eat him." Gretel began to cry, but the old Witch made her get breakfast ready. She cooked a nice meal, which the Witch and Hansel ate, while she got nothing but a crab's claw.

After breakfast the Witch hobbled off, and then Gretel ran to her brother and told him what was to be done to him. Hansel said, "Quick, Gretel, we must run away at once; but first go into the front room and bring the old woman's fairy wand." Gretel did so, and she waved it in front of Hansel's coop, and at once the front fell off and he was free. Then the children ran away.

They had not gone far when the old Witch came back to the cottage. She saw that the children had gone, and she ran to the window and looked out. Now, her eyesight was so keen that she could see for a long, long way. She spied Gretel and Hansel, and said to herself, "They have not gone very far; I shall soon overtake them."

Then she put on her magic boots and ran after the children. Every step she took was huge, and soon she drew near to the runaways. At once Gretel waved her wand, and what do you think happened? Water gushed out of the ground and spread out into a great lake. Hansel and Gretel were turned into beautiful swans, and soon were swimming about in the water. As for the old Witch, she was nowhere to be seen. Nobody knows what became of her, but I think she was probably drowned. When Gretel had been turned into a beautiful swan, she kept the magic wand in her beak. She now waved it

to and fro and suddenly the lake vanished, and the two swans were turned into children once more. Then Hansel and Gretel went back to the old Witch's house and found in a hiding place a basket full of diamonds and pearls and shining stones of all kinds and sizes. Hansel stuffed his pockets full of them, and Gretel put as many into her apron as it would hold.

Then the little white bird came to them singing sweetly and fluttering before them to show them the way out of the forest. Soon they saw their father's cottage, and then they began to run.

Oh, how pleased the father was to see his children once more! He had been the most unhappy man alive ever since the day when he had left them to die, as he thought, in the forest. He had driven his wife out of his house, and he had spent the time in mourning for his poor lost children. Hansel and Gretel now fell on their father's neck, and all three wept for joy. Then the children showed their father the diamonds, pearls and shining stones, and he told them they were worth ever so much money, and that they would never be poor again. So, after all their sorrow and trouble, Hansel and Gretel and their father found themselves rich, and lived happily ever after.

Grimm, *The Milk-White Thorn*

The Golden Goose

Once upon a time there was a man who had three sons. The youngest of these sons was thought by his father and brothers to be half-witted, and for this reason they mocked him and made fun of everything he did. But this youngest son, whose name was Peter, was not so silly after all, as this story will plainly show.

Well, one day the eldest son was sent by his father into the forest to chop wood for the winter. He was his mother's favourite, and before he started out she made him some nice pancakes and gave him a bottle of wine, so that he might not be hungry or thirsty while he was away from home. As this lad, whose name was Paul, entered the forest he met a little old man, who said: "Young sir, give me, please, one of your pancakes and a sip of wine out of your bottle, for I am fainting with hunger and thirst."

"Not I," said Paul. "If I were to give you a pancake and a drink of wine, I should have less to eat and drink myself. Not I, indeed. Just take yourself off, for you are nothing but a beggar."

The old man shook his head sadly and disappeared. Soon Paul began to cut down a tree, but his axe glanced off the trunk and cut his leg so badly that he was obliged to

limp home and have it bound up. On the way home he met the old man, who said to him: "That is the way in which I punish the greedy."

Next day the second son, whose name was Luke, was sent into the forest to do the work which his older brother had failed to do. His mother gave him a cake and a jar of cider, so that he might not be hungry or thirsty during the day. He had not gone far when he, too, met the old man, who said: "Young sir, give me, please, a piece of your cake and a sip of cider out of your jar, for I am fainting with hunger and thirst."

"Not I," said Luke. "You ought to be ashamed of yourself for asking a boy for his food and drink. Off with you, you old vagabond."

Soon the second son began to cut down a tree; but his axe stuck in the trunk, and in pulling hard at it to get it out it sprang back in his face and knocked several of his teeth out. He was so badly hurt that he went home at once, crying and moaning with the pain.

Next morning poor Peter, whom everybody called Silly Peter, asked his father to allow him to go and cut wood in the forest.

"No," said his father; "now that your clever brothers have failed, a half-witted fellow like you is not likely to succeed."

But Peter begged so hard that his father at last said: "Off with you. I suppose you won't give me any peace until you are hurt too."

Peter's mother gave him a piece of dry bread and a bottle of water, and off he went. He had not gone far before he, too, met the little old man.

"Young sir," he said, "give me, please, a crumb of your bread and a sip of water out of your bottle, for I am fainting with hunger and thirst."

"Certainly," answered Peter. "You are welcome to half my bread and half my water. Let us sit down here and I will divide it. I wish I had better food for your sake."

The boy and the old man sat down by the roadside, and Peter opened his basket. His eyes nearly jumped out of his head when he saw what it contained; for the bread had been turned into the most beautiful cake that was ever baked, and the water had been turned into the most delicious wine that was ever pressed out of grapes.

Peter and his companion made a hearty meal, and then the old man said:

"You are a kind-hearted lad. Unlike your two brothers, you gladly shared your dinner with me. Now I shall reward you. They call you silly, but you shall be rich and great. Do you see that old tree? Cut it down and at the roots you will find something very lucky. Farewell, my son, and keep your kind heart all your life."

So saying, the old man disappeared, and Peter began to chop down the tree. When it fell, he saw sitting at the roots a wonderful goose with feathers of pure gold. Peter took up the goose and, instead of going home with it, went to the nearest inn, where he stayed all night.

In the morning Peter started off with his goose under his arm. He had not gone far when a ploughman saw him, and shouted out: "I want a few feathers from that bird."

"Come and take them," cried Peter.

The man took hold of the bird's tail, but what do you think happened? His finger and thumb stuck fast, and try as he would he could not pull his hand away. He struggled with all his might, but he could not get free, and there he remained as if glued to the goose.

On they went, Peter and the unwilling ploughman, and as they crossed a field a country girl saw them. At once the ploughman cried out to her: "Come and help me to get free from this fellow."

The girl came to help him, but as soon as she touched the man her hand was held fast, and though she pulled and struggled with all her might, she too was obliged to follow Peter wherever he went.

Soon Peter and his train came to a village in which a fair was being held. In front of a show was a clown who was making the people laugh with his merry antics. When he saw Peter pass by with the ploughman and the girl, he cried out to them: "You must come into the show. You are more foolish than I am." He laid hold of the girl to try to stop her, but

to his surprise he too stuck fast and could not get free. So he also had to go wherever Peter went.

Soon they passed a chimney sweep, and the clown called out: "Come here and pull me away from this girl, and I will give you a silver crown." At once the chimney sweep took hold of the clown and tried to pull him away. But he too stuck fast, and on went Peter with the goose under his arm, followed by the ploughman, the girl, the clown, and the chimney sweep. Then they all fell a-crying and the policeman, hearing the noise, ran up to see what was the

matter. He put his hand on the chimney sweep's shoulder; but as soon as he did so he found himself held fast, and though he yelled threats and struggled with all his might, he too had to follow in Peter's train.

Hearing the hullabaloo, the policeman's wife ran to her window and, looking out, saw her husband trying to get away, but unable to do so. At once she ran out and threw her arms round the policeman. She too found herself held fast and obliged to go wherever Peter wished.

A little further on, Peter, the goose, the ploughman, the girl, the clown, the chimney sweep, the policeman and his wife, came to a city in which there was a princess who was so sad that nothing could make her smile. She was pining away, and the King, her father, was so full of grief that he was ready to give half his kingdom to the man who could make his daughter laugh. "He who makes my daughter the Princess laugh," he declared, "shall marry her and be my heir."

When Peter and his train came into the city, the people gathered round and began to roar with laughter at the strange sight. The King heard the noise and ran out of his palace. When he saw the ploughman, the girl, the clown, the chimney sweep, the policeman and his wife, all struggling to get free, their antics amused him so much that he laughed until he cried.

"Ha, ha, ha!" he said, "bring them to the Princess; and if they do not make her laugh, nothing will. Ha, ha, ha!"

So Peter and his procession passed under the window of the room in which the sad Princess sat, and one of her maids begged her to look out. She did so, and at once her sadness vanished. A smile of merriment appeared on her pale face, and she laughed aloud like the chime of sweet bells.

Never in his life had Peter heard anything so sweet, and was quite certain that he had never seen anyone half so beautiful. He fell in love with her on the spot.

"I have made her laugh," he said. "So she shall be my wife, and I shall be the King's heir."

When Peter went to the King and asked for his daughter's hand in marriage, the King was not willing to keep his word, for he thought that Peter was only a rough, common fellow and not at all fit to be his son-in-law.

"Before you can marry my daughter,"

he said, "you must bring me a man who can drink up all the wine in my cellar."

Peter was very much disappointed, but his face brightened when he thought of the old man, his friend. "He will help me, I know," thought Peter; "I will go and seek him."

So he went into the forest, and at last came to the fallen tree where he had found the goose. Here he saw an old man who looked very miserable indeed.

"Oh, oh!" he cried, "I have a most terrible thirst, and nothing seems able to quench it. I have drunk the brook dry, and I am just as thirsty as ever. What shall I do?"

"Come with me," said Peter, "and you shall drink your fill, I promise you."

So the old man went with Peter, and together they went into the King's cellar. What a thirst that man had, to be sure! He drank and drank, barrel after barrel of wine, and did not stop until there was not a drop of wine left.

Once more Peter went to the King and begged his daughter's hand in marriage. But the King was still unwilling to keep his word, and said: "Before you can marry my daughter you must bring me a man who can eat up a mountain of bread."

Once more Peter went off to the forest, and here he found a tall thin man who seemed to be in pain.

"Oh, oh!" he cried, pulling his belt in very tightly, "I am the hungriest man in the world. I have eaten all the loaves in a baker's shop, and I am hungrier than ever. What shall I do?"

"Come with me," said Peter, "and you shall eat your fill, I promise you."

So Peter took the hungry man to the mountain of bread. At once the man began to devour it, and before evening the whole mountain had disappeared.

Then Peter went to the King for the third time and begged his daughter's hand in marriage, but still the King was not willing to keep his word.

"Before you can marry my daughter," he said, "you must bring me a ship that will sail over the land just as well as it will sail over the water."

Poor Peter was much cast down, but he set off for the forest once again, for he thought, "Perhaps the little old man will help me one more time."

"Indeed I will," said a voice, and, looking round, Peter saw his friend. "I sent you the thirsty man and I sent you the hungry man, and now I will give you the ship that can travel by land and by sea. Here it is."

Peter looked, and a little way in front of him he saw a great wheeled ship with golden masts and silken sails. He thanked his friend and, jumping aboard, seized the tiller. Before you could say "Jack Robinson" his wonderful ship was in the King's courtyard.

The King was so surprised and delighted that he could no longer refuse to give his daughter to the young man who had done so much to win her. The wedding took place the next day, and Peter and his wife were the happiest couple in all the world. When the old King died, Peter took his place on the throne, and the Princess sat by his side, the loveliest queen that ever was seen.

Grimm, *The Milk-White Thorn*

Rumpelstiltzkin

There lived once upon a time a poor miller who had a very beautiful daughter. Now it happened one day that he had an audience with the King, and in order to appear a person of some importance he told him that he had a daughter who could spin straw into gold.

"Now that is a talent worth having," replied the King to the miller; "if your daughter is as clever as you say, bring her to my palace tomorrow, and I'll put her to the test."

When the girl was brought to him he led her into a room full of straw, gave her a spinning-wheel and a spindle, and said: "Now set to work and spin all night till early dawn, and if by that time you haven't spun the straw into gold you shall die." Then he closed the door behind him and left her alone inside.

The poor miller's daughter sat down, and didn't know what in the world she was to do. She had not the least idea of how to spin straw into gold, and became at last so miserable that the began to weep. Suddenly the door opened, and in stepped a tiny little man who said: "Good evening, Miss Miller-maid; why are you crying so bitterly?"

"Oh!" answered the girl, "I have to spin this straw into gold, and I haven't a notion how it's done."

"What will you give me if I spin it for you?" asked the manikin.

"I'll give you my necklace," said the girl.

The little man took the necklace, sat himself down at the wheel, and whir, whir, whir, the wheel went round three times, and the bobbin was full. Then he put on another, and whir, whir, whir, the wheel went round three times, and the second too was full; and so it went on till the morning, when all the straw was spun away, and all the bobbins were full of gold.

As soon as the sun rose the King came, and when he perceived the gold he was astonished and delighted, but his heart only lusted more than ever after the precious metal. He had the miller's daughter put into another room full of straw, much bigger than the first, and ordered her, if she valued her life, to spin it all into gold before the following morning.

The girl didn't know what to do, and began to cry; then the door opened as before, and the tiny little man appeared and said: "What will you give me if I spin the straw into gold for you?"

"I'll give you the ring from my finger," answered the girl.

The manikin took the ring, and whir! round went the spinning-wheel again, and when morning broke he had spun all the straw into glittering gold.

The King was pleased beyond measure at the sight, but his greed for gold was still not satisfied, and he had the miller's daughter brought into a yet bigger room full of straw, and said to her: "You must spin all this away in the night; but if you succeed this time you shall become my wife." "She's only a miller's daughter," he thought; "but I couldn't find a richer wife if I were to search the whole world over."

When the girl was alone the little man appeared for the third time, and said: "What will you give me if I spin the straw for you once again?"

"I've nothing more to give," answered the girl.

"Then promise me when you are Queen to give me your first child."

"Who knows what may not happen before that?" thought the miller's daughter; and besides, she saw no other way out of it, so she promised the manikin what he demanded, and he set to work once more and spun the straw into gold.

When the King came in the morning, and found everything as he had desired, he straightaway made her his wife, and the miller's daughter became a queen.

When a year had passed a beautiful son was born to her, and she thought no more of the little man, till all of a sudden one day he stepped into her room and said: "Now give me what you promised." The Queen was in a great state, and offered the little man all the riches in her kingdom if he would only leave her the child. But the

285

the other names she knew, in a string, but at each one the manikin called out: "That's not my name."

Next day she sent to inquire the names of all the people in the neighbourhood, and had a long list of the most uncommon and extraordinary for the little man when he made his appearance. "Is your name, Sheepshanks, Cruickshanks, Spindleshanks?" but he always replied: "That's not my name."

On the third day the messenger returned and announced: "I have not been able to find any new names, but as I came upon a high hill round the corner of the wood, where the foxes and hares bid each other good night, I saw a little house, and in front of the house burned a fire, and round the fire sprang the most grotesque little man, hopping on one leg and crying:

Tomorrow I brew, today
I bake,
And then the child away
I'll take;
For little deems my royal
dame
That Rumpelstiltzkin is my name!

You may imagine the Queen's delight at hearing the name, and when the little man stepped in shortly afterwards and asked: "Now, my lady Queen, what's my name?" she asked first: "Is your name Conrad?" "No." "Is your name Harry?" "No." "Is your name, perhaps, Rumpelstiltzkin?"

"Some demon has told you that, some demon has told you that," screamed the man, and in his rage drove his right foot so far into the ground that it sank in up to his waist; then in a passion he seized the left foot with both hands and tore himself in two.

Grimm, *The Blue Fairy Book*

manikin said: "No, a living creature is dearer to me than all the treasures in the world." Then the Queen began to cry and sob so bitterly that the little man was sorry for her, and said: "I'll give you three days to guess my name, and if you find it out in that time you may keep your child."

Then the Queen pondered the whole night over all the names she had ever heard, and sent a messenger to scour the land, and to pick up far and near any names he should come across. When the little man arrived on the following day she began with Kasper, Melchior, Belshazzar, and all

Goldilocks and the Three Bears

Three bears once lived by themselves in a little house in the forest. They were the huge Papa Bear, the big Mamma Bear, and the little Baby Bear. Their house had just two rooms—a big room to live in, and a small room upstairs to sleep in. Each of the Bears had a bowl and a spoon, a chair to sit on, and a bed to sleep in—all just of the right size.

A woodcutter lived near the edge of the forest, with his wife and young daughter. The little girl's hair was so fair that she was called Goldilocks. She often went into the forest with her father. Sometimes she went for a walk all alone.

One day little Goldilocks came to the Bears' house. She was a very rude little girl, I fear. First she peeped in at the window; but she saw no-one, as the Bears had gone for a walk. So she opened the door and walked in.

On the table stood three bowls full of porridge, which the Bears had left there to cool, to be ready when they came back. Goldilocks first tasted the big bowl, but the porridge was too salty. Then she tasted the middle bowl, but the porridge was too sweet. Then she tasted the little bowl, and the porridge was so good that she ate it all up.

Then she saw the three chairs. She tried to sit in the big chair, but it was too hard. She tried the middle chair, but it was too soft. Then she tried the little chair, but when she sat down in it the bottom fell out.

After this Goldilocks went upstairs to the Bears' bedroom, where she saw three beds. She was very tired from her walk, and thought it would be quite nice to take a short nap.

First she went to the big bed, but it was too high for her. She went to the middle bed, but it was too low. Then she went to

287

"Someone has been sitting in my chair, and has sat right through it," said the Baby Bear; and he began to cry. Now, no-one could be found in the room, so the Three Bears went upstairs to their bedroom, to look for "someone" there. "Someone has been in my bed," roared the big Papa Bear. "Someone has been in my bed," shouted the big Mamma Bear. "Someone has been in my bed," screamed the little Baby Bear, "and here she is still."

The roar and the shout and the scream woke Goldilocks from her nap. She sprang up, turned to the open window, and jumped out as quick as a flash.

The Three Bears also made a rush for the window. But they were in such a hurry that they all stuck fast in it, and could not get out.

Long before they got out at the door, Goldilocks was far away in the forest; and you may be sure that she ran all the way home as fast as she could.

Anon., *The Milk-White Thorn*

the little bed, and it suited her so well that she soon fell fast asleep.

Before long the Three Bears came home again quite ready for breakfast.

"Someone has been at my porridge," cried the Papa Bear in his great big, rough voice.

"Someone has been at my porridge," cried the Mamma Bear in her big, smooth voice.

"Someone has been at my porridge," cried the Baby Bear in his little, squeaky voice, "and has eaten it all up."

Then they looked all round the room to find out who had been at the porridge, and at once they saw that the chairs were all out of their places.

"Someone has been sitting in my chair," cried the great big Papa Bear.

"Someone has been sitting in my chair," said the Mamma Bear.

Why the Sea is Salt

Once upon a time, long ago, there were two brothers, one rich and the other poor. When Christmas Eve came, the poor one had not a bite in the house, either of meat or bread; so he went to his brother and begged him to give him something for Christmas Day. It was not the first time the brother had been forced to give something to him, and he was not better pleased by being asked now than he generally was.

"If you will do what I ask you, you shall have a whole ham," he said. The poor one immediately thanked him, and promised he would do this.

"Well, here is the ham, and now you must go straight to Dead Man's Hall," said the rich brother, throwing the ham to him.

"Well, I will do what I have promised," said the other, and he took the ham and set off. He travelled on and on all day, and at nightfall he came to a place where there was a bright light.

"I have no doubt this is the place," thought the poor brother with the ham. An old man with a long white beard was standing in the shed, chopping logs.

"Good evening," said the poor brother with the ham.

"Good evening to you. Where are you going at this late hour?" asked the man.

"I am going to Dead Man's Hall, if only I am on the right track," answered the poor brother.

"Oh! yes, you are right enough, for it is here," replied the old man. "When you get inside they will all want to buy your ham, for they don't get much meat to eat there: but you must not sell it unless you can get the hand-mill which stands behind the door for it. When you come out again I will teach you how to stop the hand-mill, which is useful for almost everything.

So the man with the ham thanked the other for his good advice, and rapped at the door.

When he got in, everything happened just as the old man had said it would: all the people, great and small, came round him like ants on an ant-hill, and each tried to outbid the other for the ham.

"By rights my wife and I ought to have it for our Christmas dinner, but, since you have set your hearts upon it, I must just give it up to you," said the man. "But, if I sell it, I will have the hand-mill which is standing there behind the door."

At first they would not hear of this, and haggled and bargained with the man, but he stuck to what he had said, and they were forced to give him the hand-mill. When the man came out again into the yard, he asked the old woodcutter how he was to stop the hand-mill, and when he had learnt that he thanked him and set off home with all the speed he could, but did not get there until after the clock had struck the hour of twelve on Christmas Eve.

"But wherever in the world have you been?" asked the man's wife. "Here I have sat waiting hour after hour, and have not even two sticks to lay across each other under the Christmas porridge pot."

"Oh! I could not come before; I had something of importance to see about, and a long way to go, too; but now you shall just see!" said the man, and then he set the hand-mill on the table, and ordered it first to grind light, then a tablecloth, and then meat, and beer, and everything else that was good for a Christmas Eve's supper; and the mill ground all that he ordered. "Bless me!" said his wife as one thing after another appeared; and she wanted to know where her husband had got the mill from, but he would not tell her that.

"Never mind where I got it; you can see that it is a good one, and the water that turns it will never freeze," said the man. So he ground meat and drink and all kinds of good things, to last all Christmas time, and on the third day he invited all his friends to come to a feast.

Now when the rich brother saw all that there was at the banquet and in the house, he was both vexed and very angry, for he begrudged everything his brother had. "On Christmas Eve he was so poor that he came to me and begged for a trifle and now he gives a feast as if he were both a count and a king!" he thought. "But tell me where you got your riches from," he said to his brother.

"From behind the door," said the poor brother, for he did not choose to satisfy his brother on that point; however, later in the evening, when he had taken a drop too much, he could not refrain from telling how he had come by the hand-mill. "There you see what has brought me all my wealth!" he said, and brought out the mill, and made it grind first one thing and then another. When the rich brother saw that he insisted on having the mill, and after a great deal of persuasion he got it; but he had to give three hundred dollars for it, and the poor brother was to keep it till the haymaking was over, for he thought; "If I keep it as long as that, I can make it grind meat and drink that will last many a long year."

During that time you may imagine that the mill did not grow rusty, and when harvest time came the rich brother got it, but the other had taken good care not to teach him how to stop it. It was evening when the rich man got the mill home, and in the morning he told his wife to go out and spread the hay after the mowers, and he would attend to the house himself that day, he said.

So, when dinner time drew near, he set the mill down on the kitchen table, and said: "Grind herrings and porridge, and do it both quickly and well." So the mill began to grind herrings and porridge, and first all the dishes and tubs were filled, and then it came out all over the kitchen floor. The man twisted and turned it, and did all he could to make the mill stop, but, however he turned it and screwed it, the mill went on grinding, and in a short time the porridge rose so high that the man was in danger of drowning. So he threw open the living room door, but it was not long before the mill had ground the living room full too, and it was with difficulty and danger that the man could go through the stream of porridge and get hold of the door latch. When he got the door open, he ran out, and the herrings and porridge came after him, and it streamed out over both farm and field.

Now his wife, who was out spreading the hay, began to think dinner was long in coming, and said to the women and the mowers: "Though the master does not call us home, we may as well go. It may be that he finds he is not good at making porridge, and I should do well to help him. "So they began to straggle homewards, but when they had got a little way up the hill they met the herrings and porridge, all pouring forth and winding about one over the other, and the man himself in front of the flood. "If only each of you had a hundred stomachs! Take care that you are not drowned in all this porridge!" he cried as he went by them, down to where his brother lived. Then he begged him to take the mill back again at once, for, he said: "If it grind just one more hour the whole district will be destroyed by herrings and porridge." But the brother would not take it until the other paid him three hundred dollars, and that he was obliged to do.

Now the poor brother had both the money and the mill again. So it was not long before he had a farmhouse much finer than that in which his brother lived, but the mill ground him so much money that he covered it with plates of gold; and the farmhouse lay close by the sea, so it shone and glittered far out to sea. Everyone who sailed by there now had to put in to visit the rich man in the gold farmhouse, and everyone wanted to see the wonderful mill, for the report of it spread far and wide, and there was no-one who had not heard of it.

After a long, long time there came a skipper who wished to see the hand-mill. He asked if it could make salt. "Yes, it can make salt," said the man who owned it, and when the skipper heard that he wished with all his might to have the mill, let it cost what it might, for, he thought, if he had it, he would no longer have to sail far away over the perilous sea for freights of salt. At first the man would not hear of parting with it, but the skipper begged, and at last the man sold it to him, and got many, many thousand dollars for it. When the skipper had got the mill on his back he did not stay there long, for he was so afraid that the man should change his mind, and he had no time to ask how he was to stop it grinding, but got on board his ship as fast as he could.

When he had gone a little way out to sea he took the mill on deck. "Grind salt, and grind both quickly and well," commanded the skipper. So the mill began to grind salt, and kept grinding till it spouted out like water, and when the skipper had got the ship filled he wanted to stop the mill, but, whichever way he turned it, and however much he tried, it went on grinding, and the heap of salt grew higher and higher, until at last the ship sank.

There lies the mill at the bottom of the sea, and still, day by day, it grinds on: and that is why the sea is salt.

Asbjørnsen and Möe, *The Blue Fairy Book*

The Flying Trunk

There was once a merchant who was so rich that he could have paved the whole street, and perhaps even a little side street besides, with silver. But he did not do that; he knew another way of spending his money. If he spent a shilling he got back two—such an excellent merchant he was—till he died.

Now his son inherited all this money. He lived very merrily; he went every night to the theatre, made paper kites out of five-pound notes, and played ducks and drakes with sovereigns instead of stones. In this way the money was likely to come soon to an end, and that's just what happened.

At last he had nothing left but four shillings, and he had no clothes except a pair of slippers and an old dressing-gown. His friends did not trouble themselves any more about him; they would not even walk down the street with him. But one of them who was rather good-natured sent him an old trunk with the message, "Pack up!" That was all very well, but he had nothing to pack up, so he sat on the trunk.

It was an enchanted trunk, for as soon as the lock was pressed it could fly. He pressed it, and away he flew in it up the chimney, high into the clouds, further and further away. But whenever the bottom gave a little creak he was in terror lest the trunk should go to pieces, for then he would have turned a dreadful somersault—just think of it!

In this way he arrived at the land of the Turks. He hid the trunk in a wood under some dry leaves, and then walked into the town. He could do that quite well, for all the Turks were dressed just as he was—in a dressing-gown and slippers.

He met a nurse with a little child. "Hello!" he said, "what is that great castle there close to the town? The one with the windows so high up?"

"The Sultan's daughter lives there," she answered. "It is prophesied that she will be very unlucky in her husband, and so no-one is allowed to see her except when the Sultan and Sultana are nearby."

"Thank you," said the merchant's son, and he went into the wood, sat on his trunk, flew on to the roof, and crept through the window into the Princess' room.

She was lying on the sofa asleep, and was so beautiful that the young merchant *had* to kiss her. Then she woke up and was very much frightened, but he said he was a Turkish god who had come through the air to see her, and that pleased her very much.

They sat close to each other, and he told her a story about her eyes. They were beautiful dark lakes in which her thoughts swam about like graceful mermaids. And her forehead was a snowy mountain, grand and shining. These were lovely stories.

Then he asked the Princess to marry him, and she agreed at once.

"But you must come here on Saturday," she said, "for the Sultan and the Sultana are coming to tea with me. They will be indeed proud that I receive the god of the Turks. But mind you have a really good story ready, for my parents like them immensely. My mother likes something rather moral and high-flown, and my father likes something merry to make him laugh."

"Yes, I shall only bring a fairy story for my dowry," he said, and so they parted. But the Princess gave him a sabre set with gold pieces which he could use.

Then he flew away, bought himself a new dressing-gown, and sat down in the wood and began to make up a story, for it had to be ready by Saturday, and that was no easy matter.

When he had it ready it was Saturday. The Sultan, the Sultana, and the whole Court were at tea with the Princess. He was most graciously received.

"Will you tell us a story?" asked the Sultana; "one that is thoughtful and also instructive?"

"But something that we can laugh at," said the Sultan.

"Oh, certainly," he replied, and began: "Now, listen attentively. There was once a box of matches which lay between a tinder box and an old iron pot, and they told the story of their youth.

" 'We used to be on the green fir boughs. Every morning and evening we had diamond tea, which was the dew, and all day long we had sunshine, and the little birds used to tell us stories. We were rich, because the other trees only dressed in summer, but we had green dresses in summer and winter. Then the woodcutter came, and our family was split up. We have now the task of making light for the lowest people. That is why we grand people are in the kitchen.'

" 'My fate was quite different,' said the iron pot, near which the matches lay.

" 'Since I came into the world I have been many times scoured, and have cooked much. My only pleasure is to have a good chat with my companions when I am lying nice and clean in my place after dinner.'

" 'Now you are talking too fast,' spluttered the fire.

" 'Yes, let us decide who is the grandest!' said the matches.

" 'No, I don't like talking about myself,' said the pot.

" 'Let us arrange an evening's entertainment. I will tell the story of my life.

" 'On the Baltic by the Danish shore—'

" 'What a beautiful beginning!' said all the plates. 'That is a story that will please us all.'

"And the end was just as good as the beginning. All the plates clattered for joy.

" 'Now I will dance,' said the tongs, and she danced. Oh! how high she could kick! The old chair-cover in the corner split when he saw her. The urn would have sung but she said she had a cold; she could not sing unless she boiled.

"In the window was an old quill pen. There was nothing remarkable about her except that she had been dipped too deeply into the ink. But she was extremely proud of that.

" 'If the urn will not sing,' she declared, 'outside the door hangs a nightingale in a cage who will sing.'

" '*I* don't think it is proper,' said the kettle, 'that such a foreign bird should be heard.'

" 'Oh, let us have some acting,' said everyone. 'Do let us!'

"Suddenly the door opened and the maid came in. Everyone was quite quiet. There was not a sound. But each pot knew what he might have done, and how grand he was. The maid took the matches and lit the fire with them. How they spluttered and flamed, to be sure! 'Now everyone can see,' they thought, 'that we are the grandest! How we sparkle! What a light—'

"But here they were burnt out."

"That was a delightful story!" said the Sultana. "I quite feel myself in the kitchen with the matches. Yes, now you shall marry our daughter."

"Yes, indeed," agreed the Sultan, "you shall marry our daughter on Monday." And they treated the young man as one of the family. The wedding was arranged, and the night before the whole town was illuminated. Biscuits and gingerbreads were thrown among the people, the street boys stood on tip-toe crying hurrahs and whistling through their fingers. It was all splendid.

"Now I must also give them a treat," thought the merchant's son. So he bought rockets, crackers, and all the kinds of fireworks you can think of, put them in his trunk, and flew up with them into the air.

Whirr-r-r, how they fizzed and blazed! All the Turks jumped so high that their slippers flew above their heads; such a splendid glitter they had never seen before. Now they could quite well understand that it was the god of the Turks himself who was to marry the Princess.

As soon as the young merchant came down again into the wood with his trunk he thought, "Now I will just go into the town to see how the show has taken." And it was quite natural that he should want to do this.

Oh! what stories the people had to tell! Each one whom he asked had seen it differently, but they had all found it beautiful. "I saw the Turkish god himself," said one. "He had eyes like glittering stars, and a beard like foaming water." "He flew away in a cloak of fire," said another. They were splendid things that he heard, and the next day was to be his wedding day.

Then he went back into the wood to sit in his trunk; but what had become of it?

The trunk had been burnt. A spark of the fireworks had set it alight, and the trunk was in ashes. He no longer had the means to fly, and would never be able to reach his beautiful bride.

She stood the whole day long on the roof and waited; perhaps she is waiting there still. But he wandered through the world and told stories; though they are not nearly so merry as the one he told about the matches.

Andersen, *The Pink Fairy Book*

The Swineherd

There was once upon a time a poor prince. He possessed a kingdom which, though small, was yet large enough for him to marry on, and married he wished to be.

Now it was certainly a little audacious of him to venture to say to the Emperor's daughter, "Will you marry me?" But he did venture to say so, for his name was known far and wide. There were hundreds of princesses who would gladly have said "Yes," but would she say the same?

Well, we shall see.

On the grave of the Prince's father grew a rose tree, a very beautiful rose tree. It only bloomed every five years, and then bore but a single rose, but oh, such a rose! Its scent was so sweet that when you smelt it you forgot all your cares and troubles. And he had also a nightingale which could sing as if all the beautiful melodies in the world were locked up in its little throat. The Prince determined that the Princess was to have this rose and this nightingale, and so they were both put into silver caskets and sent to her. The Emperor had them brought to him in the great hall, where the Princess was playing with her ladies-in-waiting. When she caught sight of the big caskets which contained the presents, she clapped her hands for joy. "If only it were a little pussy cat!" she said. But the rose tree with the beautiful rose came out. "But how prettily it is made!" said all the ladies-in-waiting. "It is more than pretty," said the Emperor, "it is charming!" But the Princess felt it, and then she almost began to cry. "Ugh! Papa," she said, "it is not artificial, it is *real!*"

298

"Ugh!" said all the ladies-in-waiting, "it is real!"

"Let us see first what is in the other casket before we begin to be angry," the Emperor, thought and out came the nightingale. It sang so beautifully that one could scarcely utter a cross word against it.

"*Superbe! charmant!*" said the ladies-in-waiting, for they all chattered French, each one worse than the other.

"How much the bird reminds me of the musical snuff-box of the late Empress!" said an old courtier. "Ah, yes, it sounds just the same!"

"Yes," said the Emperor; and then he wept like a little child.

"I hope that this, at least, is not real?" asked the Princess.

"Yes, it is a real bird," said those who had brought it.

"Then let the bird fly away," said the Princess; and she would not on any account allow the Prince to come.

But he was not daunted. He painted his face brown and black, drew his cap well over his face, and knocked at the door. "Good-day, Emperor," he said. "Can I get a place here as servant in the castle?"

"Yes," said the Emperor, "but there are so many who ask for a place that I don't know whether there will be one for you; but, still, I will think of you. Wait, it has just occurred to me that I want someone to look after the swine, for I have so very many of them."

And the Prince got the situation of Imperial Swineherd. He had a wretched little room close to the pigsties; here he had to stay, but the whole day he sat working, and when evening had come he had made a pretty little pot. All round it were little bells, and when the pot boiled they jingled most beautifully and played the old tune:

"Where is Augustus dear?
Alas! he's not here, here, here!"

But the most wonderful thing was, that when one held one's finger in the steam of the pot, then at once one could smell what dinner was being cooked in any fireplace in the town. That was indeed something quite different from the rose.

Now the Princess came walking past with all her ladies-in-waiting, and when she heard the tune she stood still and her face beamed with joy, for she also could play "Where is Augustus dear?" It was the only tune she knew, and she could play it with one finger.

"Why, that is the tune I play!" she said. "He must be a most accomplished swineherd! Listen! Go down and ask him what the instrument costs."

And one of the ladies-in-waiting had to go down; but she put on wooden clogs. "What will you take for the pot?" asked the lady-in-waiting.

"I will have ten kisses from the Princess," answered the Swineherd.

"Heaven forbid!" said the lady-in-waiting.

"Yes, I will sell it for nothing less," replied the Swineherd.

"Well, what does he say?" asked the Princess.

"I really hardly like to tell you," answered the lady-in-waiting.

"Oh, then you can whisper it to me."

"He is disobliging!" said the Princess, and walked away. But she had only gone a few steps when she heard the bells ring out so prettily:

"Where is Augustus dear?
Alas! he's not here, here, here."

"Listen!" said the Princess. "Ask him whether he will take ten kisses from my ladies-in-waiting."

"No, thank you," said the Swineherd. "Ten kisses from the Princess, or else I keep my pot."

"That is extremely tiresome!" said the Princess. "But you must put yourselves in front of me, so that no-one can see."

And so the ladies-in-waiting placed themselves in front and then spread out their dresses; so the Swineherd got his ten kisses, and she got the pot.

What happiness that was! Throughout the whole night and the whole day the pot was made to boil; there was not a fireplace in the whole town where they did not know what was being cooked, whether it was at the chancellor's or at the shoemaker's.

All the ladies-in-waiting danced and clapped their hands. "We know who is going to have soup and pancakes; we know

who is going to have sausages and porridge —isn't it interesting?"

"Yes, very interesting!" said the first lady-in-waiting.

"But don't say anything about it, for I am the Emperor's daughter."

"Oh, no, of course we won't!" replied everyone.

The Swineherd—that is to say, the Prince (though they did not know he was anything but a true Swineherd)—let no day pass without making something, and one day he made a rattle which, when it was turned round, played all the music for dancing which had ever been known since the world began.

"But that is *superbe!*" said the Princess as she passed by. "I've never heard a more beautiful composition. Listen! Go down and ask him what this instrument costs; but I won't kiss him again."

"He wants a hundred kisses from the Princess," said the lady-in-waiting who had gone down to ask him.

"I believe he is mad!" said the Princess, and then she went on; but she had only gone a few steps when she stopped.

"One ought to encourage art," she said. "I am the Emperor's daughter! Tell him he shall have, as before, ten kisses; the rest he can take from my ladies-in-waiting."

"But we don't at all like being kissed by him," said the ladies-in-waiting.

"That's nonsense," said the Princess; "and if I can kiss him, you can too. Besides, remember that I give you board and lodging."

So the ladies-in-waiting had to go down to him again.

"A hundred kisses from the Princess," he said, "or each keeps his own."

"Put yourselves in front of us," she said then; and so all the ladies-in-waiting put themselves in front, and he began to kiss the Princess.

"What can that commotion be by the pigsties?" asked the Emperor, who was standing on the balcony. He rubbed his eyes and put on his spectacles. "Why, those are the ladies-in-waiting playing their games; I must go down to them." So he took off his shoes, which were shoes though he had trodden them down into slippers. What a hurry he was in!

As soon as he came into the yard the Emperor walked very softly, and the ladies-in-waiting were so busy counting the kisses and seeing fair play that they never noticed the Emperor. He stood on tip-toe.

"What is that?" he said, when he saw the kissing; and then he threw one of his slippers at their heads just as the Swineherd was about to take his eighty-sixth kiss.

"Be off with you!" said the Emperor, for he was very angry. And the Princess and the Swineherd were driven out of the empire.

Then she stood still and wept; the Swineherd was scolding, and the rain was streaming down.

"Alas, what an unhappy creature I am!" sobbed the Princess. "If only I had taken the beautiful Prince! Alas, how unfortunate I am!"

And the Swineherd went behind a tree, washed the black and brown off his face, threw away all his old clothes, and then stepped forward in his splendid clothes, looking so beautiful that the Princess was obliged to curtsy.

"I now come to this. I despise you!" he said. "You would have nothing to do with a noble Prince; you did not understand the rose or the nightingale, but you could kiss the Swineherd for the sake of a toy. This is what you get for it!" And he went into his kingdom and shut the door in her face, and she had to stay outside singing:

"Where's my Augustus dear?
Alas! he's not here, here, here!"

Andersen, *The Yellow Fairy Book*

301

Little Red Riding-Hood

Once there was a little village girl, the prettiest ever seen. Her mother was very fond of her, and her grandmother likewise. The old woman made for her a little hood, which suited the girl so well that ever after she went by the name of Little Red Riding-Hood.

One day, when her mother was making cakes, she said, "My child, you shall go and see your grandmother, for I hear she is not well; and you shall take her some of these cakes and a pot of butter."

Little Red Riding-Hood was delighted to go, though it was a long walk; but she was a good child and very fond of her kind grandmother.

Passing through a wood, she met a great wolf, who was most eager to eat her up but dared not because of a woodcutter who was busy close by. So he only came and asked her politely where she was going.

The poor child, who did not know how dangerous it is to stop and speak to wolves, replied, "I am going to see my grandmother, and to take her a cake and a pot of butter which my mother has sent her."

"Is it very far from here?" asked the Wolf.

"Oh, yes, it is just above the mill which you may see up there— the first house you come to in the village."

"Well," said the Wolf, "I will go there also, to inquire after your excellent grandmother. I will go one way and you the other, and we will see who can be there first."

So he ran as fast as he could, taking the shortest road. However, the little girl took the longest; for she stopped to pluck roses in the wood, to chase butterflies and gather the prettiest flowers she could find— she was such a happy little soul.

The Wolf was not long in reaching the grandmother's door. He knocked, Toc—toc, and the grandmother said, "Who is there?"

"It is your granddaughter, Little Red Riding-Hood," replied the wicked beas imitating the girl's soft voice; "I bring you a cake and a pot of butter which my mother has sent you."

The grandmother, who was ill in her bed, said, "Very well, dear; pull the string and the latch will open."

The Wolf pulled the string—the door flew open; he leaped in, attacked the poor old woman, and ate her up in less than no time, tough as she was, for he had not tasted anything for more than three days.

Then he carefully shut the door and, laying himself down snugly in the bed, waited for Little Red Riding-Hood. It was not long before she came and knocked, Toc—toc, at the door.

"Who is there?" said the Wolf; and the girl, hearing his gruff voice, felt sure that her poor grandmother must have caught a cold and be very ill indeed. So she answered cheerfully, "It is your granddaughter, Little Red Riding-Hood, who brings you a cake and a pot of butter which my mother has sent you."

Then the Wolf, softening his voice as much as he could, said, "Pull the string and the latch will open."

So Little Red Riding-Hood pulled the string and the door opened. The Wolf, on seeing her enter, hid himself as much as he could under the quilt, and said in a whisper, "Put the cake and the pot of butter on the shelf, and then come to bed, for it is very late." Little Red Riding-Hood did not think so; but to please her grandmother she began to get ready for bed, when she was very much astonished to find how different the old woman looked from ordinary.

"Grandmother, what great big arms you have!" she said, almost in a whisper.

"That is to hug you better, my dear."

"Grandmother, what great big ears you have!"

"That is to hear you better, my dear."

"Grandmother, what great big eyes you have!"

"That is to see you better, my dear."

"Grandmother, what a great big mouth you have!"

"That is to eat you all up," cried the wicked Wolf; and he was going to do so, when the door opened and a man rushed in. It was the woodcutter with his axe. In less than no time he had killed the Wolf, and Little Red Riding-Hood was saved.

Perrault, *The Milk-White Thorn*

Toads and Diamonds

There was once upon a time a widow who had two daughters. The eldest was so much like her in the face and temperament that whoever looked upon the daughter saw the mother. They were both so disagreeable and so proud that there was no living with them.

The youngest, who was the very picture of her father for courtesy and sweetness of temperament, was also one of the most beautiful girls ever seen. As people naturally love their own likeness, this mother doted on her eldest daughter, and at the same time had a horrible aversion for the youngest— she made her eat in the kitchen and work continually.

Among other things, this poor child was forced twice a day to fetch water a long way from the house, and bring home a pitcher full of it. One day, as she was at this fountain, there came to her a poor woman, who begged her to let her drink.

"Oh! yes, with all my heart," said this pretty little girl; and rinsing the pitcher, she took up some water from the clearest place of the fountain, and gave it to her, holding up the pitcher all the while, that she might drink more easily.

The good woman having drunk, said to her: "You are so pretty, my dear, so good and so mannerly, that I cannot help giving you a gift." For this was a fairy, who had taken the form of a poor country woman, to see how far the civility and good manners of this pretty girl would go. "I will give you as a gift," continued the Fairy, "that, at every word you speak, there shall come out of your mouth either a flower or a jewel."

When this pretty girl came home her mother scolded her for staying so long at the fountain.

"I beg your pardon, Mamma," said the poor girl, "for not making more haste." And in speaking these words there came out of her mouth two roses, two pearls and two diamonds. "Well, what is this I see there?" said her mother, quite astonished. "I think I see pearls and diamonds come out of the girl's mouth! How does this happen, child?"

This was the first time she ever called her child. The poor girl told her everything frankly, not without dropping out infinite numbers of diamonds. "Truly," cried the mother, "I must send my child there. Come here; look what

comes out of your sister's mouth when she speaks. Would you not be glad, my dear, to have the same gift given to you? You have nothing else to do but go and draw water out of the fountain, and when a certain poor woman asks you to let her drink, to give it to her very civilly."

"It would be a fine sight indeed," said this ill-bred girl, "to see me draw water."

"You shall go!" said the mother; "this minute." So away she went, but grumbling all the way, taking with her the best silver tankard in the house.

She was no sooner at the fountain than she saw coming out of the wood a lady most gloriously dressed, who came up to her and asked to drink. This was, you must know, the very Fairy who appeared to her sister, but had now taken the air and dress of a princess, to see how far this girl's rudeness would go.

"Have I come here," replied the proud, saucy girl, "to serve you with water? I suppose the silver tankard was brought purely for your ladyship, was it? However, you may drink out of it, if you have a fancy."

"You are not very mannerly," answered the Fairy, without putting herself in a rage. "Well, then, since you have so little breeding, and are so disobliging, I give you as a gift that at every word you speak there shall come out of your mouth a snake or a toad."

As soon as her mother saw her coming she cried out: "Well, Daughter?"

"Well, Mother?" answered the pert girl, throwing out of her mouth two vipers and two toads.

"Oh! mercy," cried the mother; "what is this I see? Oh! it is that wretch her sister who has brought about all this; but she shall pay for it;" and immediately she ran to beat her. The poor child fled away from her, and went to hide herself in the forest.

The King's son, then on his return from hunting, met her, and seeing her so very pretty, asked her what she was doing there alone and why she cried.

"Alas! sir, my mamma has turned me out-of-doors."

The King's son, who saw several pearls and diamonds come out of the girl's mouth, desired her to tell him how that happened. She told him the whole story; and so the King's son fell in love with her, and, considering that such a gift was worth more than any marriage portion, conducted her to the palace of the King his father, and there married her.

As for her sister, she made herself so much hated that her own mother turned her out; and the miserable wretch, having wandered about for a good while without finding anybody to take her in, went to a corner of the wood, and there died.

Perrault, *The Blue Fairy Book*

The Steadfast Tin Soldier

There were once upon a time five-and-twenty tin soldiers—all brothers, as they were made out of the same old tin spoon. Their uniform was red and blue, and they shouldered their guns and looked straight in front of them. The first words that they heard in this world, when the lid of the box in which they lay was taken off, were: "Hurrah, tin soldiers!" from a little boy, clapping his hands; they had been given to him because it was his birthday, and now he began setting them out on the table. Each soldier was exactly like the others in shape, except just one, who had been made last when the tin had run short; but there he stood as firmly on his one leg as the others did on two, and he is the one that became famous.

There were many other toys on the table on which they were being set out, but the nicest of all was a pretty little castle made of cardboard, with small windows through which you could see into the rooms. In front of the castle stood some little trees surrounding a tiny mirror which looked like a lake. Wax swans were floating about and reflecting themselves in it. That was all very pretty; but the most beautiful thing was a little woman, who stood in the open doorway. She was cut out of paper, but she had on a dress of the finest muslin, with a scarf of narrow blue ribbon draped round her shoulders, fastened in the middle with a glittering rose made of gold paper, which was as large as her head. The little woman was stretching out both her arms, for she was a dancer, and was lifting up one leg so high in the air that the Tin Soldier couldn't find it anywhere, and thought that she, too, had only one leg.

"That's the wife for me!" he thought; "but she is so grand, and lives in a castle, while I have only an old box with four-and-twenty others. This is no place for her! But I must make her acquaintance." Then he stretched himself out behind a snuff-box

306

that lay on the table; from there he could watch the dainty little woman, who continued to stand on one leg without losing her balance.

When the night came all the other tin soldiers went into their box, and the people of the house went to bed. Then the toys began to play at visiting, dancing and fighting. The tin soldiers rattled in their box, for they wanted to be out too, but they could not raise the lid. The nutcrackers played at leap-frog, and the slate-pencil ran about the slate; there was such a noise that the canary woke and began to talk to them, in poetry too! The only two who did not stir from their places were the Tin Soldier and the Dancer. She remained on tip-toe, with both arms outstretched; he stood steadfastly on his one leg, never moving his eyes from her face.

The clock struck twelve, and crack! off flew the lid of the snuff-box; but there was no snuff inside, only a little black imp—that was the beauty of it.

"Hullo, Tin Soldier!" said the imp. "Don't look at things that aren't intended for the likes of you!" But the Tin Soldier took no notice, and seemed not to hear.

"Very well then, wait till tomorrow!" said the imp.

When it was morning, and the children had got up, the Tin Soldier was put in the window; and whether it was the wind or the little black imp, I don't know, but all at once the window flew open and out fell the little Tin Soldier, head over heels, from the third-storey window! That was a terrible fall, I can tell you! He landed on his head with his one leg in the air, his gun wedged between two paving stones.

The nursery maid and little boy came down at once to look for him, but, though they were so near him that they almost trod on him, they did not notice him. If the Tin Soldier had only called out "Here I am!" they must have found him; but he did not think it fitting for him to cry out, because he had on his uniform.

Very soon it began to drizzle; then the drops came faster, and there was a regular downpour. When it was all over, two little street boys came along.

"Just look!" exclaimed one. "Here is a tin soldier! He shall sail up and down in a boat!"

They quickly made a little boat out of newspaper, put the Tin Soldier in it, and made him sail up and down the gutter; both boys ran along beside him, clapping their hands. What great waves there were in the gutter, and what a swift current! The paper boat tossed up and down, and in the middle of the stream it went so quickly that the Tin Soldier trembled; but he remained steadfast, showed no emotion, and looked straight in front of him, shouldering his gun. All of a sudden the boat passed under a long tunnel that was as dark as his box had been.

"Where can I be coming to now?" he wondered. "Oh, dear! This is the black imp's fault! Ah, if only the little woman were sitting beside me in the boat, it might be twice as dark for all I should care!" Suddenly there came along a great water rat that lived in the tunnel. "Have you a passport?" asked the rat. "Out with your passport!" But the Tin Soldier was silent, and grasped his gun more firmly. The boat sped on, and the rat behind it. Ugh! how he showed his teeth, as he cried to the chips of wood and straw: "Hold him, hold him! he has not paid the toll! He has not shown his passport!"

But the current became swifter and stronger. The Tin Soldier could already see daylight where the tunnel ended; but in his ears there sounded a roaring enough to frighten any brave man. Only think! at the end of the tunnel the gutter discharged itself into a large canal; that would be just as dangerous for him as it would be for us to go down a waterfall.

Now he was so near to it that he could not hold on any longer. On went the boat, the poor Tin Soldier keeping himself as stiff as he could: no-one should say of him afterwards that he had flinched. The boat whirled three, then four times round, and became filled to the brim with water: it began to sink! The Tin Soldier was standing up to his neck in water, and deeper and deeper sank the boat, and softer and softer grew the paper; now the water was over his head. He was thinking of the pretty little Dancer, whose face he should never see again, and there sounded in his ears, over and over again:

"Forward, forward, soldier bold!
Death's before you, grim and cold!"

The paper tore in two, and the soldier fell—but at that moment he was swallowed by a great fish. Oh! how dark it was inside, even darker than in the tunnel, and it was really very close quarters! But there the steadfast little Tin Soldier lay full length, shouldering his gun.

Up and down swam the fish, then he made the most dreadful contortions, and became suddenly quite still. Then it was as if a flash of lightning had passed through him; the daylight streamed in, and a voice exclaimed, "Why, here is the little Tin

Soldier!" The fish had been caught, taken to market, sold and brought into the kitchen, where the cook had cut it open with a large knife.

She took up the Tin Soldier between her finger and thumb, and carried him into the room, where everyone wanted to see the hero who had been found inside a fish; but the Tin Soldier was not at all proud. They put him on the table, and—no, but what strange things do happen in this world!—the Tin Soldier was in the same room in which he had been before! He saw the same children, and the same toys on the table; and there was the same grand castle with the pretty little Dancer. She was still standing on one leg with the other high in the air; she too was steadfast. That touched the Tin Soldier, he was nearly going to shed tin tears; but that would not have been fitting for a soldier. He looked at her, but she said nothing.

All at once one of the little boys took up the Tin Soldier, and threw him into the stove, giving no reasons; but doubtless the little black imp in the snuff-box was at the bottom of this too.

There the Tin Soldier lay, and felt a heat that was truly terrible; but whether he was suffering from actual fire, or from the ardour of his passion, he did not know. All his colour had disappeared; whether this had happened on his travels or whether it was the result of trouble, who can say? He looked at the little woman, she looked at him, and he felt that he was melting; but he remained steadfast. Suddenly a door opened, the draught caught up the little Dancer, and off she flew like a fairy to the Tin Soldier in the stove, burst into flames— and that was the end of her! Then the Tin Soldier melted down into a little lump, and when next morning the maid was taking out the ashes, she found him in the shape of a heart. There was nothing left of the little Dancer but her golden rose, burnt as black as a cinder.

Andersen, *The Yellow Fairy Book*

Dick Whittington

Dick Whittington was a very little boy when his father and mother died; so little indeed, that he never knew them, nor the place where he was born. He strolled about the country as ragged as a colt, till he met with a waggoner who was going to London, and who gave him leave to walk all the way by the side of his waggon without paying anything for his passage. This pleased the little Whittington as he wanted to see London very much, for he had heard that the streets were paved with gold, and he was willing to get a bushel of it; but how great was his disappointment, poor boy! when he saw the streets covered with dirt instead of gold, and found himself in a strange place, without a friend, without food and without money.

Though the waggoner was so charitable as to let him walk up by the side of the waggon for nothing, he took care not to know him when they came to town, and the poor boy was, in a little time, so cold and so hungry that he wished he was sitting in a good kitchen and by a warm fire in the country.

In this distress he asked charity of several people, and one of them told him "Go to work you idle rogue."

"That I will," says Whittington, "with all my heart; I will work for you if you will let me."

The man, who thought this savoured of cleverness and impertinence (though the poor lad intended only to show his readiness to work), gave him a blow with a stick which broke his head so that the blood ran down.

In this situation, and fainting for want of food, he laid himself down at the door of Mr Fitzwarren, a merchant, where the cook saw him, and, being an ill-natured woman, ordered him to go about his business or she would pour a bucket of water on him. At this time Mr Fitzwarren came from the Exchange, and began also to scold the poor boy, bidding him to go to work.

Whittington answered that he should be glad to work if anybody would employ him, and that he should be able to work if he could get some food to eat, for he had had nothing for three days, and he was a poor country boy, and knew nobody, and nobody would employ him.

He then endeavoured to get up, but he was so very weak that he fell down again. The merchant felt sorry for the boy and ordered the servants to take him in and give him some food and drink, and let him help the cook to do any dirty work that she had to set him about. People are too quick to reproach those who beg with being idle, but give themselves no concern to put them in the way of getting business to do, or considering whether they are able to do it, which is not charity.

But we return to Whittington, who would have lived happily in this family had he not been bumped about by the cross cook, who must be always basting or roasting, and when the spit was idle employed her hands upon beating poor Whittington! At last Miss Alice, his master's daughter, was informed of it, and then she took compassion on the poor boy, and made the servants treat him kindly.

Besides the bad temper of the cook, Whittington had another difficulty to get over before he could be happy. He had, by order of his master, a bed placed for him in a garret, where there were a number of rats and mice that often ran over the poor boy's nose and disturbed his sleep. After some time, however, a gentleman who came to his master's house gave Whittington a penny for brushing his shoes. This he put into his pocket, being determined to invest it to the best advantage; and the next day, seeing a woman in the street with a cat under her arm, he ran up to her and asked the price of it. The woman (as the cat was a good mouser) asked a deal of money for it, but on Whittington's telling her that he had but a penny in the world, and that he wanted a cat dearly, she let him have it.

This cat Whittington concealed in the garret, for fear she should be beaten by his mortal enemy the cook, and here she soon killed or frightened away the rats and mice, so that the poor boy could at last sleep soundly.

Soon after this the merchant, who had a ship ready to sail, called for his servants, as his custom was, in order that each of them might venture something to try their luck; and whatever they sent was to pay neither freight nor customs duty, for the good man thought justly that he would be blessed the more for his readiness to let the poor share in his fortune.

All the servants appeared except poor Whittington, who, having neither money nor goods, could not think of anything to send to try his luck; but his good friend Miss Alice, thinking his poverty kept him away, ordered him to be called.

She then offered to invest something for him, but the merchant told his daughter that would not do, it must be something of his own. Poor Whittington said he had nothing but a cat which he had bought for a penny that was given to him. "Fetch your cat, boy," replied the merchant, "and send her." Whittington brought poor puss and delivered her to the captain, with tears in his eyes, for he said he should now be disturbed by the rats and mice as much as ever. All the company laughed at the adventure except Miss Alice, who pitied the poor boy and gave him something to buy another cat.

While puss was beating the billows at sea, poor Whittington was severely beaten at home by his tyrannical mistress the cook, who used him so cruelly, and made such games of him for sending his cat to sea, that at last the poor boy determined to run away from his place, and, having packed up the few things he had, he set out very early in the morning. He travelled as far as Holloway, and there sat down on a stone to consider which way to go; but while he was ruminating, Bow bells, of which there were only six, began to ring; and he thought the bells said to him:

> *"Turn again, Whittington,*
> *Thrice Lord Mayor of London."*

"Lord Mayor of London!" he said to himself; "what would I not endure to be Lord Mayor of London, and ride in such a fine coach? Well, I'll go back again, and bear all the pummelling and ill-usage of Cicely rather than miss the opportunity of being Lord Mayor!" So home he went, and happily got into the house and about his business before Cicely the cook made her appearance.

We must now follow Miss Puss to the coast of Africa. How perilous are voyages at sea, how uncertain the winds and the waves, and full of accidents!

The ship which had the cat on board was long beaten at sea, and at last, by contrary winds, driven on a part of the coast of Barbary which was inhabited by Moors. These people received our countrymen with civility, and therefore the captain, in order to trade with them, showed them samples of the goods he had on board, and sent some of them to the King of the country, who was so well pleased that he sent for the captain to his palace. Here the goods were placed, according to the custom of the country, on rich carpets, embroidered with gold and silver; and the King and Queen being seated at the upper end of the room, dinner was brought in, which consisted of many dishes; but no sooner were the dishes put down but an amazing number of rats and mice came from all quarters, and devoured all the food in an instant.

The captain, in surprise, turned round to the nobles and asked if these vermin were not offensive. "Oh! yes," they replied, "very offensive; and the King would give half his treasure to be freed of them, for they not only destroy his dinner, as you can see, but they assault him in his chamber, and even in his bed, so that he is obliged to be watched while he is sleeping, for fear of them."

On hearing this, the captain jumped for joy; he remembered poor Whittington and his cat, and told the King he had a creature on board the ship that would despatch all these vermin immediately. The King's heart heaved so high at the joy which this news gave him that his turban dropped off his head. "Bring this creature to me," he said; "vermin are dreadful in a Court, and if she will perform what you say I will load your ship with gold and jewels in exchange for her."

The captain, who certainly knew his business, took this opportunity to set forth the merits of Miss Puss. He told his Majesty that it would be inconvenient to part with her, as, when she was gone, the rats and mice might destroy the goods in the ship—however, to oblige his Majesty he would fetch her.

"Run, run," commanded the Queen; "I am impatient to see the dear creature."

Away flew the captain, while another dinner was being provided, and returned with the cat just as the rats and mice were devouring that also. He immediately put down Miss Puss, who killed a great number of them.

The King rejoiced greatly to see his old enemies destroyed by so small a creature, and the Queen was highly pleased, and desired the cat might be brought near that she might look at her. Upon which the captain called "Pussy, pussy, pussy!" and she came to him. He then presented her to the Queen, who started back, and was afraid to touch a creature who had made such a havoc among the rats and mice; however, then the captain stroked the cat and called "Pussy, pussy!" He then put her down on the Queen's lap, where she, purring, played with her Majesty's hand, and then sang herself to sleep.

The King having seen the exploits of Miss Puss, and being informed that her kittens would stock the whole country, bargained with the captain for the whole ship's cargo, and then gave them ten times as much for the cat as all the rest amounted to. On which, taking leave of their Majesties and other great personages at Court, they sailed with a fair wind for England.

The morn had scarcely dawned when Mr Fitzwarren arose to count over the cash and settle the business for that day. He had just entered the counting house, and seated himself at the desk,

when somebody came, tap, tap, tap at the door. "Who's there?" said Mr Fitzwarren.

"A friend," answered the other.

"What friend can come to the door at this unseasonable time?"

"A real friend is never unseasonable," answered the other. "I come to bring you good news of your ship *Unicorn*." The merchant bustled up in such a hurry that he forgot his gout; instantly opened the door, and who should be seen waiting but the captain, with a cabinet of jewels, and a cargo list, for which the merchant lifted up his eyes and thanked heaven for sending

him such a prosperous voyage. Then they told him of the adventures of the cat, and showed him the cabinet of jewels which they had brought for young Whittington. Upon which the merchant cried out with great earnestness, but not in the most poetical manner:

"Go, *send him in, and tell him of his fame,*
And call him Mr Whittington by name."

It is perhaps not in our power to prove him a good poet, but he was a good man, which was a much better character; for when some who were present told him that this treasure was too much for such a poor boy as Whittington, he said; "God forbid that I should deprive him of a penny; it is his own, and he shall have it to a farthing." He then ordered Mr Whittington in, who was at this time cleaning the kitchen and would have excused himself from going into the counting house, saying the room was swept and his shoes were dirty and full of hobnails. The merchant, however, made him come in, and ordered a chair to be set for him. Thinking they intended to make sport of him, as had been too often the case in the kitchen, he begged his master not to mock a poor simple fellow who intended them no harm, but let him go about his business. The merchant, taking him by the hand, said: "Indeed, Mr Whittington, I am in earnest with you, and sent for you to congratulate you on your great success. Your cat has procured you more money than I am worth in the world, and may you long enjoy it and be happy!"

At length, being shown the treasure, and convinced by them that all of it belonged to him, he fell upon his knees and thanked God for his care of such a poor and miserable creature. He then laid all the treasure at his master's feet, who refused to take any part of it, but told him he heartily rejoiced at his prosperity, and hoped the wealth he had acquired would be a comfort to him, and would make him happy. Whittington then applied to his mistress, and to his good friend Miss Alice, who refused to take any part of the money, but told him she heartily rejoiced at his good success, and wished him all the happiness in the world. He then gave presents to the captain, and the ship's crew for the care they had taken of his cargo. He distributed presents to all the servants in the house, not forgetting even his old enemy the cook, though she little deserved it.

After this Mr Fitzwarren advised Mr Whittington to dress himself in the manner of a gentleman, and made him the offer of his house to live in till he could provide himself with a better one.

Now it came to pass when Mr Whittington's face was washed, his hair curled, and he dressed in a rich suit of clothes, that he turned out a smart young fellow; and, as wealth contributes much to give a man confidence, he in a little time dropped his sheepish behaviour,

and soon grew a sprightly and good companion, so that Miss Alice, who had formerly pitied him, now fell in love with him.

When her father saw they loved each other he proposed a match between them, to which both parties cheerfully consented, and the Lord Mayor, Court of Aldermen, Sheriffs, the Company of Stationers, the Royal Academy of Arts, and a number of eminent merchants attended the ceremony.

History further relates that they lived very happily, had several children, and died at a good old age. Mr Whittington served Sheriff of London and was three times Lord Mayor of London.

Anon., *The Blue Fairy Book*

Henny-Penny

One day Henny-Penny was picking up corn in the cornyard when—whack!—something hit her on the head. "Goodness gracious me!" said Henny-Penny, "the sky's a-going to fall; I must go and tell the king."

So she went along and she went along and she went along till she met Cocky-Locky. "Where are you going, Henny-Penny?" says Cocky-Locky. "Oh! I'm going to tell the king the sky's a-falling," says Henny-Penny. "May I come with you?" says Cocky-Locky. "Certainly," says Henny-Penny. So Henny-Penny and Cocky-Locky went to tell the king the sky was a-falling.

They went along, and they went along, and they went along, till they met Ducky-Daddles. "Where are you going to, Henny-Penny and Cocky-Locky?" says Ducky-Daddles. "Oh! we're going to tell the king the sky's a-falling," said Henny-Penny and Cocky-Locky. "May I come with you?" says Ducky-Daddles. "Certainly," says Henny-Penny and Cocky-Locky. So Henny-Penny, Cocky-Locky and Ducky-Daddles went to tell the king the sky was a-falling.

So they went along, and they went along, and they went along, till they met Goosey-Poosey. "Where are you going

to, Henny-Penny, Cocky-Locky and Ducky-Daddles?" said Goosey-Poosey. "Oh! we're going to tell the king the sky's a-falling," said Henny-Penny and Cocky-Locky and Ducky-Daddles. "May I come with you?" said Goosey-Poosey. "Certainly," says Henny-Penny, Cocky-Locky and Ducky-Daddles. So Henny-Penny, Cocky-Locky, Ducky-Daddles and Goosey-Poosey went to tell the king the sky was a-falling.

So they went along, and they went along, and they went along, till they met Turkey-Lurkey. "Where are you going, Henny-Penny, Cocky-Locky, Ducky-Daddles and Goosey-Poosey?" says Turkey-Lurkey. "Oh! we're going to tell the king the sky's a-falling," said Henny-Penny, Cocky-Locky, Ducky-Daddles and Goosey-Poosey. "May I come with you, Henny-Penny, Cocky-Locky, Ducky-Daddles and Goosey-Poosey?" said Turkey-Lurkey. "Oh, certainly, Turkey-Lurkey," said Henny-Penny, Cocky-Locky, Ducky-Daddles and Goosey-Poosey. So Henny-Penny, Cocky-Locky, Ducky-Daddles, Goosey-Poosey and Turkey-Lurkey all went to tell the king the sky was a-falling.

So they went along, and they went along, and they went along, till they met Foxy-Woxy, and Foxy-Woxy said to Henny-Penny, Cocky-Locky, Ducky-Daddles, Goosey-Poosey and Turkey-Lurkey: "Where are you going, Henny-Penny, Cocky-Locky, Ducky-Daddles, Goosey-Poosey and Turkey-Lurkey?" And Henny-Penny, Cocky-Locky, Ducky-Daddles, Goosey-Poosey and Turkey-Lurkey said to Foxy-Woxy: "We're going to tell the king the sky's a-falling." "Oh! but

this is not the way to the king, Henny-Penny, Cocky-Locky, Ducky-Daddles, Goosey-Poosey and Turkey-Lurkey," says Foxy-Woxy: "I know the proper way; shall I show it to you?" "Oh, certainly, Foxy-Woxy," said Henny-Penny, Cocky-Locky, Ducky-Daddles, Goosey-Poosey and Turkey-Lurkey. So Henny-Penny, Cocky-Locky, Ducky-Daddles, Goosey-Poosey, Turkey-Lurkey and Foxy-Woxy all went to tell the king the sky was a-falling.

So they went along, and they went along, and they went along, till they came to a narrow, dark hole. Now this was the door of Foxy-Woxy's cave. But Foxy-Woxy said to Henny-Penny, Cocky-Locky, Ducky-Daddles, Goosey-Poosey and Turkey-Lurkey: "This is the short way to the king's palace: you'll soon get there if you follow me. I will go first and you come after, Henny-Penny, Cocky-Locky, Ducky-Daddles, Goosey-Poosey and Turkey-Lurkey." "Why, of course, certainly, without doubt, why not?" said Henny-Penny, Cocky-Locky, Ducky-Daddles, Goosey-Poosey and Turkey-Lurkey.

So Foxy-Woxy went into his cave,

and he didn't go very far, but turned round to wait for Henny-Penny, Cocky-Locky, Ducky-Daddles, Goosey-Poosey and Turkey-Lurkey. So at last at first Turkey-Lurkey went through the dark hole into the cave. He hadn't gone far when "Hrumph", Foxy-Woxy snapped off Turkey-Lurkey's head and threw his body over his left shoulder. Then Goosey-Poosey went in, and "Hrumph", off went her head and Goosey-Poosey was thrown beside Turkey-Lurkey. Then Ducky-Daddles waddled down, and "Hrumph", snapped Foxy-Woxy, and Ducky-Daddles' head was off and Ducky-Daddles was thrown alongside Turkey-Lurkey and Goosey-Poosey. Then Cocky-Locky strutted down into the cave, and he hadn't gone far when "Snap, Hrumph!" went Foxy-Woxy, and Cocky-Locky was thrown alongside Turkey-Lurkey, Goosey-Poosey and Ducky-Daddles.

But Foxy-Woxy had made two bites at Cocky-Locky, and when the first snap only hurt Cocky-Locky, but didn't kill him, he called out to Henny-Penny. But she turned tail and off she ran home, so she never told the king the sky was a-falling.

Anon., *English Fairy Tales*

The Three Billy-Goats Gruff

Once upon a time there were three billy-goats, who were to go up to the hillside to make themselves fat, and the name of all three was 'Gruff'.

On the way up was a bridge over a stream they had to cross, and under the bridge lived a great big ugly troll, with eyes as big as saucers, and a nose as long as a poker.

First of all came the youngest Billy-Goat Gruff to cross the bridge.

"Trip, trap! trip, trap!" went the bridge.

"WHO'S THAT tripping over my bridge?" roared the Troll.

"Oh! it is only I, the tiniest Billy-Goat Gruff; and I'm going up to the hillside to make myself fat," said the Billy-goat, with such a small voice.

"Now, I'm coming to gobble you up," said the Troll.

"Oh, no! please don't take me. I'm too little, that I am," said the Billy-Goat; "wait a bit till the second Billy-Goat Gruff comes; he's much bigger."

"Well, be off with you!" said the Troll.

A little while later came the second Billy-Goat Gruff to cross the bridge.

"TRIP, TRAP! TRIP, TRAP! TRIP, TRAP!" went the bridge.

"WHO'S THAT tripping over my bridge?" roared the Troll.

"Oh! it's the second Billy-Goat Gruff, and I'm going up to the hillside to make myself fat," said the Billy-Goat, who hadn't such a small voice.

"Now, I'm coming to gobble you up," said the Troll.

"Oh, no! don't take me; wait a little till the big Billy-Goat Gruff comes; he's much bigger."

"Very well, be off with you!" said the Troll.

But just then up came the big Billy-Goat Gruff.

"TRIP, TRAP! TRIP, TRAP! TRIP, TRAP!" went the bridge, for the Billy-Goat was so heavy that the bridge creaked and groaned under him.

"WHO'S THAT tramping over my bridge?" roared the Troll.

"IT IS I! THE BIG BILLY-GOAT GRUFF," said the Billy-Goat, who had an ugly hoarse voice of his own.

"Now, I'm coming to gobble you up," roared the Troll.

"*Well, come along! I've got two spears,*
And I'll poke your eyeballs out at your ears;
I've got, besides, two curling-stones,
And I'll crush you to bits, body and bones."

That was what the big Billy-Goat said, and so he flew at the Troll and poked his eyes out with his horns, and crushed him to bits, body and bones, and tossed him out into the stream, and after that he went up to the hillside. There the Billy-Goats got so fat they were scarcely able to walk home again; and if the fat hasn't fallen off them, why they're still fat; and so:

"*Snip, snap, snout,*
This tale's told out."

Asbjørnsen and Möe,
Popular Tales from the Norse

The Nightingale

The palace of the Emperor of China was the most splendid in the world, all made of priceless porcelain, but so brittle and delicate that you had to take great care how you touched it. In the garden were the most beautiful flowers, and on them were tied silver bells which tinkled, so that you could not help looking at the flowers. The garden was so large that even the gardener himself did not know where it ended. If you ever got beyond it, you came to a stately forest. The forest sloped down to the sea, and in these trees there lived a nightingale. She sang so beautifully that even the poor fisherman who had so much to do stood and listened when he came at night to cast his nets. "How beautiful it is!" he said; but he had to attend to his work, and forgot about the bird. But when she sang the next night and the fisherman came there again, he said the same thing, "How beautiful it is!"

From all the countries round came travellers to the Emperor's town, who were astonished at the palace and the garden. But when they heard the Nightingale they all said, "This is the finest thing after all!"

Learned scholars wrote many books about the town, the palace, and the garden. But they did not forget the Nightingale; she was praised the most. Some of the books reached the Emperor. He sat in his golden chair, and read and read. He nodded his head every moment, for he liked reading the brilliant accounts of the town, the palace, and the garden. "However, the Nightingale is better than all," he saw written.

"What is that?" exclaimed the Emperor. "I don't know anything about this Nightingale! Fancy reading for the first time about it in a book!"

And he called his First Lord to him. He was so proud that if anyone of lower rank than his own ventured to speak to him, he would say nothing but "P!"

"Here is a most remarkable bird which is called a nightingale!" said the Emperor. "They say it is the most glorious thing in my kingdom. Why has no-one ever said anything to me about it?"

"I have never before heard it mentioned!" said the First Lord. "I will look for it and find it!"

But where was it to be found? The First Lord ran up and down stairs, through the halls and corridors; but none of those he met had ever heard of the Nightingale. And the First Lord ran again to the Emperor, and told him that it must be an invention.

"Your Imperial Majesty cannot really believe all that is written!"

"But the book in which I read this," said the Emperor, "is sent me by His Great Majesty the Emperor of Japan; so it cannot be untrue, and I will hear the Nightingale! She must be here this evening! She has my gracious permission to appear, and if she does not, the whole Court shall be trampled under foot after supper!"

The First Lord ran up and down stairs, through the halls and corridors, and half the Court ran with him, for they did not want to be trampled under foot. Everyone was asking after the wonderful Nightingale which all the world knew of, except those at Court.

At last they met a poor little girl in the kitchen, who said to them, "Oh! I know the Nightingale well. I have permission to carry the scraps over from the Court meals to my poor sick mother, and when I am going home at night, tired and weary, then I hear the Nightingale singing! It brings tears to my eyes, and I feel as if my mother were kissing me!"

"Little kitchenmaid!" said the First Lord, "you shall have leave to see the Emperor at dinner, if you can lead us to the Nightingale."

And so they all went into the wood where the Nightingale was wont to sing.

When they were on the way there they heard a cow mooing.

"Oh!" said the Courtiers, "now we have found her! What a wonderful power for such a small beast to have!"

"No; that is a cow mooing!" said the little kitchenmaid. "We are still quite a long way off!"

Then the frogs began to croak in the marsh. "Splendid!" said they. "Now we hear her; it sounds like a little church bell!"

"No, no; those are frogs!" said the little kitchenmaid. "But I think we shall soon hear her now!"

Then the Nightingale began to sing.

"There she is!" cried the little girl. And she pointed to a little dark grey bird up in the branches.

"Is it possible!" said the First Lord. "How ordinary she looks! She must surely have lost her feathers because she sees so many distinguished men round her!"

"Little Nightingale," the little kitchen-maid called out, "our Gracious Emperor wants you to sing before him!"

"With the greatest of pleasure!" said the Nightingale; and she sang so gloriously that it was a pleasure to listen.

"It sounds like glass bells!" said the First Lord. "She will be a great success at Court."

"Shall I sing once more for the Emperor?" asked the Nightingale, thinking that the Emperor was there.

"My esteemed little Nightingale," said the First Lord, "I have the great pleasure to invite you to Court this evening, where His Gracious Imperial Highness will be enchanted with your charming song!"

"It sounds best in the green wood," said the Nightingale; but still, she came gladly when she heard that the Emperor wished it. At the palace everything was splendidly prepared. The porcelain walls and floors glittered in the light of many thousand gold lamps; the most gorgeous flowers which tinkled out well were placed in the corridors. All the bells jingled so much that one could not hear oneself speak. The whole Court was there, and the little kitchenmaid was allowed to stand behind the door, now that she was a Court cook.

The Nightingale sang so gloriously that the tears came into the Emperor's eyes and ran down his cheeks. The Emperor was so delighted that he said she should wear his gold slipper round her neck. But the Nightingale told him she had had enough

reward already. "I have seen tears in the Emperor's eyes—that is a great reward for me. An Emperor's tears have such power!" Then she sang again with her gloriously sweet voice.

"That is most charming!" said all the ladies round. And they all took to holding water in their mouths that they might gurgle whenever anyone spoke to them. Then they thought themselves nightingales.

The Nightingale had to stay at Court now; she had her own cage, and permission to walk out twice in the day and once at night.

She was given twelve servants, who each held a silken string which was fastened round her leg. There was little pleasure in flying about like this.

One day the Emperor received a parcel on which was written 'The Nightingale'. "Here is another new book about our famous bird!" said the Emperor.

However, is was not a book, but a little mechanical toy—an artificial nightingale which was like the real one, only that it was set all over with diamonds, rubies and sapphires. When it was wound up, it could sing the piece the real bird sang, and moved its tail up and down, and glittered with silver and gold. Round its neck was a little velvet collar on which was written, 'The Nightingale of the Emperor of Japan is nothing compared to that of the Emperor of China'.

"This is magnificent!" they all said, and the man who had brought the clockwork bird received on the spot the title of Bringer of the Imperial First Nightingale.

"Now they must sing together; what a duet we shall have!" And so they sang together, but their voices did not blend, for the real Nightingale sang in her way and the clockwork bird sang waltzes.

"It is not its fault!" declared the bandmaster; "it keeps very good time and is quite after my style!"

Then the artificial bird had to sing alone. It gave just as much pleasure as the real one, and then it was so much prettier to look at; it sparkled like bracelets and necklaces. Three-and-thirty times it sang the same piece without being tired. People would have heard it again, but the Emperor thought that the living Nightingale should sing now—but where was she? No-one had noticed that she had flown out of the open window away to her green woods.

"What *shall* we do!" said the Emperor.

And all the Court scolded, and said that the Nightingale was very ungrateful. "But we have still the best bird!" they said and the artificial bird had to sing again, and that was the thirty-fourth time they had heard the same piece. And the bandmaster praised the bird tremendously; he assured them it was better than a real nightingale, not only because of its beautiful plumage and diamonds, but inside as well. "For see, my Lords and Ladies and your Imperial Majesty, with the real Nightingale one can never tell what will come out, but all is known about the artificial bird. You can explain it, you can open it and show people where the waltzes lie, how they go, and how one follows the other!"

"That's just what we think!" said everyone; and the bandmaster received permission to show the bird to the people the following Sunday. They should hear it sing, commanded the Emperor. They all said "Oh!" and held up their forefingers and nodded time. But the poor fisherman who had heard the real Nightingale said: "This one sings well enough, the tunes glide out; but there is something wanting—I don't know what!"

The real Nightingale was banished from the kingdom. The artificial bird was put on silken cushions by the Emperor's bed, all the presents which it received, gold and precious stones, lay round it, and it was given the title of Imperial Night-singer. And the bandmaster wrote a work of twenty-five volumes about the artificial bird. It was so learned, long, and so full of the hardest Chinese words that everyone said they had read it and understood it; for once they had been very stupid about a book, and had been trampled under foot in consequence.

So a whole year passed. The Emperor, the entire Court, and all the people knew every single note of the artificial bird's song by heart. But they liked it all the better for this; they could even sing with it. However, one evening, when the artificial bird was singing its best, something in the bird went crack. Something snapped! Whir-r-r! all the wheels ran down and then the music ceased. The Emperor sprang up, and had his physician summoned, but what could *he* do! Then the clockmaker came, and, after a great deal of talking and examining, he put the bird somewhat in order, but he said that it must be very seldom used as the works were nearly worn out, and it was impossible to put in new ones. Here was a calamity! Only once a year was the artificial bird allowed to sing, and even that was almost too much for it.

Five years passed, and then a great sorrow came to the nation. The Chinese look upon their Emperor as everything, and now he was ill, and not likely to live it was said. Already a new Emperor had been chosen, and the people stood outside in the street and asked the First Lord how the old Emperor was. "P!" was all he said, and he shook his head.

Cold and pale lay the Emperor in his splendid bed; the whole Court believed him dead, and one after the other left him to pay their respects to the new Emperor. Everywhere in the halls and corridors cloth was laid down so that no footstep could be heard, and everything was still—very, very still. And nothing came to break the silence.

The Emperor longed for something to come along and relieve the monotony of this deathlike stillness. If only someone would speak to him! If only someone would sing to him.

"Music! music!" cried the Emperor. "You little bright golden bird, sing! I gave you gold and jewels; I have hung my gold slipper round your neck with my own hand—sing! do sing!" But the bird was silent. There was no-one to wind it up, and so it could not sing. And all was silent, so terribly silent!

All at once there came in at the window the most glorious burst of song. It was the little living Nightingale, who, sitting outside on a bough, had heard the need of her Emperor and had come to sing to him of comfort and hope. And as she sang the blood flowed quicker and quicker in the Emperor's weak limbs, and life began to return.

"Thank you, oh, thank you!" said the Emperor. "You divine little bird! I know you. I chased you from my kingdom, and you have given me life again! How can I reward you?"

"You have done that already!" replied the Nightingale. "I brought tears to your eyes the first time I sang. They are jewels that rejoice a singer's heart. But now you should sleep and get strong again." And the Emperor fell into a deep, calm sleep as she sang.

The sun was shining through the window when he awoke, strong and well. None of his servants had come back yet, for they thought he was dead. But the Nightingale sat and sang to him.

"You must always stay with me!" said the Emperor. "You shall sing whenever you like, and I will break the artificial bird into a thousand pieces."

"Don't do that!" said the Nightingale. "He did his work as long as he could. I cannot build my nest in the palace and live here; but let me come whenever I like. I will sit in the evening on the bough outside the window, and I will sing you something that will make you feel happy and grateful. I will sing of joy, and of sorrow; I will sing of the evil and the good which lies hidden from you. The little singing-bird flies all around, to the poor fisherman's hut, to the farmer's cottage, to all those who are far away from you and your Court. I love your heart more than your crown. Now I will sing to you again; but you must promise me one thing—"

"Anything!" said the Emperor, standing up in his Imperial robes, which he had himself put on.

"One thing I beg of you! Don't tell anyone that you have a little bird who tells you everything. It will be much better not to!" Then the Nightingale flew away.

The servants came in to look at their dead Emperor. The Emperor said, "Good morning!"

Andersen, *The Yellow Fairy Book*

Snow White

Once upon a time, in the middle of winter when the snowflakes were falling like feathers, a queen sat at a window framed in black ebony and sewed. She pricked her finger with the needle, and three drops of blood fell on the snow outside, and she thought to herself: "Oh! what wouldn't I give to have a child as white as snow, as red as blood, and as black as ebony!"

And her wish was granted, for not long after a little daughter was born to her, with skin as white as snow, lips and cheeks as red as blood, and hair as black as ebony. They called her Snow White, and not long after her birth the Queen died.

After a year the King married again. His new wife was a beautiful woman, but so proud and overbearing that she couldn't stand any rival to her beauty. She possessed a magic mirror, and when she used to ask:

"Mirror, mirror, hanging there,
Who in all the land's most fair?"
it always replied:
"You are most fair, my Lady
Queen,
None fairer in the land is seen."
Then she was quite happy, for she knew the mirror always spoke the truth.

Snow White was growing prettier and prettier every day, and when she was seven years old she was fairer than the Queen. One day when the Queen asked her mirror the usual question, it replied:
"My Lady Queen, you are fair,
'tis true,
But Snow White is fairer far
than you."
Then the Queen flew into the most awful rage and turned every shade of green in her jealousy. Every day her envy, hatred and malice grew, for envy and jealousy are like evil weeds which spring up and choke the heart. At last, calling a huntsman to her, she said: "Take the child out into the wood, kill her, and bring me back her lungs and liver, that I may know for certain she is dead." The huntsman led Snow White out into the wood,

326

but as he was drawing out his knife to slay her, she began to cry and said: "Oh, dear huntsman, spare my life, and I will promise to fly forth into the wood and never to return home."

And because she was so young and pretty the huntsman took pity on her and said: "Well, run along, poor child." For he thought to himself: "The wild beasts will soon eat her up."

And his heart felt lighter because he hadn't had to do the deed himself. As he turned away a young boar came running past, so he shot it, and brought its lungs and liver home to the Queen as proof that Snow White was dead. And the wicked woman ate them up, thinking she had made an end of Snow White for ever.

Now when the poor child found herself alone in the big wood the very trees around her seemed to assume strange shapes, and she felt so frightened she didn't know what to do. Then she began to run over the sharp stones, and through the bramble bushes, and the wild beasts ran past her, but they did her no harm. She ran as far as

her legs would carry her, and as evening approached she saw a little house, and she stepped inside to rest. Everything was very small in the little house, but cleaner and neater than anything you can imagine. In the middle of the room there stood a little table, with seven little plates and forks and spoons and knives and tumblers on it. Against the wall were seven little beds, each covered with snow-white covers. Snow White felt so hungry and thirsty that she ate a bit of bread and a little porridge from each plate, and drank a drop of wine out of each tumbler. Feeling tired and sleepy she lay down and fell fast asleep.

When it got quite dark the masters of the little house returned. They were seven dwarfs who worked in the mines, deep in the heart of the mountain. They lit their seven little lamps, and saw Snow White fast asleep.

"Goodness gracious!" they cried, "what a beautiful child!"

And they were so enchanted by her beauty that they let her sleep on in the little bed. But the seventh Dwarf slept with his companions one hour in each bed, and in this way he managed to pass the night.

In the morning Snow White awoke, but when she saw the seven Dwarfs she felt very frightened. But they were so friendly and asked her what her name was in such a kind way, that she replied: "I am Snow White."

"Why did you come to our house?"

Then she told them how her stepmother had wished her put to death, and how the huntsman had kindly spared her life, and how she had run the whole day till she had come to their little house.

The Dwarfs then asked her: "Will you stay and keep house for us, cook, make the beds, do the washing, sew and knit? If you keep everything neat and clean, you shall want for nothing."

"Yes," answered Snow White, "I will gladly do all you ask."

Every morning the Dwarfs went into the mountain to dig for gold, and in the evening, Snow White always had their supper ready. But during the day the girl was left quite alone, so the good Dwarfs warned her: "Beware of your stepmother. She will soon find out you are here, and whatever you do don't let anyone into the house."

Now the Queen, after she thought she had eaten Snow White's lungs and liver, believed that she was once more the most beautiful woman in the world; so stepping before her mirror one day she said:

"Mirror, mirror, hanging there,
Who in all the land's most fair?"
and the mirror replied:
"My Lady Queen, you are fair,
'tis true,
But Snow White is fairer far
than you.
Snow White who dwells with the
seven little men,
Is as fair as you, as fair again."
The Queen was nearly struck dumb with horror, for the mirror always spoke

the truth, and she knew now that Snow White was still alive. She pondered all day and all night how she might destroy her. Eventually she stained her face and dressed herself up as an old peddler wife, so that she was quite unrecognisable. In this guise she went over the seven hills till she came to the house of the seven Dwarfs. There she knocked at the door, calling out: "Fine wares to sell, fine wares to sell!"

Snow White peeped out of the window, and called out: "What have you to sell?"

"Laces of every shade and description," she answered; and she held one up that was made of brightly coloured silk.

"Surely I can let the honest woman in," thought Snow White; so she unbarred the door and bought the pretty lace.

"Come," said the old woman, "I'll lace you up properly."

The old woman laced her so tightly that it took Snow White's breath away, and she fell down dead.

"Now you are no longer the fairest," said the wicked old woman, and then she hastened away.

In the evening, the seven Dwarfs came home, and saw their dear Snow White lying on the floor, as still as a dead person. They lifted her up tenderly, and when they saw how tightly laced she was they cut the lace in two, and she began to breathe a little and gradually came back to life. When the Dwarfs heard what had happened, they said to Snow White: "The old peddler wife was none other than the wicked old Queen. In future you must let no-one in, if we are not at home."

The wicked old Queen went straight to her mirror and said:

"Mirror, mirror, hanging there,
Who in all the land's most fair?"
and the mirror answered:

*"My Lady Queen, you are fair,
'tis true,
But Snow White is fairer far than
you.
Snow White who dwells with the
seven little men,
Is as fair as you, as fair again."*

When she heard this she became as pale as death. "This time," she said to herself, "I will think of something that will make an end of her once and for all."

And by the witchcraft which she understood so well she made a poisonous comb; then she assumed the form of another old woman. So she went over the seven hills till she reached the house of the seven Dwarfs, and knocking at the door called out: "Fine wares for sale."

Snow White looked out of the window and said: "You must go away, for I may not let anyone in."

"But surely you are not forbidden to look out?" said the old woman, and she held up the poisonous comb for her to see.

It pleased the girl so much that she opened the door. The old woman said: "Now I'll comb your hair properly for you." Poor Snow White thought no evil, but hardly had the comb touched her hair than the poison worked and she fell down on the floor unconscious.

"Now, my fine lady, you're really done for this time," said the wicked woman, and she made her way home as fast as she could.

Fortunately it was now near evening, and the seven Dwarfs soon returned home. When they saw Snow White lying dead on the ground, they at once suspected that her wicked stepmother had been at work again; so they searched till they found the poisonous comb, and the moment they pulled it out of her head Snow White came to herself again, and told them what had happened. Then they warned her once more to open the door to no-one.

The Queen went straight to her mirror and asked:

*"Mirror, mirror, hanging there,
Who in all the land's most fair?"*

and it replied:

*"My Lady Queen, you are fair,
'tis true,
But Snow White is fairer far
than you.*

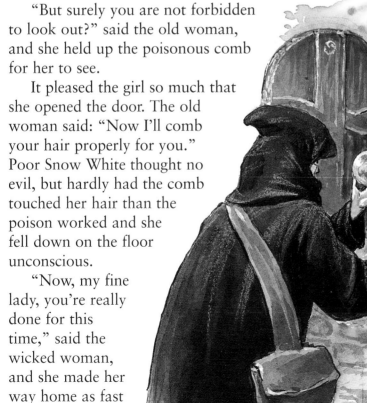

Snow White who dwells with the
seven little men,
Is as fair as you, as fair again.*"

When she heard these words she shook
with rage. "Snow White shall die," she
cried; "even if it costs me my own life."

Then she made a poisonous apple.
Outwardly it looked beautiful, white with
red cheeks, so that everyone who saw it
longed to eat it, but anyone who might do
so would die on the spot. She stained her
face and dressed herself up as a peasant,
and so she went over the seven hills to the
house of the seven Dwarfs. She knocked at
the door, as usual, but Snow White put her
head out of the window and called out: "I
may not let anyone in, the seven Dwarfs
have forbidden me to do so."

"Are you afraid of being poisoned?"
asked the old woman. "See, I will cut this
apple in half. I'll eat the white cheek and
you can eat the red."

But the apple was so cunningly made
that only the red cheek was poisonous.
Snow White longed to eat the tempting
fruit, and when she saw that the peasant
woman was eating it herself, she couldn't
resist, and stretching out her hand she took
the poisonous half. But hardly had the first
bite passed her lips than she fell down dead.
Then the eyes of the cruel Queen sparkled
with glee, and laughing aloud she cried:
"As white as snow, as red as blood, and as
black as ebony, this time the Dwarfs won't
be able to bring you back to life."

When she got home she asked the
mirror:

*"Mirror, mirror, hanging there,
Who in all the land's most fair?"*
and this time it replied:

*"You are most fair, my Lady
Queen,
None fairer in the land is seen."*

Then her jealous heart was at rest—at
least, as much at rest as a jealous heart can
ever be.

When the little Dwarfs came home in
the evening they found Snow White lying
on the ground, and she neither breathed
nor stirred. They looked round everywhere
to see if they could find anything poisonous
about. They unlaced her bodice, combed
her hair, but all in vain; the child was dead
and remained dead. Then they placed her
on a bier, and all the seven Dwarfs sat
round it, weeping and sobbing for three
whole days and three whole nights. At last
they made up their minds to bury her, but
she looked as blooming as a living being,
and her cheeks were still such a lovely
colour, that they said: "We can't hide her
away in the black ground."

So they had a coffin made entirely of
transparent glass, and they laid her in it,
and wrote on the lid in golden letters that
she was a royal princess. Then they put the
coffin on the top of the mountain, and one
of the Dwarfs always remained beside it
and kept watch over it.

Snow White lay a long time in the coffin, and she always looked the same, just as
if she were fast asleep. She remained as
white as snow, as red as blood, and her hair
as black as ebony.

One day a prince came to the wood and
passed by the Dwarfs' house. He saw the
coffin on the hill, with the beautiful Snow
White inside it, and when he had read what
was written on it in golden letters, he said
to the Dwarf: "Give me the coffin. I'll give
you whatever you like for it."

But the Dwarf said: "No; we wouldn't
part with it for all the gold in the world."

"Well, then," he replied, "give it to me
because I can't live without Snow White. I
will cherish it as my dearest possession."

He spoke so sadly that the good Dwarfs had pity on him and gave him the coffin, and the Prince asked his servants to bear it away on their shoulders. As they were going down the hill they stumbled over a bush and jolted the coffin so violently that the poisonous bit of apple Snow White had swallowed fell out of her throat. She gradually opened her eyes, lifted up the lid of the coffin, and sat up alive and well.

"Oh! dear me, where am I?" she cried.

The Prince answered joyfully, "You are with me," and he told her all that had happened, adding, "I love you better than anyone in the whole wide world. Will you come with me to my father's palace and be my wife?"

Snow White consented at once, and the marriage was celebrated with great pomp and splendour.

Now Snow White's wicked stepmother was one of the guests invited to the wedding feast. When she had dressed herself very gorgeously for the occasion, she went to the mirror and said:

"Mirror, mirror, hanging there,
Who in all the land's most fair?"
and the mirror answered:
"My Lady Queen, you are fair,
'tis true,
But Snow White is fairer far
than you."

When the wicked woman heard these words she was beside herself with rage and mortification. At first she didn't want to go to the wedding at all, but at the same time she felt she would never be happy till she had seen the young Queen. As she entered Snow White recognised her and nearly fainted with fear; but red-hot iron shoes had been prepared for the wicked old Queen, and she was made to get into them and dance till she fell down dead.

Grimm, *The Red Fairy Book*

Little One Eye, Little Two Eyes, and Little Three Eyes

There was a woman who had three daughters. The eldest was called Little One Eye, because she had only one eye in the middle of her forehead; the second, Little Two Eyes, because she had two eyes like other people; and the youngest, Little Three Eyes, because she had three eyes, one of them being in the middle of the forehead, and the other two in the usual place.

Now, because Little Two Eyes looked no different from other people, her sisters and mother could not bear even to look at her. They said, "You with your two eyes are no better than anybody else; you do not belong to us." They knocked her about, and gave her shabby clothes, and food that was left over from their own meals; in short, they made life difficult for her whenever they could.

It happened that Little Two Eyes had to go out into the fields to look after the goat; but she was still quite hungry, because her sisters had given her so little to eat. She sat down on a small hill and began to cry, and cried so much that two little streams ran down out of each eye. And as she looked up once in her sorrow, a woman stood near her, who asked, "Little Two Eyes, why do you cry?"

Little Two Eyes answered, "Have I not need to cry? Because I have two eyes, like other people, my sisters and my mother cannot bear me; they push me out of one corner into the other, give me shabby clothes, and nothing to eat but what they leave. Today they have given me so little that I am still quite hungry."

The wise woman said, "Little Two Eyes, dry your eyes, and I will tell you something which will keep you from ever being hungry again. Only say to your goat:
'Little goat, bleat;
Little table, rise,'
and a neatly laid table will stand before you with the most delicious food on it, so that you can eat as much as you like.

"When you are satisfied and do not want the table any more, only say:
'Little goat, bleat;
Little table, away,'
and it will all disappear before your eyes." Then the wise woman herself disappeared out of sight.

Little Two Eyes thought, "I must see at once if it is true what she has said, for I am much too hungry to wait." So she said:
"Little goat, bleat;
Little table, rise."

Scarcely had she uttered the words, when there stood before her a little table, covered with a white cloth, on which was laid a plate, a knife and fork, and a silver spoon. The most delicious food was there also, and smoking hot, as if it had just come from the kitchen.

Then Little Two Eyes said the shortest grace that she knew, began to eat, and found it very good. And when she had had enough, she said just as the wise woman had taught her:
"Little goat, bleat;
Little table, away."

In an instant the little table, and all that stood on it, had disappeared again.

"That is a beautiful, easy way of housekeeping," thought Little Two Eyes, and was quite happy and merry. In the evening, when she came home with her goat, she found a little dish with food, which her sisters had put aside for her; but she did not touch anything—she had no need. On the next day she went out again with her goat, and let the few crusts that had been given to her remain uneaten.

The first time and the second time the sisters took no notice; but when the same thing happened every day, they noticed it, and said, "All is not right with Little Two Eyes; she always leaves her food, and she used formerly to eat up everything that was given her; she must have found other ways of dining."

In order to discover the truth, they resolved that Little One Eye should go with Little Two Eyes when she drove the goat into the meadow, and see what she did there, and whether anybody brought her anything to eat and drink. So when Little Two Eyes set out again, Little One Eye came to her and said, "I will go with you into the field and see that the goat is taken proper care of, and driven to good pasture."

But Little Two Eyes saw what Little One Eye had in her mind, and drove the goat into some long grass, saying, "Come, Little One Eye, we will sit down; I will sing you something."

Little One Eye sat down, being tired from the walk and from the heat of the sun, and Little Two Eyes kept on singing:

"Are you awake, Little One Eye?
Are you asleep, Little One Eye?"

Then Little One Eye shut her one eye and fell asleep. And when Little Two Eyes saw that Little One Eye was fast asleep, and could not tell anything, she said:

"Little goat, bleat;
Little table, rise,"

and seated herself at her table, and ate and drank till she was satisfied. Then she called out again:

"Little goat,
bleat;
Little table,
away."

and instantly everything disappeared.

Little Two Eyes now woke Little One Eye and said, "Little One Eye, you pretend to watch, and fall asleep over it, and in the meantime the

goat could have run all over the world; come, we will go home."

Then they went home, and Little Two Eyes let her little dish once again stand untouched; and Little One Eye, who could not tell the mother why her sister would not eat, said, as an excuse, "Oh, I fell asleep out there."

The next day the mother said to Little Three Eyes, "This time *you* shall go and see if Little Two Eyes eats out-of-doors, and if anyone brings her food and drink, for she must eat and drink secretly."

Then Little Three Eyes went to Little Two Eyes and said, "I will go with you and see whether the goat is taken proper care of, and driven to good pasture."

But Little Two Eyes saw what Little Three Eyes had in her mind, and drove the goat into long grass, and said as before, "We will sit down here, Little Three Eyes; I will sing you something."

Little Three Eyes seated herself, being tired from the walk and the heat of the sun, and Little Two Eyes began the same song again, and sang:

> "*Are you awake, Little Three Eyes?*"

But instead of singing the words as she should:

> "*Are you asleep, Little* Three *Eyes?*"

she sang:

> "*Are you asleep, Little* Two *Eyes?*"

and went on singing:

> "*Are you awake, Little Three Eyes? Are you asleep, Little* Two *Eyes?*"

So the two eyes of Little Three Eyes fell asleep, but the third did not go to sleep, because it was not spoken to in the song. Little Three Eyes, to be sure, shut it, and pretended to be going to sleep, but only through slyness; for she winked with it, and

could see everything quite well. And when Little Two Eyes thought that Little Three Eyes was fast asleep, she said her little sentence:

> "*Little goat, bleat;*
> *Little table, rise,*"

ate and drank heartily, and then told the little table to go away again:

> "*Little goat, bleat;*
> *Little table, away.*"

But Little Three Eyes had in fact seen everything.

Then Little Two Eyes came to her, woke her and said, "Ah! Little Three Eyes, have you been asleep? You keep watch well! Come, we will go home."

When they got home, Little Two Eyes again did not eat, and Little Three Eyes said to the mother: "I know why the proud thing does not eat. When she says to the goat out there:

> '*Little goat, bleat;*
> *Little table, rise,*'

there stands a table before her, which is covered with the very best food, much better than we have here; and when she is satisfied, she says:

> '*Little goat, bleat;*
> *Little table, away,*'

and everything is gone again: I have seen it all exactly. She put two of my eyes to sleep with her little verse, but the one on my forehead remained awake."

Then the envious mother cried out, "Shall *she* be better off than we are?" and she fetched a butcher's knife and stuck it into the poor goat's heart, so that it fell down dead.

When Little Two Eyes saw that, she went out full of grief, sat on a small hill, and wept bitter tears. All at once the wise woman stood near her again and said, "Little Two Eyes, why do you cry?"

"Shall I not cry?" answered she. "My mother has killed the little goat that laid the table so beautifully every day when I said your little verse; now I must suffer hunger and thirst again."

The wise woman said, "Little Two Eyes, I will give you some good advice; beg your sisters to give you the heart of the goat, and bury it in the ground in front of the house door, and then see what happens to you." Then she disappeared, and Little Two Eyes went home and said to her sisters, "Dear sisters, give me some part of my goat; I don't ask for anything good, only give me the heart."

Then they laughed and said, "You can have that, if you do not want anything else." Little Two Eyes took the heart, and buried it quietly in the evening in front of the house door, following the advice of the wise woman.

Next morning, when the sisters woke and went to the house door together, there stood a most splendid tree, with leaves of silver, and fruit of gold hanging between them. Nothing more beautiful or charming could be seen in the wide world.

But they did not know how the tree had come there in the night. Little Two Eyes alone noticed that it had grown out of the heart of the goat, for it stood just where she had buried it in the ground.

Then the mother said to Little One Eye, "Climb up, my child, and gather us some fruit from the tree."

So Little One Eye climbed up, but

when she wanted to seize a golden apple, the branch sprang out of her hand: this happened every time, so that she could not gather a single apple, though she tried as much as she could.

Then the mother said, "Little Three Eyes, you climb up; you can see better with your three eyes than Little One Eye can."

Little One Eye scrambled down, and Little Three Eyes climbed up. But Little Three Eyes was no cleverer, and might look about her as much as she liked—the golden apples always sprang back from her grasp. At last the mother became impatient, and climbed up herself, but she could touch the fruit just as little as Little One Eye or

Little Three Eyes; she always grasped the air. Then Little Two Eyes said, "I will go up myself; perhaps I shall succeed better." "You!" cried the sisters. "With your two eyes, what can you do?" But Little Two Eyes climbed up, and the golden apples did not spring away from her, but dropped by themselves into her hand, so that she could gather one after the other, and she brought down a whole apron full.

Her mother took them from her, and instead of her sisters, Little One Eye and Little Three Eyes, behaving better to poor Little Two Eyes after this, they were only envious because she alone could get the fruit, and behaved still more cruelly to her.

One day as they stood together by the tree, a young knight came by. "Quick, Little Two Eyes," cried the two sisters, "creep under, so that we may not be ashamed of you;" and they threw over poor Little Two Eyes, in a great hurry, an empty cask that stood just by the tree, and pushed beside her the golden apples which she had broken off.

Now, as the Knight came nearer, he proved to be a handsome prince, who stood still, admired the beautiful tree of gold and silver, and said to the two sisters: "To whom does this beautiful tree belong? She who gives me a branch of it shall have whatever she wishes."

Then Little One Eye and Little Three Eyes answered that the tree was theirs, and they would break off a branch for him. They both gave themselves a great deal of trouble, but it was of no use, for the branches and fruit sprang back from them every time. Then the Knight said: "It is very strange that the tree belongs to you, and yet you have not the power of gathering anything from it."

They insisted, however, that the tree was their own property. But as they spoke, Little Two Eyes rolled a few golden apples from under the cask, so that they ran to the feet of the Knight; for Little Two Eyes was angry that Little One Eye and Little Three Eyes did not tell the truth.

When the Knight saw the apples he was astonished, and asked where they came from. Little One Eye and Little Three Eyes answered that they had another sister, who might not show herself because she had only two eyes, like other common people. But the Knight desired to see her, and called out, "Little Two Eyes, come out." Then Little Two Eyes came out of the cask quite comforted, and the Knight was astonished at her great beauty, and said: "You, Little Two Eyes, can certainly gather me a branch from the tree?"

"Yes," answered Little Two Eyes, "I can do that, for the tree belongs to me." And she climbed up and easily broke off a branch, with its silver leaves and golden fruit, and handed it to the Knight.

Then the Knight said, "Little Two Eyes, what shall I give you for it?"

"Oh," said Little Two Eyes, "I suffer hunger and thirst, sorrow and want, from early morning till late evening; if you would take me with you and free me, I should be happy."

Then the Knight lifted Little Two Eyes on to his horse, and took her home to his castle; there he gave her beautiful clothes, food, and drink, as much as she wanted; and because he loved her so much he married her, and the marriage was celebrated with great joy.

Now, when Little Two Eyes was taken away by the handsome Knight, the two sisters envied her very much for her happiness. "The splendid tree remains for us, however," thought they; "and even though we cannot gather any fruit from it, everyone will stand still before it, come to us, and praise it." But the next morning the tree had disappeared, and all their hopes with it.

Little Two Eyes lived happily for a long time. Once two poor women came to her at the castle and begged alms. Then Little Two Eyes looked in their faces and recognised her sisters, Little One Eye and Little Three Eyes, who had fallen into such poverty that they had to wander about and seek their bread from door to door.

Little Two Eyes, however, welcomed them, and was very good to them, and took care of them; for they both repented from their hearts the evil they had done to their sister in their youth.

Grimm, *The Milk-White Thorn*

Tom Thumb

Long, long ago, in the time of the good King Arthur, there lived a very wise man called Merlin. He was the most skilful enchanter in the world at that time. This famous Wizard was able to take upon himself the form of any man he chose.

Dressed like a beggar, he was one day travelling along a country road. Feeling very tired, he stopped at a wayside cottage to ask for some bread and a drink of milk.

The owner of the cottage, who was a ploughman, gave him a hearty welcome; and his wife brought the Wizard fresh milk in a wooden bowl, and some brown bread on a platter.

The Wizard was greatly pleased with the meal and with the kindness of his hosts. But though the cottage was clean and tidy, and husband and wife seemed very healthy, it was plain that they were not as happy as such good people ought to have been. Merlin put many questions to them, and they told him that they would be much happier if they had a child to love and take care of. If only she had a son, the woman said, even if the child were no bigger than a man's thumb, she would be one of the happiest women in the whole world.

Merlin soon afterwards left the cottage, after thanking the worthy couple for their kindness. As he walked along he began to smile at the idea of a boy no bigger than a man's thumb. Then he went to the Fairy Queen and told her of the poor woman's wish. Queen Mab was also much amused at the thought, and she promised Merlin to send the ploughman's wife a boy no bigger than her husband's thumb. This she did; and when the child lay in its tiny cradle she paid a visit to the ploughman's cottage, and left behind some clothing for the little fellow. There was an oak leaf to serve for a hat, a tiny shirt made of a spider's web, and a jacket woven of thistledown. There was also a pair of shoes, made from a mouse's skin, tanned with the downy hair.

The years went by, yet Tom Thumb, as the child had been named by Queen Mab, did not grow any bigger than his father's thumb. But as he grew older he became very cunning and full of tricks of all kinds. He would play with the boys at a game of cherry stones; and when he had lost all his own he would creep into the wallets of his playmates and steal some of theirs. One day a young boy found him doing this, and dragged him out.

"Aha!" he cried, "I have caught you at last, and you shall have your reward." Then he put Tom back into the wallet and, drawing the string tight, gave it a hearty shake. Tom was badly bruised from the cherry stones, and quite dazed. He cried out with pain, and was now ready to promise never to play this trick any more.

Not long afterwards his mother was making a pudding. Tom, wishing to see how it was made, climbed up to the edge of the bowl; and he fell heels over head into the pudding, unseen by his mother. Soon he was wrapped up in the pudding-cloth, and put into the pot to boil! The flour had filled the boy's mouth so that he could not cry out. But when he felt the hot water he kicked and struggled so much that his mother thought the fairies had got into the pudding. So she took it out of the pan and flung it down near the cottage door.

A poor man who was passing at the moment lifted up the pudding, put it into his bag, and walked away with it. Tom had now got the flour out of his mouth, and set up a dismal cry. This filled the man with such fear that he flung down the pudding and ran off. The pudding-cloth was torn open with the fall and Tom crept out, covered with batter. He made his way home with great trouble, and his mother washed him in a teacup filled with warm water, kissed him, and put him to bed.

Soon after this Tom's mother took the boy with her to milk the cow. The wind was very strong, and she was afraid he would be blown away; so she tied him to a thistle with a piece of fine thread.

The cow soon saw his oak-leaf hat and, having a taste for oak leaves, took poor Tom and the thistle in one mouthful. Soon the little fellow was dancing about within the cow's mouth, doing his best to avoid her teeth, and crying at the top of his voice, "Mother! Mother!"

"Where are you, my child?" cried the ploughman's wife in great distress.

"Here, Mother," came the reply from the red cow's mouth.

The poor woman began to cry and wring her hands; but the cow, feeling something unusual in her mouth, opened it and let Tom drop out. His mother caught him in her apron and, wrapping him up, ran home with him as fast as she could.

Not long afterwards Tom's father made him a whip of barley straw with which to drive the cattle. Walking in the fields one day, Tom slipped his foot and rolled into a furrow. A raven flying overhead saw him, picked him up, and carried him to the top of a giant's castle which stood by the seashore.

Tom was now in a state of great fear, and did not know what to do. After a while Grumbo the Giant came out to walk on the terrace. Soon he caught sight of Tom, and picking him up he looked at him severely. But Tom kicked so hard that the Giant threw him into the sea. A large fish caught him and swallowed him at once. At the same moment, along came a boat in which sat a fisherman who had been sent to catch fish for King Arthur's table.

He hooked the fish that had swallowed poor Tom, and it was taken to the cook, who cut it open. Out stepped the little fellow, as cheerful as ever; and great was the surprise of the cook.

Tom was soon taken to the King, who was greatly pleased with him and made him his dwarf. In time he became a great favourite at court, and amused the King and Queen by his tricks. When the King rode out on horseback he often took Tom with him. And whenever a shower came on, the little fellow always crept into the King's breast-pocket, where he slept till the rain was over.

One day King Arthur asked Tom about his parents. He wished to know whether they were as small as their son, and how they made a living. Tom said that his father and mother were as tall as other people, and that they were very poor.

On hearing this, the King took Tom to his treasury, where all his money and jewels were kept. Then he told him he might have as much money as he could carry home to his parents. Tom ran off at once to get a little purse, and was given a threepenny piece to put into it!

This was all that he could carry; in fact, the little fellow found it was no easy matter to get it upon his back. Then he set out for his father's house, but he had to rest more than a hundred times by the way. After two days and two nights of weary travel Tom reached his home in safety.

His mother ran out to meet him and carried him into the house. He was glad to get home, but he was greatly tired. So his mother placed him in a walnut shell by the fireside, and feasted him for three days on a hazel nut. But this made him ill, for a whole nut used to serve him for a month.

Tom soon got well again; but as the weather was very bad, he could not set out for King Arthur's palace. So his mother made a little parasol of paper, and tied Tom to the handle. Then she gave him a puff into the air with her mouth, and the wind soon carried him to the castle of the King.

Arthur, the Queen, and all the knights who sat at the King's Round Table, were very glad to see Tom again. And the little fellow went through many fine tricks to please them—so many, indeed, that he grew very weary and seemed like to die.

Then the Queen of the Fairies, hearing that he was ill, came to the palace in a coach drawn by flying mice; placing Tom by her side, she drove him through the air till she came to her own home. Here he rested, and was so well fed and tended by the Queen's maidens that he soon became quite well again. Then the Fairy Queen sent him back to King Arthur's palace.

She caused a light breeze to come up, and on it she placed Tom. He floated on it like a cork on the water, and was carried in a few moments to the palace.

Just as he floated over the courtyard the cook happened to be taking to the King a great bowl of spiced wine. Into this Tom fell with a splash, and spilt a great deal of the wine over the cook's jacket.

The cook was very angry, and she told the King that Tom had jumped into the bowl out of mischief. King Arthur was angry too when he heard this, and he gave orders to his men to cut off poor Tom's head.

Tom Thumb was now in great fear, and did not know what to do. As he walked about the palace kitchen he saw a miller sitting at a table yawning. With one bound he jumped into his mouth.

The miller was so angry with him that he opened the window and threw him into the river. A large salmon snapped him up in a moment. Then a fisherman caught the salmon, and sold it to a knight, who sent it as a present to King Arthur. The cook found Tom as before, and took him to the King. But his Majesty was very busy at the moment, and gave orders for Tom to be kept in prison until he wanted him.

The cook now put him into a mouse-trap. After a week had passed Tom was sent for by the King, who not only forgave him for what he had not done, but made him a knight. He was now to be known as Sir Thomas Thumb.

The King ordered a new suit of clothes to be prepared for him. His shirt was made of a butterfly's wings, his boots of chicken skin. Then a lovely mouse was fitted with a saddle for the new knight to take his rides.

One day Tom Thumb was riding by a farmhouse when a large cat saw him, made

a spring, and seized both him and his steed. She then ran up a tree with them; but Tom drew his sword, and set upon her so fiercely that she let them both fall. One of the King's nobles who was passing caught Tom in his hat and took him home at once to the royal palace.

Not long afterwards the Fairy Queen took Tom off to Fairyland, where he stayed for some years. During that time King Arthur and his chief nobles died. Tom now wished to go once more to Court, so the Fairy Queen sent him as before. The new King was named Thunstone, and he and all his knights flocked to see the little man.

King Thunstone asked who he was and where he came from and Tom Thumb said:

"My name is Tom Thumb,
From the fairies I've come.

to Tom Thumb. So she told the King that the little knight had been very rude to her. This was not true, and Tom knew it was only a made-up story. But when the King sent for him he was so much afraid that he hid himself in an empty snail shell. There he lay for some time, till he was nearly dead with hunger.

At last he peeped out. Seeing a fine large butterfly near him, he placed himself astride of it, and was at once carried up into the air. The butterfly flew from bush to bush and from field to field. At last it came to the palace garden, where the King and Queen spent a merry time in trying to catch it. Then, alas! poor Sir Thomas fell from his seat into a watering pot, in which he was almost drowned.

When the Queen saw him she flew into a great rage, and said that he should be at once beheaded; and he was again put into a mouse-trap, to wait until the time came for putting him to death. But the cat, seeing something alive in the trap, rolled it about until the wires broke, and so set Tom free once more.

The King now took him again into favour; but the adventures of Sir Thomas Thumb were now almost at an end. One day he was sitting in the palace garden when an enormous spider attacked him. Sir Thomas drew his sword and fought like a hero. But the spider was the victor, and soon the brave little knight lay dead upon the ground.

The King, his knights, and even the Queen were sorry at his death. A white marble stone was raised over his grave, on which was written the story of his life, so that all should know the wonder of it.

Anon., *The Milk-White Thorn*

When King Arthur lived,
This Court was my home.
In me he delighted,
By him I was knighted.
Did you never hear of Sir Thomas Thumb?"

The new King was so pleased with the little knight that he ordered a small chair to be made, in which Tom could sit on the dinner table; also a palace of gold, about nine inches high, with a door an inch and a half wide, for him to live in.

Now the new Queen grew very angry when she saw the favour that was shown

Sleeping Beauty

Once there was a royal couple who grieved very much because they had no children. When at last, after waiting a long time, the Queen presented her husband with a little daughter, his Majesty showed his joy by giving a christening feast so grand that nothing like it had ever been known before. He invited all the fairies in the land—there were seven altogether—to be godmothers to the little Princess, hoping that each might bestow on her some good gift, as was the custom of good fairies in those days.

At the end of the ceremony all the guests returned to the palace, where there was set before each Fairy Godmother a fine covered dish, with an embroidered table-napkin, and a knife and fork of pure gold, studded with diamonds and rubies. But, alas! as they placed themselves at table, there entered an old fairy who had never been invited, because more than fifty years since she had left the country on a pleasure trip and had not been heard of until this day.

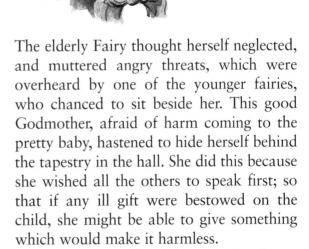

His Majesty, being much troubled, desired a dish to be placed before her, but it was of common ware, for he had ordered from his jeweller only seven gold dishes for the seven fairies that he had invited.

The elderly Fairy thought herself neglected, and muttered angry threats, which were overheard by one of the younger fairies, who chanced to sit beside her. This good Godmother, afraid of harm coming to the pretty baby, hastened to hide herself behind the tapestry in the hall. She did this because she wished all the others to speak first; so that if any ill gift were bestowed on the child, she might be able to give something which would make it harmless.

The six now offered their good wishes—which, unlike most wishes, were sure to come true. The fortunate little Princess was to grow up the fairest woman in the world; to have a temper sweet as an angel; to be perfectly graceful and gracious; to sing like a nightingale; to dance like a leaf on a tree; and to possess every virtue under the sun.

Then the old Fairy's turn came. Shaking her head spitefully, she uttered the wish that when the baby grew up into a young lady, and learned to spin, she might prick her finger with the spindle and at once die of the wound.

At this the guests shuddered, and some of the more tender-hearted began to weep. The parents were almost out of their wits with grief; but the wise Fairy appeared from behind the curtain, saying cheerfully: "Your Majesties may comfort yourselves; the Princess shall not die. I have no power to alter the ill-fortune just wished her by my sister—her finger must be pierced; and she shall then sink, not into the sleep of death, but into a sleep that will last a hundred years. After that time is ended, the son of a king will find her, kiss her, awaken her, and marry her."

Immediately all the fairies vanished.

The King, in the hope of avoiding his daughter's fate, issued an order forbidding all persons to spin, and even to have spinning-wheels in their houses, on pain of instant death. But it was all in vain.

One day, when she was just fifteen years of age, the King and Queen left their daughter alone in one of their castles. Wandering about at her will, the maiden came to an old tower, climbed to the top of it, and there found a very old woman—so old and deaf that she had never heard of the King's order—busy with her wheel.

"What are you doing, my good old woman?" said the Princess.

"I'm spinning, my pretty child."

"Ah, how charming! Let me try if I can spin also."

She had no sooner taken up the spindle than the point pierced her finger. Though it was only a small wound, she fainted away at once, and dropped silently the floor.

The poor frightened old woman called for help. Soon came the ladies-in-waiting, who tried every means to restore their young mistress; but all their care was useless. She lay, beautiful as an angel, the colour still lingering in her lips and cheeks; her dress softly stirred with her breath: only her eyes were closed fast. When the King her father and the Queen her mother beheld her like this they knew regret was idle—all had happened as the

344

cruel Fairy meant. But they also knew that their daughter would not sleep for ever. They sent away all the doctors and all the attendants, and themselves sorrowfully laid her upon a bed of embroidery, in the most elegant apartment of the palace. There the Princess slept, and looked like a sleeping angel still.

When this misfortune happened, the kindly young Fairy who had saved the Princess by changing her sleep of death into this sleep of a hundred years, was twelve thousand leagues away. But being informed of everything, she arrived speedily, in a chariot of fire drawn by dragons. The King was startled by the sight, but nevertheless went to the door of his palace, and, with a sad face, gave her his hand to help her to climb down.

The Fairy approved of all he had done. Then, being a fairy of common sense and foresight, she suggested that the Princess, awakening after a hundred years in this ancient castle, might be a good deal put out to find herself alone, especially with a young prince by her side. Accordingly, without asking any one's leave, she touched with her magic wand all the people of the palace, except the King and Queen: governesses, ladies of honour, waiting-maids, gentlemen, cooks, kitchen-girls, pages, footmen—down to the horses that were in the stables, and the grooms that attended them, she touched each and all.

She even touched the little fat lap-dog, Puffy, who had laid himself down beside his mistress on her splendid bed. He, like all the rest, fell fast asleep in a moment. The very spits that were before the kitchen fire ceased turning, and the fire itself went out, and everything became as silent as if it were the middle of the night, or as if the palace were a palace of the dead.

The King and Queen—having kissed their daughter and wept over her a little, but not too much, she looked so sweet and content—departed from the castle, giving orders that it was to be approached no more. The command was unnecessary; for in a quarter of an hour there sprang up around it a wood so thick and thorny that neither beasts nor men could by any means get through there. Above this dense mass of forest could only be seen the top of the high tower where the lovely Princess slept.

A great many changes happen in a hundred years. The King, who never had a second child, died, and his throne passed into another royal family. So entirely was the story of the poor Princess forgotten that when the reigning King's son, being one day out hunting and stopped in the chase by the thorny briers round the castle, inquired what wood it was and what were those towers which he saw appearing out of the midst of it, no-one could answer him. At length an old peasant was found who remembered having heard his grandfather say to his father that in this tower was a princess, as beautiful as the day, who was doomed to sleep there for one hundred years, until awakened by a king's son, who was to be her bridegroom.

At this the young Prince, who had the spirit of a hero, determined to find out the truth for himself. He leapt from his horse and began to force his way through the thick wood. To his amazement the stiff branches all gave way, and the ugly thorns sheathed themselves of their own accord, and the brambles buried themselves in the earth to let him pass. They closed behind him, allowing none of his servants to follow; but, ardent and young, he went boldly on alone.

The first thing he saw was enough to smite him with fear. Bodies of men and

horses lay stretched on the ground; yet the men had faces, not death-white, but red as peonies, and beside them were glasses half filled with wine, showing that they had gone to sleep while drinking.

Next he entered a large court, paved with marble, where stood rows of guards presenting arms, but motionless as if cut out of stone; then he passed through many chambers where gentlemen and ladies, all in the costume of a hundred years before, slept at their ease, some standing, some sitting. The pages were lurking in corners, the ladies of honour were stooping over their embroidery frames, or listening to the gentlemen of the Court, but all were as silent as statues.

Their clothes, strange to say, were fresh and new as ever; and not a particle of dust or spider-web had gathered over the furniture, though it had not known a broom for a hundred years. Finally the astonished Prince came to an inner chamber and saw the fairest sight his eyes had ever beheld. A young girl of wonderful beauty lay asleep on an embroidered bed, and she looked as if she had only just closed her eyes.

Trembling, the Prince approached and knelt beside her. Some say he kissed her, but as nobody saw it, and she never told, we cannot be quite sure of the fact. However, as the end of the time had come, the Princess awakened at once and, looking at him with tender eyes, said drowsily, "Is it you, my Prince? I have waited for you for a very long time."

Charmed with these words, and even more with the tone in which they were uttered, the Prince assured the Princess that he loved her more than his own life. Nevertheless, he was the more shy of the two; for, thanks to the kind Fairy, the Princess had had plenty of time to dream of him during her century of slumber, while he had never even heard of her till an hour before. For a long time did they sit talking, and yet had not said half of what they wished to say. Their only interruption was the barking of the little lap-dog, Puffy, who had awakened when his mistress did, and now began to be exceedingly jealous that the Princess did not notice him as much as she used to.

Meantime all the attendants, whose enchantment was also broken, not being in love, were ready to die of hunger after their fast of a hundred years. A lady of honour announced that dinner was served; then the Prince handed his beloved Princess at once to the great hall where they beheld a fully laden table. She did not wait to dress for dinner, being already perfectly and magnificently attired, though in a fashion somewhat out of date. However, the Prince had the politeness not to notice this, nor to remind her that she was dressed exactly like her royal grandmother, whose portrait still hung on the palace walls.

During the banquet a concert was given by the attendant musicians; and considering they had not touched their instruments for a century, they played extremely well. They ended with a wedding march: for that very evening the marriage of the Prince and the Princess was celebrated; and though the bride was nearly one hundred years older than the bridegroom, it is remarkable that the fact would never have been found out by anyone who did not know it.

Perrault, *The Milk-White Thorn*

Jack and the Beanstalk

Once upon a time there was a poor widow who lived in a little cottage with her only son Jack. He was a thoughtless boy, but very affectionate and kind-hearted. There had been a hard winter, and after it the poor woman had suffered from fever. Jack did no work, and they grew dreadfully poor. The widow saw that there was no means of keeping Jack and herself from starvation but by selling her cow; so one morning she said to her son: "You must take the cow to market for me, and sell her."

On the way, he met a butcher who had some beautiful beans in his hand. Jack stopped to look at them, and the butcher told the boy that they were of great value, and persuaded the silly lad to sell the cow for these beans.

When he brought them home to his mother instead of the money, she was very vexed and shed many tears, scolding Jack for his folly. He was very sorry and mother and son went to bed very sadly that night; their last hope seemed gone.

At daybreak Jack rose and went out into the garden. "At least," he thought, "I will sow the wonderful beans. Mother says they are just common scarlet-runners, and nothing else; but I may as well sow them."

That day they had very little dinner, and went sadly to bed.

Next day Jack got up and went out into the garden. The beans had grown up in the night, and climbed up and up till they covered the high cliff that sheltered the cottage, and disappeared above it! The stalks had twined and twisted themselves together till they formed a ladder.

"I wonder where it ends," said Jack to his mother; "I think I'll climb up and see."

Jack instantly began to climb, and went up and up till everything he had left behind him—the cottage, the village—looked quite little, and still he could not see the top of the Beanstalk.

After climbing higher and higher, till he grew afraid to look down for fear he should be giddy, Jack at last reached the top of the Beanstalk and found himself in a beautiful country, with beautiful meadows covered with sheep. Not far from the place where he had got off the Beanstalk stood a strong castle.

While Jack was standing looking at the castle, a very strange-looking woman came out of the wood. She wore a pointed cap of red satin, her hair streamed loose over her shoulders, and she walked with a staff. Jack took off his cap and made her a bow.

"If you please, ma'am," said he, "is this your house?"

"No," said the old lady. "Listen, and I will tell you the story of that castle."

"Once upon a time there was a noble knight, who lived in this castle, which is on the borders of Fairyland. He had a fair and beloved wife: and his neighbours, the little people, bestowed on him many excellent and precious gifts.

"Rumour whispered of these treasures; and a monstrous giant, who was a very wicked being, resolved to obtain possession of them. So he bribed a false servant to let him inside the castle when the knight was in bed and asleep, and he killed him as he lay.

"The lady was not to be found. She had gone with her infant son, to visit her old nurse. The next morning, one of the servants at the castle, who had managed to escape, came to tell the poor lady of the sad fate of her husband.

"The lady consented to remain at her nurse's house as the best place of concealment; for the servant told her the Giant had vowed, if he could find her, he would kill both her and her baby. Years rolled on. The old nurse died, leaving her cottage to her poor lady, who dwelt in it, working as a peasant for her daily bread.

"Jack, that poor lady is your mother. This castle was once your father's, and must again be yours."

"My mother! What ought I to do? My poor father! My dear mother!"

"You must win it back for your mother. But the task if a very difficult one and full of peril, Jack. Have you courage to undertake it?"

"I fear nothing when I know I'm doing right," replied Jack.

"Then," said the lady in the red cap, "you are one of those who slay giants. Remember, all the Giant possesses is really yours." As she ceased speaking, the lady of the red hat suddenly disappeared, and of course Jack knew she was a fairy.

He went up and blew the horn which hung at the castle door. The door was opened by a frightful giantess, with one great eye in the middle of her forehead. As soon as Jack saw her he turned to run away, but she caught him and dragged him into the castle.

"Ho, ho!" she laughed terribly. "I shan't let you go. I am weary of my life. I am so over-worked, and I don't see why I should not have a page as well as other ladies. And you shall be my boy. You shall clean the knives, and black the boots, and make the fires, and help me when the Giant is out. When he is at home I must hide you, for he has eaten up all my pages, and you would be a dainty morsel, my little lad."

While she spoke she dragged Jack right into the castle. The poor boy was very much frightened. But he struggled to be brave and make the best of things. "I am quite ready to help you, and do all I can

349

to serve you," he said, "only I beg you will be good enough to hide me from your husband, for I should not like to be eaten at all."

"That's a good boy," said the Giantess, nodding her head; "Come here, child; go into my wardrobe: he never ventures to open that; you will be safe there." And she opened a huge wardrobe which stood in the great hall, and shut him in it. However, the keyhole was so large that it admitted plenty of air, and he could see everything that took place through it. By and by Jack heard a heavy tramp on the stairs, like the lumbering along of a great cannon, and then a voice like thunder cried out:

"Fe, fi, fo, fum,
I smell the blood of an Englishman.
Be he living, or be he dead,
I'll grind his bones to be my
bread."

"Wife," cried the Giant, "I know there is a man in the castle. Let me have him for breakfast."

"You are grown old and stupid," cried the lady in her loud tones. "It is only a nice fresh steak off an elephant, that I have cooked for you, which you smell. There, sit down and make a good breakfast."

And she placed a huge dish before him of savoury steaming meat, which made him forget his idea of an Englishman being in the castle. When he had breakfasted he went out for a walk; and then the Giantess opened the door, and made Jack come out to help her. He helped her all day. She fed him well, and when evening came put him back in the wardrobe.

The Giant came in to supper. Jack watched him through the keyhole, and was amazed to see him put half a fowl at a time into his mouth.

When the supper was ended he told his wife bring him at once his hen that laid the golden eggs. "It lays as well as it did when it belonged to that paltry knight," he said; "indeed I think the eggs are heavier than ever."

The Giantess soon returned with a little brown hen, which she placed on the table before her husband.

Then he took up the brown hen and said to her: "Lay!" and she instantly laid a golden egg.

"Lay!" said the Giant again; and she laid another.

"Lay!" he repeated the third time; and again a golden egg lay on the table.

By and by the Giant put the hen down on the floor, and soon after was fast asleep, snoring so loud that it sounded like claps of thunder.

Jack pushed open the door of the wardrobe and crept out; very softly he stole across the room and, picking up the hen, made haste to the door; he opened it, shut and locked it after him, and ran back to the Beanstalk, which he descended as fast as his feet would move.

When his mother saw him enter the house she wept for joy, for she had feared that the Fairies had carried him away, or that the Giant had found him. But Jack put the brown hen down before her, and told her how he had been in the Giant's castle, and all his adventures. She was very glad to see the hen, which would make them rich once more.

Jack made another journey up the Beanstalk to the Giant's castle one day while his mother had gone to market; but first he dyed his hair and disguised himself. The old woman did not know him again, and dragged him in as she had done before, to help her do the work; but presently she heard her husband coming, and hid him in

350

the wardrobe, not thinking that it was the same boy who had stolen the hen. She told him to stay quite still there, or the Giant would eat him.

Then the Giant came in saying:

"Fe, fi, fo, fum,
I smell the blood of an
Englishman.
Be he living, or be he
dead,
I'll grind his bones to be
my bread."

"Nonsense!" replied the wife, "it is only a roasted bullock for your supper; sit down and I will bring it up to you at once."

As soon as they had finished their meal, the Giantess rose and said: "Now, my dear, I am going up to my room to finish the story I am reading. If you want me call for me."

"Before you go," said the Giant, "bring me my money bags, that I may count my golden pieces before I sleep."

She went and soon returned with two large bags over her shoulders. "There," she said; "that is all that is left of the knight's money. When you have spent it you must take another baron's castle."

"That he shall not, if I can help it," thought Jack.

The Giant took out heaps and heaps of golden pieces, and counted them. Leaning back in his chair he fell fast asleep, snoring.

Jack stole softly out of the wardrobe, and taking up the bags of money (which were his very own, because the Giant had stolen them from his father), he ran off, and with great difficulty climbing down the Beanstalk, laid the bags of gold on his mother's table.

After a time Jack made up his mind to go again to the Giant's castle. So he climbed the Beanstalk once more, and blew the horn at the Giant's gate. The Giantess soon opened the door; she was very stupid, and did not know him again. She told him to come in, and again hid him away in the wardrobe.

By and by the Giant came home, and as soon as he had crossed the threshold he roared out:

"Fe, fi, fo, fum,
I smell the blood of an Englishman.
Be he living, or be he dead,
I'll grind his bones to be my
bread."

"You stupid old Giant," said his wife, "you only smell a nice sheep, which I have grilled for your dinner."

And the Giant sat down, and his wife brought him a whole sheep for his dinner.

When he had eaten it all up, he said: "Now bring me my harp, and I will have a little music while you take your walk."

The Giantess returned with a beautiful harp. The framework was all sparkling with diamonds and rubies, and the strings were all of gold.

"This is one of the nicest things I took from the knight," said the Giant. "I am very fond of music, and my harp is a faithful servant."

So he drew the harp towards him and said: "Play!" and the harp played a very soft, sad air.

"Play something merrier!" said the Giant; and the harp played a merry tune.

"Now play me a lullaby," roared the Giant; and the harp played a sweet lullaby, to the sound of which its master fell asleep.

Then Jack stole softly out of the wardrobe, and seized the harp and ran away with it; but as he jumped over the threshold the harp called out: *Master! Master!*" and the Giant woke up.

With a tremendous roar he sprang from his seat, and in two strides had reached the door. But Jack was very nimble. He fled like lightning with the harp, talking to it as he went (for he saw it was a fairy), and telling it he was the son of its old master, the knight.

Still the Giant came on so fast that he was quite close to poor Jack, and had stretched out his great hand to catch him. But, luckily, just at that moment he stepped on a loose stone, stumbled, and fell flat on the ground.

This accident gave Jack time to get on the Beanstalk and hasten down it; but just as he reached their own garden he beheld the Giant descending after him.

"Mother! Mother!" cried Jack, "make haste and give me the axe."

His mother ran to him with a hatchet in her hand, and Jack with one tremendous blow cut through the Beanstalk.

"Now, Mother, stand out of the way!" said he.

Down came the Giant with a terrible crash, and as he fell on his head, he broke his neck, and lay dead at the feet of the woman he had so much injured.

And Jack and his mother lived happily ever after.

Anon., *The Red Fairy Book*

The Fairy's Two Gifts

In olden times, when the fairies lived on earth in the forms of human beings, a good Fairy, once wandering for some distance, became tired, and night came on before she could find shelter. At last she saw before her two houses just opposite each other—one large and beautiful, which belonged to a rich man; the other, small and wretched in appearance, which was owned by a poor peasant.

The Fairy thought, "I shall not be much trouble to the rich man." So she went up to the door of the beautiful house, and knocked. The rich man opened a window, and asked the stranger what she wanted.

"I beg you to give me a night's lodging," she replied.

Then the owner of the beautiful house looked at the wanderer from head to foot, and he saw that she was dressed in ragged clothes, but he could not see how much gold she had in her pocket. So he shook his head and said, "I cannot take you in—my rooms are full of valuable things, and if I were to admit into my house everyone who knocks at my door, I should soon have to take the beggar's staff myself. You must seek for what you want elsewhere."

Then he shut down the window, and left the good Fairy standing outside.

She turned her back on the grand house and went across to the other. Scarcely had she knocked, when the poor man opened the door, and begged the wanderer to enter.

"You must remain all night with us," he said: "it is already quite dark, and you cannot attempt to go further."

The Fairy was pleased so she stepped in, and the wife of the poor man came forward to welcome her, and led her in and told her to make herself quite comfortable.

"We have not much," she said, "but what there is, we will give you with all our hearts."

She placed the potatoes on the fire, and, while they were cooking milked the goat, that the visitor might have a little milk. As soon as the cloth was laid the Fairy seated herself at the table and ate with them, and the poor fare tasted good, because it was shared amid contentment and peace.

When bedtime came, the wife called her husband away privately and said: "Dear husband, let us for tonight make up a straw bed for ourselves, that the traveller may lie in our bed and rest; after walking the whole day she must be tired."

"With all my heart," he replied; "I will go and ask her to do so."

The good Fairy would not at first accept this kind offer, but at length she could not refuse. The poor man and his wife, therefore, slept on their bed of straw, and the Fairy rested comfortably in the bed.

In the morning she found the wife cooking a breakfast for her of the best they had. The Fairy again took her place at the table, the sun shone brightly into the room, and the faces of the poor people wore such a happy, contented expression that she was sorry to leave them.

As she rose to go she said farewell, and thanked them for their hospitality. At the door she turned and said: "As you have been so kind to me when you thought I was poor and in need, therefore I will show you that I have power to reward you. Three times shall your wish be granted you."

"What greater blessings can I wish for," said the husband, "but that we two, as long as we live, may be healthy and strong, and that we may always have our simple daily wants provided for? I cannot think of a third wish."

"Would you not like a new house instead of this old one?" she asked.

"Oh yes," they both cried; "if we have these three wishes granted we shall want nothing more."

Then the Fairy changed the old house into a new one, and promising them the fulfilment of their other wishes, went on her way. About noon the owner of the fine house happened to look out of his window, and saw with surprise opposite a pretty new cottage with red tiles, on the spot where the old house once stood. He stared at it for some time, and at last called his wife, and said to her: "Tell me how this can have happened: yesterday there stood an old, wretched-looking hut; today, this beautiful new cottage. Run over and ask how it has all come about."

The wife went over to ask the poor man to explain this wonderful change.

"Yesterday evening," he said, "came a poor traveller to our door who begged for a night's lodging. She was very poorly clad, but we gave her all we had, and our bed. This morning when she left us she offered to grant us the fulfilment of three wishes. We wished for continued health and our daily food as the greatest blessings, and at last she changed our old hut into this new and beautiful cottage."

On hearing this, the rich man's wife ran hastily back, and told her husband what she had heard. "I could tear myself to pieces," he exclaimed. "Oh, if I had only known! That stranger came here first, such a shabby-looking woman she was, and begged me to give her a night's lodging, but I refused her."

"Never mind," said his wife; "now make haste, ride after this woman; if you can overtake her you can ask her to grant you three wishes also."

The rich man followed this good advice, saddled his horse, rode after the traveller, and at last overtook her. He spoke to her then most gently and kindly, and hoped that she would not take it amiss that he had not admitted her the evening before. "I assure you," he said, "I was only looking for the key of the house door, and in the meantime you went away; if you should pass our way again you must stay with us."

"Yes," she replied, "I will do so, if I ever pass your house again."

Then the rich man asked the woman if she would not grant him three wishes. "I would grant you this willingly," replied the Fairy, "but I do not think it would be good for you; you have nothing to wish for."

The rich man replied that he could easily find something to wish for that would bring him good fortune, if he only knew that his wishes would be accomplished.

"Very well," said the Fairy; "ride home, and your three wishes shall be granted."

The rich man had obtained his desire, and he rode homewards, thinking deeply of what the wishes should be. He allowed the bridle to hang so loosely that his horse began to dance about till his thoughts were all so scattered that he could not collect them again. He struck the horse and said, "Be quiet, Bess," but the animal pranced and reared till he was nearly thrown off. At last he became angry, and cried out, "What do you mean by it? I wish your neck was broken."

No sooner had he spoken the words than his horse fell under him, and lay dead, and so was his first wish fulfilled. He was a greedy man and so he would not leave the saddle and bridle behind him. He cut the straps, hung them on his back, and prepared to walk home. "We have still two wishes remaining," he said, and comforted himself with the thought.

As he now walked along through the hot sand, with the burning noonday sun shining upon him, he became fretful with the heat and fatigue. The saddle dragged him back, and he could not decide what to wish for. "If I were to wish for all the riches and treasures in the world," he said to himself, "what would be the use? I should not know which to choose. Then he sighed, and said, "If I were only like the Bavarian peasant, who had three wishes offered him. First he wished for a draught of beer; the second time for as much beer as he could drink; and the third time for a whole cask. Each time he thought he had gained what he wanted, but afterwards it seemed to him like nothing."

Presently, there came to him a thought of how happy his wife must be, sitting in their cool room at home, and enjoying something very nice. It vexed him so much not to be there with her, that, without a thought of the consequences, he exclaimed, "Ah! I wish this heavy saddle would slip from my back, and that she was sitting upon it, not able to move."

As the last word fell from his lips, the saddle and bridle vanished, and he became aware that his second wish was fulfilled.

He ran home, for he wanted to sit alone in his chamber and think of something great for his last wish. But when he opened the door, there sat his wife on the saddle, screaming and lamenting that she was fixed, and could not get down.

"Make yourself quite happy," he said.

"I can wish for all the riches in the world to be ours; and my wish will be accomplished if you will only remain sitting there."

"But," she replied angrily, "you stupid head, what would be the use of all those riches to me if I am obliged to sit always on this saddle? No, no; you wished me here, and now you must wish me off again."

He was obliged, therefore, much against his will, to utter as his third wish that his wife might be set free, and the wish was immediately granted.

The rich and selfish man had, therefore, no other result from his three wishes than anger, vexation, trouble, and the loss of his horse. The poor man, who was charitable and kind to others, had gained happiness and contentment for the rest of his days.

Grimm, *Grimm's Fairy Tales*

The Tailor and the Bear

There once lived a princess who was so very haughty that when a suitor came she would have nothing to do with him unless he could solve one of her riddles; and if he tried, and did not succeed, he was dismissed with mockery and contempt. She allowed it to be generally known, however, that the man who could find out her riddle should be her husband.

Now, it happened that three tailors came to the town in which the Princess lived. The two eldest, who had done so many fine stitches, and guessed all sorts of puzzling riddles, were sure of being able to guess what the Princess propounded; it was not possible such clever people could fail. The third Tailor, however, was a useless little fellow, who knew scarcely anything of his trade; yet he fancied he might be lucky as well as any of them, and wished to try. But the other two said to him: "You had better stay at home with your half-witted head; you will never guess anything."

The little Tailor, however, was not to be diverted from his purpose. He said he had set his heart upon it, and he would go as well as everybody else. So they all three informed the Princess that they were ready to receive the riddle if she would lay it before them. They said that the right people had arrived at last—people who had fine understanding, and could thread a needle with anyone!

The Princess immediately sent for them, and propounded the riddle. "I have two different sorts of hair on my head," she said; "what colour are they?"

"If you were old, I should have to say the colours were black and white, like the clothes people call pepper and salt," replied one.

"You are wrong," said the Princess, and she turned to the second.

"The hairs are neither black nor white," he replied, "but brown and red, like my father's holiday coat."

"Wrong again," said the Princess, turning to the third; "most certainly these are not the answers."

Then the little Tailor stepped boldly forward, and said: "The Princess has a silver and a golden hair on her head, and they, of course, are of different colours."

When the Princess heard this she turned pale, and almost fell down with fright. The little Tailor had guessed her riddle, and she had firmly believed that not a man upon earth could do so.

When she at last recovered herself, she said: "You have guessed my riddle, but I am not won yet; you must do something more than this before I can be your wife. Down in the stable there lives a bear; you must spend the entire night with him, and if in the morning you are still alive, I will be your wife."

She thought as she said this that she should easily get rid of the little Tailor; for the Bear had never yet allowed anyone to escape alive when once he had them in his power. The Tailor, however, did not allow himself to be frightened; he went away, feeling quite contented, and saying: "Boldly ventured is half won."

When evening arrived, the little Tailor was taken down to the stables where the Bear lived. The Bear was quite ready to bid him welcome with a pat of his paw.

"Gently, gently, friend; I will soon make you quiet," thought the Tailor. So he sat down, made himself quite comfortable, as if he had no care, pulled some nuts out of his pocket, cracked them, and ate the kernels quite at his ease.

When the Bear saw this, he began to wish for nuts also, and asked the Tailor to give him some. The Tailor put his hand in his pocket and brought out a handful of what appeared to be nuts, but were really pebbles. The Bear stuck them in his muzzle, and rolled them about in his teeth, but he could not crack them, try as he would.

"What a stupid blockhead I certainly must be," thought the Bear, "not to be able to crack a nut." So he said to the Tailor, "Crack my nuts for me, will you?"

"Now, what a fellow you are," said the Tailor, "with such a great muzzle as yours, and yet not to be able to crack a nut."

He took the pebble from the Bear and, quickly changing it for a nut, put it in his mouth, and in a moment crack it went.

"I really must try to do that myself," said the Bear.

So the little Tailor gave him again more pebbles, and the Bear worked hard, and bit with all his strength, but, as you may be sure, without success; the Tailor, meanwhile, keeping him in a good humour by pretending to crack the stones for him, but always very cleverly changing them for real nuts.

Presently the little Tailor took a violin from under his coat, and began to play upon it. On this, the Bear, who understood music, could not help standing up and beginning to dance, and, after he had danced for a little while, he was so pleased with the music that he said to the Tailor: "Is it very difficult to learn to play upon that fiddle?"

"Oh, no; quite easy," replied the Tailor. "Look here, I lay my left hand on the strings, and with my right I draw the bow across them, making all sorts of sounds."

"I must learn to play it," said the Bear, "for then I shall be able to dance whenever I like. What do you think about it? Will you undertake to teach me?"

"With all my heart," replied the Tailor, "if you have the ability for it. But first show me your paws; the nails are tremendously long, and I must cut them a little before you begin to play."

In a corner of the stable stood a vice, which the Tailor brought out, and told the Bear to place his foot upon it. As soon as he did so, the Tailor screwed it so tight that he could not move. Then he left the Bear grumbling, and said: "Wait a little while till I bring the scissors."

The Bear might grumble as much as he liked now, the Tailor did not care; he felt safe, so he laid himself down in the corner on a bundle of straw, and went fast asleep.

During the night the Princess heard the growling, and she felt sure that the Bear was growling for joy over the little Tailor, of whom he was making a meal. So she rose in the morning quite contented; but when she went to the stable and peeped in, she was astonished. There stood the Tailor, as safe and sound as a fish in the water.

She could not say a single word against him, for she had spoken openly about the arrangement, and the King even ordered a carriage to take her to the church to be married to the Tailor. The Princess was not really unwilling, for she admired the young man's courage; so they entered the King's carriage, and drove off to church together. Meanwhile, the other Tailors, who envied his good fortune, made one more effort to destroy it. They went to the stable, set the

growling and snorting behind it, and in her terror she cried out, "Oh, the Bear is behind, and if he overtakes us we shall be lost." The Tailor was quite prepared and self-possessed; he stood on his head, and, sticking his legs through the window, cried out, "Bear, do you see the vice? If you don't go away now, you shall be screwed down and never again set free."

When the Bear heard this, he turned round and ran back with all his might. Our young Tailor travelled with his bride to the church, where they were happily married, and on their return the Princess took him by the hand and led him into the castle, where they continued to live in peace and were as happy as two skylarks. Whoever will not believe this story is true must pay a forfeit of one hundred dollars.

Grimm, *Grimm's Fairy Tales*

Bear's feet free from the vice, and no sooner did he regain his liberty than he immediately set off in a rage to run after the carriage. The Princess heard him

Scheherazade

The Sultan Schahriar had a wife whom he loved more than all the world, and his greatest happiness was to surround her with splendour, and to give her the finest dresses and the most beautiful jewels. It was therefore with the deepest shame and sorrow that he accidentally discovered, after several years, that she had deceived him completely, and her whole conduct turned out to have been so bad that he felt himself obliged to carry out the law of the land, and order the Grand-Vizier to put her to death. The blow was so heavy that his mind almost gave way, and he declared that he was quite sure that at bottom all women were as wicked as the Sultana, if you could only find them out, and that the fewer the world contained the better. And so every evening he married a fresh wife and had her strangled the following morning before the Grand-Vizier, whose duty it was to provide these unhappy brides for the Sultan. The poor man fulfilled his task with reluctance, but there was no escape, and every day saw a girl married and a wife dead.

This behaviour caused great horror in the town, where nothing was heard but cries and lamentations. In one house was a father weeping for the loss of his daughter, in another perhaps a mother trembling for the fate of her child; and instead of the blessings that had formerly been heaped on the Sultan's head, the air was now full of curses.

The Grand-Vizier himself was the father of two daughters, the elder sister called Scheherazade, and the younger Dinarzade. Dinarzade had no particular gifts to distinguish her from other girls, but her sister was clever and courageous in the highest degree. Her father had given her the best teachers in philosophy, medicine, history and the fine arts, and besides all this, her beauty excelled that of any girl in the kingdom of Persia.

One day, when the Grand-Vizier was talking to his eldest daughter, who was his delight and pride, Scheherazade said to him, "Father, I have a favour to ask of you. Will you grant it to me?"

"I can refuse you nothing," replied he, "that is just and reasonable."

"Then listen," said Scheherazade. "I am determined to stop this barbarous practice of the Sultan's, and to deliver the girls and mothers from the awful fate that hangs over them."

"It would be an excellent thing to do," answered the Grand-Vizier, "but how do you propose to accomplish it?"

"My Father," answered Scheherazade, "you have to provide the Sultan daily with a fresh wife, and I implore you, by all the affection you bear me, to allow the honour to fall upon me."

"Have you lost your senses?" exclaimed the Grand-Vizier, starting back in horror. "What has put such a thing into your head? You ought to know by this time what it means to be the Sultan's bride!"

"Yes, my Father, I know it well," replied she, "and I am not afraid to think of it. If I fail, my death will be a glorious one, and if I succeed I shall have done a great service to my country."

"It is of no use," said the Grand-Vizier, "I shall never consent. If the Sultan was to order me to plunge a dagger in your heart,

I should have to obey. What a task for a father! Ah, if you do not fear death, fear at any rate the anguish you would cause me."

"Once again, my dear Father," replied Scheherazade, "will you grant me what I ask?"

"What, are you still so obstinate?" exclaimed the Grand-Vizier. "Why are you so resolved upon your own ruin?"

But the daughter absolutely refused to attend to her father's words, and at length, in despair, the Grand-Vizier was obliged to give way. He went sadly to the palace to tell the Sultan that the following evening he would bring him Scheherazade.

The Sultan received this news with the greatest astonishment. "How ever have you made up your mind," he asked the Grand-Vizier, "to sacrifice your own daughter to me?"

"Sire," answered the Grand-Vizier, "it is her own wish. Even the sad fate that awaits her could not hold her back."

"Let there be no mistake, Vizier," said the Sultan. "Remember that you will have to take her life yourself. If you refuse, I swear that your head shall pay forfeit."

"Sire," returned the Vizier, "Whatever the cost, I will obey you. Though a father, I am also your subject." So the Sultan told the Grand-Vizier he might bring his daughter as soon as he liked.

The Vizier took back this news to Scheherazade, who received it as if it had been the most pleasant thing in the world. She thanked her father warmly for yielding to her wishes, and, seeing him still bowed down with grief, told him that she hoped he would never repent having allowed her to marry the Sultan. Then she went to prepare herself for the marriage, and begged that her sister Dinarzade should be sent for to speak to her.

When they were alone, Scheherazade said: "My dear Sister; I want your help in a very important affair. My father is going to take me to the palace, to celebrate my marriage with the Sultan. When his Highness receives me, I shall beg him, as a last favour, to let you sleep in our chamber, so that I may have your company during the last night I am alive. If, as I hope, he grants me my wish, be sure that you wake me an hour before the dawn, and speak to me in these words: 'My Sister, if you are not asleep, I beg you, before the sun rises, to tell me one of your charming stories.' Then I shall begin, and I hope by this means to deliver the people from the terror that reigns over them." Dinarzade replied that she would do with pleasure what her sister wished.

When the usual hour arrived the Grand-Vizier took Scheherazade to the palace, and left her alone with the Sultan, who told her to raise her veil and was amazed at her beauty. But seeing her eyes full of tears, he asked what was the matter. "Sire," replied Scheherazade, "I have a sister who loves me as tenderly as I love her. Grant me the favour of allowing her to sleep this night in the same room, as it is the last night we shall be together." Schahriar consented to Scheherazade's petition, and Dinarzade was sent for.

An hour before daybreak Dinarzade woke up, and exclaimed, as she had promised, "My dear Sister, if you are not asleep, tell me, before the sun rises, one of your charming stories. It is the last time I shall have the pleasure of hearing you."

Scheherazade turned to her husband, the Sultan. "Will your Highness permit me to do as my sister asks?" said she.

"Willingly," the Sultan answered. And so Scheherazade began.

Anon., *The Arabian Nights Entertainments*

Aladdin and the Wonderful Lamp

There once lived a poor tailor, who had a son called Aladdin, a careless, idle boy who would do nothing but play all day in the streets. This so grieved the father that he died; yet, in spite of his mother's tears and prayers, Aladdin did not mend his ways. One day, when he was playing in the streets as usual, a stranger asked him his age, and if he was not the son of Mustapha the tailor.

"I am indeed, sir," replied Aladdin; "but he died a long while ago."

The stranger, who was a famous African magician, kissed him, saying: "I am your uncle. Go to your mother and tell her I am coming."

Aladdin ran home and told his mother all about his newly found uncle.

"Indeed, child," she said, "your father had a brother, but I always thought he was dead." However, she prepared supper and told Aladdin to seek his

uncle, who came laden with wine and fruit. He kissed the place where Mustapha used to sit, telling Aladdin's mother not to be surprised at not having seen him before, as he had been forty years out of the country. He then turned to Aladdin and asked him his trade; the boy hung his head, while his mother burst into tears. On learning that Aladdin was idle and would learn no trade, he offered to take a shop for him and stock it with merchandise.

Next day the Magician led Aladdin a long way outside the city gates. At last they came to two mountains divided by a narrow valley. "We will go no further," said

the false uncle. "I will show you something wonderful; gather up sticks while I kindle a fire."

When it was lit the Magician threw on it a powder, at the same time saying some magical words. Then the earth trembled a little and opened in front of them, disclosing a square flat stone with a brass ring in the middle to raise it by. Aladdin tried to run away, but the Magician caught him and gave him a blow that knocked him down. "What have I done, Uncle?" he said piteously; then the Magician said more kindly: "Fear nothing, but obey me. Beneath this stone lies a treasure which is to be yours, and no-one else may touch it, so you must do exactly as I tell you."

At the word treasure Aladdin forgot his fears, and grasped the ring as he was told. The stone came up quite easily, and some steps appeared.

"Go down," said the Magician; "at the foot of those steps you will find an open door leading into three large halls. Tuck up your gown and go through them without touching anything, or you will die instantly. These halls lead into a garden of fine fruit trees. Walk on till you come to a niche in a terrace where stands an old lamp. Pour out the oil it contains and bring it to me." He drew a ring from his finger and gave it to Aladdin, wishing him good fortune. Aladdin found everything as the Magician had said, gathered some fruit off the trees, and, having got the lamp, arrived at the mouth of the cave. The Magician cried out: "Make haste and give me the lamp." This Aladdin refused to do until he was out of the cave. The Magician flew into a terrible rage and, throwing some more powder on to the fire, he said something, and the stone rolled back into its place. The Magician had read in his magic books of a wonderful lamp which would make him the most powerful man in the world. Though he alone knew where to find it, he could only receive it from the hand of another. He had picked out the foolish Aladdin for this purpose, intending to get the lamp and kill him afterwards. Now he left Persia in a rage.

Scheherazade, at this point seeing that it was now day, and knowing that the Sultan always rose early to attend the Council, stopped speaking.

"Indeed, Sister," said Dinarzade, "this is a wonderful story."

"The rest is still more wonderful," replied Scheherazade, "and you would say so, if the Sultan would allow me to live another day, and would give me leave to tell it to you the next night."

Schahriar, who had been listening to Scheherazade with pleasure, said to himself, "I will wait till tomorrow; I can always have her killed when I have heard the end of her story."

All this time the Grand-Vizier was in a terrible state of anxiety. But he was much delighted when he saw the Sultan enter the council chamber without giving the terrible command that he was expecting.

The next morning, before daybreak, Dinarzade said to her sister, "Dear Sister, if you are awake I beg you to go on with your story."

The Sultan did not even wait for Scheherazade to ask his leave. "Finish," he said. "I am curious to hear the end."

So Scheherazade went on with the story.

This happened every morning. The Sultana told a story, and the Sultan let her live to finish it.

For two long days Aladdin remained in the dark. At last he clasped his hands in prayer, and in so doing rubbed the ring, which the Magician had forgotten to take from him. Immediately an enormous and frightful genie rose out of the earth, saying: "I am the Slave of the Ring, and will obey you in all things."

Aladdin fearlessly replied: "Deliver me from this place!" then the earth opened, and he found himself outside. As soon as his eyes could bear the light he went home and told his mother what had passed, and showed her the lamp and the fruits he had gathered in the garden, which were in reality precious stones. He then asked for some food.

"Alas! child," she said, "I have nothing in the house, but I have spun a little cotton and will go and sell it."

Aladdin told her to keep her cotton, for he would sell the lamp instead. As it was very dirty she began to rub it with a cloth, that it might fetch a higher price. Instantly a hideous genie appeared, and asked what she would have. She fainted away, but Aladdin, snatching the lamp, said boldly: "Fetch me something to eat!" The Genie returned with a silver bowl, twelve silver plates containing rich food, two silver cups, and two bottles of wine.

Aladdin's mother, when she came to herself, asked where the splendid feast had come from. "Ask not, but eat," replied Aladdin. So they sat at breakfast till it was dinner time, and Aladdin told his mother about the lamp. She begged him to sell it, and have nothing to do with devils. "No," said Aladdin, "since chance has made us aware of its virtues, we will use it, and the ring likewise, which I shall always wear on my finger." When they had eaten all the Genie had brought, Aladdin sold one of the silver plates, and so on until none was left. He then called up the Genie, who gave him another set of plates, and they lived this way for many years.

One day Aladdin heard an order from the Sultan proclaiming that everyone was to stay at home and close their shutters while the Princess, his daughter, went past. Aladdin peeped through a chink. The Princess looked so beautiful that Aladdin fell in love with her at first sight. He went home so changed that his mother was frightened. He told her he loved the Princess so deeply that he could not live without her, and meant to ask for her hand in marriage. His mother burst out laughing, but Aladdin at last prevailed upon her to go before the Sultan and carry his request.

Aladdin's mother fetched a napkin and laid in it the magic fruits from the enchanted garden to please the Sultan. She went up to the foot of the throne and remained kneeling until the Sultan said to her: "Rise, good woman, and tell me what you want."

When she hesitated, the Sultan ordered her to speak freely, promising to forgive her beforehand for anything she might say. She then told him of her son's great love for the Princess. The Sultan asked her kindly what she had in the napkin, and then she unfolded the jewels and presented them. He was thunderstruck, and turning to the Vizier said: "What do you say? Ought I not to bestow the Princess on one who values her at such a price?"

The Sultan then turned to Aladdin's mother, saying: "Good woman, your son must first send me forty basins of gold brimful of jewels. Go and tell him that I await his answer."

The mother of Aladdin bowed low and went home, thinking all was lost. She gave Aladdin the Sultan's message, adding: "He may wait long enough for your answer!"

"Not so long, Mother, as you think," her son replied. He summoned the Genie, and in a few moments the jewels filled up the small house and garden.

When the Sultan saw Aladdin's jewels he came down from his throne, embraced

Aladdin, and led him into a hall where a feast was spread, intending to marry him to the Princess that very day. But Aladdin refused, saying, "I must first build a palace fit for her," and took his leave.

Once home, he said to the Genie: "Build me a palace of the finest marble, set with jasper, agate and other precious stones. In the middle you shall build me a large hall with a dome, its four walls of gold and silver, each side having six windows, whose lattices must be set with diamonds and rubies. There must be stables and horses and grooms and slaves; go and see about it at once!"

The palace was finished by next day. That night the Princess said good-bye to her father, and set out for Aladdin's palace. She was charmed at the sight of Aladdin and told him that, having seen him, she willingly obeyed her father.

After the wedding had taken place Aladdin led her into the hall, where a feast was spread, and she supped with him, after which they danced till midnight.

Meanwhile, far away in Africa the Magician remembered Aladdin, and by his magic arts discovered that he had escaped, and had married a princess, with whom he was living in great honour and wealth. He knew that the poor tailor's son could only have accomplished this by means of the lamp, and travelled night and day, bent on Aladdin's ruin. As he passed through the town he heard people talking everywhere about a marvellous palace.

"Forgive my ignorance," he pleaded, "what is this palace you speak of?"

"Have you not heard about Prince Aladdin's palace," came the reply, "the greatest wonder of the world?"

Having seen the palace, the Magician knew that it had been raised by the Genie of the Lamp, and became half mad with rage. He determined to get hold of the lamp, and again plunge Aladdin into the deepest poverty.

Unluckily, Aladdin had gone hunting for eight days, which gave the Magician plenty of time. He bought a dozen copper lamps, put them into a basket, and went to the palace, crying: "New lamps for old!" followed by a jeering crowd.

The Princess sent a slave to find out what the noise was about, who came back laughing, so that the Princess scolded her.

"Madam," replied the slave, "who can help laughing to see an old fool offering to exchange fine new lamps for old ones?"

Another slave, on hearing this, said: "There is an old one on the shelf there which he can have." Now this was the magic lamp. The Princess, not knowing its value, laughingly told the slave to take it and make the exchange.

She went and said to the Magician: "Give me a new lamp for this one." He snatched it and told the slave to take her choice, amid the jeers of the crowd. Little he cared, but went on his way shouting about his lamps. He walked out of the city gates to a lonely place, where he remained till nightfall, when he pulled out the lamp and rubbed it. The Genie appeared, and at the Magician's command carried him, together with the palace and the Princess in it, to a lonely place in Africa.

Next morning the Sultan looked out of the window towards Aladdin's palace and rubbed his eyes, for it was gone. He sent for the Vizier and asked what had become of the palace. The Vizier looked out too, and was lost in astonishment. He put it down to enchantment, and the Sultan sent thirty men on horseback to fetch Aladdin in chains. They met him riding home, bound him, and forced him to go with them on foot. The people, however, who loved him, followed, armed, to see that he came to no harm. He was carried before the Sultan, who ordered the executioner to cut off his head. The executioner made Aladdin kneel down, bandaged his eyes, and raised his scimitar to strike. At that instant the Vizier, who saw that the crowd had forced their way into the courtyard and were scaling the walls to rescue Aladdin, called to the executioner to stay his hand. The people, indeed, looked so threatening that the Sultan gave way and ordered Aladdin to be unbound, and pardoned him in the sight of the crowd.

Aladdin now begged to know what he had done. "False wretch!" said the Sultan, "come here," and showed him from the window the place where his palace had once stood. Aladdin was so amazed that he could not say a word. "Where is my palace and my daughter?" demanded the Sultan. "For the first I am not so concerned, but you must find my daughter or lose your head."

Aladdin begged for forty days in which to find her, promising if he failed, to return and suffer death at the Sultan's pleasure. His prayer was granted, and he went forth sadly from the Sultan's presence. He came to the banks of a

river, and knelt down to say his prayers before throwing himself in. In so doing he rubbed the magic ring he still wore. The Genie he had seen in the cave appeared, and asked his will.

"Save my life, Genie," replied Aladdin, "and bring my palace back."

"That is not in my power," said the Genie; "I am only the Slave of the Ring; you must ask the Genie of the Lamp."

"Even so," said Aladdin, "but you can take me to the palace, and set me down under my dear wife's window." He at once found himself in Africa, under the window of the Princess, and fell asleep out of sheer weariness.

The next morning, as the Princess was dressing, one of her women looked out and saw Aladdin. The Princess ran and opened the window, and at the noise she made Aladdin looked up. After he had kissed her

367

Aladdin said: "I beg of you, Princess, tell me what has become of an old lamp I left on the shelf in the hall of four-and-twenty windows, when I went hunting."

"Alas!" she said, "I am the innocent cause of our sorrows," and told him of the exchange of the lamp.

"Now I know," cried Aladdin, "that we have to thank the African Magician for this! Where is the lamp?"

"He carries it about with him," said the Princess. "He wishes me to marry him, saying that you were beheaded by my father's command; but I only reply with my tears. If I persist, I doubt not but he will use violence."

Aladdin comforted her, and left her for a while. Having bought a certain powder, he returned to the Princess, who let him in by a side door. "Put on your most beautiful dress," he said to her, "and receive the Magician with smiles. Invite him to sup with you, and say that you wish to taste the wine of his country. He will go for some and while he is gone I will tell you what to do."

She listened carefully to Aladdin, and when he left her she invited the Magician to sup with her, saying: "I would like to taste the wines of Africa." The Magician flew to his cellar, and the Princess put the powder Aladdin had given her in her cup. When he returned she asked him to drink her health, handing him her cup in exchange for his, as a sign she was reconciled to him.

Before drinking, the Magician made her a speech in praise of her beauty, but the Princess cut him short, saying: "Let us drink first, and you shall say what you will afterwards." She set her cup to her lips and kept it there, while the Magician drained his to the dregs and fell back lifeless.

The Princess then opened the door to Aladdin, and flung her arms round his neck. He went to the dead Magician, took the lamp out of his vest, and told the Genie to carry the palace and all in it back home. This was done at once, and the Princess in her chamber only felt two little shocks, and little thought she was at home again.

After this Aladdin and his wife lived in peace. He succeeded the Sultan when he died, and reigned for many years, leaving behind him a long line of kings!

Anon., *The Blue Fairy Book*

368

The Voyages of Sindbad the Sailor

In the times of the Caliph Haroun-al-Raschid there lived in Bagdad a poor porter named Hindbad, who on a very hot day was sent to carry a heavy load from one end of the city to the other. Before he had accomplished half the distance he was so tired that, finding himself in a quiet street where the pavement was sprinkled with rose-water, and a cool breeze was blowing, he set his burden upon the ground, and sat down to rest in the shade of a grand house. Very soon he decided that he could not have chosen a pleasanter place; a most delicious perfume came from the open windows and mingled with the scent of the rose-water which steamed up from the hot pavement. Within the palace he heard some music, as of many instruments cunningly played, and the melodious warble of nightingales and other birds, and by this, and the appetising smell of many dainty dishes of which he presently became aware, he judged that feasting and merry-making were going on. He wondered who lived in this magnificent house which he had never seen before, the street in which it stood being one which he seldom had occasion to pass. To satisfy his curiosity he went up to some splendidly dressed servants who stood at the door, and asked one of them the name of the master of the mansion.

"What," replied he, "do you live in Bagdad and not know that here lives the noble Sindbad the Sailor, that famous traveller who sailed over every sea upon which the sun shines?"

The porter, who had often heard people speak of the immense wealth of Sindbad, could not help feeling envious of one whose lot seemed to be as happy as his own was miserable. Casting his eyes up to the sky he exclaimed aloud: "Consider, O Mighty Creator of all things, the difference between Sindbad's life and mine. Every day I suffer a thousand hardships and misfortunes, and have hard work to get even enough bad barley bread to keep myself and my family alive, while the lucky Sindbad spends money right and left and

lives upon the fat of the land! What has he done that you should give him this pleasant life—and what have I done to deserve so hard a fate?

So saying he stamped upon the ground like one beside himself with misery and despair. Just at this moment a servant came out of the palace, and taking him by the arm said, "Come with me. The noble Sindbad, my master, wishes to speak to you."

Hindbad was not a little surprised at this summons, and feared that his carelessly spoken words might have drawn upon him the displeasure of Sindbad, so he tried to excuse himself with the excuse that he could not leave the burden which had been entrusted to him in the street. However, the servant promised him that it would be taken care of, and urged him to obey the call so pressingly that at last the porter was obliged to yield.

He followed the servant into a vast room, where a great company was seated round a table covered with all sorts of delicacies. In the place of honour sat a tall, grave man whose long white beard gave him a venerable air. Behind his chair stood a crowd of attendants eager to minister to his every need. This was the famous Sindbad himself. The porter, more than ever alarmed at the sight of so much magnificence, tremblingly saluted the noble company. Sindbad, making a sign to him to approach, caused him to be seated at his right hand, and himself heaped choice morsels upon his plate, and poured out for him a draught of excellent wine, and presently, when the banquet drew to a close, spoke to him familiarly, asking his name and occupation.

"My lord," replied the porter, "I am called Hindbad."

"I am glad to see you here," continued Sindbad. "And I will answer for the rest of the company that they are equally pleased, but I wish you to tell me what it was you said just now in the street." For Sindbad, passing by the open window before the feast began, had heard his complaint and therefore had sent for him.

At this question Hindbad was covered with confusion and, hanging down his head, replied, "My lord, I confess that, overcome by weariness and ill-humour, I uttered indiscreet words, which I pray you to pardon me."

"Oh!" replied Sindbad, "please do not imagine that I am so unjust as to blame you. On the contrary, I understand your situation and can pity you. However, you appear to be mistaken about me, and I wish to set you right. You doubtless imagine that I have acquired all the wealth and luxury that you see me enjoy without difficulty or danger, but this is far indeed from being the case. I have only reached this happy state after having for years suffered every possible kind of toil and danger.

"Yes, my noble friends," he continued, addressing the company, "I assure you that my adventures have been strange enough to deter even the most avaricious men from seeking wealth by crossing the seas. Since you have, perhaps, only heard confused accounts of my voyages, and the dangers and wonders that I have met with by sea and by land, I will now give you a true account of some of them, which I think you will be pleased to hear."

As Sindbad was relating his adventures chiefly on account of the porter, he ordered, before beginning his tale, that the burden which had been left in the street should be carried by some of his own servants to the place for which Hindbad had set out at first, while he remained to listen to the story.

First Voyage

I had inherited considerable wealth from my parents, and being young and foolish I at first squandered it recklessly on every kind of pleasure, but presently, finding that riches speedily take wings if managed as badly as I was managing mine, and remembering also that to be old and poor is misery indeed, I began to consider how I could make the best of what still remained to me. So I sold all my household goods by public auction, and joined a company of merchants who traded by sea, embarking with them at Balsora in a ship which we had fitted out between us.

We set sail and took our course towards the East Indies by the Persian Gulf, having the coast of Persia upon our left hand and upon our right the shores of Arabia Felix. I was at first much troubled by the uneasy motion of the vessel, but speedily recovered my health, and since that hour have been no more plagued by sea-sickness.

From time to time we landed at various islands, where we sold or exchanged our merchandise, and one day, when the wind dropped suddenly, we found ourselves becalmed close to a small island like a green meadow, which only rose slightly above the surface of the water. Our sails were furled, and the Captain gave permission to all who wished to land for a while and amuse themselves. I was among the number, but when after strolling about for some time we lit a fire and sat down to enjoy the meal which we had brought with us, we were startled by a sudden and violent trembling of the island, while at the same moment those left upon the ship set up an outcry bidding us come on board for our lives, since what we had taken for an island was nothing but the back of a sleeping whale.

Those who were nearest to the boat threw themselves into it, others sprang into the sea, but before I could save myself the whale plunged suddenly into the depths of the ocean, leaving me clinging to a piece of the wood which we had brought to make our fire. Meanwhile a breeze had sprung up, and in the confusion that ensued on board our vessel in hoisting the sails and taking up those who were left in the boat and clinging to its sides, no-one missed me and I was left at the mercy of the waves. All that day I floated up and down, now beaten this way, now that, and when night fell I despaired for my life; but, weary as I was, I clung to my frail support, and great was my joy when the morning light showed me that I had drifted against an island.

The cliffs were very high and steep, but luckily for me some tree roots protruded in places, and by their aid I climbed up at last, and stretched myself upon the turf at the top, where I lay, more dead than alive, till the sun was high in the heavens. By that time I was extremely hungry, but after some searching I came upon some edible herbs and a spring of clear water, and much refreshed I set out to explore the island. Presently I reached a great plain where a grazing horse was tethered, and as I stood looking at it I heard voices talking apparently underground, and in a moment a man appeared who asked me how I came upon the island. I told him my adventures, and heard in return that he was one of the grooms of Mihrage, King of the island, and that each year they came to feed their master's horses in this plain. He took me to a cave where all his companions were assembled, and when I had eaten the food they set before me, they told me to think myself fortunate to have come upon them when I did, since they were going back to their master the next day, and without their aid I could certainly never have found my way to the inhabited part of the island.

Early the next morning we set out, and when we reached the capital I was graciously received by the King, to whom I related my adventures, and he ordered that I should be well cared for and provided with such things as I needed. Being a merchant I sought out men of my own profession, and particularly those who came from foreign countries, as I hoped in this way to hear news from Bagdad, and find out some means of returning there, for the capital was situated upon the seashore, and visited by vessels from all parts of the world.

One day after my return, as I went down to the quay, I saw a ship which had just cast anchor and was discharging her cargo. Drawing nearer I presently noticed that my own name was marked on some of the packages and, after having carefully examined them, I felt sure that they were indeed those which I had put on board our ship at Balsora. I then recognised the Captain of the vessel, but as I was certain that he believed me to be dead, I went to him and asked who owned the packages that I was looking at.

"There was on board my ship," he replied, "a merchant of Bagdad named Sindbad. One day he and several of my other passengers landed upon what we supposed to be an island, but which was really an enormous whale floating asleep upon the waves. No sooner did it feel upon its back the heat of the fire which had been kindled, than it plunged into the depths of the sea. Several of the people who were upon it perished in the waters, and among others this unlucky Sindbad. This merchandise is his, but I have resolved to dispose of it for the benefit of his family if I should ever chance to meet with them."

"Captain," said I, "I am that Sindbad whom you believe to be dead, and these are my possessions!"

When the Captain heard these words he exclaimed, "What is the world coming to? In these days there is not an honest man to be met with. Did I not with my own eyes see Sindbad drown, and now you have the audacity to tell me that you are he! I should have taken you to be a just man, and yet for the sake of obtaining that which does not belong to you, you are ready to invent this horrible falsehood."

"Have patience, and do me the favour to hear my story," said I.

"Speak then," replied the Captain, "I'm all attention."

So I told him of my escape and of my fortunate meeting with the King's grooms, and how kindly I had been received at the palace. Very soon I began to see that I had made some impression upon him, and after the arrival of some of the other merchants, who showed great joy at once more seeing me alive and well, he declared that he also recognised me.

Throwing himself upon my neck, he said, "Heaven be praised that you have escaped from so great a danger. As to your goods, take them and dispose of them as you please." I thanked him, and praised his honesty, begging him to accept several bales of merchandise in token of my gratitude, but he would take nothing. Of the choicest of my goods I prepared a present for King Mihrage, who was at first amazed, having known that I had lost my all. However, when I had explained to him how my bales had been miraculously restored to me, he graciously accepted my gifts, and in return gave me many valuable things. I traded so successfully upon our homeward voyage that I arrived in Balsora with about one hundred thousand sequins.

My family received me with as much joy as I felt upon seeing them once more. I bought land and built a great house in which I resolved to live happily, and in the enjoyment of all the pleasures of life to forget my past sufferings.

Here Sindbad paused and commanded the musicians to play again, while the feasting continued until evening. When the time came for the porter to depart, Sindbad gave him a silk purse containing one hundred sequins, saying, "Take this, Hindbad, and go home, but tomorrow come again and you shall hear more of my adventures."

The porter retired quite overcome by so much generosity, and you may imagine that he was well received at home, where his wife and children thanked their lucky stars that he had found such a benefactor.

The next day Hindbad, dressed in his best, returned to the voyager's house, and was received with open arms. As soon as all the guests had arrived the banquet began as before, and when they had feasted long and merrily, Sindbad addressed them thus: "My friends, I beg that you will listen while I relate the adventures of my second voyage, which you will find even more astonishing than the first."

Second Voyage

I had resolved, as you know, on my return from my first voyage, to spend the rest of my days quietly in Bagdad, but very soon I grew tired of such an idle life and longed once more to find myself upon the sea. I therefore embarked for the second time in a good ship with other merchants whom I knew to be honourable men. We went from island to island, often making excellent bargains, until one day we landed at a spot which, though covered with fruit trees and abounding in springs of excellent water, appeared to be uninhabited. While my companions wandered here and there gathering flowers and fruit, I sat down in a shady place and, having heartily enjoyed the provisions and the wine I had brought with me, I fell asleep, lulled by the murmur of a clear brook which flowed close by.

How long I slept I know not, but when I opened my eyes and started to my feet I perceived with horror that I was alone and that the ship was gone. I rushed to and fro like one distracted, uttering cries of despair, and when from the shore I saw the vessel under full sail just disappearing upon the horizon, I wished bitterly enough that I had been content to stay at home in safety. But I presently took courage and looked about for a means of escape. When I had climbed a tall tree I first of all directed my anxious glances towards the sea; but, finding nothing hopeful there, I turned landward, and my curiosity was excited by a huge dazzling white object, so far off that I could not make out what it might be.

Descending from the tree I hastily collected what remained of my provisions and set off as fast as I could go towards it. As I drew near it seemed to me to be a white ball of immense size and height, and when I could touch it, I found it marvellously smooth and soft. As it was impossible to climb it—for it presented no foothold—I walked round it seeking some opening, but there was none. I counted, however, that it was at least fifty paces round. By this time the sun was near setting, but suddenly it fell dark, something like a huge black cloud came over me, and I saw with amazement that it was a bird of extraordinary size which was hovering near. Then I remembered that I had often heard the sailors speak of a wonderful bird called a roc, and it occurred to me that the white object which had so puzzled me must be its egg.

Sure enough the bird settled slowly down upon it, and I cowered close beside the egg in such a position that one of the bird's feet, which was as large as the trunk of a tree, was just in front of me.

Taking off my turban I bound myself securely to the huge claw with the linen in the hope that the roc, when it took flight next morning, would bear me away with it from the desolate island. And this was precisely what did happen. As soon as dawn appeared the bird rose into the air carrying me up till I could no longer see the earth, and then suddenly it descended so swiftly that I almost lost consciousness. When I became aware that the roc had settled and that I was once again upon solid ground, I hastily unbound my turban from its foot and freed myself, and that not a moment too soon; for the bird, pouncing upon a huge snake, killed it with a few blows from its powerful beak, and seizing it up rose into the air once more and soon disappeared from my view. When I had looked about me I began to doubt if I had gained anything by quitting the desolate island.

The valley in which I found myself was deep and narrow, and surrounded by

mountains which towered into the clouds and were so steep and rocky that there was no way of climbing up their sides. As I wandered about, seeking anxiously for some means of escaping from this trap, I observed that the ground was strewn with diamonds, some of them of an astonishing size. This sight gave me great pleasure, but my delight was speedily dampened when I saw also numbers of horrible snakes so long and so large that the smallest of them could have swallowed an elephant with ease. Fortunately for me they seemed to hide in caverns of the rocks by day, and only came out by night, probably because of their enemy the roc.

All day long I wandered up and down the valley, and when it grew dusk I crept into a little cave. Having blocked up the entrance to it with a stone, I ate part of my little store of food and lay down to sleep, but all through the night the serpents crawled to and fro, hissing horribly, so that I could scarcely close my eyes for terror. I was thankful when the morning light appeared, and when I judged by the silence that the serpents had retreated to their dens I came tremblingly out of my cave and wandered up and down the valley once more, kicking the diamonds contemptuously out of my path, for I felt that they were indeed vain things to a man in my situation. At last, overcome with weariness, I sat down on a rock, but I had hardly closed my eyes when I was startled by something which fell to the ground with a thud close beside me.

It was a huge piece of fresh meat, and as I stared at it several more pieces rolled over the cliffs in different places. I had always thought that the stories the sailors told of the famous valley of diamonds, and of the cunning way which some merchants had devised for getting at the precious stones,

were mere travellers' tales, but now I saw that they were surely true. These merchants came to the valley at the time when the eagles, which keep their eyries in the rocks, had hatched their young. The merchants then threw great lumps of meat into the valley. These, falling with so much force upon the diamonds, were sure to take up some of the precious stones with them when the eagles pounced upon the meat and carried it off to their nests to feed their broods. Then the merchants, scaring away the parent birds, would secure their treasures.

Until this moment I had looked upon the valley as my grave, but now I took courage and began to devise a means of escape. I began by picking up the largest diamonds I could find and storing them in my leather wallet; this I tied securely to my belt. I then chose the piece of meat which seemed most suited to my purpose, and with the aid of my turban bound it firmly to my back; this done I lay down upon my face and awaited the coming of the eagles.

I soon heard the flapping of their mighty wings above me, and felt one of them seize upon my piece of meat, and me with it, and rise slowly towards his nest, into which he presently dropped me. Luckily for me the merchants were on the watch, and setting up their usual outcries they rushed to the nest scaring away the eagle. Their amazement was great when they discovered me, and also their disappointment, and they fell to abusing me for having robbed them of their usual profit. Addressing myself to the one who seemed most aggrieved, I said: "I am sure, if you knew all I have suffered, you would show more kindness towards me, and as for diamonds, I have enough here of the very best for you and me and all your company." So saying I showed them to him. The others all crowded round me, wondering at my adventures and admiring the trick by which I had escaped from the valley, and when they had led me to their camp and examined my diamonds, they assured me that in all the years that they had carried on their trade they had seen no stones to be compared with them for size and beauty.

I found that each merchant chose a nest, and took his chance of what he might find in it. So I begged the one who owned the nest to which I had been carried to take as much as he would of my treasure, but he contented himself with one stone, and that by no means the largest, assuring me that with such a gem his fortune was made, and he need toil no more. I stayed with the merchants for several days, and then as they were journeying homewards I gladly accompanied them. Our way lay across high mountains infested with frightful serpents, but we had the good luck to escape them and came at last to the seashore.

We set sail and at last reached Balsora, from where I hastened to Bagdad, where my first action was to bestow large sums of money upon the poor, after which I settled down to enjoy tranquilly the riches I had gained with so much toil and pain.

Having thus related the adventures of his second voyage, Sindbad again bestowed a hundred sequins upon Hindbad, inviting him to come on the following day and hear how he fared upon his third voyage. The other guests also departed to their homes, but all returned at the same hour next day, including the porter, whose former life of hard work and poverty had already begun to seem to him like a bad dream. Again after the feast was over did Sindbad claim the attention of his guests and began the account of his third voyage.

Third Voyage

After a very short time the pleasant easy life I led made me quite forget the perils of my two voyages. Moreover, as I was still in the prime of life, it pleased me better to be up and doing. So once more providing myself with the rarest and choicest merchandise of Bagdad, I conveyed it to Balsora, and set sail with other merchants I knew for distant lands. We had touched at many ports and made much profit, when one day upon the open sea we were caught by a terrible wind which blew us completely out of our reckoning, and lasting for several days finally drove us into harbour on a strange island.

"I would rather have come to anchor anywhere than here," said our Captain. "This island and those adjoining it are inhabited by hairy savages, who are certain to attack us, and we dare not resist these dwarfs, since they swarm like locusts, and if one of them is killed the rest will fall upon us, and speedily make an end of us."

These words caused great consternation among all the ship's company, and only too soon we were to find out that the Captain spoke truly. There appeared a vast multitude of hideous savages, covered with reddish fur. Throwing themselves into the waves, they surrounded our vessel. Chattering meanwhile in a language we could not understand, and clutching at ropes and gangways, they swarmed up the ship's side with such speed and agility that they almost seemed to fly.

You may imagine the rage and terror that seized us as we watched them, neither daring to hinder them nor able to speak a word to deter them from their purpose, whatever it might be. Of this we were not left long in doubt. Hoisting the sails, and cutting the cable of the anchor, they sailed our vessel to an island which lay a little further off, where they drove us ashore; then they made off to the place from which they had come, leaving us helpless upon a shore avoided with horror by all mariners for a reason which you will soon learn.

Turning away from the sea we wandered miserably inland, finding as we went various herbs and fruits which we ate, feeling that we might as well live as long as possible though we had no hope of escape. Presently we saw in the distance what seemed to be a splendid palace, towards which we turned our weary steps, and when we reached it we saw that it was a castle, lofty and strongly built. Pushing back the heavy ebony doors we entered the courtyard, but upon the threshold of the great hall beyond it we paused, frozen with horror, at the sight which greeted us. On one side lay a huge pile of human bones and on the other spits for roasting! Overcome with despair we sank trembling to the ground, and lay there without speech or motion. The sun was setting when a loud noise aroused us, the door of the hall was violently burst open and a horrible giant entered. He was as tall as a palm tree, and perfectly black, and had one eye, which flamed like a burning coal in the middle of his forehead. His teeth were long and sharp and grinned horribly, while his lower lip hung down upon his chest, and he had ears like elephant's ears, which covered his shoulders, and nails like the claws of some fierce bird.

At this terrible sight our senses left us and we lay like dead men. When at last we came to ourselves, the Giant sat examining us attentively with his fearful eye. Presently, when he had looked at us enough, he came towards us and, stretching out his hand, took me by the back of the neck, turning me this way and that. Feeling that I was mere skin and bone, however, he set me down again and went on to the next, whom he treated in the same fashion. At last he came to the Captain and, finding him the fattest of all, he took him up in one hand and stuck him upon a spit and proceeded to kindle a huge fire at which he presently roasted him. After the Giant had supped he lay down to sleep, while we lay shivering with horror the whole night. When day broke he awoke and went out, leaving us in the castle.

When we believed him to be really gone we started up bemoaning our horrible fate until the hall echoed with our despairing cries. Though we were numerous and our enemy was alone it did not occur to us to kill him, and indeed we should have found that a hard task, even if we had thought of it, and no plan could we devise to deliver ourselves. So at last, submitting to our sad fate, we spent the day in wandering up and down the island eating such fruits as we could find. When night came we returned to the castle, having sought in vain for any other place of shelter. At sunset the Giant returned, supped upon one of our unhappy comrades, slept till dawn, and then left us as before. Our condition seemed so frightful that several of my companions thought it would be better to leap from the cliffs and perish in the waves rather than await so miserable an end; but I had a plan of escape which I now unfolded to them, and which they at once agreed to attempt.

"Listen, my brothers," I added. "Plenty of driftwood lies along the shore. Let us make several rafts, and carry them to a suitable place. If our plot succeeds, we can wait for the chance of some passing ship to rescue us. If it fails, we must quickly take to our rafts; frail as they are, we have more chance of saving our lives with them than we have if we remain here."

All agreed with me, and we spent the day in building rafts, each capable of carrying three persons. At nightfall we returned to the castle, and very soon in came the Giant, and one more of our number was sacrificed. But the time of our vengeance was at hand! As soon as he had finished his horrible meal he lay down to sleep as before, and when we heard him begin to snore I, and nine of the boldest of my comrades, rose softly, and took each a spit, which we made red-hot in the fire, and then we plunged them into the Giant's eye, completely blinding him. Uttering a terrible cry, he sprang to his feet clutching in all directions to try to seize one of us, but we had all fled different ways as soon as the deed was done, and thrown ourselves flat upon the ground in corners where he was not likely to touch us with his feet.

After a vain search he fumbled about till he found the door, and then fled out of it howling frightfully. As for us, when he was gone we made haste to leave the fatal castle, and, stationing ourselves beside our rafts, we waited to see what would happen. Our idea was that if, when the sun rose, we saw nothing of the Giant, and no longer heard his howls, which still came faintly through the darkness, growing more and more distant, we should conclude that he was dead, and that we might safely stay upon the island and need not risk our lives upon the frail rafts. But alas! morning light showed us our enemy approaching, supported on either hand by two giants nearly as large and fearful as himself, while a crowd of others followed close upon their heels. Hesitating no longer, we clambered upon our rafts and rowed with all our might out to sea. The Giants, seeing their prey escaping them, seized up huge pieces of rock and, wading into the water, hurled them after us with such good aim that all the rafts except the one I was upon were swamped, and their luckless crews drowned, without our being able to do anything to help them. Indeed I and my two companions had all we could do to keep our own raft beyond the reach of the Giants, but by hard rowing we at last reached the open sea. Here we were at the mercy of the winds and waves, which tossed us to and fro all that day and night, but the next morning we found ourselves near an island, upon which we gladly landed.

There we found delicious fruits, and having satisfied our hunger we lay down to rest upon the shore. Suddenly we were aroused by a loud rustling noise. Starting up, we saw that it was caused by an immense snake which was gliding towards us over the sand. So swiftly it came that it had seized one of my comrades before he had time to fly, and in spite of his cries and struggles speedily crushed the life out of him in its mighty coils and proceeded to swallow him. By this time my other companion and I were running for our lives to some place where we might hope to be safe from this new horror, and seeing a tall tree we climbed up into it, having first provided ourselves with a store of fruit off the surrounding bushes. When night came I fell asleep, but only to be awakened once more by the terrible snake, which after hissing horribly round the tree at last reared itself up against it. Finding my sleeping comrade who was perched just below me, the snake swallowed him also, and crawled away leaving me half dead with terror.

When the sun rose I crept down from the tree with hardly a hope of escaping the dreadful fate which had overtaken my comrades; but life is sweet, and I determined to do all I could to save myself. All day long I toiled with frantic haste and collected quantities of dry brushwood, reeds and thorns, which I tied into bundles. I piled them firmly one upon another until I had a kind of tent in which I crouched like a mouse in a hole when she perceives the cat coming. You may imagine what a fearful night I passed, for the snake returned eager to devour me, and glided round and round my frail shelter seeking an entrance. Every moment I feared that it would succeed in pushing aside some of the bundles, but happily for me they held together, and when it grew light my enemy retired, baffled and hungry, to his den. As for me I was more dead than alive! Shaking with fright and half suffocated by the poisonous breath of the monster, I came out of my tent and crawled down to the sea, feeling that it would be better to plunge from the cliffs and end my life at once than pass such another night of horror. But to my joy and relief I saw a ship sailing by, and by shouting wildly and waving my turban I managed to attract the attention of her crew.

A boat was sent to rescue me, and very soon I found myself on board surrounded by a wondering crowd of sailors and merchants eager to know by what chance I found myself on that desolate island. After I had told my story they regaled me with the choicest food the ship afforded, and the Captain, seeing that I was in rags, generously bestowed upon me one of his own coats. After sailing about for some time and touching at many ports we came at last to the island of Salahat, where sandalwood grows in abundance. Here we anchored, and as I stood watching the merchants disembarking their goods and preparing to sell or exchange them, the Captain came up to me and said: "I have here, Brother, some merchandise belonging to a passenger of mine who is dead. Will you do me the favour to trade with it, and when I meet with his heirs I shall be able to give them the money, though it will be only just that you shall have a portion for your trouble."

I consented gladly, for I did not like standing by idle. He pointed the bales out to me, and sent for the person whose duty it was to keep a list of the goods that were on the ship. When this man came he asked in what name the merchandise was to be registered.

"In the name of Sindbad the Sailor," replied the Captain.

At this I was greatly surprised, but looking carefully at him I recognised him to be the Captain of the ship upon which I had made my second voyage, though he had altered much since that time. As for him, believing me to be dead it was no wonder that he had not recognised me.

"So, Captain," said I, "the merchant who owned those bales was known as Sindbad?"

"Yes," he answered. "He belonged to Bagdad, and joined my ship at Balsora, but by mischance he was left behind on a desert island where we had landed to fill up our water-casks, and it was not until four hours later that he was missed. By that time the wind had freshened, and it was impossible to put back for him."

"You suppose him to have perished then?" said I.

"Alas! yes," he answered.

"Why, Captain!" I cried, "look well at me. I am that Sindbad who fell asleep upon the island and awoke to find himself abandoned!"

The Captain stared at me in amazement, but was eventually convinced that I was indeed speaking the truth, and rejoiced greatly at my escape.

"I am glad to have that piece of carelessness off my conscience at any rate," said he. "Now take your goods, and the profit I have made for you upon them, and may you prosper in future."

I returned to Bagdad with so much money that I could not count it, besides treasures without end. I gave largely to the poor, and bought much land to add to what I already possessed, and thus ended my third voyage.

When Sindbad had finished his story he gave another hundred sequins to Hindbad, who then departed with the other guests; but the next day when they had all reassembled, and the banquet was ended, their host continued his adventures.

Fourth Voyage

Not even all that I had gone through could make me contented with a quiet life. I soon wearied of its pleasures, and longed for change and adventure. Therefore I set out once more, but this time in a ship of my own, which I built and fitted out at the nearest seaport. I wished to be able to call at whatever port I chose, taking my own time; but as I did not intend carrying enough goods for a full cargo, I invited several merchants of different nations to join me. We set sail with the first favourable wind, and after a long voyage upon the open seas we landed on an unknown island which proved to be uninhabited. We determined, however, to explore it, but had not gone far when we found a roc's egg, as large as the one I had seen before and very nearly hatched, for the beak of the young bird had already pierced the shell. In spite of all I could say to deter them, the merchants who were with me fell upon it with their hatchets, breaking the shell, and killing the young roc. Then lighting a fire upon the ground they hacked morsels from the bird, and proceeded to roast them while I stood by aghast.

Scarcely had the merchants finished their ill-omened feast when the air above us was darkened by two mighty shadows. The Captain of my ship, knowing by experience what this meant, cried out to us that the parent birds were coming, and urged us to get on board with all speed. This we did, and the sails were hoisted, but before we had travelled far, the rocs reached their despoiled nest and hovered above it, uttering frightful cries when they discovered the mangled remains of their young one. For a moment we lost sight of them, and were hoping that we had escaped when they reappeared and soared into the air directly over our vessel. We saw that each held in its claws an immense rock ready to crush us. There was a moment of suspense, then one bird loosed its hold and the huge block of stone hurtled through the air, but thanks to the presence of mind of the helmsman, who turned our ship violently in another direction, it fell into the sea close beside us, till we could nearly see the bottom. We had hardly time to draw a breath of relief before the other rock fell with a mighty crash right in the midst of our luckless vessel, smashing it into a thousand fragments, and crushing or hurling into the sea, both passengers and crew. I myself went down with the rest, but had the good fortune to rise unhurt, and by holding on to a piece of driftwood with one hand and swimming with the other I kept myself afloat and was washed up by the tide on to an island. Its shores were steep and rocky, but I scrambled up safely and threw myself down to rest upon the green turf.

When I had somewhat recovered, I began to examine the spot in which I found myself, and truly it seemed to me that I had reached a garden of delights. There were trees everywhere, and they were laden with flowers and fruit, while a crystal stream wandered in and out under their shadow. When night came I slept sweetly, though the remembrance that I was alone in a strange land made me sometimes start up and look around me in alarm, and then I wished heartily that I had stayed at home. However, the morning sunlight restored my courage, and I once more wandered among the trees, but always wondering anxiously as to what I might see next. I had penetrated some distance into the island when I saw an old man bent and feeble sitting upon the river bank, and at first I took him to be some shipwrecked mariner like myself. Going up to him I greeted him in a friendly way, but he only nodded his head at me in reply. I then asked what he was doing there, and he made signs to me that he wished to get across the river to gather some fruit, and seemed to beg me to carry him on my back. Pitying his age and feebleness, I took him up, and wading across the stream I bent down that he might more easily reach the bank, and told him to get down. But instead of allowing himself to be set upon his feet (even now it makes me laugh to think of it!), this creature who had seemed to me so decrepit leapt nimbly upon my shoulders, and hooking his legs round my neck gripped me so tightly that I was almost choked, and so overcome with terror that I fell unconscious to the ground.

When I recovered, my enemy was still in his place, though he had released his hold enough to allow me breathing space, and seeing me revive he prodded me first with one foot and then with the other, until I was forced to get up and stagger about with him under the trees while he gathered and ate the choicest fruits. This went on all day, and even at night, when I threw myself down half dead with weariness, the terrible old man held on tight to my neck, nor did he fail to greet the first glimmer of morning light by drumming upon me with his heels, until I was forced to wake and resume my dreary march with rage and bitterness in my heart.

One day I passed a tree under which lay several dry gourds, and catching one up I amused myself for a time with scooping out its contents and pressing into it the juice of several bunches of grapes which hung from every bush. When the gourd was full I left it propped in the fork of a

tree, and a few days later, carrying the hateful old man that way, I snatched at my gourd as I passed it and enjoyed a draught of excellent wine so good and refreshing that I even forgot my detestable burden, and began to sing and caper.

The old mam was not slow to perceive the effect which my drink had produced and that I carried him more lightly than usual, so he stretched out his skinny hand and seizing the gourd first tasted its contents cautiously, then drained them to the very last drop. The wine was strong and the gourd large, so he also began to sing after a fashion, and soon I had the delight of feeling the iron grip of his goblin legs unclasp, and with one vigorous effort I threw him to the ground, from which he never moved again. I was so glad to have at last got rid of this uncanny old man that I ran leaping and bounding down to the seashore, where, by the greatest good luck, I met with some mariners who had anchored off the island to enjoy the delicious fruits, and to renew their supply of water.

They listened to the story of my escape with amazement, saying: "You fell into the hands of the Old Man of the Sea, and it is a mercy that he did not strangle you as he has everyone else upon whose shoulders he has managed to perch himself. This island is well known as the scene of his evil deeds, and no merchant or sailor who lands upon it cares to stray far away from his comrades." After we had talked for a while they took me back with them on board their ship, where the Captain received me kindly, and we soon set sail and since that time I have rested from my labours, and given myself up wholly to my family and friends.

Thus Sindbad ended the story of his last voyage, and turning to Hindbad he added: "Well, my friend, and what do you think now? Have you ever heard of anyone who has suffered more hardships, or had more narrow escapes than I have? Is it not just that I should now enjoy a life of ease and tranquillity?"

Hindbad drew near, and kissing his hand respectfully replied, "Sir, you have indeed known fearful perils; my troubles have been nothing compared to yours. Moreover, the generous use you make of your wealth proves that you deserve it. May you live long and happily in the full enjoyment in it."

Sindbad then gave Hindbad a hundred sequins, and henceforward counted him among his friends; also he caused him to give up his profession as a porter, and to eat daily at his table that he might all his life remember Sindbad the Sailor.

Anon., *The Arabian Nights Entertainments*

Ali Baba and the Forty Thieves

In a town in Persia there dwelt two brothers, one named Cassim, the other Ali Baba. Cassim was married to a rich wife and lived in plenty, while Ali Baba had to maintain his wife and children by cutting wood in a neighbouring forest and selling it in the town. One day, when Ali Baba was in the forest, he saw a large troop of men on horseback, coming towards him in a cloud of dust. He was afraid they were robbers, and climbed into a tree for safety. When they came up to him and dismounted, he counted forty of them. They unbridled their horses and tied them to trees. The finest man among them, whom Ali Baba took to be their Captain, went a little way among some bushes, and said: "Open, Sesame!" so plainly that Ali Baba heard him. A door opened in the rocks, and having made the troop go in, he followed them, and the door shut again by itself. They stayed some time inside, and Ali Baba, fearing they might come out and catch him, was forced to sit patiently in the tree. At last the door opened again, and the Forty Thieves came out. As the Captain went in last he came out first, and made them all pass by him; he then closed the door, saying: "Shut, Sesame!" Every man mounted his horse, the Captain put himself at their head, and they returned as they came.

Then Ali Baba climbed down and went to the door concealed among the bushes, and said: "Open, Sesame!" and it flew open. Ali Baba, who expected a dull, dismal place, was greatly surprised to find it large and well lighted, and shaped in the form of a vault, which received the light from an opening in the ceiling. He saw rich bales of merchandise—silk, brocades all piled together, and gold and silver in heaps, and money in leather purses. He went in and the door shut behind him. He did not look at the silver, but brought out as many bags of gold as he thought his asses, which were browsing outside, could carry, loaded them with the bags, and hid it all with pieces of wood. Using the words: "Shut, Sesame!" he closed the door and went home.

Then he drove his asses into the yard, shut the gates, carried the money bags to his wife, and emptied them out before her. He ordered her to keep the secret, and he would go and bury the gold. "Let me first measure it," replied his wife. "I will go and borrow a measure from someone, while you dig the hole."

So she ran to the wife of Cassim and borrowed a measure. Knowing Ali Baba's poverty, the sister was very curious to find out what sort of grain his wife wished to measure, and artfully put some fat at the bottom of the measure. Ali Baba's wife went home and set the measure on the heap of gold, and filled and emptied it often, to her great content. She then carried it back to her sister, without noticing that a piece of gold was sticking to it, which Cassim's wife perceived directly

her back was turned. She grew curious, and said to Cassim when he came home: "Cassim, your brother is richer than you. He does not count his money, he measures it." He begged her to explain this riddle, which she did by showing him the piece of money and telling him where she found it.

Then Cassim grew so envious that he could not sleep, and went to his brother in the morning before sunrise. "Ali Baba," he said, showing him the gold piece, "you pretend to be poor and yet you measure gold." By this time Ali Baba saw that through his wife's folly Cassim and his wife knew their secret, so he confessed all and offered Cassim a share. "That I expect," answered Cassim; "but I must know where to find the treasure, otherwise I will tell all, and you will lose all." Ali Baba, more out of kindness than fear, told him of the cave, and the very words to use.

Cassim left Ali Baba, meaning to go ahead of him and get the treasure for himself.

He rose very early next morning, and set out with ten mules loaded with great chests. He soon found the place, and the door in the rock. He said: "Open, Sesame!" and the door opened and shut behind him. He could have feasted his eyes all day on the treasures, but he now hastened to gather together as much of it as possible; but when he was ready to go he could not remember what to say for thinking of his great riches. Instead of "Sesame," he said: "Open, Barley!" and the door remained fast. He named several different sorts of grain, all but the right one, and the door still stuck fast. He was so frightened at the danger he was in that he had as much forgotten the word as if he had never heard it.

About noon the robbers returned to their cave and saw Cassim's mules roving about with great chests on their backs. This gave them the alarm; they drew their sabres and went to the door, which opened when their Captain said: "Open, Sesame!" Cassim, who had heard the trampling of their horses' feet, resolved to sell his life dearly, so when the door opened he leapt out and threw the Captain down. In vain, however, for the robbers with their sabres soon killed him. On entering the cave they saw all the bags laid ready, and could not imagine how anyone had got in without knowing their secret. They cut Cassim's body into four quarters, and nailed them up inside the cave, in order to frighten anyone who should venture in, and went away in search of more treasure.

As night drew on Cassim's wife grew very uneasy, and ran to her brother-in-law and told him where her husband had gone. Ali Baba did his best to comfort her, and set out to the forest in search of Cassim. The first thing he saw on entering the cave was his dead brother. Full of horror, he put the body on one of his asses, and bags of gold on the other two, and, covering everything with some wood, returned home. He drove the two asses laden with gold into his own yard, and led the other to Cassim's house. The door was opened by the slave Morgiana, whom he knew to be both brave and cunning. Unloading the ass, he said to her: "This is the body of your master, who has been murdered, but we must bury him as though he had died in his bed. I will speak with you again, but now tell your mistress I have come." The wife of Cassim, on learning the fate of her husband, broke out into cries and tears, but Ali Baba offered to take her to live with him and his wife if she would promise to keep his secret and leave everything to Morgiana; she agreed, and dried her eyes.

Morgiana, meanwhile, found a chemist and asked him for some lozenges. "My poor master," she said, "can neither eat nor speak, and no-one knows what his illness is." She carried home the lozenges, then returned next day weeping, and asked for an essence only given to those just about to die. Thus, in the evening, no-one was surprised to hear the wretched shrieks and cries of Cassim's wife and Morgiana, telling everyone that Cassim was dead. The next day Morgiana went to an old cobbler near the gates of the town who opened his stall early, put a piece of gold in his hand, and told him to follow her with his needle and thread. Having bound his eyes with a handkerchief, she took him to the room where the body lay, pulled off the bandage and ordered him to sew the quarters together, after which she covered his eyes again and led him home. Then they buried Cassim, and Morgiana his slave followed him to the grave, weeping and tearing her hair, while Cassim's wife stayed at home crying and lamenting. Next day she went to live with Ali Baba, who gave Cassim's shop to his eldest son.

The Forty Thieves, on their return to the cave, were astonished to find Cassim's body gone as well as some of their money bags. "We are certainly discovered," declared the Captain, "and shall be ruined if we cannot find out who it is that knows our secret. Two men must have known it; we have killed one man, we must now find the other. One of you who is bold and artful must go into the city dressed as a traveller, and discover who we have killed, and whether men talk of the strange manner of his death. If the messenger fails he must lose his life, lest we be betrayed." One of the thieves started up and offered to do this, and after the rest had highly praised him for his bravery he disguised himself, and happened to enter the town at daybreak, just near Baba Mustapha's stall. The thief greeted him, saying: "Honest man, how can you possibly see to stitch at your age?"

"Old as I am," replied the cobbler, "I have very good eyes, and you will believe me when I tell you that I sewed a dead body together in a place where I had less light than I have now."
The robber was over-joyed at his good fortune and, giving him a piece of gold, desired to be shown the house where he stitched up the dead body. At first Mustapha refused, saying that he had been blindfolded; but when the robber gave him another piece of gold he began to think he might remember the turnings if he were blindfolded as before. This plan succeeded; the robber partly led him, and was partly guided by him, in front of Cassim's house, then he marked the door with a piece of chalk. Then, well pleased, he said good-bye to Baba Mustapha and returned to the

forest. By and by Morgiana, going out, saw the mark the robber had made, guessed that some mischief was brewing, and fetching a piece of chalk marked two or three doors on each side, without saying anything to her master or mistress.

The thief, meantime, told his comrades of his discovery. The Captain thanked him, and told him to show him the house he had marked. But when they came to it they saw that five or six of the houses were chalked in the same manner. The guide was so surprised that he knew not what answer to make, and when they returned he was at once beheaded for having failed. Another robber was despatched, and, having won over Baba Mustapha, marked the house in red chalk; but Morgiana being again too clever for them, the second messenger was put to death also.

The Captain now resolved to go himself, but, being wiser than the others, he did not mark the house, but looked at it so closely that he could not fail to remember it, He returned, and ordered his men to go into the neighbouring villages and buy nineteen mules, and thirty-eight leather jars, all empty, except one which was full of oil. The Captain put one of his men, fully armed, into each, rubbing the outside of the jars with oil from the full vessel. Then the nineteen mules were loaded with thirty-seven robbers in jars, and the jar of oil, and reached the town by dusk. The Captain stopped his mules in front of Ali Baba's house, and said to Ali Baba, who was sitting outside for coolness: "I have brought oil from a distance to sell at tomorrow's market, but it is now so late that I do not know where to pass the night, unless you will do me the favour to take me in."

Though Ali Baba had seen the Captain of the robbers in the forest, he did not recognise him in the disguise of an oil merchant. He welcomed the man, opened his gates for the mules to enter, and went to Morgiana to bid her prepare a bed and supper for his guest. He brought the stranger into his hall, and after they had eaten went again to speak to Morgiana in the kitchen, while the Captain went into the yard under pretence of seeing to his mules, but really to tell his men what to do. Beginning at the first jar and ending at the last, he said to each man: "As soon as I throw some stones from the window of my chamber, cut the jars open with your knives and come out, and I will be with you in a trice." He returned to the house, and Morgiana led him to his chamber.

Morgiana then told Abdallah, her fellow slave, to begin cooking some broth for her master, who had gone to bed. Meanwhile her lamp went out, and she had no more oil in the house. "Do not be uneasy," said Abdallah; "go into the yard and take some out of one of those jars." Morgiana thanked him for his advice, took the oil pot, and went into the yard. When she came to the first jar the robber inside said softly: "Is it time?"

Any other slave but Morgiana, on finding a man in the jar instead of the oil she wanted, would have screamed and made a noise; but she, knowing the danger that her master was in, thought of a plan, and answered quietly: "Not yet, but soon." She went to all the jars, giving the same answer, till she came to the jar of oil. She now saw that her master, thinking to entertain an oil merchant, had let thirty-eight robbers into his house. She filled her oil pot, went back to the kitchen, and, having lit her lamp, went again to the oil jar and filled a large kettle full of oil. When it boiled she went and poured enough oil into every jar to stifle and kill the robber inside. When this brave deed was done she went back to the kitchen, put out the fire and the lamp, and waited to see what would happen.

In a quarter of an hour the Captain of the robbers awoke, got up and opened the window. As all seemed quiet he tossed down some little pebbles which hit the jars. He listened, and as none of his men seemed to stir he grew uneasy, and went down into the yard. On going to the first jar and saying: "Are you asleep?" he smelt the hot boiled oil, and knew at once that his plot to murder Ali Baba and his household had been discovered. He found that all the gang were dead, and, missing the oil out of the last jar, became aware how they had died. He then forced the lock of a door leading into a garden, and climbing over several walls made his escape. Morgiana heard and saw all this, and, rejoicing at her success, went to bed and fell asleep.

At daybreak Ali Baba arose, and, seeing the oil jars there still, asked why the merchant had not taken his mules with him. Morgiana told him to look in the first jar and see if there was any oil. Seeing a man, he started back in terror. "Have no fear," said Morgiana; "the man cannot harm you: he is dead." When he had recovered somewhat from his astonishment, Ali Baba asked what had become of the merchant. "Merchant!" replied she, "he is no more a merchant than I am!" and she told him the whole story, assuring him that it was a plot of the robbers of the forest, of whom only three were left, and that the white and red chalk marks had something to do with it. Ali Baba thanked Morgiana and said that he owed her his life. They then buried the thirty-eight bodies in Ali Baba's garden, while the mules were sold in the market.

The Captain returned to his lonely cave, which seemed frightful to him without his lost companions, and resolved to avenge them by killing Ali Baba. He dressed himself carefully, and went into the town, where he took lodgings in an inn. In the course of a great many journeys to the forest he had carried away many rich things and much fine linen, and so set up a shop opposite that of Ali Baba's son. He called himself Cogia Hassan, and as he was both polite and well dressed he soon made friends with Ali Baba's son, and through him with Ali Baba, whom he was continually asking to dine with him. Ali Baba, wishing to return his kindness, invited him into his house and received him smiling, thanking him for his kindness to his son. When the merchant was about to take his leave Ali Baba stopped him, saying: "Where are you going, sir, in such haste? Will you not stay and dine with me?"

The merchant refused, saying that he had a reason; and, on Ali Baba's asking him what that was, he replied: "It is, sir, that I can eat no food that has any salt in it."

"If that is all," replied Ali Baba, "let me tell you that there shall be no salt in either the meat or the bread that we eat tonight."

He went to give this order to Morgiana, who was surprised. "Who is this man," she said, "who eats no salt with his meat?"

"He is an honest man, Morgiana," returned her master; "therefore do as I tell you." But she could not withstand a desire to see this strange man, so she helped Abdallah to carry up the dishes, and saw in a moment that Cogia Hassan was the robber captain, and carried

a dagger under his garment. "I am not surprised," she said to herself, "that this wicked man, who intends to kill my master, will eat no salt with him; but I will hinder his plans."

She sent up the dinner by Abdallah, while she made ready for one of the boldest acts that could be thought of. When the dessert had been served, Cogia Hassan was left alone with Ali Baba and his son, whom he meant to make drunk and then to murder them. Morgiana, meanwhile, put on a head-dress like a dancing girl's, and clasped a girdle round her waist, from which hung a dagger with a silver hilt. She then said to Abdallah: "Take your drum, and let us go and divert our master, his son and his guest." Abdallah took his drum and played before Morgiana until they came to the door, where Abdallah stopped playing and Morgiana made a low curtsy.

"Come in, Morgiana," said Ali Baba, "and let Cogia Hassan see what you can do;" and, turning to Cogia Hassan, he said: "She's my slave and my housekeeper."

Cogia Hassan was by no means pleased, for he feared that his chance of killing Ali Baba was gone for the present; but he pretended great eagerness to see Morgiana. Abdallah began to play and Morgiana to dance. After she had performed several dances she drew her dagger and made passes with it, sometimes pointing it at her own breast, sometimes at her master's, as if it were part of the dance. Suddenly, out of breath, she snatched the drum from Abdallah with her left hand and, holding the dagger in her right, held out the drum to her master. Ali Baba and his son put a piece of gold into it, and Cogia Hassan, seeing that she was coming to him, pulled out

his purse to make her a present, but while he was putting his hand into it Morgiana plunged the dagger into his heart.

"Unhappy girl!" cried Ali Baba and his son, "what have you done to ruin us?"

"It was to preserve you, master, not to ruin you," answered Morgiana. "See here," opening the false merchant's garment and showing the dagger; "see what an enemy you have entertained! Remember, he would eat no salt with you, and what more would you have? Look at him! he is both the false oil merchant and the Captain of the Forty Thieves."

Ali Baba was so grateful to Morgiana for saving his life that he gave her her freedom and offered her to his son in marriage, who readily consented, and a few days later their wedding was celebrated with great splendour. At the end of a year Ali Baba, hearing nothing of the two remaining robbers, judged they were dead, and set out to the cave. The door opened when he said: "Open, Sesame!" He went in, and saw that nobody had been there since the Captain left it. He brought away as much gold as he could carry, and returned to town. He told his son the secret of the cave, which his son handed down in his turn, so the children and grandchildren of Ali Baba were rich to the end of their lives.

Anon., *The Blue Fairy Book*

Aesop's
Fables

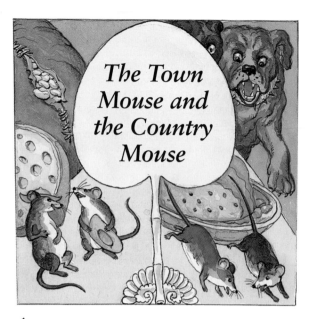

The Town Mouse and the Country Mouse

A Town Mouse once went on a visit to his Cousin in the country. He was rough and ready, this Cousin, but he loved his town friend and made him welcome. Beans and bacon, cheese and bread, were all he had to offer, but he offered them freely. The Town Mouse turned up his long nose at this country fare, and said: "I cannot understand, Cousin, how you can put up with such poor food; come with me to the town and I will show you how to live."

No sooner said than done: the two mice set off for the town and arrived at the Town Mouse's residence late at night.

"You will want some refreshment after our journey," said the polite Town Mouse, and took his friend into the grand dining room. There they found the remains of a fine feast, and soon the two mice were eating up jellies and cakes and all that was nice.

Suddenly they heard growling. "What is that?" said the Country Mouse.

"It is only the dogs of the house," the other answered.

"Only!" said the Country Mouse. "I do not like that music at my dinner." Just at that moment the door flew open, in came two huge mastiffs, and the two mice had to scamper down and run off. "Good-bye, Cousin," said the Country Mouse.

"What! going so soon?" said the other.

"Yes," he replied:

"Better beans and bacon in peace than cakes and ale in fear."

The Dog and the Shadow

It happened that a Dog had got a piece of meat and was carrying it home in his mouth to eat it in peace. On his way home he had to cross a bridge across a running brook. As he crossed, he looked down and saw his own shadow reflected in the water beneath. Thinking it was another dog with another piece of meat, he made up his mind to have that also. So he made a snap at the shadow in the water, but as he opened his mouth the piece of meat fell out, dropped into the water and was never seen again.

Beware lest you lose the substance by grasping at the shadow.

The Goose that Laid the Golden Eggs

One day a countryman going to the nest of his Goose found there an egg all yellow and glittering. When he took it up it was as heavy as lead and he was going to throw it away, because he thought a trick had been played on him. But he took it home on second thoughts, and soon found to his delight that it was an egg made of pure gold. Every morning the same thing occurred, and he soon became rich by selling his eggs. As he grew rich he grew greedy; and thinking to get at once all the gold the Goose could give, he killed it and opened it only to find nothing there.

Greed often over-reaches itself.

The Fox and the Crane

At one time the Fox and the Crane were on visiting terms and seemed very good friends. So the Fox invited the Crane to dinner, and for a joke put nothing before her but some soup in a very shallow dish. This the Fox could easily lap up, but the Crane could only wet the end of her long bill in it, and left the meal as hungry as when she began. "I am sorry," said the Fox, "the soup is not to your liking."

"Pray, do not apologise," answered the Crane. "I hope you will return this visit, and come and dine with me soon." So a day was appointed when the Fox should visit the Crane; but when they were seated at table all that was for their dinner was contained in a very long-necked jar with a narrow mouth, in which the Fox could not insert his snout, so all he could manage to do was to lick the outside of the jar.

"I will not apologise for the dinner," said the Crane:

"One bad turn deserves another."

The Bat, the Birds and the Beasts

A great battle was about to be fought between the Birds and the Beasts. When the two armies were facing one another, the Bat could not make up his mind which one to join. The Birds that passed his perch said: "Come with us," but he replied, "I am a Beast." Later on, some beasts passing beneath him looked up and said: "Come with us," but he replied, "I am a Bird."

Luckily, at the last moment the Birds and Beasts made peace and did not fight a battle. Then the Bat came to the birds wishing to join in the celebrations, but they all turned against him and he had to fly away. Then he went over to the Beasts, but they wanted to tear him to pieces. The Bat only just managed to escape. "Ah," said the Bat, "now I see that:

He that is neither one thing nor another has no friends."

The Lion and the Bullfrog

A Lion went past a pool of water one day and heard a dreadful roaring noise coming from the reeds on the farther shore. He could see nothing, but he was sure that a gigantic monster must be roaring at him, about to attack. The Lion ran for his life.

The noise was coming from a small Bullfrog in the reeds, but the Lion did not have the courage to go over and find out.

Imaginary fears are the worst.

The Boy who Cried Wolf

There was once a young Shepherd Boy who tended his sheep at the foot of a mountain near a dark forest. It was rather lonely for him all day, so he thought upon a plan by which he could get a little company and some excitement. He rushed down towards the village calling out "Wolf, Wolf," and the villagers came out to meet him, and some of them stopped with him for a considerable time. This pleased the Boy so much that a few days later he tried the same trick, and again the villagers came to his help.

However, shortly after this a Wolf actually did come out from the forest, and began to worry the sheep, and the Boy of course cried out "Wolf, Wolf", still louder than before. But this time the villagers, who had been fooled twice before, thought the Boy was again deceiving them, and nobody stirred to come to his help. So the Wolf made a good meal off the Boy's flock, and when the Boy complained, the wise man of the village said:

"A liar will not be believed, even when he speaks the truth."

The Wind and the Sun

The Wind and the Sun were disputing which was the stronger. Suddenly they saw a traveller coming down the road, and the Sun said: "I see a way to decide our dispute. Whichever of us can cause that traveller to take off his cloak shall be regarded as the stronger. You begin." So the Sun retired behind a cloud, and the Wind began to blow as hard as it could upon the traveller. But the harder he blew the more closely did the traveller wrap his cloak round him, till at last the Wind had to give up in despair. Then the Sun came out and shone in all his glory upon the traveller, who soon found it too hot to walk with his cloak on.

Kindness achieves more than severity.

The Boaster

A Man used to boast all the time of what he had done. He boasted wherever he was, whether he stayed at home or went to the market or walked along the street. In the end, someone said to him: "I am tired of hearing about what you have done. Let me see you do it now instead of talking about it!" The Boaster was silent after that.

Deeds, not words.

The Lion and the Mouse

Once when a Lion was asleep a little Mouse began running up and down upon him; this soon wakened the Lion, who placed his huge paw upon him, and opened his big jaws to swallow him.

"Pardon, O King," exclaimed the little Mouse: "forgive me this time, I shall never forget it; who knows, I may be able to do you a turn one of these days." The Lion was so tickled at this idea that he lifted up his paw and let him go.

Some time later the Lion was caught in a trap, and the hunters who desired to carry him alive to the King tied him to a tree while they went in search of a wagon to carry him on. Just then the little Mouse happened to pass by and, seeing the sad plight in which the Lion was, went up to him and soon gnawed away the ropes that bound the King of the Beasts.

"Was I not right?" said the little Mouse.

Little friends may prove great friends.

The One-Eyed Doe

A Doe had had the misfortune to lose one of her eyes, and could not see anyone approaching her on that side. So to avoid any danger she always used to feed on a high cliff near the sea, with her good eye looking towards the land. By this means she could see when the hunters approached her on land, and often escaped by this means. But the hunters found out that she was blind in one eye and, hiring a boat, rowed under the cliff where she used to feed and shot her from the sea. "Ah," she cried with her dying voice, "I thought of the dangers of the land, but not those of the sea. That was my undoing."

Misfortune often attacks us from an unexpected quarter.

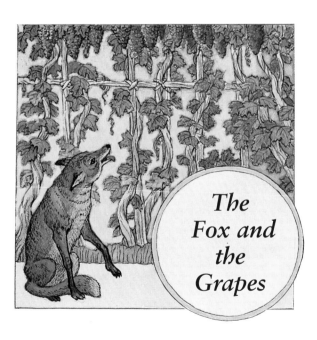

The Fox and the Grapes

One very hot summer's day a Fox was strolling through an orchard till he came to a bunch of Grapes just ripening on a vine which had been trained over a lofty branch. "Just the thing to quench my thirst," he said. Drawing back a few paces, he took a run and a jump, and just missed the bunch. Turning round again with a one, two, three, he jumped up, but with no greater success. Again and again he tried to reach the tempting morsel, but at last had to give it up, and walked away with his nose in the air, saying: "I am sure they are sour."

It is easy to despise what you cannot get.

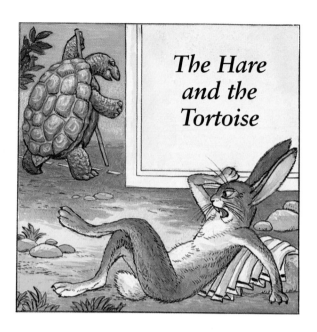

The Hare and the Tortoise

The Hare was once boasting of his speed before the other animals. "I have never yet been beaten," he said, "when I put forth my full speed. I challenge anyone here to race with me."

The Tortoise said quietly, "I accept your challenge."

"That is a good joke," said the Hare; "I could dance round you all the way."

"Keep your boasting till you've beaten," answered the Tortoise. "Shall we race?"

So a course was fixed and a start was made. The Hare darted almost out of sight at once, but soon stopped and, to show his contempt for the Tortoise, lay down to have a nap. The Tortoise plodded on and plodded on, and when the Hare awoke from his nap, he saw the Tortoise just near the winning-post and could not run up in time to save the race. Then said the Tortoise:

Slow and steady wins the race.

The Two Crabs

One fine day two Crabs came out from their home to take a stroll on the sand. "Child," said the mother, "you are walking very ungracefully. You should accustom yourself to walking straight forward without twisting from side to side."

"Pray, Mother," said the young one, "do but set the example yourself, and I will follow you."

Example is the best teacher.

The Boy and Fortune

A Boy was weary and fell asleep right at the edge of a deep well so that he was almost falling in. The goddess Fortune appeared to him and touched him on the shoulder, saying, "Wake up, wake up. If you had fallen into the well, people would have blamed not your foolishness but me, Fortune."

Fortune is not to blame for our carelessness.

The Two Pots

Two Pots had been left on the bank of a river, one of brass, and one of earthenware. When the tide rose they both floated off down the stream. Now the earthenware pot tried its best to keep aloof from the brass one, which cried out: "Fear nothing, friend, I will not strike you."

"But I may come in contact with you if I come too close;" said the other, "and whether I hit you, or you hit me, I shall suffer for it."

Equals make the best friends.

401

King Log and King Stork

The Frogs were living happily in a marshy swamp that just suited them; they splashed about caring for nobody and with nobody troubling them. But some of them thought this was not right, that they should have a king and a constitution, so they determined to send up a petition to Jove. "Mighty Jove," they cried, "send unto us a king that will rule over us and keep us in order." Jove laughed at their croaking, and threw down a huge Log, which came splashing down into the swamp.

The Frogs were very frightened by the commotion, and all rushed to the bank to look at the monster; but after a time, seeing that it did not move, one or two of the very boldest of them ventured out towards the Log, and even dared to touch it; still it did not move. Finally, the greatest hero of the Frogs jumped on the Log and commenced dancing up and down on it, thereupon all the Frogs came and did the same; and for some time the Frogs went about their business every day without taking the slightest notice of their new King Log.

But this did not suit them, so they sent another petition to Jove, and said to him: "We want a real king; one that will really rule over us." This made Jove angry, so he sent among them a big Stork that soon set to work gobbling them all up. Then the Frogs repented when too late.

Better no rule than cruel rule.

The Peacock and Juno

A Peacock once placed a petition before Juno desiring to have the voice of a nightingale, but Juno refused his request. "Fate has given to all their destined gifts: you have been given beauty, the eagle strength, and the nightingale song," she said. When the Peacock persisted, and pointed out that he was her favourite bird, Juno said:

"Be content with your lot; one cannot be first in everything."

Nonsense Verse

Nonsense Poems

by Edward Lear

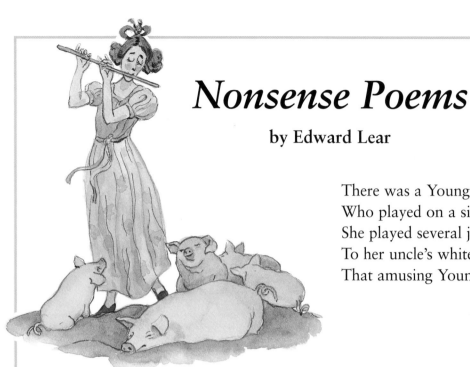

There was a Young Lady of Bute,
Who played on a silver-gilt flute;
She played several jigs,
To her uncle's white pigs,
That amusing Young Lady of Bute.

There was an Old Man of Berlin,
Whose form was uncommonly thin;
Till he once, by mistake,
Was mixed up in a cake,
So they baked that Old
Man of Berlin.

There was an Old Person of Dutton,
Whose head was as small as a button;
So, to make it look big,
He purchased a wig,
And rapidly rushed about Dutton.

There was a Young Lady of Welling,
Whose praise all the world was a-telling;
She played on a harp,
And caught several carp,
That accomplished Young Lady
of Welling.

There was an Old Man with a beard,
Who said, "It is just as I feared!—
Two Owls and a Hen,
Four Larks and a Wren,
Have all built their nests in my beard!"

There was an Old Man of Aosta,
Who possessed a large cow, but he
lost her;
But they said, "Don't you see,
She has rushed up a tree?
You invidious Old Man of Aosta!"

There was an Old Man of Melrose,
Who walked on the tips of his toes;
But they said, "It ain't pleasant,
To see you at present,
You stupid Old Man of Melrose."

There was an Old Man of Coblenz,
The length of whose legs was
immense;
He went with one prance,
From Turkey to France,
That surprising Old Man
of Coblenz.

There was a Young Lady of Norway,
Who casually sat in a doorway;
When the door squeezed her flat,
She exclaimed, "What of that?"
This courageous Young Lady of Norway.

There was an Old Man with a flute,
A "sarpint" ran into his boot;
But he played day and night,
Till the "sarpint" took flight,
And avoided that man with a flute.

There was a Young Lady whose nose,
Was so long that it reached to her toes;
So she hired an old lady,
Whose conduct was steady,
To carry that wonderful nose.

There was an Old Man of Moldavia,
Who had the most curious behaviour;
For while he was able,
He slept on a table,
That funny Old Man of Moldavia.

There was an Old Lady whose folly,
Induced her to sit in a holly;
Whereupon, by a thorn,
Her dress being torn,
She quickly became melancholy.

There was an Old Person of Anerley,
Whose conduct was strange and
unmannerly;
He rushed down the Strand,
With a pig in each hand,
But returned in the evening to Anerley.

There was a Young Lady whose bonnet
Came untied when the birds sat upon it;
But she said, "I don't care!
All the birds in the air
Are welcome to sit on my bonnet!"

There was an Old Man on a hill,
Who seldom, if ever, stood still;
He ran up and down
In his grandmother's gown,
Which adorned that Old Man on a hill.

There was an Old Man of Nepaul,
From his horse had a terrible fall;
But, though split quite in two,
With some very strong glue,
They mended that Man of Nepaul.

There was a Young Lady whose chin,
Resembled the point of a pin;
So she had it made sharp,
And purchased a harp,
And played several tunes with her chin.

The Owl and the Pussy-Cat

by Edward Lear

I

The Owl and the Pussy-Cat went to sea
In a beautiful pea-green boat,
They took some honey, and plenty
of money,
Wrapped up in a five-pound note.
The Owl looked up to the stars
above,
And sang to a small guitar,
"O lovely Pussy! O Pussy,
my love,
"What a beautiful Pussy
you are,
"You are,
"You are!
"What a beautiful Pussy
you are!"

II

Pussy said to the Owl, "You elegant fowl!
"How charmingly sweet you sing!
   "O let us be married! too long we
   have tarried:
      "But what shall we do for a ring?"
   They sailed away for a year and a day,
      To the land where the Bong-tree
      grows,
         And there in a wood a Piggy-
         wig stood,
         With a ring at the end of his nose,
      His nose,
   His nose,
With a ring at the end of his nose.

III

"Dear Pig, are you willing to sell for one
shilling,
"Your ring?" Said the Piggy, "I will."
So they took it away, and were married
next day,
By the Turkey who lives on the hill.
They dined on mince, and slices
of quince,
Which they ate with a runcible
spoon;
And hand in hand, on
the edge of the sand,
They danced by the
light of the moon,
The moon,
The moon,
They danced by the
light of the moon.

The Jumblies

by Edward Lear

I

They went to sea in a Sieve, they did,
In a Sieve they went to sea:
In spite of all their friends could say,
On a winter's morn, on a stormy day,
In a Sieve they went to sea!
And when the Sieve turned round
and round,
And every one cried, "You'll all be
drowned!"
They called aloud, "Our Sieve ain't
big,
"But we don't care a button! we don't
care a fig!
"In a Sieve we'll go to sea!"
Far and few, far and few,
Are the lands where the Jumblies live;
Their heads are green, and their hands
are blue,
And they went to sea in a Sieve.

II

They sailed away in a Sieve, they did,
In a Sieve they sailed so fast,
With only a beautiful pea-green veil
Tied with a riband by way of a sail,
To a small tobacco-pipe mast;
And every one said, who saw them go,
"O won't they be soon upset, you know!
"For the sky is dark, and the voyage is long,
"And happen what may, it's extremely wrong
"In a Sieve to sail so fast!"
Far and few, far and few,
Are the lands where the Jumblies live;
Their heads are green, and their hands
are blue,
And they went to sea in a Sieve.

III

The water it soon came in, it did,
The water it soon came in;
So to keep them dry, they wrapped their feet
In a pinky paper all folded neat,
And they fastened it down with a pin.
And they passed the night in a crockery-jar,
And each of them said, "How wise
we are!
"Though the sky be dark, and the
voyage be long,
"Yet we never can think we were
rash or wrong,
"While round in our Sieve we spin!"
Far and few, far and few,
Are the lands where the Jumblies live;
Their heads are green, and their
hands are blue,
And they went to sea in a Sieve.

And no end of Stilton Cheese.
Far and few, far and few,
Are the lands where the Jumblies live;
  Their heads are green, and their
  hands are blue,
  And they went to sea in a Sieve.

VI

  And in twenty years they all came
  back,
  In twenty years or more,
  And every one said, "How tall they've
    grown!
"For they've been to the Lakes, and the
Terrible Zone,
"And the hills of the Chankly Bore;"
And they drank their health, and gave
them a feast
Of dumplings made of beautiful yeast;
And every one said, "If we only live,
"We too will go to sea in a Sieve,—
"To the hills of the Chankly Bore!"
Far and few, far and few,
Are the lands where the Jumblies live;
Their heads are green, and their hands
are blue,
And they went to sea in a Sieve.

IV

And all night long they sailed away;
And when the sun went down,
They whistled and warbled a moony song
To the echoing sound of a coppery gong,
In the shade of the mountains brown.
"O Timballo! How happy we are,
"When we live in a sieve and a crockery-jar.
"And all night long in the moonlight pale,
"We sail away with a pea-green sail,
"In the shade of the mountains brown!"
Far and few, far and few,
Are the lands where the Jumblies live;
Their heads are green, and their hands
are blue
And they went to sea in a Sieve.

V

They sailed to the Western Sea, they did,
To a land all covered with trees,
And they bought an Owl, and a useful Cart,
And a pound of Rice, and a Cranberry Tart,
And a hive of silvery bees.
And they bought a Pig, and some green
Jackdaws,
And a lovely Monkey with lollipop paws,
And forty bottles of Ring-Bo-Ree,

The Dong with a Luminous Nose

by Edward Lear

Slowly it wanders,—
pauses,—creeps,—
Anon it sparkles,—flashes
and leaps;
And ever as onward it
gleaming goes
A light on the Bong-tree stems it throws.
And those who watch at that midnight
hour
From Hall or Terrace, or lofty Tower,
Cry, as the wild light passes along,—
"The Dong!—the Dong!
"The wandering Dong
through the forest goes!
"The Dong! the Dong!
"The Dong with a
luminous Nose!"

When awful darkness and silence reign
Over the great Gromboolian plain,
Through the long, long wintry nights;—
When the angry breakers roar
As they bear on the rocky shore;—
When Storm-clouds brood on the
towering heights
Of the Hills of the Chankly Bore:—

Then, through the vast and gloomy dark,
There moves what seems a fiery spark,
A lonely spark with silvery rays
Piercing the coal-black night,—
A meteor strange and bright:—
Hither and thither the vision strays,
A single lurid light.

Long years ago
The Dong was happy and gay,
Till he fell in love with a Jumbly Girl
Who came to those shores one day.
For the Jumblies came in a Sieve, they did,—
Landing at eve near the Zemmery Fidd
Where the Oblong Oysters grow,
And the rocks are smooth and gray.
And all the woods and the valleys rang
With the Chorus they daily and nightly
sang,—
"Far and few, far and few,
Are the lands where the Jumblies live;
Their heads are green, and their hands
are blue,
And they went to sea in a Sieve."

Happily, happily passed those days!
While the cheerful Jumblies staid;
They danced in circlets all night long,
To the plaintive pipe of the lively Dong,
In moonlight, shine, or shade.
For day and night he was always there
By the side of the Jumbly Girl so fair,
With her sky-blue hands, and her sea-
green hair,
Till the morning came of that hateful day
When the Jumblies sailed in their Sieve
away,
And the Dong was left on the cruel shore
Gazing—gazing for evermore,—
Ever keeping his weary eyes on
That pea-green sail on the far horizon,—
Singing the Jumbly Chorus still

As he sat all day on the grassy hill,—
"Far and few, far and few,
Are the lands where the Jumblies live;
Their heads are green, and their hands
are blue,
And they went to sea in a Sieve."

But when the sun was low in the West,
The Dong arose and said,—
"What little sense I once possessed
"Has quite gone out of my head!"
And since that day he wanders still
By lake and forest, marsh and hill,
Singing—"O somewhere, in valley or plain
"Might I find my Jumbly Girl again!
"For ever I'll seek by lake and shore
"Till I find my Jumbly Girl once more!"

Playing a pipe with silvery squeaks,
Since then his Jumbly Girl he seeks,
And because by night he could not see,
He gathered the bark of the
Twangum Tree
On the flowery plain that grows.
And he wove him a wondrous Nose,—
A Nose as strange as a Nose could be!
Of vast proportions and
painted red,
And tied with cords to the back of
his head.
—In a hollow rounded space
it ended
With a luminous lamp within
suspended
All fenced about
With a bandage stout
To prevent the wind from
blowing it out;—
And with holes all round
to send the light,
In gleaming rays on the
dismal night.

And now each night, and all night long,
Over those plains still roams the Dong;
And above the wail of the Chimp
and Snipe
You may hear the squeak of his
plaintive pipe
While ever he seeks, but seeks in vain
To meet with his Jumbly Girl again;
Lonely and wild—all night he goes,—
The Dong with a luminous Nose!
And all who watch at the midnight hour,
From Hall or Terrace, or lofty Tower,
Cry, as they trace the Meteor bright,
Moving along through the dreary night,—
"This is the hour when forth he goes,
"The Dong with a luminous Nose!
"Yonder—over the plain he goes;
"He goes!
"He goes;
"The Dong with a luminous Nose!"

The Pobble who has no Toes

by Edward Lear

I

The Pobble who has no toes
Had once as many as we;
When they said, "Some day
you may lose them all,"
He replied—"Fish fiddle
de-dee!"
And his Aunt
Jobiska made him drink,
Lavender water tinged with pink,
For she said, "The world in general knows
"There's nothing so good for a
Pobble's toes!"

II

The Pobble who has no toes
Swam across the Bristol Channel;
But before he set out he wrapped his nose,
In a piece of scarlet flannel.
For his Aunt Jobiska said, "No harm
"Can come to his toes if his
nose is warm;

"And it's perfectly known that a Pobble's
toes,
"Are safe—provided he minds his nose."

III

The Pobble swam fast and well,
And when boats or ships came near him,
He tinkledy-binkledy-winkled a bell,
So that all the world could hear him.
And all the Sailors and Admirals cried,
When they saw him nearing the further side—
"He has gone to fish, for his
Aunt Jobiska's,
"Runcible Cat with
crimson whiskers!"

IV

But before he touched the
shore,
The shore of the Bristol Channel,
A sea-green Porpoise carried away
His wrapper of scarlet flannel.
And when he came to observe his feet,
Formerly garnished with toes so neat,
His face at once became forlorn
On perceiving that all his toes were gone!

V

And nobody ever knew
From that dark day to the present,
Whoso had taken the Pobble's toes,
In a manner so far from pleasant.
Whether the shrimps or crawfish gray,
Or crafty Mermaids stole them away—
Nobody knew; and nobody knows,
How the Pobble was robbed of his twice
five toes!

VI

The Pobble who has no toes
Was placed in a friendly Bark,
And they rowed him back, and carried
him up,
To his Aunt Jobiska's park.
And she made him a feast at his earnest wish
Of eggs and buttercups fried with fish—
And she said—"It's a fact the whole
world knows,
"That Pobbles are happier without
their toes."

The Table and the Chair

by Edward Lear

I

Said the Table to the Chair,
"You can hardly be aware
"How I suffer from the heat,
"And from chilblains on my feet!
"If we took a little walk,
"We might have a little talk!
"Pray let us take the air!"
Said the Table to the Chair.

II

Said the Chair unto the Table,
"Now you *know* we are not able!
"How foolishly you talk,
"When you know we *cannot* walk!"
Said the Table with a sigh,
"It can do no harm to try;
"I've as many legs as you,
"Why can't we walk on two?"

III

So they both went slowly down,
And walked about the town
  With a cheerful bumpy sound,
  As they toddled round and
  round.
  And everybody cried,
  As they hastened to their side,
  "See! the Table and the Chair
  "Have come out to take the air!"

419

IV

But in going down an ally,
To a castle in the valley,
They completely lost their way,
And wandered all the day.
Till, to see them safely back,
They paid a Ducky-quack,
And a Beetle, and a Mouse,
Who took them to their house.

V

Then they whispered to each other,
"O delightful little brother!
"What a lovely walk we've taken!
"Let us dine on Beans and Bacon!"
So the Ducky and the leetle
Browny-Mousy and the Beetle,
Dined, and danced upon their heads,
Till they toddled to their beds.

The Duck and the Kangaroo

by Edward Lear

I

Said the Duck to the Kangaroo,
"Good gracious! how you hop!
"Over the fields and the water too,
"As if you never would stop!
"My life is a bore in this nasty pond,
"And I long to go out in the world beyond!
"I wish I could hop like you!"
Said the Duck to the Kangaroo.

II

"Please give me a ride on your back!"
Said the Duck to the Kangaroo.
"I would sit quite still, and say nothing
but 'Quack',
"The whole of the long day through!
"And we'd go to the Dee, and the
Jelly Bo Lee,
"Over the land, and over
the sea—
"Please take me a ride!
O do!"
Said the Duck to
the Kangaroo.

III

Said the Kangaroo to the Duck,
"This requires some little reflection;
"Perhaps on the whole it might bring
me luck,
"And there seems but one objection,
"Which is, if you'll let me speak so bold,
"Your feet are unpleasantly wet and cold,
"And would probably give me the roo—
          "Matiz!" said the Kangaroo.

IV

Said the Duck, "As I sat on the rocks,
"I have thought over that completely,
"And I bought four pairs of worsted socks,
"Which fit my web-feet neatly.
"And to keep out the cold I've bought a cloak,
"And every day a cigar I'll smoke,
"All to follow my own dear true
"Love of a Kangaroo!"

V

Said the Kangaroo, "I'm ready!
"All in the moonlight pale,
"But to balance me well, dear Duck, sit steady!
"And quite at the end of my tail!"
So away they went with a hop and a bound,
And they hopped the whole world three times round;
And who so happy—O who,
As the Duck and the Kangaroo?

Nonsense Numbers

*O*NE old ox
opening oysters.

*T*WO toads totally tired
trying to trot to Tetbury.

THREE tawny tigers
taking tea.

FOUR fat frogs
fanning fainting flies.

FIVE ferocious foxes
following feeble fowls.

*S**IX*** sage serpents
singing silly songs.

*S**EVEN*** smart salmon
snapping silly shrimps.

*E**IGHT*** elegant elephants
eagerly eating eggs.

NINE nimble nightingales
nudging naughty newts.

TEN toy-terriers
travelling the tootling train.

More Nonsense Numbers

The animals went
in one by one,
the elephant munching
a caraway bun.

The animals went
in two by two,
the great giraffe
and the kangaroo.

The animals went
in three by three,
the Persian cat and
the bumble bee.

The animals went
in four by four,
the hippopotamus
stuck in the door.

The animals went
in five by five,
the bees were grand
and came in a hive.

The animals went
in six by six,
the poodle dog
with his many tricks.

The animals went
in seven by seven,
some from Somerset
some from Devon.

The animals went
in eight by eight,
the crocodile ran,
he thought he'd be late.

The animals went
in nine by nine,
the polar bear
and the porcupine.

The animals went
in ten by ten,
the crowing cock
and the bantam hen.

The animals went
in twenty by twenty,
shut the door quickly
I think we have plenty.

Nonsense Alphabet

By Edward Lear

A

A was once an Apple-pie,
Pidy
Widy
Tidy
Pidy
Nice insidy
Apple-pie.

B

B was once a little Bear,
Beary!
Wary!
Hairy!
Beary!
Taky cary!
Little Bear!

C

C was once a little Cake,
Caky
Baky
Maky
Caky
Taky Caky
Little Cake.

D

D was once a little Doll,
Dolly
Molly
Polly
Nolly
Nursy Dolly
Little Doll!

E

E was once a little Eel,
Eely
Weely
Peely
Eely
Twirly Tweely
Little Eel.

F

F was once a little Fish,
Fishy
Wishy
Squishy
Fishy
In a Dishy
Little Fish!

G

G was once a little Goose,
Goosy
Moosy
Boosey
Goosey
Waddly woosy
Little Goose!

H

H was once a little Hen,
Henny
Chenny
Tenny
Henny
Eggsy-any
Little Hen?

I

I was once a Bottle of Ink,
Inky
Dinky
Thinky
Inky
Blacky Minky
Bottle of Ink!

J

J was once a Jar of Jam,
Jammy
Mammy
Clammy
Jammy
Sweety—Swammy
Jar of Jam!

K

K was once a little Kite,
Kity
Whity
Flighty
Kity
Out of Sighty—
Little Kite!

L

L was once a little Lark,
Larky!
Marky!
Harky!
Larky!
In the Parky
Little Lark!

M

M was once a little Mouse,
Mousey
Bousey
Sousy
Mousy
In the Housy
Little Mouse!

N

N was once a little Needle,
Needly
Tweedly
Threedly
Needly
Wisky—wheedly
Little Needle!

O

O was once a little Owl,
Owly
Prowly
Howly
Owly
Browny Fowly
Little Owl!

P

P was once a little Pump,
Pumpy
Slumpy
Flumpy
Pumpy
Dumpy, Thumpy
Little Pump!

Q

Q was once a little Quail,
Quaily
Faily
Daily
Quaily
Stumpy-taily
Little Quail!

R

R was once a little Rose,
Rosy
Posy
Nosy
Rosy
Blows-y—grows-y
Little Rose!

S

S was once a little Shrimp,
Shrimpy
Nimpy
Flimpy
Shrimpy
Jumpy—jimpy
Little Shrimp!

T

T was once a little Thrush,
Thrushy
Hushy
Bushy
Thrushy
Flitty—Flushy
Little Thrush!

U

U was once a little Urn,
Urny
Burny
Turny
Urny
Bubbly—burny
Little Urn!

V

V was once a little Vine,
Viny
Winy
Twiny
Viny
Twisty-twiny
Little Vine!

W

W was once a Whale,
Whaly
Scaly
Shaly
Whaly
Tumbly-taily
Mighty Whale!

X

X was once a great King Xerxes,
Xerxy
Perxy
Turxy
Xerxy
Linxy Lurxy
Great King Xerxes!

Y

Y was once a little Yew,
Yewdy
Fewdy
Crudy
Yewdy
Growdy grewdy
Little Yew!

Z

Z was once a piece of Zinc,
Tinky
Winky
Blinky
Tinky
Tinkly Minky
Piece of Zinc!

Text Acknowledgements

Many nursery rhymes and verses cannot be attributed to an author. We acknowledge below the rhymes and verses whose authorsip we could ascertain.

Robert Louis Stevenson:
A Good Play
Bed in Summer
Block City
Foreign Lands
Looking-Glass River
My Shadow
Nest Eggs
North-West Passage
Picture Story-Books in Winter
Singing
The Flowers
The Little Land
The Moon
The Swing
The Unseen Playmate
The Wind
Whole Duty of Children

Kate Greenaway:
Prince Finikin
Somewhere Town
Tea for Two
The Cats Have Come to Tea
The Daisies
The Dancing Family
The Four Princesses
The Little Jumping Girls
The Proud Girl
When We Went Out with Grandmamma

Dr Heinrich Hoffmann:
Shock-Headed Peter
The Story of Cruel Frederick
The Story of Flying Robert
The Story of Johnny Head-in-Air
The Story of the Man that Went Out Shooting

R. André:
Alderman Poppy
Froggy's Banquet
General Cock-a-Doodle
Mister Gooseberry's Barber
Mister Sunflower
Monsieur Renard's Gloves
Old Maid Hollyhock
Sunflower Cymbals
The Battle of the Bee and the Snapdragon
The Butterflies Lawn Tennis
The Cobweb Harp
The Doormouse Juggler

Illustration Acknowledgements

R. André: pp. 7 (bottom), 110–115, 440, 442.

E. V. Boyle: pp. 2, 147, 149, 153, 155, 159, 161, 165, 167, 169, 171, 177, 180–185, 439, 445.

Randolph Caldecott: pp. 9, 84–100,

Walter Crane: pp. 5 (middle), 136, 137, 394 (bottom), 395 (bottom), 396, 398 (top), 399 (top), 400 (bottom), 401, 402, 438, 444.

Richard Doyle: pp. 3, 6, 8, 186–193, 437, 441, 448.

Kate Greenaway: pp. 7 (top), 60–67, 194–202, 446.

Dr Heinrich Hoffman: pp. 50–59.

Lialia and Valentin Varetsa: pp. 4, 5 (top and bottom), 22 (top), 28–41, 68–83, 101–109, 116–135, 140–145, 173, 179, 209, 211, 213, 215, 216, 217, 219, 221, 223, 224, 225, 227, 229, 230, 233, 234, 235, 237, 239, 241–247, 249–252, 254–257, 259, 261, 263–267, 269, 270, 271, 273, 274, 275, 277, 278, 279, 281, 283, 284–293, 295–298, 300–310, 313–319, 321, 322, 324–327, 329, 331, 333, 335–339, 341–344, 346, 347, 349, 351, 352, 361, 362, 363, 365, 367, 368, 369, 372, 375, 379, 383–386, 388, 389, 391, 392, 393, 394 (top), 395 (top), 397, 398 (bottom), 399 (bottom), 400 (top), 403–422, 431–435, 447.

Text Sources

Anon. (date unknown). *The Milk-White Thorn*. London: Thomas Nelson & Sons.

Austin, Sarah (1872). *The Story without an End*. London: Sampson Low, Marston, Low, and Seale.

Browning, Robert (date unknown). *The Pied Piper of Hamelin*. London: Frederick Warne and Co.

Doyle, Richard (1842). *Jack the Giant Killer*. London: Eyre and Spottiswoode.

Lang, Andrew (ed.) (1889). *The Blue Fairy Book*. London: Longmans, Green & Co.

Lang, Andrew (ed.) (1890). *The Red Fairy Book*. London: Longmans, Green & Co.

Lang, Andrew (ed.) (1892). *The Green Fairy Book*. London: Longmans, Green & Co.

Lang, Andrew (ed.) (1894). *The Yellow Fairy Book*. London: Longmans, Green & Co.

Lang, Andrew (ed.) (1897). *The Pink Fairy Book*. London: Longmans, Green & Co.

Lang, Andrew (ed.) (1898). *The Arabian Nights Entertainments*. London: Longmans, Green & Co.

Lang, Andrew (ed.) (1906). *The Orange Fairy Book*. London: Longmans, Green & Co.

Paull, H. B. (translator) *Grimm's Fairy Tales*. London: Frederick Warne and Co.

Index of First Lines in Nursery Rhymes

General Index

Published by Global Book Publishing Pty Ltd
1/181 High Street, Willoughby, 2068 NSW Australia
Phone (612) 9967 3100, Fax (612) 9967 5891

ISBN 1 74048 078 3

Managing Editor: Marie-Louise Taylor
Art Director: Stan Lamond
Designers: Kathie and Susie Baxter-Smith
Typesetter: Dee Rogers

Film separation by
Pica Colour Separation Overseas Pte Ltd, Singapore
Printed by
Sing Cheong Printing Co. Ltd, Hong Kong

For permission to reproduce any of the illustrations
in this book, please contact Gordon Cheers at
Global Book Publishing Pty Ltd